Secret Song

Also by Catherine Coulter
in Large Print:

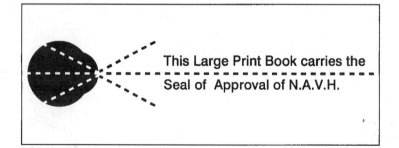

This Large Print Book carries the
Seal of Approval of N.A.V.H.

Secret Song

Medieval Song Quartet #3

Catherine Coulter

Thorndike Press • Thorndike, Maine

Copyright © Catherine Coulter, 1991
Medieval Song Quartet Series

Published in 2000 by arrangement with Signet, a division of
Penguin Putnam Inc.

Thorndike Press Large Print Basic Series.

The tree indicium is a trademark of Thorndike Press.

The text of this Large Print edition is unabridged.
Other aspects of the book may vary from the original edition.

Set in 16 pt. Plantin by Elena Picard.

Printed in the United States on permanent paper.

Library of Congress Cataloging-in-Publication Data

Coulter, Catherine.
    Secret song / by Catherine Coulter.
        p. cm. — (Medieval song quartet ; 3)
    ISBN 0-7862-2357-X (lg. print : hc : alk. paper)
    1. Great Britain — History — 13th century — Fiction.
2. Large type books. I. Title.
PS3553.O843 S43 2000
    813′.54—dc21   99-055837

To my parents,
Charles and Elizabeth Coulter,
who passed along
what talent genes I can lay claim to.
All my love and thanks.

Prologue

Near Grainsworth Abbey
March 1275

Daria wished the heavy clouds overhead would free the snow. She wanted the misery of freezing snow blowing into her face, stinging her eyes, mixing with the burning tears.

But as the afternoon lengthened, the weather simply grew colder, the wind more vicious, twisting and ripping through the few naked-branched oak trees that lined the narrow road, but it didn't snow.

She hunched down in her miniver-lined cloak and closed her eyes. Her mare, Henrietta, plodded onward, her head bowed, keeping rhythm with the destrier's pace ahead of her. Every few minutes, Drake, Lord Damon's master-at-arms, would swivel about to see that she still rode docilely behind him, that she hadn't somehow fled without him noticing, that she was keeping herself silent and submissive and obedient. Drake wasn't a bad man, or cruel, but he was her uncle's minion, and he always carried out his master's orders without hesitation or question. Also, she knew, it would never occur to him to question his master's right to dispose of his niece in any way that suited him. She was naught but a female and thus all decisions were made for her and around her.

She had no choices. She knew now that she'd never had a choice. She simply hadn't realized it so starkly before. Before, Daria, the child, had had to obey only occasional commands from her uncle, nothing of the magnitude that would make her want to crawl away and die. After all, what could a man want with a child? But now she was seventeen, more than old enough to be weighed and judged and a value set on her. She was no longer a child and her uncle had seen it and acted on it. A girl went from her father — or in this case, her uncle — to her husband. From one man to another. Chattel of one man to be chattel of another. No choice, no argument. It was as the man dictated, as the man ordered. She felt tears again, and hated them, for crying was useless. Crying meant that there was hope, and there wasn't any of that to be had.

Daria dashed her palm over her eyes, and when she opened them again she saw in her mind's eye her uncle Damon, as clear to her as the armored back of Drake, who rode directly in front of her. She saw him in his bed-chamber and she heard his voice, deep and clear and indifferent, his words of a month ago still as fresh as if he'd spoken them but moments before. No, she thought now, he hadn't been indifferent, not at all. It had been an act. He'd been looking forward to this — to humiliating her and then telling her what he'd planned for her. No, her uncle was never indifferent in his cruelty. He relished it.

He'd been sitting up in his fur-covered bed, Cora, one of the castle serving wenches, naked beside him. Upon Daria's entrance into Lord Damon's bedchamber, Cora had giggled and slithered down beside him, pulling the white rabbit furs over her naked shoulders. He appeared not to care that the furs left his own chest bare. He appeared not to care that he was naked and in his bed with his mistress in front of his niece. Of course he'd planned it. There was no doubt in her mind. Daria had said nothing, merely waited for him to tell her why he'd sent for her. He in turn was silent for many moments, negligently stroking his right hand over Cora's shoulder.

Daria had closed her eyes, knowing he did this for her benefit, to show her yet again that a female was naught but what a man wanted her to be.

Daria had felt the familiar feelings of hate, revulsion, and helplessness surge through her. She loathed her uncle and he knew it, and she guessed it amused him, this silent hatred of hers. This *meaningless* silent hatred of hers. What did he want? For her to scream at him, to cry, to cower in humiliation and embarrassment? She stood perfectly still. She'd learned patience with him. She'd learned to wait silent as a rock, giving him no encouragement.

She didn't move. Her expression didn't change.

Suddenly he seemed to tire of his game. He pulled the furs higher over Cora and told her to be still and turn her back to him. "I tire of your sheep's face," he added, his eyes all the while on his silent niece.

"You sent for me," Daria said finally, holding her voice as calm and emotionless as she was trying to hold her body.

"Aye, I did. You're more than full grown, Daria. You turned seventeen two months ago. My silly little Cora here — already quite a woman — is only fifteen. You should have a babe suckling at your breast by now, as do most females. Aye, I've held you here overlong. But I had to wait, you see, wait for just the offer I wished." He smiled then, showing all his very white teeth. "At least next month you will finally have a husband to plow that little belly of yours. And he'll do it enthusiastically, I doubt it not."

She paled and stepped back. She couldn't help it.

He laughed. "Doesn't the thought of a husband please you, niece? Or do you fear and dislike all men? Don't you wish to escape me and become mistress in your own keep?"

She stared at him, mute.

"Answer me, you silly girl!"

"Aye."

"Good. It will be done. When you leave me, Daria, tell your mother I wish to see her. Cora has but whetted my appetite."

Daria didn't move this time, and after a moment, Damon merely shrugged, as if tiring of baiting her. Daria knew he forced her mother, her gentle, sweet mother — his dead half-brother's wife — and had taken her since the accidental death of his half-brother, James of Fortescue, in a tourney in London some four years before. But her mother, Lady Katherine, had never said a word to Daria, never complained, never cried. She was told she was to go to the lord and she went without comment, without objection, to Damon, and later emerged, still silent, her eyes cast down, her mouth sometimes swollen and bruised-looking. But Daria knew; all the servants spoke of it and she'd overheard them. This was the first time he had spoken openly of it before to her. But he wanted her to know, she guessed, but she wouldn't do what he wanted, she wouldn't plead with him, she wouldn't beg him to spare her mother. She said instead, "Who is to be my husband?"

"So you do have some interest, do you? You will doubtless be happy about my choice for you." He paused and she saw the malicious gleam in his pale blue eyes. She knew she wouldn't like it and so did he. She waited, silent and still and cold, wishing now she'd kept her mouth shut and hadn't asked. She didn't want to know, not yet. But Damon said, his voice relishing his words, "Why, it is Ralph of Colchester, eldest son of the Earl of Colchester. They visited Reymerstone, don't you remember? Last November. Ralph told me he is most pleased with you, as is his father."

"Not Ralph of Colchester! No! You would not, he is loathsome! He raped Anna again and again and he got her with child and —"

Damon roared with laughter. She'd finally reacted and he was pleased with himself. "Aye, I know it," he said, still laughing, shaking the big bed with his mirth. "I made him a wager, you see. I told him that his father and I wanted him to get you with child immediately, and to see if he was capable, I gave him Anna, who was ready to be bred in any case. He impregnated her quickly. I was pleased and relieved, as was his father."

Daria just looked at him, stunned and repelled, but not really surprised. She heard herself ask, "What did you offer as your wager with him?"

Damon laughed again. "So there is still a portion of defiance in you? Well, no matter now. I wagered your mother's gold necklace. The one my half-brother gave her upon their marriage." He watched her face closely.

She gave him no more satisfaction. She'd given him more than enough. She said instead, shrugging, "It is of very little value."

She looked at him, and for an instant, just a brief moment, she thought she saw some resemblance to her father in him. But she wasn't certain. She couldn't remember her father clearly anymore, even though it had been only four years since his death. But her father had been gone so often, for long stretches of time, and he hadn't particularly noticed her even on his rare visits to Fortescue Hall, for she was naught but a girl, a female whose only worth lay in a marriage advantageous to him. Still, surely he hadn't been as vile as his elder half-brother, surely.

And now it was Damon, his half-brother, who would gain the advantages of her marriage.

"What did you offer Ralph and his father? All my inheritance?"

"Why, certainly, most of it, but I dislike your impertinent tongue. Hold it quiet or I will have your mother brought here and she will tell you the value of obedience to me. Aye, Colchester will have most of your immense dowry and I will have the Colchester land that will extend my boundaries all the way to the North Sea. It is precisely what I wanted, what I've waited for so patiently. Actually, I will tell you why I allowed you to become so aged. The boy, Ralph, was mightily ill last year and I didn't know if he would survive; his father was concerned that even if he did survive, he wouldn't still have potent seed. But I was content to wait. He did survive, as did his seed, and aye, little Daria, I have got what I wanted, all of it."

" 'Tis my money, my inheritance! All that my father owned, he gave to me. You take everything, and 'twas not yours to take!"

His face darkened and he threw back the furs. He came to his feet, standing naked by his bed. Cora stared at him as he strode to

14

Daria. For a moment Daria believed he would strike her, but he didn't. He'd never struck her. It wasn't his way. He just smiled at her now, but she knew that it was rage burning bright in his eyes, not amusement.

"Go now," he said at last. "Even you have managed to offend me, which is surprising. Your mother will prepare for your trip to Colchester. You will have wagons full of household items, as every bride should. You are the Reymerstone heiress; thus I have been more than generous with you. I would not wish to make a niggardly impression or leave any person in doubt of my affection for you, for I want no questions. You will leave in three weeks. I will come in time for your wedding, of course. And if you are obedient, I just might bring your mother with me. Well, why don't you say something? No? Leave me, then!"

She stared at him a moment, not at his body — for the very hardness of him, all that pale blond hair that covered him, frightened her — but at his hated face. Then she turned and walked from the chamber.

All she saw, all she could comprehend, was that Ralph of Colchester was to be her husband.

Her mother had held her, petted her whilst she cried, but she'd told her that any marriage — even to Ralph of Colchester — was better than remaining here. She must face it and behave as a lady ought, with dignity and acceptance. With a smooth, serene countenance.

And that was that. But Daria had despised the twenty-year-old Ralph of Colchester with his weak chin and his bowed thin legs and his leering expressions. And she'd seen what he'd done to Anna, fourteen-year-old Anna, naught but a child herself really, big-breasted, and pretty and stupid. She hadn't deserved to be raped repeatedly, but she had been, for the entire week's visit. Twice a day Ralph had raped her. And the men had laughed and clapped the miserable youth on his shoulder and told him his rod was sure and true.

Finally, Daria thought, bringing herself back to the present, raising her face skyward. Snowflakes were falling now, each one falling more quickly than the last, blanketing Drake, his men, and all the wagons in pure white. As the flakes struck her face, she felt the numbing cold of them pierce more and more deeply into her. Henrietta stumbled and snorted and Daria patted her neck. She wondered if Ralph would allow her to ride once they were wedded. She wondered if he would rape her twice a day as he had Anna.

Drake turned, shouting back to her that they would shortly arrive at the Cistercian Abbey of Grainsworth, where they would pass the night.

They were soon forced to form a single-file column, for the road narrowed dramatically, bounded on both sides by huge rocks and tumbled boulders, stark and bold.

When the attack came, it was all the more terrifying because Drake and his dozen men couldn't see their enemy; nor could they defend themselves, held apart in their long line, their horses screaming and lunging in terror. They fell, one by one, struck by the arrows shot from behind the rocks. Some of the men were wearing armor, but it didn't matter, they were rained with arrows and eventually an arrow found its mark in the man's neck or in his face. Other men wore padded jerkins, and they were killed more quickly. But none of them had a chance against an enemy hidden behind rocks and shooting through a thick veil of white snow.

Oddly enough, after the first shock of the attack, Daria wasn't afraid. She knew deep inside her that she wouldn't die. Not today, not by an arrow shot through her chest. When only Daria and her maid, Ena, remained, when all the screams died away and the white air was cleansed of arrows and men's cries, did their attackers emerge, un-scathed. They were shouting and laughing at the ease of their victory. Daria saw their leader immediately, a huge man, and he was laughing the loudest as he directed his men to loot the dead, collect the horses, and see to the wagons.

He took off his helmet. He had the red-dest hair she'd ever seen.

1

Reymerstone Castle, Essex, England
Near the North Sea
Early May 1275

Roland de Tournay found the seat of the Earl of Reymerstone easily enough. The castle dominated the rock-strewn promontory that jutted out like a tongue into the Thirgby River that flowed nearly a mile into the North Sea. The castle was in the Norman style, built by the present earl's great-grandfather, and was more stark and weathered than comfortable, still more of a fortification and a garrison than a residence. Yet the present earl had lined the pockets of many merchants to add comfort to the austere gray stone castle, luxuries such as thick tapestries to blanket the stone walls and keep out the damp from the North Sea, Flanders carpets in bright scarlets and royal blues, beautiful embroidered cushions for the three chairs, each made by an artisan of great skill. The dozen trestle tables and their long benches in the great hall, however, had not changed in three generations, and past living of all the common men and women who had shared their meals on the gnarled old tables still showed clearly, all the scuffs, all the knife-carved initials, all the old grease.

The great hall of Reymerstone was impressive, Roland decided as he waited for the emergence of the Earl of Reymerstone, Damon Le Mark. Roland knew he was being studied by several serving wenches and sent them a wink that caused giggles and pert smiles. He saw a female hurrying toward him, this one a lady, possibly the mistress of Reymerstone. She was in her thirties, brown-eyed, hair a dull red and of slight stature. She'd once been very pretty. Now she looked faded and tired, her shoulders slightly bowed. She looked beaten down. Her expression, however, when she looked at him, suddenly changed and she looked furtively around her, then approached him quickly, her step light and quick as a girl's.

"You are Roland de Tournay, sir?" she asked in a low voice that was soft and cultured.

"Aye, my lady. I come at the invitation of the Earl of Reymerstone, your husband."

"He will be here shortly. He is otherwise occupied just now." What did that mean? Roland wondered. The woman continued, "I am Lady Katherine of Fortescue, the current earl's sister-in-law. His half-brother was my husband."

"Your husband was James of Fortescue? I had heard he'd fallen by accident in a tourney, just before he was to leave with Edward for the Holy Land. My sympathies, my lady."

She again nodded her bowed head. Roland frowned. Couldn't she look at him, eye-to-eye? Could she possibly be frightened of him?

"Do you know why Lord Reymerstone asked me to come here?"

Her head came up then and he saw the strain in her fine eyes. And there was something else — fear, perhaps, which brought him fully alert.

"It concerns my daughter," she said quickly, glancing behind her. She grabbed his sleeve. "You must find my child and bring her back safely, you must! Ah, here he comes. I daren't remain. I will leave you now, sir."

She glided silently away, gone into the

gaggle of serving wenches before the earl had seen her.

Roland had a moment to study the Earl of Reymerstone as he strode toward him. He was a tall man, in his late thirties, lean of build, a full head of white-blond hair, his eyes the palest of blues. His stubborn chin was beardless, his expression was obstinate. He didn't look to be an easy man. He looked to be a man who got his own way, by any means necessary. Roland had survived many of his adult years by correctly summing up a man's character. He'd seldom been wrong in the past five years. Indeed, his only huge mistake had been in his dealings with a woman. A lady, so very young, so very fair, and he a young man of very tender years. He shook off the memory of Joan of Tenesby.

The earl gave Roland a brief nod and Roland knew he'd been weighed in those short minutes as well. "You have come in good time, thank the saints, de Tournay. Come and sit with me. We have much to discuss."

Roland accepted a cup of ale and waited for his host to come to the point.

"I will pay you well," Damon Le Mark said, and raised his own cup for a toast. Roland sent him a bland look and asked, "Whom do I have to kill?"

The earl laughed. "I do not seek to hire an assassin. Any enemy I have I will slay myself. I hire a man who's known for his ingenuity, his ability with languages, and his skill at changing his appearance to suit any situation in which he finds himself. Is it not true that you were accepted in the company of Barbars himself in the Holy Land? That you passed yourself off as a Saracen for two years? That you masqueraded as a Muslim with such finesse even the most devout didn't know you for what you were?"

"You are well-informed." Roland wasn't about to deny the earl's recital. He wasn't vain; nor was he foolishly modest. For the most part, it was true. Odd how the very attributes Roland held to be in his favor sounded vile on the earl's lips. He waited, more interested now. The earl's need must be great. The task must be beyond his own abilities, and it irked him.

Damon Le Mark knew he must suffer the arrogance and impertinence of the young man seated in front of him, a young man who, in addition to his reputation for boldness and cunning, was passing handsome, his lean face well sculpted, his black hair thick and gleaming, his dark eyes bright with intelligence. But he was swarthy as a savage Irishman, and didn't look to be a man of particular wealth or refinement. Damon Le Mark also reminded himself that this man was of no inborn worth at all despite his birth and his heritage. He held no title and, more important, no land. He was a man who made his way by playacting and deceit, and yet he, a man his superior in every way, must be gracious, and he must offer him a great deal of money. It was galling.

"I'm always well-informed," the earl said. "It took my couriers a good deal of time to locate you."

"I received your message in Rouen. I was passing the winter there very pleasantly."

"So I hear." He'd been told by his own man that de Tournay had been living with a very pretty young widow in Rouen.

"Her name was Marie," Roland said easily, and sipped at his ale. It was warm and dark and very smooth. "But do not mistake me. I was ready to come home, very nearly. As soon as the weather grew warmer."

"To earn money by guile?"

"Yes, if need be, though I believe that wit is more to the point than guile. Would you not agree?"

The earl knew he'd been insulting when he shouldn't have. He retrenched, shrugging. "Ah, it's those other things that must interest me, de Tournay, for I wish you not to do them just yet. The reason I asked you here is vital. It concerns my beloved niece, Daria. I will be brief. She was kidnapped on her journey to Colchester, where she was to wed Ralph of Colchester. All twelve of the men in her train were butchered in an ambush. All the wagons carrying her wedding goods were stolen. I want you to rescue her and I will pay you very well."

"Has a ransom been demanded?"

The earl's eyes narrowed and he bared his teeth. "Oh, aye, the damnable impertinent whoreson! I would that you would kill him as well, but I suppose that the rescue of my dearest niece must take precedence."

"Who stole her?"

"Edmond of Clare."

"The Marcher Baron? How very odd." Roland fell silent. It was more than odd. The Marcher Barons, their power and existence granted to them by the great Duke William himself nearly two hundred years before, had little reason to stray from their strongholds unless it was to press west to garner more Welsh land and butcher more Welsh outlaws. It was their responsibility to contain the Welsh, and this they did with endless vigor and impressive continuity. They were in effect little kings, holding immense power in their own feudal kingdoms.

It galled King Edward no end, this power outside himself, and Roland knew he planned to curtail their immense influence by defeating the Welsh once and for all by building royal castles all along the northern coast of the country. "I'll push the malignant little lordlings until they're on bended knee to me, pleading with me to leave them something!" he'd said once, pounding a table with his fist and sending it in splinters to the floor. Roland continued after a moment, "Edmond of Clare's stronghold is between Chepstow and Trefynwy, bordering the southeast corner of Wales. Why would he come across the width of England to kidnap your niece?"

The earl kept a stubborn silence. The impertinence of the knave, asking him these questions. He was furious but he contained himself. He couldn't anger de Tournay, for the man wasn't his to command. De Tournay could leave. Still, he refused to tell him the truth of the matter. He laid the matter on another's shoulders, saying finally, "Clare despises the Earl of Colchester. He wanted revenge so he stole my niece. He wants nearly all her dowry as ransom or he will rape her until she is with child before he returns her to me."

"What did Colchester do to Clare to

merit such a chilling revenge?"

Damon Le Mark's face paled and his hand shook. He wanted to thrash de Tournay for his infernal curiosity. He smiled and Roland felt the chill of that smile to his bones. This was not a man to guard your back. Damon shrugged. "I understand Colchester accidentally killed Clare's brother some five years ago. I know none of the actual facts of the incident, and it was Colchester's decision not to tell me more. Now, will you rescue my niece?"

This was doubtless a lie, but Roland let it go. Probably closer to the mark was that the Earl of Reymerstone had killed Edmond of Clare's brother. "When was she stolen?"

"On March the third."

A black eyebrow shot upward. "You wait a long time to reply to Clare's demands."

"I did not wait here doing nothing until my men had found you in that silly Frenchwoman's bed!"

"On the contrary," Roland said with no heat, "Marie wasn't at all silly. What did you do?"

"I made two attempts, and both failed, or rather the men I sent to bring her back to me were fools and blundered. I discovered that my second attempt failed but two days ago. Clare returned one of my men alive with a new message and a new demand."

Roland waited, knowing he wasn't going to like hearing what Clare wanted now.

"The whoreson now wants to wed my niece. He still wants her dowry as well, of course. If I don't send my own priest to him carrying all her dowry with him by the last day of May, he says he will rape her, then give her to his soldiers for their sport. Then, if she still lives, he will have her used until she is with child. Then he will throw her in a ditch."

"I wonder why he wishes to marry her," Roland said, stroking his chin.

"He wishes to humiliate me further!"

"Your niece — is she beautiful as well as rich? Would her face and physical gifts charm him as does her dowry?"

And in that instant, Roland saw quite clearly just what the earl thought of his niece. Living in Reymerstone with this man for master could not have been pleasant. Roland wondered where the mother stood in all this mess.

"She is well-enough-looking, I suppose," Damon said finally, shrugging. "She is but a female, nothing more. Her tongue is impertinent upon occasion, but nothing a strong man can't control. She must continually be reminded that obedience and submission are what are expected of her. As I said, she needs a strong man."

And you saw yourself nicely in that role. "I met her mother. I imagine she was once quite lovely. Does the daughter have her coloring?"

The earl merely shrugged. "No, the girl has dark hair, filled with autumn colors, and her eyes are the oddest green. Pure but dark. Her features resemble her mother's but they are less coarse, more finely drawn."

"I find it fascinating that Clare demands you send your own priest. Do you know why?"

"Clare is a religious zealot. He is a man controlled and dominated by his fanaticism. If he requests I send a priest, it is because he believes a priest will not cheat him of the dowry money, that the priest will fairly wed him to my niece. He does not seem to realize that priests are as venal a company as any. Will you try to rescue her before the whoreson ravishes her? Before the last day of May?"

"You don't believe he's raped her already?"

"No." This was said grudgingly but firmly. Interesting, Roland thought as he said, "Why not? After all, what does a man's religious beliefs have to do with his lust?"

"Edmond of Clare keeps his word, at least that is his reputation. But if you haven't rescued her by the end of May, he will do exactly as he says he will, whether he wishes to or not. I know him well enough, and 'tis true."

Roland held off giving the earl his answer that evening, even though he knew he would go to Tyberton and he knew exactly how he would present himself. The coin he would earn for this rescue would give him sufficient funds to purchase Sir Thomas's small keep, Thispen-Ladock, and the surrounding rich grazing lands in Cornwall. And that was what he wanted. He would no longer be beholden to any man for his survival. When this was over, when the wretched niece was returned to her uncle, Roland would use his wits to further himself, not be at the behest of another. He wanted to remain in England; he wanted to be master of his castle and his own lands, and once he rescued this girl from Edmond of Clare, he would have his wish. It mattered not that Damon Le Mark had lied to him throughout; it mattered not that it was more than likely he, Damon Le Mark, and not the fat Earl of Colchester, who had killed Clare's brother.

That night Roland was given one of the serving wenches to warm his bed and his blood. She was clean and sweet-smelling and he took her three times during the long night, for he was hungry for a woman after being absent for several weeks from Marie's enthusiastic ardor, and he gave her pleasure as well and wished he could remember her name the following morning to thank her.

He said to the earl as he mounted his destrier, a stark black Arab named Cantor, "As I told you, I will rescue your niece and I will do it long before the deadline Clare has set. You, however, must swear to me that you will try no more schemes on your own. They might endanger me and my plans."

The earl frowned and pulled on his ear, a lifelong habit that had left one earlobe a bit longer than the other, but finally agreed. Roland wondered if his word meant anything. He doubted that it did in the normal course of events. However, a good deal of coin was now in Roland's possession, half of the payment he was to receive. Perhaps that would keep Le Mark out of the game.

"Nor will you send a priest or your niece's dowry. There will be no need."

The earl's pale eyes gleamed. "You have great confidence, de Tournay."

"I will rescue her. Count out the rest of my coin, my lord, for I shall surely return to claim it."

Roland prepared to whip Cantor about,

31

when the earl called after him, "De Tournay! If the girl is not a virgin, I don't wish to have her back. You can kill her if you wish to. It matters not to me."

Slowly Roland stilled his destrier and dismounted to stand facing the earl. He was sickened but not oversurprised. "I don't understand you. What matter if the girl is ravished? Her dowry remains the same size, does it not? Her dowry doesn't constrict even if her maidenhead is gone."

"All changes if she is not chaste."

"For that matter, how do I know if she's been ravished? How would you know?"

"I would examine her myself." The earl paused, then said, fury facing his voice, "That damned fool Colchester says he won't have her for his son if she isn't pure. His foul mother gave his father the pox and killed him because of the men she took to her bed. He's terrified that if Daria is ravished, she'll kill his precious son with disease as well."

Roland was seeing the earl thrusting his fingers into the girl's body to feel if her maidenhead were still intact. To humiliate another thus was incomprehensible to him, particularly a girl who had no recourse but to accept the shame of it.

"Colchester isn't the only unwedded man

in the kingdom," Roland said mildly. "Wed her to another. She's an heiress, I gather. Most men aren't so absolute in their requirements for a wife, I doubt."

"She is to wed Colchester, none other. It is the only match I will accept."

And then, finally, Roland understood. The Earl of Reymerstone had made an agreement with the Earl of Colchester, and what he would gain in the marriage mattered more to him than the dowry. Roland wondered what the bargain was that the two men had struck.

"If she's a virgin when I rescue her, she will be a virgin when she arrives here."

"Excellent. If she isn't, then I will kill her and you as well, de Tournay, and I will keep her dowry for myself, since there is nothing else for me."

Roland believed he would most certainly try. He nodded curtly and remounted Cantor. He was on his way to London now, to see the king; then he would ride to Cornwall. He needed to see Graelam de Moreton; then he wanted to visit Thispen-Ladock, just to look at the stone walls and the green hills, just to stroll through the inner bailey and speak to all the people, and know that what he was doing would make this possible for him. He had the time, and in the next two weeks he would make all his plans. He would travel northward from Cornwall to the southeast corner of Wales to Tyberton Castle, domain of the Clares since Duke William's conquest of England. He knew now how he would present himself to Edmond of Clare. He smiled, seeing himself in this new role. He also admitted, his smile widening, that he had a bit of studying to do before he arrived at Tyberton Castle.

Tyberton Castle, on the River Wye
May 1275

Ena lightly slapped the folds of Daria's silk gown into a more pleasing shape. "There, 'tis lovely ye are now. But the man will find ye lovely as well, the good Lord above knows that. Ye'll take care, won't ye, little mistress?"

"Aye," Daria said. Ena's warnings, admonitions, and portents were daily fare and their impact had dimmed with repetition. Edmond of Clare was surely bent on ravishment, and today would be the day. But he didn't ravish her, and the days went by. Slowly, so very slowly. She wished to heaven that Ena wouldn't call her "little mistress." It was what he called her, and she hated it. She'd been here since the twelfth of March, nearly two months now, and she wanted to scream with the boredom, the fear, with the awful tension that would never leave her. She was a prisoner and she didn't know what her captor wanted of her. At the beginning, she'd spoken from her terror, not measuring the possible consequences of her words. She asked him, fear making her voice harsh, "If you ransom me, will you let me go? Is it just my dowry you want? Why don't you say something? Why don't you tell me?"

Edmond of Clare had slapped her, not really all that hard, but hard enough so that she'd felt the pain of it throughout her body and she'd reeled with the force of it, nearly falling to her knees. He watched the pain take her for a few moments, then said easily, this matter of her impertinence duly handled, "You will do as I tell you and you will ask me no more questions. Now, little mistress, would you like to eat some delicious stewed lamb?"

He baffled her. She feared him, yet he hadn't struck her since that first time. Of course she'd tried to give him no provocation. She saw violence in him, leashed in her presence, but she could feel it, just as she'd always felt it in her Uncle Damon. She saw his control tested once when a servant had spilled some thickly sauced meat on his arm. She saw the vein jump in his throat, saw his clenched fists, but his voice issued forth mild, and his reproof was gentle. Then why, she'd wondered, had the servant looked like he was shortly to die and was wonderfully surprised when he hadn't?

She still didn't know anything. If he was ransoming her, as she had to assume that he was, she didn't know what he'd demanded; she didn't know if her uncle had responded. She didn't know anything, and it was infuriating and frustrating. And then she would think: all he did was slap me. And she decided she would ask him again. She wouldn't demand, she would ask softly, something she should have learned to do with her uncle. Ah, but it galled her to be the supplicant.

Ena stepped back and folded her arms over her scrawny chest. "Ye've grown, a good inch taller ye are, and look at yer ankles, poking out over yer feet, and that gown of yers pulls across yer breasts. Ye must have new gowns, at least cloth so ye can sew yerself something that will fit ye. Ask the earl to fetch ye some nice woolen cloth —"

"That's quite enough, Ena. I won't demand cloth for new gowns. I care not if my ankles offend you — it matters not to me."

"Ah, if only we could leave here and ye could wed with Ralph of Colchester as ye were supposed to."

Daria shivered at that gruesome thought. "I would rather become a nun."

These sarcastically spoken impious words brought a loud groan from Ena and a quick crossing over her chest. "Ralph of Colchester was to be yer husband! If he was weak, he would still have been yer husband, and that makes all the difference. He's no savage marauder who should have been a priest, a crazy man who holds ye prisoner and makes ye pray in his damp chapel until yer knees are cramped and bruised red!"

"I wonder," Daria mused aloud, ignoring her maid, "I do wonder if Ralph of Colchester will still wish to marry me. 'Tis a matter of the size of my dowry, I think, not the question of my virtue or my captor's virtue. That and how much his father needs my coin. 'Tis an interesting question, though. Mayhap I'll ask the earl."

That brought a louder shriek from Ena, and Daria lightly patted her arm. "Nay, I jest. Don't carry on so." She turned and walked to the narrow window, only a narrow arrow slit actually, with a skin hanging above it to be lowered when the weather was foul. For the past three days the sun had shone down warm and bright.

But Daria shivered. She stared down into the inner bailey of Tyberton Castle. It was a huge fortress, its denizens numbering into the hundreds, and there were people and animals and filth everywhere. The only time there was quiet was on Sundays. The earl held services and all were required to attend for the endless hours. Until a week ago.

Edmond of Clare was devoutly religious. He spent the hours from five in the morning until seven on his knees in the cold Tyberton chapel. Then his priest held a private Mass for him and only for him, for which all the castle folk were grateful. The earl had been on a rampage for the past four days, for his priest had left Tyberton during a storm one night and no one knew why.

Daria knew why, as, she suspected, did most of the inhabitants of Tyberton, though they would never say so. The priest had no calling for such sacrifice as Clare demanded. He was fat and lazy and all the services had finally ground him down. He'd hated the cold dark chapel, hated the endless hours of absolving the Earl of Clare. Daria had heard him mumble about it, complaining bitterly that he would die of frozen lungs before the winter was out.

Well, now the chapel was empty. There

was no mumbled illiterate Latin service to suffer through, no chilled bones from the damp cold air blowing through the thick gray stones from the River Wye. No more suffering for the nose, for the priest had smelled as foul as the refuse pile at the back of the castle. The fellow was gone. All were relieved except the earl.

Daria had found it odd, though, that the earl, such a fanatic in matters of the soul, didn't speak a bit of Latin. The priest had slurred his words, creating them from the sounds he knew the earl would accept, for he himself couldn't pronounce half of them properly and the earl seemed not to notice.

Daria spoke and read Latin, as did her mother, who'd been her teacher. She'd said nothing to the earl about it.

She turned at the knock on her small chamber door. It was one of the earl's men, a thin-faced youth named Clyde who had the habit of looking at Daria as if she were a Christmas feast and he a man begging to stuff himself. She simply stared at him, not moving.

"The earl wishes to see ye," he said, and as he spoke, his eyes traveled down her body, stopping only when they reached the pointed toes of her leather slippers.

She merely nodded, still not moving,

waiting for Clyde to leave, which he finally did, his expression sour. Once she'd moved to do his bidding, only to feel his hands on her as she passed him.

"Ye be careful, young mistress," Ena hissed in her ear. "Ye stay out of his reach. Pray until yer tongue falls out, but keep away from him."

"Please," Daria said, shook off Ena's hand, and left the chamber. She lifted her skirts as she stepped carefully down the deeply cut stone steps that wound downward into the great hall of Tyberton. There were only three men in the hall and one of them was Edmond of Clare. He was speaking in a low voice to his master-at-arms, a Scotsman named MacLeod. Daria watched Edmond make a point with his hands, and shivered, remembering when his right hand, palm open, had struck her cheek. He was a big man, with the fierce red hair of his Scottish mother and the dark Celtic eyes of his father. His complexion was white as a dead man's. He usually spoke softly, which made it all the more unsettling when he suddenly exploded in a rage. He was a giant of a man, his chest the width of a tree trunk, the lower part of his pale white face covered with a curling red beard. He was handsome in a savage sort of way, Daria would give him that, but she'd heard that his wife, dead for only six months now, her infant son with her, had lived in fear of him. She was inclined to believe it.

She didn't move, but rather waited until he noticed her, which he did. "Come hither," he called. "I have gained us a new priest. His name is Father Corinthian and he will say Mass for us tomorrow. He is a Benedictine."

Daria walked forward, noticing the priest in his cheap wool cowl for the first time. "Father," she said.

"My child," said Father Corinthian. He pulled back the hood from his monk's cowl and took her hand. Daria felt a shock that drove the color from her face. She wanted to pull her hand away, but she didn't. She looked into the priest's dark eyes and she knew him.

She knew him to the very depths of her, and it was as terrifying as it was unexpected, this amazing and overwhelming knowledge, and she was consumed with dark feelings that she couldn't comprehend and that made her reel with their force. Here was something that was fearful yet real, and it was overpowering. For the first time in her life, Daria fainted, collapsing in a heap to the rush-strewn floor.

2

Daria awoke with Ena crouched over her, her face parchment white, her lips trembling with fear and prayers.

"I'm all right," Daria said, and then turned her face away. But she wasn't all right; something had happened that she didn't understand. It was frightening. No, nothing was all right.

"But, little mistress, what happened? The earl just carried you here. He said naught. Did he speak harshly to you or strike you in front of that new priest? Did you speak sharply to him? Did he — ?"

"Please, Ena, take your leave. The earl did nothing to me. I wish to rest. Leave me now."

The old woman sniffed and retreated to the far corner of the chamber. Daria stared toward the narrow window. A shaft of bright sunlight knifed through, illuminating dust motes in its wake. What had happened to her in the great hall was inexplicable. The priest, that beautiful young man who was a Benedictine, a young man who was dedicated to God . . . and she'd somehow known him, recognized him, felt his very being deep inside of her. How could that be? It made no sense.

It had happened but once before in her seventeen years, this prescience, this foreknowledge, this tide of feeling that had been the curse of her grandmother, a bent old woman who'd died howling curses at her son and daughters. A crazy old woman with wild stringy hair and mad eyes, eyes the same color green as were hers.

When Daria was twelve her mother had told her that her father would be coming home to them shortly to visit with them until he left for the Holy Land. He was currently in London, fighting in a tourney. It was in that instant Daria saw her father, handsome and awesomely forbidding in his gleaming silver armor, astride his destrier, and he was charging, his visor down, lance at the ready. She saw him as clearly as she saw her mother who stood in front of her, staring and silent. She saw his lance buffeted to the side, saw him lifted off his destrier's back and flung into the dirt. She saw the other man's destrier rear back in fright and come crashing down on her father's head. She heard the crunching of the metal, the smashing of bone, and she screamed with the sight of it, the sound of it, the dark feel of it in her mind, the bloody horror of it. And she'd told her mother what she'd seen, but her mother had somehow known she was seeing something, and she was already as pale as the wimple that hid her beautiful auburn hair. "No," her mother had whispered; then she'd left Daria, nearly running, and Daria had known her mother was afraid of her in that moment.

And the word had reached them five days later. Her father's body followed three days after that, and he was buried on the family hillock, his body never again seen by his wife because the destrier had smashed his skull under his hooves.

Now it had happened again. Only this time it wasn't death and terror and pain that wouldn't cease. This time it was a strange shock of recognition, a *knowing* of another person she'd never seen before. She didn't understand what it meant or how to account for it or explain it. Was this poor young priest to die? She didn't think so, but she simply didn't know. But she'd looked at him and felt something deep within her move, open, and then he'd taken her hand as any priest might, and the touch of him had pierced into her, leaving her naked and raw, confused feelings flooding through her.

And like a lackwit, she'd fainted. She'd fainted in front of the earl, and she'd known even as she'd felt herself falling that she was still gaping at the young priest.

There came a knock on the chamber door. Daria turned to see Ena speed to the door and open it slightly to peer out. She heard Edmond of Clare's voice. He pushed Ena out of his way, nearly knocking the old woman to the floor, and strode into the room.

"You're awake," he said, looking down at her from his great height. "What happened to you? Are you sickening with something?"

She shook her head, fearing in that moment what might come out of her mouth if she spoke.

"Then what?"

Should she tell him that her grandmother had died mad, died cursed as a witch, and that mayhap she was a witch too? Tell him that the priest who'd shriven her grandmother had been pale and stammering with fear in the presence of that mad old woman? "I am sorry to upset you. I just suddenly felt faint. The Benedictine priest . . . he is to remain here at Tyberton?"

"Aye. I wanted you to meet him, but you fell at our feet, and the poor young fellow was naturally concerned. You frightened him, and now I must wonder if you did it apurpose, to beg his help, mayhap? To beg his assistance to help you escape me?"

"No."

"I did not really think so. You haven't the guile, Daria, to gain your ends through perfidy."

She stared at him, wondering how he could come to believe she was so transparent. She prayed a moment would come when she would best him with her perfidy.

"He appears a pious and learned young man," Edmond of Clare continued after a moment. "The Benedictines spawn dedicated priests, from what I hear. He will remain here in my service."

"What is his name?"

"He said the name given him at the Benedictine abbey was Father Corinthian. He will hold a Mass for us on the morrow morning. You and I will attend, no one else. My soul is needful of cleansing. As for yours, your sheltered youth sustains you, but still God's word will not come amiss to your ears."

Daria didn't want to see the young priest again, and yet at the same time she wanted to see him, touch him, just once more, just to see if the first time had been a vague aberration, an accident brought about by her fear and frustration at her captivity.

He was a priest, this man who wasn't a man. He was God's man, God's weapon, God's gift to man. "I will come to the chapel," she said, and Edmond of Clare stared down at her silently for another long moment, lightly touched his fingers to her hair. "So soft you are," he said, then left her.

She lay there frozen. There was no meanness in his look or his light touch, but a certain tenderness, and it terrified her. It wasn't lust, yet there was lust in it, and something else far more harmful as well. She closed her eyes. Her heart pounded loudly.

That evening at the late meal, she came slowly into the great hall, glad for its loudness, its sheer number of people, for their very presence was a sort of protection for her. She saw Edmond already seated in his great chair, the new priest seated at his left. The chair to his right — her chair — was empty. Her step lagged. She couldn't take her eyes off the priest. She saw in the rich light of the flambeaux that his dark hair shone clean and silky. He was dressed simply, but unlike other priests she'd known, both he and his clothing were clean. Even in the loose tunic, she could tell that he was lean and well-formed; his didn't seem to be the body of a man who partook only of spiritual exercise. He looked fit and active, a man who could just as easily take his place as a knight and a warrior. But his face held her and she couldn't take her eyes off him as she walked slowly through the throngs of people to the dais. His features were finely hewn, from his arched black brows to the cleft in his chin. He was nearly dark as an Arab, his eyes nearly black as his hair. As he spoke, he used his hands, eloquent narrow hands, to make a point. His expression was intelligent, and more than that, it was clever. He was a priest, surely, but he was a handsome man, and to look upon him gave one pleasure. Suddenly he looked up and saw her, and his face stilled.

To her utter stupefaction, she felt that same shock of recognition explode inside her. She felt bare and exposed, yet she realized in that moment that he didn't see what was there for him to see and understand and take. Aye, take. She saw him stare at her, and he cocked his head to one side in silent question. He had felt nothing; he must believe her mad.

She quickly lowered her eyes and made her way quietly to her chair.

Edmond of Clare nodded at her, saw that her trencher was filled, then turned his attention back to the priest. He didn't appear to have noticed anything amiss.

Roland chewed for a long while on the stewed piece of beef. He needed to give himself time to regain his wits. He saw Daria seat herself on Clare's right, saw her lower her eyes to her trencher.

He heard Clare ask him a question, and he responded. He'd escaped from Clare's company as soon as he could this afternoon after the girl had fallen into a faint at his feet. He'd seen the utter bewilderment in her eyes when she'd turned to look at him, the obvious shock she felt upon seeing him, touching his hand. It was passing strange, and he was inclined to think the girl bereft of wits. It was as if she'd known him, as if she recognized him, but that wasn't possible. He'd never seen her before in his life. And he would have remembered.

She was passing fair. He'd found her pleasant to look at, surely, nothing more or less. Her features were clear and delicately drawn, satisfying the taste of most men, and yet she wasn't beautiful in the purity and perfection of her features. There was strength in her face, a natural vitality that was now dimmed from her captivity. Her dark hair was as her uncle had described it — filled with the rich deep colors of autumn — but even her hair appeared dulled. Her eyes were a pure green that seemed to lighten or darken with her changing mood. This afternoon they'd been as dark as the turbulent Irish Sea in the dawn. Now they were light and soft. She was reed slender, slight of build, but her chin was held high, showing her dignity, her training as a lady. But there was strength and courage in her, he knew it. There was a hollowness in her cheeks, a drawn look about her, again a sign of her captivity.

Perhaps he could even understand why Edmond of Clare wanted to take her as his wife. Perhaps the man had seen the promise in her, the grit. Even as he thought it, Roland shook his head. No, the earl saw a young girl in splendid health who would produce him a string of fine sons. If he were lucky, she wouldn't die in childbed as had his first two wives. Then Roland saw again in his mind's eye her insensible shock upon seeing him. Perhaps it was an attack of bile on her part and not a lack of wit. He prayed it was so. He'd even questioned himself as to his role; had she perhaps seen through him?

Seen him as a fraud and a liar? Not believed him a priest for the barest second?

Edmond of Clare put further questions to him, and he replied easily and fluently, for he'd studied his role for the past two weeks, bending on it with all his concentration. He couldn't afford to make mistakes. His life hung in the balance, as did hers. He rather liked the name Father Corinthian; it had a very Eastern sound to it that pleased the aesthetic part of him. But this wretched girl . . . whatever had been wrong with her this afternoon? He would get her out of here soon and he'd get her home even sooner.

He shivered and took another bite of the overly salted stewed beef. He had to find out if she was still a virgin. He thought that she was. From what he knew already of Edmond of Clare, the man, whatever else he was, appeared to understand honor. The girl didn't look in the least abused.

What she did look was bewildered. She didn't face him once during the long meal. Roland determined he would discover the cause of her stupefaction as soon as possible. He passed his evening discussing theological questions with Edmond of Clare. What seemed to prey on the earl's mind was the issue of man's loyalty to another man versus his loyalty to God. Roland quickly discovered that the earl wasn't a stupid man. He also quickly learned that the earl spent the bulk of his time immersing his mind in religious matters, and thus knew more about Church dogma than did Roland. If Roland hadn't been so facile of tongue, he would have found himself several times in grave difficulties.

At one point the earl leaned back in his chair and stroked his thick fingers through his equally thick red beard. "You met the young lady, Daria," he said at last. "I intend to wed her the last day of this month."

"Ah," Roland said, smiling. "That brings up an interesting question, does it not? A man's loyalty to a woman, namely his wife."

"Absurd," said Edmond of Clare, shrugging. "Women are of little worth, save as vessels for a man's seed, and my first two wives failed even at that. They both died, taking their infants with them. You would think they could have left the babes alive, but they didn't, curse their selfishness. But Daria, the girl looks healthy and fit to bear me sons."

Roland felt astonishment at the earl's words. He'd heard men vow before their peers that women were naught but chattel, but to say a woman was selfish because her babe died with her? It passed all bounds.

"Who is she?" he asked, taking a sip of wine from his flagon. "She already seems the mistress, since she is obviously a lady."

The earl answered readily, without hesitation, "The niece of a man I have wanted to kill for five years. But with her as my wife, he will be safe from me, curse his rotted soul. It is the compromise I am willing to make. She also brings me a great dowry. I suppose I must forget my revenge upon the uncle with the niece as my wife. Unless, of course, I can get my hands on him with no one knowing of it." The earl fell silent, his expression brooding, as if he weren't completely pleased with the bargain he had made. He said suddenly, "Is it your belief, Father, that if a man fully intends to marry a woman, it is still a sin for him to bed the woman before they are joined in God's eyes?"

Roland felt no astonishment at this question. He felt a surge of raw anger, and oddly enough, a bit of amusement. Edmond of Clare was a man who hated to give in to lust, and if he did, he wanted it condoned and excused by God. But if he did take Daria before Roland could get her away from Tyberton . . . Roland wasn't stupid or naive, and he knew that Damon Le Mark, once he knew for a certainty she was no longer a virgin, would kill her just as he'd said he would. He wanted her back only because of Colchester and what the marriage would bring him, the coveted lands to extend his own acres. And it was only the lands that drew him more than the great dowry. But Colchester wouldn't have her marry his son if her maidenhead had been rent, and thus Damon Le Mark would have to content himself with her money. To get it, he would have to rid himself of his niece.

Roland brought his wits to bear on the earl's question. He said with all the firmness a priest should have at his command, and prayed it was enough, "A man's lust is a matter that should not concern his wife or the lady who will soon be his wife. If he must needs slake his lust, he should do it on another female, one of lesser account."

Edmond of Clare muttered something under his breath but presented no arguments. The interminable evening finally ended in his saying prayers over the assembled men and women of Tyberton. He wanted to impress the Benedictine priest. He fancied he did it well. He noticed that most of the people remaining in the hall appreciated his efforts toward their spiritual salvation. Only a few of the louts fidgeted and leaned from one side to the other. He would see them punished.

Roland bade the girl, Daria, good night, and watched her leave the hall. He prayed he'd saved the girl's maidenhead for another day with his priestly edict. He slept that night in a small niche off the solar, warm enough, but he would wager that in the dead of winter a man's bones would be chilled to the marrow pressed against the cold damp stones, even wrapped in a dozen blankets.

It was six o'clock in the morning and Roland was clean and cowled and vigorously awake. Latin hummed on his tongue. Since he was a small boy, Roland had always preferred the early mornings. His mind was sharper, his wits more acute, his body supple and strong and ready for action. He made his way quickly to the damp and depressing chapel.

The Tyberton chapel was long and narrow, with several wooden carved saints decorating the nave, each rivaling the other in varying stages of gruesome martyrdom. It was damp and cold in the chapel and Roland could feel the early-morning fog from the River Wye waft through the thick gray stones. He thought again of his goal: the keep and the lands he was purchasing in Cornwall. The keep itself was small, but it was finely built and was safe and snug and warm, situated nearer the southern coast rather than the savage and barren northern coast. It would be his once he'd returned the girl safely to her uncle and collected the other half of his fee. By all the saints, he wished this were over and he was there, tilling his own fields, repairing his own walls, filling his own granaries.

He waited impatiently for the earl and Daria to arrive, the Mass filtering through his mind. He knew much of it by heart now, not that it mattered overmuch. Edmond of Clare spoke no Latin, just parroted the responses; he'd made sure of that when he'd questioned the earl's former priest, a fat lout who was delighted to take the coin offered to escape Tyberton and its fanatic owner. As for the rest of the castle denizens, they could scarce speak the King's English, from what Roland had heard.

The girl, Daria, came first into the chapel. She was dressed warmly, a thick wool cloak covering her gown. It was apparent that she'd been in this chapel many times before. Her head was covered by a soft white wimple. Her eyes were downcast. She was either very religious or she was purposefully avoiding looking at him. He stared hard at her until she finally looked up. He saw uncertainty writ clear on her face, blank surprise in her eyes as she looked at him. And there it was again, that odd way she stared at him. He started to speak, but Edmond of Clare strode in at that moment. He offered Daria his arm and escorted her to the first bench facing the nave and the priest.

"Father," Edmond said, his voice low and sonorous and infinitely respectful.

Roland nodded benignly. "Be seated, my children, and we will praise the Lord's bounty and laud his beneficence on the Feast of Devotion." He crossed himself and regarded his two supplicants with bland favor. Once they were seated, he began, his voice fluent and low:

Nos autem gloriari oportet in cruce Domini nostri Jesu Christi: in quo est salus, vita, et resurrectio nostra: per quem salvati, et liberati sumus.

Daria felt the pure sweet tones of the Latin fill her. He spoke beautifully, his voice low and soothing. It was obvious to her that he was learned, unlike many priests, who were illiterate, for he understood what he was saying and gave feeling to the sentiments. As he spoke, she translated his words in her mind.

". . . But it behooves us to glory in the cross of our Lord Jesus Christ: in whom is our salvation, life, and resurrection: by whom we are saved and delivered . . ."

Alleluia, alleluia. Deus misereatur nostri, et benedicat nobis: illuminet vultum suum super nos, et misereatur nostri. Gloria Patri.

It was beautiful, the words and his voice, and she couldn't take her eyes from his face, his beautiful face that wasn't a man's face, not really, but the face of God at this moment, his speech God's speech, the near-hypnotic movement of his hands binding her and making the earl beside her draw in his breath with the moving beauty of it. ". . . Alleluia, alleluia. May God have mercy on us and bless us: may he cause the light of his countenance to shine upon us, and may he have mercy on us. Glory to the Father."

Hoc enim sentite in vobis, quod et in Christo Jesu: Qui cum in forma Dei esset, non rapinam arbitratus est esse se aequalem Deo: sed semetipsum . . .

The words continued to flow from his mouth through her mind: ". . . Let this mind be in you, which was also in Christ Jesus: who, being in the form of God, thought it

not robbery to be equal with God: but emptied himself . . ."

Father Corinthian paused, oddly, then re-
sumed, his voice lower, his pace quickened.

Neque auribus neque oculie satis consto . . .

Daria's head whipped up and she stared
at him. His look was limpid, his hands
raised, even as he repeated yet again:

Neque auribus neque oculie satis consto . . .

No, it wasn't possible, yet she hadn't mistaken his words. Her lips parted and she
stared at him, even as he said again, in Latin,
"I am losing my eyesight and getting deaf."

Hostis in cervicibus alicuinus est . . .

She whispered the words in English, "The
foe is at our heels."

Nihil tibi a me postulanti recusabo . . .
Optate mihi contingunt . . . Quid de me
fiet? . . . Naves ex porta solvunt . . . Nostri
circiter centum ceciderunt . . . Dulce
lignanum, dulces clavos, dulcia ferens
pondera: quae sola fuisti digna sustinere
regem caelorum, et Domininum. Alleluia.

"I will refuse you nothing . . . My wishes are being fulfilled . . . What will become of me? . . . The ships sail from the harbor . . . About a hundred of our men fell . . . Sweet wood, sweet nails, bearing a sweet weight: which alone wert worthy to bear the king of heaven and the Lord. Alleluia."

Daria's expression was one of astonishment and amazement. She quickly realized that the earl, his head raised in proud arrogance before his God, his eyes closed in exaltation, hadn't realized that his new priest, his learned and erudite Benedictine, had been having a fine time mixing the Mass with a layman's Latin. But he hadn't done it in the manner of the last priest. No, this man was educated, and he had the ability to juggle and to substitute, but . . .

The remainder of the Mass went quickly, and the priest seemed to have gathered his memory together, for he made no more references to foes or cut-off heads.

He blessed the earl and Daria, saying, his arms raised, "Dominus vobiscum," and the earl replied by rote to the priest's exhortation of the Lord be with you with "Et cum spiritu tuo."

Father Corinthian looked at Daria expectantly, and she said softly, "Capilli horrent."

Roland nearly lost his ale and bread and

60

his bland expression, so taken aback was he. There was no expression on her face as she repeated, not the expected "Et cum spiritu tuo" but again "Capilli horrent."

His hair stands on end.

The little twit knew Latin! By all the saints, she was mocking him, she could give him away! He looked appalled, as well he might; then he caught himself as he heard her say clearly, "Bene id tibi vertat."

He bowed his head, her words buzzing with the Latin Mass in his mind. *I wish you all success in the matter.*

Roland stepped back and raised his hands. "Deo gratias." He smiled at the earl, who looked as if God himself had just conferred honors upon him.

"Thank you, Father, thank you. My soul rejoices that you are here." The earl rubbed his large hands together. "Aye, I feared whilst there was no man of God in my castle, feared for my own soul and the souls of my people."

He turned to Daria and said, his tone disapproving, "You said something I did not recognize as a response. What was it?"

She didn't pale; she didn't change expression. She said, "It was nonsense. I couldn't remember what to repeat, and thus conjured up the sounds. I am sorry, my lord, Father, it was disrespectful of me."

The earl's face grew even more stiff with disapproval. " 'Tis blasphemous to do such a thing. I shall have the good Father Corinthian teach you the proper responses, and you will learn them now. It is shameful not to know them, Daria."

She bowed her head submissively.

"Yes, my lord."

"Your uncle was remiss in his responsibilities toward you. You will spend the next hour with Father Corinthian."

"Yes, my lord."

The earl nodded once again to Roland and took his leave. They were alone in the dank chapel.

"Who are you?"

"That is quick and to the point," Roland remarked, his eyes on the closed chapel door. "Let me make certain no one is about outside."

"It wouldn't matter if there were a dozen men listening at the door. This wretched chapel is sound as a crypt, the door nearly as thick as the stone of the walls."

Nonetheless Roland strode to the door, opened it, and slowly closed it again. He turned to face her.

"Who are you?" she repeated.

"You speak Latin."

"Yes, I speak Latin. 'Twas something you didn't expect."

"No I didn't. You didn't give me away to the earl. May I assume that you still wish to escape him?"

She nodded and asked again, "Who are you?"

"I am sent by your uncle to rescue you. As you know now, I am no Benedictine priest."

She gave him a dazzling, perfectly wicked smile that rocked him back on his heels. He thought he'd made a perfectly adequate priest, damn her impertinence. He was frowning, but she forestalled him. "But you are an educated man, unlike the previous priest, who could barely string together sounds that resembled Latin. The earl, of course, didn't know any better. Did you get rid of him?"

"Yes, 'twas quite easy, for he was miserable here at Tyberton, and most willing to accept a bit of coin for his absconding. You recognized me, then, yesterday when you fainted? You knew I was no priest from just looking at me? That is why you turned so pale and collapsed?"

She shook her head and looked embarrassed. "I don't know why . . . that is, I didn't know you then, and yet I did know you, perhaps even better than I know myself." That sounded like utter drivel, she thought. She ground to a painful halt and looked up at him for his reaction. Again, that shock of knowledge, that feeling that he was there, deep inside her, part of her, and she took a step back. She wasn't making sense and he would think her utterly mad.

"What is it? Do I frighten you?"

"Yes," she said. "I don't understand this."

Roland chose for the moment to ignore her mysterious words. Indeed he didn't understand any of what she'd said and didn't have time at present to seek enlightenment. "As I said, I am here to rescue you."

"I don't wish to marry Ralph of Colchester. He is lewd and weak and without character."

Roland frowned at her. "That is something that has nothing to do with me. Your uncle is paying me to bring you back, and that is what I shall do. What happens to you then is up to your uncle. He is your guardian. It is his decision. No female should have the power to decide who her husband will be. It would lead the world into chaos."

"This world you men have ruled since the beginning of time stews continuously in chaos. What more harm or disaster could women bring to bear?"

"You speak from ignorance. Mayhap your

uncle isn't wise or compassionate, but it is the way of things. It's natural that you submit."

Daria sighed. He was naught but a man, like all the other men who had come into her life. Men ruled and women obeyed. It was a pity and it brought her pain, which she promptly dismissed. This man whom she knew, this man who didn't know her, also didn't care what happened to her. Why should he? This absurd recognition was all on her side, these bewildering feelings had naught to do with him. It came to her then that once he'd gotten her free of Edmond of Clare, she could then escape from him. He cared not, after all, what became of her.

"You have not yet told me your name."

"You may call me Roland."

"Ah, like Charlemagne's fearsomely brave Roland. When do we leave, sir?"

3

Roland rocked back on his heels at that. "Just like that? You believe me? You will go with me? You require no more proof?"

Daria shook her head, smiling at him, that dazzling, innocent, yet strangely knowing smile. "Of course I believe you. I am pleased you aren't a priest."

"Why?"

She wanted to tell him that she was delighted that he was just a man, a man of the world, and not a man of God, but she didn't. He would truly believe her mad. She shook her head again, saying, "My mother, did you see her? Is she all right? You went to Reymerstone Castle?"

"Yes, and your mother appeared well. You have something of the look of her, not her coloring, but something of her expression. If I recall aright, your father was dark as a Neapolitan."

"You knew my father?"

"As a young man in King Edward's company, aye, I knew him, as did most of the young knights. Sir James was brave and trustworthy. It is a pity he died so inopportunely. Edward missed him sorely in the Holy Land."

The chapel door suddenly opened and the earl reappeared. "Well, girl? Tell me the correct response."

Daria didn't change expression. She repeated swiftly, her eyes lowered meekly, "Et cum spiritu tuo."

The earl nodded. "Well said. I am pleased with you. I have never agreed that women had not the ability to learn, and you have proved me correct. Do you agree with your brothers, Father?"

Roland looked benignly upon Daria as he would upon a dog who had just performed a trick well. He smiled to himself as he said in a pontifical voice, "Women can learn to mouth words — in any language — if they are allowed sufficient time for repetition. 'Tis doubtful she gleans the true meaning, but God is understanding and forgiving of his most feeble creation."

The earl nodded and Daria ground her teeth.

"You will come with me now, Daria," the

earl continued. "A tinker is here and I wish you to select a piece of finery you wish to have. You will become my wife at the end of the month, and thus I wish to show you my favor."

She stared at him dumbfounded, and Roland waited, tense and anxious, but she said nothing, merely nodded and followed the earl docilely from the chapel. Only when they were alone did she touch the earl's sleeve to gain his attention. She looked up at him, her expression puzzled, and said, unable to keep her surprise to herself, "This is why you kidnapped me, my lord? You wished to wed me?"

The incredulity in her voice was understandable, as was her question, though it bordered on impertinence. He decided to deal gently with her this time. "Nay, little one, I took you in revenge against your uncle, who is a man I detest above most men. At first I demanded your dowry as a ransom. Then, your graceful presence has made my heart quicken in my breast, and I changed my demand to him. He will send me his own priest and your dowry by the end of May and we will be wedded. Then he will be safe from my vengeance." He frowned even as the words came out of his mouth. "Mayhap not. Mayhap I shall change my mind, for Damon Le Mark is a poisonous snake to be crushed."

"What did you tell him you would do if he refused your demand? Did you threaten to murder me?"

The earl reacted swiftly, for this was beyond what in his mind was permissible for a woman, particularly for a woman who would be his wife. He struck her with his open palm on her cheek and she reeled backward, her shoulder striking the doorway, sending pain jolting through her body.

"Keep your pert tongue in your mouth, Daria! I will tell you what you need to know, and it will be enough for you. No more of your insolence — it displeases me, as it must displease our Lord."

It was odd this rage she felt. It wasn't the same she felt toward her uncle. This rage burned hot within her, but she also saw Edmond of Clare as apart from the awful anger he'd brought her. Her uncle was purposely cruel. Worse, he pleased himself with cruelty and the suffering of others, whereas Edmond of Clare simply saw her — a female — as a being to be constantly corrected and admonished, for her benefit, not because it gave him demented pleasure. He believed devoutly in God, at least in a God that suited his own convictions and expectations, and saw it as his duty to teach her the proper way of behaving. Her rage simmered and she sought to control it.

Roland held himself back in the shadows. It required all his control to do so. He'd heard her question of Clare and seen him strike her.

He didn't particularly wish to, but he found that he admired her in that moment. He saw the grit in her that would grow stronger as she gained years, if only she would be given the least encouragement and opportunity. She didn't cry. She didn't speak. She merely straightened her clothing and stood there stolid and silently proud, waiting for the earl to tell her his bidding. Roland wondered how many times he'd struck her during her captivity, to show her a woman's place. He must get her away from here, quickly. Not only was the earl growing perilously close to ravishing her, he just might injure her badly in a fit of rage.

During the remainder of the day, Roland examined the castle and found the escape route he would use. He learned that Daria had her maid with her, but he knew the older woman would hold them back and they wouldn't have a good chance of escaping if they took her with them. The old woman would have to stay here. If Daria protested, he would simply . . . What would he do? Strike her, as did Edmond of Clare? He shook his head on that thought.

That evening the earl again monopolized him so that he had no opportunity of speaking privately with Daria. She no longer looked at him as if he were some sort of specter to be gawked at, or a man she'd seen before, perhaps in another place or in another time. Still, though, she tended to avoid his eyes, and it bothered him because he didn't understand her.

"There is a debate that fascinates me," the earl began as he moved a chess piece on the board between them.

Roland moved his king's pawn forward in answer and waited. He'd learned the value of patience, the value of allowing the other man to speak first.

"Do women have souls? What do the Benedictines offer as their belief?"

"It is a matter of some debate, as you know. Even the Benedictine order finds itself in contention on the matter." Roland moved out his king's knight in reply to the earl's pawn move.

"True, true, but surely you, as a Benedictine, believe that women should be chastised for disobedience, for ill temper, for sloth or impiety?"

"Certainly, but 'tis a husband who applies the proper chastisement."

The earl drew back, his thick red brows knitting. "She is nearly my wife. She is young and thus malleable, but still, because she carries the perversity of her gender, and the blood of a man whose heart rots with sin — I speak of her uncle, of course — she grows more impertinent as the days pass. She needs a man's correction. I wish only to provide her proper guidance now."

"She is not yet your wife."

"Does it matter, if she has not a soul, what she is? Wife, harlot, maid?"

Roland's fingers tightened around his queen's bishop. He slowly moved the piece to the knight-five square. "It is my belief that women are creatures of God just as are men. They are made as we are — they possess arms, legs, a heart, a liver. They are the weaker, true, in body and mayhap in spirit as well. But they do have worth. They birth children and protect them with their lives, and thus their claim to God's grace is as great as is a man's. After all, my lord earl, we are unable to procreate ourselves; we are unable to suckle our children. 'Twas God who bestowed upon them these gifts, and it is these gifts that speak to our continuity and thus our immortality."

"You beset me with vain sophistry, Father, and address not my concern. Surely women are vessels, and they have breasts that carry milk, and wombs that hold babes, but are they more? I do not see their birthing us as God's gift to them, for they often die doing it. It also wastes a man's time. The two wives I have held as my own knew not honor or loyalty or fierceness of spirit. They were weak both of body and of mind. I never saw them as more than the means to continue myself."

Roland remembered Joan of Tenesby. He saw her clearly in that moment and could swear, right now, that her fierceness of spirit had exceeded any man's he'd ever known. She'd destroyed those around her with an arrogance and ruthlessness that staggered him with numbing awareness even now, nearly six years later.

"But you lust after the young Daria, do you not? You bought her finery from the tinker because you wished to please her, to flatter her vanity. But it was your vanity that enjoyed your purchases."

"You twist words, Father. This talk of vanity is an absurdity. As for my lust for the girl, well, God wills it so. If we were not driven to take what the female holds, we would not continue; thus it is our lust that is the true gift from God. God gives them to us and it is our right to use them when they are able. Indeed, it is our responsibility to beget our children in their wombs."

Roland smiled and said easily, even as he moved his king's bishop, "Nay, my lord earl, 'tis you who are gifted with facile argument. You would make a good bishop." Roland suddenly realized that to move his bishop would irrevocably cripple the earl's position on the chessboard. He quickly retracted it.

"Leave it," the earl said, not seeing the danger from the move. Roland replaced the piece and sat back in his chair.

But the earl wasn't interested in the game, but in expressing his own views. He tugged on his ear, cleared his throat, saying finally, "There is another matter, Father. Something that has bothered my spirit for many weeks now. Daria is young, as I said, but I find her occasionally frivolous, impious, exhibiting a woman's vanity. I can break her of these habits. But I now find that I doubt her virtue. You see, I know her uncle well, and he is a vile lecher. And I wonder again and again: Is she still a maiden? Or did her uncle give her to Ralph of Colchester when he visited Reymerstone Castle?"

Roland was shaking his head even before he said quickly, "Nay, her uncle would have protected her, not offered her to Colchester. Doubt it not."

The earl shook his head, unconvinced, not wanting to be convinced, Roland realized in a flash of insight. "I have little trust for women. They seduce men with their beauty and their modest manners, which are really practiced and sly. Perhaps that is how she gained Colchester's favors. I must know before I wed her, I must know, and I will know."

"You must believe me, my lord. The girl is a maid. Her uncle would never have allowed Colchester to have her. She would have lost her worth, her good name, more, the good name of her family. It matters not that he is a vile lecher. He isn't stupid, is he?"

The Earl of Clare only shrugged. He didn't want to acknowledge the truth of his priest's words, Roland realized. Roland looked grim as he said, "Then what you want, my lord, is for the Church to bless your forcing of her before you take her to wive. You want the Church to bless this mad scheme of yours. Truly, my lord earl, I cannot condone that. There is another solution, another way to have your question answered. You will allow me to ask her. I can see through falsehood, my lord. It is a gift I have. I will know if she lies or not. I will tell you true."

"And you will believe, Father, the words that flow from her mouth, or will you examine her for the truth of her vow?"

Roland very nearly rocked back in his chair with surprise and distaste. The earl seemed as vile as did Damon Le Mark. Did the earl really expect a man of God to examine a woman to discover if she still possessed a maidenhead? He managed to say steadily enough, his eyes meeting the earl's straightly, "I will know, when she tells me, whether she speaks the truth."

Roland waited, his fingers so tense they whitened on his black queen. Finally the earl nodded.

"You will speak to her, then. Do it now, Father. I must know."

But the earl did not wish Roland to leave him to his task until they had finished their game of chess. Roland wanted to trounce the earl but he guessed it would not hold him in good stead. Thus, he blundered deliberately, setting his queen in the path of the earl's white knight. It was over quickly.

"You play well, Father, but not as well as I. I will continue to give you instruction."

Roland drew on priestly reserves that must contain, he thought, a goodly supply of humility and deceit. He nodded gravely. " 'Twill be an honor to be so instructed."

His meekness pleased the earl, and he added, "And I will think on your words, Father."

Roland yet again inclined his head. Ten minutes later he was lightly knocking on Daria's bedchamber door.

It was opened by the maid, Ena.

"Is your mistress within?"

The old woman nodded. "He's sent you to her, Father?"

"Aye. I will speak with her. Alone."

The maid looked quickly back at Daria, then left the bedchamber.

Daria was on her feet and hurrying toward him. "What has happened? Do we leave now? What do — ?"

"Hush," he said, and took her hands in his, squeezing them. "The earl sends me here to speak with you. He wishes me to ensure that you are still a virgin."

She blinked at him.

It was answer enough, and he smiled down at her. "I know, think no more about it. The earl has unusual views regarding God's interest in his — the earl's — lust. Come, we must speak, and quickly, for I doubt not that he will soon come to see the result of my question."

He was still holding her hands and she felt his vitality flow through into her and it made her tremble with anticipation. He seemed to sense something, and released her hands. He took a step back, saying quickly, "I distrust the earl. He desires you mightily. Indeed he has spoken to me of taking you before you are wedded. I have tried to dissuade him, but I don't know if God's wishes will take precedence over his lust for you, for as I said, he regards his wishes as one and the same as God's. We are leaving Tyberton tonight. Listen to me, for we haven't much time."

Roland spoke low and quick, but he wasn't quick enough, for the door burst open and the earl strode into the bedchamber. He looked from his priest to Daria. They stood apart, and it seemed to him that Father Corinthian was speaking earnestly to her. It seemed innocent enough, but he asked, his voice filled with suspicion, "Well, Father? Is she still a maid?"

"She is a maid," Roland said.

"That is what she tells you."

"No man has touched me!"

"You are a woman and are born with lies trembling on your tongue. I wish to believe you, Father, but I find myself beset with doubts. When you left me, I heard one of my men telling another that all the castle wenches wish to bed you. I will admit that I saw you not as a man before but solely as a priest. Perhaps I yield to false tidings, and if I do, God will surely punish me for it, yet I see you now as a man alone with her."

Roland quickly assumed his most pious pose. "Believe me, I do not see your betrothed as a woman. I see her only as one of God's creatures, nothing more."

Roland spoke calmly, yet his heart pounded in his breast. He realized that the earl wasn't entirely sane.

Edmond of Clare drew a deep steadying breath. He'd behaved badly, he knew it. He'd let his jealousy of his Benedictine priest overcome his Christian sense. He would whip the man who'd spoken irreverently of the priest. But he found himself looking again at Daria. Her cheeks were very pale, her eyes dilated. He realized that it mattered not what she'd said to the priest or what the priest believed. He had made up his mind and he knew God approved his actions.

"I would examine her now," Edmond said, advancing on her. "You will remain to testify that I do not ravish her, Father. And if she isn't a virgin, you will also so testify so that I can then do as I will with her, for it matters not what a whore wishes."

Roland cleared his throat and his voice

rang stern and hard. "I forbid it, my son."

The earl stared at him as if he'd lost his wits. "I am lord here, Father Corinthian, and no other man, even be he a man of God, has the right to gainsay me, for my word is law. Do you understand me? Come, you will be my witness."

But Daria wasn't to submit without a struggle. She grabbed up her skirts and ran from the earl. He caught her quickly, his heavy arm around her waist, and he lifted her, carrying her to the narrow cot, and threw her down upon her back, knocking the breath out of her.

"Damn you, girl, hold still!" He lifted his hand to strike her into submission, saw the priest standing rigid with disapproval near to him, and slowly lowered his hand. He leaned down, his face close to hers. "Do as I tell you or I will beat you when the priest is gone."

He'd spoken softly, so that only she heard him. She felt his spittle on her throat. He was both enraged and determined.

"Please, my lord," she said, "please don't shame me. I am a maid. What have I done to deserve your distrust? Please do not shame me."

The earl paid no attention. He was as determined as he was excited, his groin

80

twisting with painful need. He wanted to touch her, thrust his finger inside her, feel her soft woman's flesh. He felt sweat break out on his forehead, sweat from his growing lust. Daria felt one of his large hands on her belly, his fingers splayed outward, holding her flat, and his other hand was pulling at her wool skirt, yanking it up, ripping it in his haste, and she felt the chill air on her thighs. She cried out and began to struggle, frantically trying to jerk away from him. His large hand clamped about her knee and squeezed. She cried out against the sudden pain.

"Make no more struggles! Lie still and I will be through quickly."

But she couldn't make herself lie there like a helpless creature, motionless and obedient to his will, whilst he humiliated her, and looked at her and touched her. Not with Roland standing so close, looking wild and furious and nearly savage with rage. Then she realized if she continued to fight him, Roland would attack him and most likely all would be lost. And Roland would die.

To acquiesce to this, the humiliation of it threatened to choke her, but she forced herself to still, closing her eyes against the knowledge of what he was going to do to her. It cost her dearly, but she held herself perfectly rigid, enduring because she had to endure. The earl looked up at her, then grunted, pleased with her surrender.

And Roland understood. He hated watching this, hated the earl's hand touching her. He saw his large hand press her legs wide apart, saw his finger disappear between her thighs, and knew he was touching her. He shook with the compulsion to kill him, yet he knew, as did Daria, that they would have little or no chance to escape, not if he gave in to his fury and killed the earl now. He forced himself to stand there stiff and tense and mute, watching, and it was the hardest thing he had ever done in his life. The earl's face was flushed dark with lust and his breathing was loud in the chamber.

Daria whimpered when one of the earl's thick fingers thrust inside her. As he probed deeper into her, she cried out with the pain of his roughness. He frowned at her and continued deeper, widening her, preparing her for his sex, for he had every intention of taking her soon, regardless. But he knew she was a maid, aye, he knew, but he'd wanted to touch her, to feel her soft flesh.

Finally he withdrew his finger from her body, and his hand from beneath her skirts. He jerked her gown down over her legs, "She is a maid," he said, and he looked down into her face as he spoke.

"Open your eyes, damn you! I will take you to wive and you will be loyal and obedient to me, your lord and your husband. Do you understand me, Daria? Even though you are flesh of your uncle's lewd flesh, it matters not, for you will forget his loathsome nature and bind yourself to me and become what I demand."

The earl rose and looked down at her again. "Rise and straighten yourself. Father, you are my witness that she is still a virgin. Now that it is proved, let us leave her alone."

Roland nodded and his eyes dropped. He very nearly leapt on the earl in that moment, for he saw that his sex bulged against the cloth of his tunic, thick and hard.

He didn't look at Daria, for he couldn't bear to see on her pale face the misery he knew she felt. He forced himself to nod again, and motioned the earl to go ahead of him out of the bedchamber. He knew deep down that the earl would return to ravish her. If the Benedictine priest, Father Corinthian, had not been here bearing witness, the earl would have continued what he was doing. He would have ravished her. But he would return. He would return tonight; Roland knew it. He knew he must get her away from Tyberton first or he would have failed.

Still his rage made him tremble, and he was relieved that the earl didn't turn to address some question to him or he might still have wrapped his hands around Edmond of Clare's neck and wrung the life out of him.

Daria scrambled up from the bed and raced to the door. She forced herself to crack the door open and look out. The earl and Roland were gone. She retreated again, closing the door. There was no key to keep him out. She didn't yet know of Roland's plan for their escape, only that he would come for her. She began to pace, feeling so shamed, so humiliated at what he'd done to her that she couldn't bear being within herself, being at one with her body. She wasn't aware that tears were streaming down her face until Ena slipped into the chamber and gasped at the sight of her.

"He's ravished you! And that miserable priest with him! I knew he wasn't a priest, too pretty he is, too lean and hungry! Aye, both of them —"

Daria, maddened beyond control, turned on the old woman in a fury and yelled, "Shut your stupid mouth, you miserable old crone! I will hear no more of your filth!"

It was shock that made Ena obey her mistress. Never had the girl spoken thus to her, and she could but stare at her.

"Leave me! I don't wish to see your hag's face until the morning. Go!"

The old woman scuttled out. Alone once again, Daria stared at the closed door. She felt only a bit of guilt, for Ena had become more and more unstable during their months of captivity. Once she was gone, if she managed to escape, the old woman would be safe enough here. She knew the earl wouldn't waste his time killing her.

She paced until her leg cramped. She sat down on her bed and began rubbing her calf. What to do? Wait for Roland to appear? She simply didn't know. She supposed she had no choice but to remain here until he came for her. Or, she thought, rising quickly, she could try to escape herself. The door wasn't locked. Perhaps she could slip by the guards; perhaps she could race through the inner bailey and no one would attempt to stop her; perhaps . . . It was ridiculous and she knew it.

She'd nurtured such ridiculous plans frequently during her confinement. There was no escape for her; she knew it. Then, she wondered, how could Roland get her out of here? He'd said tonight. But how? She saw no way, no glimmer of a chance.

She was crying again, feeling again the earl's callused fingers digging into her flesh, touching her, pushing against her until his finger entered her, probed inside her, and the pain mixed with the humiliation of it caused her to cry out, covering her face in her hands. And Roland had watched.

It was too much. Something inside her gave way and she suddenly felt outside herself; she felt as outside and as gray as the failing dusk, and filled with numb purpose. She rose and walked slowly toward the narrow window. She measured its width with her hands. She climbed up on a stool and tried to stick her head through the opening. It was too small even for her head. She pushed harder, bruising her temples. Staggering pain coursed through her head. She scrambled off the stool, her hands pressed against her temples, and she stared down at it and then at the window and was horrified. She'd wanted to leap through it; she'd wanted to kill herself. She drew a breath and forced herself to suck in air slowly and deeply. She'd lost her reason. Slowly she lay down on her narrow bed. She closed her eyes. She would remain calm. She would wait; she had no choice. The pain in her head subsided.

She didn't know how many hours passed, if hours indeed did slip by. Perhaps it was a succession of minutes that crept by her, so very slowly, until she wanted to scream. The chamber grew dark with the night; soon the one lone candle gutted.

There was but a quarter-moon to glimmer in the night sky, and its light cast no shadows into the chamber. It was dark and silent. She heard the door open softly. She heard a man's step, a man's steady breathing.

"I cannot wait longer for you," he said, coming to a halt beside her cot. "I am here to become your husband. I have prayed long in the chapel. God approves my actions. You will take me and accept me and obey me."

4

She'd known he would come, and strangely enough, she wasn't paralyzed by fear. She listened to him speak, and some part of her marveled at his ability to bring God to his side, be the matter one of piety or lust. She listened but heard no sound of a key turning in the lock. She knew there was a key, for he'd locked her in the first several weeks of her captivity.

Then he hadn't bothered this time, for he'd seen no reason to. She heard his heavy breathing, heard his footfall as he approached the bed. She heard him trip over the single stool and curse; then he called out, "Have you no candle? I wish to see you. Where is the candle?"

Very slowly, very deliberately, Daria rolled to her side to the far side of the cot. She eased off the side and came onto her hands and knees on the hard stone floor. Could he see her somehow? Hear her heart pounding?

"Daria?" His own breathing was deep and harsh, and she knew he was feeling for her on the bed. She crawled slowly, silently, toward the door.

He yelled her name, knowing now that she wasn't lying there on the bed waiting for him. He roared, wheeling about, and he again tripped over the stool. He kicked it from his path and in the next instant he threw the door open. Dim light from the single flambeau in the corridor wall cast shadows into the chamber. And he saw her, kneeling, her arms over her chest, staring up at him, pale and still.

The earl wondered if he should beat her now for her attempt to escape him; then he thought better of it. Perhaps if he struck her he would hurt her and she would not give him her full attention when he took her. No, he wanted all her attention, he wanted her to look at him when he thrust into her, drove through her maiden's barrier. His heart pounded and his loins grew swollen and heavy.

"Get up," he said, not moving. He was standing there, his arms crossed over his chest, his legs spread, blocking her, he knew, and there was nothing she could do save obey him. But she couldn't.

She didn't move.

"Obey me, now, or you will feel the chastisement of my hand."

Daria believed him. Slowly she got to her feet. She stood there silent and waiting. He smiled at her and held out his hand. "Come, Daria. Be not afraid of me, sweetling. You will be my wife, after all. I offer you this honor willingly and with all my heart and with our Lord's blessing. I will visit pain upon you tonight, but you will open to me willingly and you will accept my seed into your womb. Perhaps you will know some pleasure, but I trust it will not be over-abundant. I do not want you to forget yourself like some women do. They are not good women; they are unworthy. My first wife was a whore, abandoned in her cries and demands, but you . . . you will be just what I want."

His words had held her in thrall, and when he moved so quickly and grabbed her arm, she finally shrieked, "No! Get away from me, I don't want this!"

Surprisingly, his hold on her arm gentled. "Fear not, Daria. You are blessed amongst women. God and man will it so. It will be my duty to take you as often as I am able, and

90

you will come to wish for me, surely, in your sweet way, and to ask me prettily to take you. Women are to bend to their husbands; it is in your nature to do so."

He stopped a moment and gave her a look filled with such certainty that she wondered for an instant if she were not somehow amiss in her view of him and the world itself and not accepting something that was truly an honor bestowed upon her. Then she laughed. She'd thought to jump out of that window if only she'd fit through it. She no longer cared. She leaned back her head and spit at him, full in the face.

In the next moment he jerked her to the bed and threw her upon her face. His hand at the small of her back held her still. The chamber door stood open, but he didn't care. He wanted to see her and he wasted no more time. She was his and he would do just as he pleased. He would honor her in marriage and take her now because he couldn't bear to wait longer. He'd already waited too long, been too careful in his deliberations regarding her. He ripped up her gown, baring her to her waist. He stood then and looked down at her sprawled legs, the rounded buttocks, the narrow waist. His loins ached and prodded. His breath hitched. He wiped her spittle from his face.

He spread his open hands over her buttocks, kneading and caressing, and he marveled at the softness and the whiteness of a woman's flesh.

She made a sound deep in her throat and tried to roll away from him. It was nothing, this woman's token resistance of hers. He merely wrapped his hands around her waist and flipped her onto her back. He pulled up her gown and again forced himself to slow, to study this wondrous gift that he had brought to himself. He stared at the mound of dark hair that covered her woman's flesh. He touched her and felt her flinch. He lifted his hand and said, "Now. Open your legs, Daria. I wish to see you."

Instead, she lifted her legs, rolled up on her shoulders, and struck him in the chest with her feet. He grunted with pain and surprise and tumbled backward.

But he caught her, easily, so easily, and she knew she would weaken soon and there could be but one conclusion.

She was screaming at him, kicking when there was naught but air to kick, for he was standing now beside the bed, watching her flailing, holding his hands over his chest, trying to regain his breath. And he was still staring down at her. Then he laughed, a low satisfied laugh. He was amused by her foolish efforts. Even as he unfastened the knot on his chausses he laughed. As he freed his manhood, he stopped laughing and looked at her. He saw her eyes lower, saw that she was staring at him, and was pleased, for he was hard and erect, his sex thrusting out from his groin. He was a good size, many women had told him so, and he wanted some healthy fear from her, at least that first time.

He came down on top of her, pinning her thrashing legs beneath his weight. She felt his sex between her legs, shoving upward, and she closed her eyes against the awful pain she knew would come when he managed to shove himself inside her. She struck his shoulders with her fists, scratched and pounded at his muscled arms. It did her no good at all. Her arm jerked back for yet another blow, this one to his head, when her hand brushed against the brass candle holder atop the small table beside the cot. A fierce joy went through her. She clutched its rough base, raised it as high as she could, and brought it down on his head.

The earl had reared back, his member held in his own hand to guide himself into her, and the blow struck the side of his head. The pain was searing and it rattled him. He fell sideways, still pinning her beneath him.

She heard him groan, then fall silent. She struck him again and felt a slight shudder go through him. Then she dropped the candlestick. She tried to push him off her. She heaved and prodded, but she couldn't move him. He was deadweight on her.

She felt tears sting her eyes. She was so close to escape and she was still trapped by him. It wasn't fair, it wasn't . . .

"What in God's name have you done?"

At the sound of Roland's low voice, her tears dried, though she still wanted to cry, but in relief. "Please, hurry, get him off me!"

Roland quickly pushed the earl off her and let him roll onto the floor. He saw that her gown was shoved up to her waist and that her legs were parted and bare. He didn't want to ask, but he did. "Are you all right? Did he . . . did he hurt you?" His own voice flattened, for he'd been late, mayhap too late to help her. The earl had been over her and she'd been naked and . . . When she shook her head violently, he felt such relief his belly cramped.

She was very pale and shaking. He still looked at her, wondering what to say, wondering if he should stick his dagger into the earl's heart, for it was what he wanted to do. He'd prayed he wasn't too late as he'd rushed up the narrow stone stairwell, prayed more devoutly than a Benedictine priest would have done.

He shook his head. He, her rescuer, hadn't done a bloody thing. She'd saved herself.

"Quickly, Daria, rip up your gown. We will bind him and gag him. Hurry, we don't have much time."

She didn't hesitate. She ripped off wide pieces of the precious dark blue wool, watching Roland from the corner of her eye as he bound the earl tightly.

Once the gag was in his mouth, Roland rolled him unceremoniously under the narrow bed.

"Now," he said, rising, "nearly done. You must change now, quickly."

Daria stared at the boy's clothes he thrust into her hands. Then she smiled.

"Hasten, we haven't much time." He lightly touched his fingertips to her cheek. "I know things are moving quickly, but you will be safe now. We will speak later."

He turned his back to her and stationed himself at the open chamber door. He wanted to close the door but knew she needed some light to dress herself in the unfamiliar clothing. He heard her breathing, her clumsy movements. He kept his eyes on the steep circular stairwell just across from the bedchamber. He'd drugged the supper ale in its wooden kegs, but still he couldn't be certain that all the earl's men had drunk enough to knock them out. To his enormous chagrin, the earl hadn't touched any drink. He'd been too intent on getting to Daria. He hadn't wanted to risk impotence with her. Roland listened. It was quiet as a tomb, ominously quiet to his ears.

"Are you dressed yet?"

"Aye," she said, appearing suddenly at his side. Roland turned to look at her. The boy's clothes disguised the woman's curves of her body but she still looked very much a female. Quickly he sat her down on the bed and braided her hair. He tied it with a bit of cloth from her shredded gown, then thrust the boy's cap over her head, bringing it nearly to her eyebrows. He removed a wrapped cloth from his tunic and she saw that it contained mud.

He smeared the mud over her eyebrows to make them black slashes across her brow, then daubed more mud on her face. He grinned. "Wondrous filthy you are now, my lad."

He grabbed her hand and pulled her up. "Listen to me carefully, Daria. You will not open your mouth. You will keep your head down and stay close behind me. When I tell you to do something, you will do it quickly and silently."

It was then she saw that he was still in his priest's garb.

"I'm ready and I will do just as you say."

He patted her filthy cheek, nodding. He'd never in his life rescued a female and he wasn't certain what she would do, or how she would respond. Mayhap faint at a critical moment, mayhap shriek. But Daria appeared to have herself well in control, at least for the moment. He looked once again at the steep shadowed stairwell, then motioned for her to follow him.

When they reached the bottom steps, Daria stared around the great hall. Scores of people were snoring, filling the hall with a low rumbling sound, the ones who sat at the trestle tables slumped forward, their heads beside their trenchers.

"Will they die? Did you poison them?"

He shook his head. "I but drugged their ale. They sleep like innocent babes. They'll awaken on the morrow with aching heads but nothing more. Hush, now."

There were some who were awake, but their eyes were vague and they gave only cursory glances at the priest and the dirty boy with him. One man even called out, his words slurred, "Father, bless me for I have drunk too much and all I see are vipers and they rollick and twist around me. They are evil, Father."

"Bless you, my son, but you deserve every viper that strikes at you. At least you are still awake, whilst your friends have succumbed."

The man looked puzzled, then quietly he fell forward, knocking himself out with the blow, and Daria wondered if he'd cracked his head.

But outside there were many who were fully alert. Roland slowed his pace. He nodded and spoke to the men who crossed his path, seemingly at his ease, taking his time. He saw several of the women look at him with eager invitation and he made his expression austere.

"Where do you go tonight, Father?"

It was the head stableman and he was looking curiously at the filthy boy who was trailing after the priest.

Roland said easily, "You see this little cockscomb here? I am taking this fiend of a boy back to his father for the thrashing he deserves. He wanted to become a knight! He is part Welsh, a bastard shucked off one of Chepstow's masters, and he can't speak clearly enough for even God to understand him. Can you imagine such a thing as the earl accepting this young fool? Well, the boy will go back to his own father and get a good flogging."

The stableman laughed. "Serves him right, the young savage," he said, and stepped back into the stable. Roland followed him quickly, motioning for Daria to stay still. She did, but she didn't want to. She heard only a soft thudding sound from within the stable. She froze, wondering if Roland needed help, but then he appeared again, and he was smiling at her. "Another man resting soundly. Stay here and keep watch."

Soon he reappeared and he was leading a horse. It wasn't much of a horse, certainly not one of the fighting men's mighty destriers. Roland swung easily onto the horse's bare back and gave her his hand. "Come, we must hurry."

She stared in wonder at the back of his head. Did he think to simply ride through the mighty gates of Tyberton Castle? He did. There were a half-dozen guards patrolling, but it was to the porter that Roland spoke.

"Blessed even', good Arthur. I take this scruffy simpleton back to his father at Chepstow, on the earl's order. Would you open the gate for me?"

And to Daria's astonishment, Arthur chuckled, spit on the dry earth, and said, "Aye, by the looks of him, Father, he'll not survive a sound thrashing, the skinny little offal. What'd he do? Piss in the earl's wine?" And he cackled at his own wit.

"He wanted to free the earl's prisoner, the girl, Daria, so she would feel pity for him and let him seduce her. The earl wanted to begin his wedding night soon, so I am his deputy with this foolish boy. I take him because I feared the earl might kill him in his haste to bed the girl and for the boy's impure thoughts."

Arthur laughed and nodded. "Aye, be gone wi' ye, Father. I'll wait for ye to return. Be certain to call loudly when ye near the castle so none of the earl's soldiers lets fly an arrow through yer heart."

"Thank you, my friend. I will hurry. See that the master is not disturbed this night!"

And Arthur cackled anew as he opened the gates. "A pretty little piece she is," he said, his words nearly incomprehensible through his chuckling. "Aye, pretty and tender as a young chick. The earl will fair enjoy himself riding her!" The last sound Daria heard from Tyberton Castle was the laughter of Arthur, the porter. They rode through the portcullis into the outer bailey and out the great oak gates. Several men nodded, but none said anything or moved to stop them. It was that easy. Daria pressed her cheek against Roland's back. "I begin to believe you a magician, Roland. Everything passed so simply. I have thought and thought these past two months and believed I would never escape him."

"I'm very good," Roland said, grinning over his shoulder at her. "I learned long ago that the best ruses were ones that stuck as close as possible to the truth. Well, mayhap I did enjoy myself a bit with the truth this time. I will say we were very lucky. However, once the earl frees himself and sobers up all his men from their drugged ale, he will be after us. We must not tarry."

"I do not wish to tarry," she said, and clasped her arms around his waist. "But this animal, Roland, he looks to have the speed of and strength of a snail."

"Be patient. My own destrier awaits us nearby."

"Will you take me back to my uncle?"

"Not yet. It wouldn't be the wisest course. First we will beset the earl with confusion."

He dug his heels into the horse's sides and the beast broke into a thumping trot.

They rode for only about an hour, northeast, into Wales. Finally Roland pulled the horse off the narrow dusty road heavily bordered with hedgerows and yew bushes and drew up before a small hut of daub and wattle surrounded with sagging, very old outbuildings. A man emerged quickly and strode toward them. Roland smiled at Daria and said, "We will mount my horse now." He helped her down and told her to wait.

Roland walked with the man behind the hut, soon to reappear leading a magnificent animal, lean and strong, black as midnight, and proud-looking as a king.

Daria saw money change hands. The man grinned and said, "Aye, aye, *lle pum buwch, lle pum buwch.*"

Roland gave him a friendly buffet on his shoulder and turned to toss Daria onto his destrier's broad back. The horse merely shifted, not moving, accepting her weight with no fuss. Roland mounted, then said to the man, "Do not forget it is to the southwest you will ride. You will wear my monk's robe and ride this mount at least two hours. Then leave the horse and the robe where our good earl will find them."

The man nodded, spit on the ground beside him, and gave a small salute to Roland.

Daria stared at the man who had come to Tyberton to rescue her. How could she have ever believed him a priest? The other women at the castle had felt he was a man, a man of this earth, a man of the flesh, but she hadn't. He was now wearing a tunic of rough rust-colored wool, belted at his waist with a wide leather strap upon which hung his sword and a dagger. He looked dangerous and he looked intensely alive. She pressed her cheek against his back and accepted the newness of him into her.

As they rode from the hut, she asked, "What did he say? Something over and over again when you gave him money."

"You have a good ear. He said that now he has a place of four cows. In other words, he can now support four cows with the money I gave him for his aid."

To Roland's astonishment, she repeated quite clearly, *"Lle pum buwch."*

"You have learned some Welsh, then, during your two months at Tyberton?"

He felt her shake her head against his shoulder. "No, the earl hates the Welsh. He forbade any of their language to be spoken at Tyberton. If ever he heard anything that sounded foreign, he had the speaker flogged. Besides, he kept me isolated." With those words, she fell silent.

It had been drizzling lightly before. Now it stopped and the sky was hung with dark clouds promising more rain before midnight. Always it rained in Wales, always. Roland tightened the straps of the two bags over his horse's back.

Some minutes later, he realized that Daria was asleep. She was limp against his back and he felt her sliding sideways. He quickly caught her sliding hands and brought them together, holding them over his waist with one of his. He looked around him at the cloud-hung sky and the towering, twisted sessile oaks that seemed to close in on them. The air was pungent with the smell of the sea and the smell of damp moss. It would begin to rain again soon. He sighed, hoping it would stay dry until they drew nearer to Trefynwy. Then they would turn east and travel through the Black Mountains, unforgiving hostile peaks and naked ridges, where they would be safe from anyone trying to find them. He said aloud to himself, to Daria, even though she slept, "I am pleased with you." He meant it. She trusted him so much that she was actually able to sleep whilst fleeing. It was remarkable.

He grinned, raising his face to the cool night breeze. His destrier, Cantor, snorted, and Roland slowed him. They still had a distance to go before Roland would be content to halt and rest for a while. It was doubtful that the earl would discover their trail very soon, if at all. Roland had purposefully planned to travel northward through Wales, knowing the earl wouldn't seriously consider searching in the country he so despised. An Englishman would decide that only a madman would escape willingly into Wales.

Roland laughed softly, pleased with his strategies, for there was something very important the earl didn't know, and wouldn't find out.

He remained pleased until the thunder began to rumble overhead. Wales, the land of endless rain, he thought, staring up at the dark clouds overhead. He had wanted to reach Abergavenny by morning, but now he knew he couldn't. A raindrop slid off his forehead. He cursed quietly, tightened his hold on Daria's wrists, for she'd slipped to the side, and knew he had to find them shelter until it stopped raining.

He knew he was lucky in the terrain in which they now traveled. There were thick forests, which provided not only cover from anyone trying to find them but also some protection from the rain that was now coming down more quickly and more furiously. He knew also of caves in the area. If he wasn't mistaken, there was one of moderate size near to Usk, off the road, just to the west of them. He knew Daria was awake now, he felt her shiver against his back. He dug in one of his leather bags and pulled out a leather jerkin. "Here, we'll hold this over our heads. It will be some protection."

"I have heard that it rains here more than anywhere else on the earth," she said.

"That's very likely," he said, wondering where she'd gotten her information. "Certainly more than in the Holy Land." The leather jerkin over their heads, Roland continued, to distract both of them from the sodden cold rain, "You will be my deaf-mute little brother whilst we are in Wales."

"Do you speak the Welsh tongue, Roland?"

"Aye, I do. It is one of my talents, this ability to learn languages easily and quickly."

"Then teach me, for I do not like to keep silent all the time."

He almost laughed, for the Welsh language was the most difficult he had learned, more difficult even than Arabic. It was on the tip of his tongue to tell her she wasn't able when he said instead, "What was it that farmer said?"

"*Lle pum buwch.* Now I will have a place for four cows."

Roland had never before met another person who had his talent for languages. He still wasn't convinced at her ability, even though the Latin she'd spoken was fluent and smooth.

"Just teach me enough so that I do not have to be deaf or mute."

Well, why not? he thought. For the next hour he taught her simple phrases, and he had to admit to being wrong. She was perhaps even more adept than he was at picking up the essence of a language, at finding patterns that no one else ever realized were there. By the time he found a suitable cave, one that was empty of mountain lions and bears, they were both sodden from the rain and Daria spoke limited but very Welsh-sounding words and phrases.

"We will wait here until it stops raining — *if* it stops raining. This cursed country does pour rain down all the time."

"Aye, but the smells, Roland," she said, sucking in air deeply. "The salt of the sea, the moss from the very rocks themselves, the heather and bracken. It is such a very *living* smell."

That was true, but he said nothing. He settled Cantor, then turned to look down at his charge. She was very wet and shivering with the cold. He pulled out his last clean leather jerkin from one of his bags. "Put it on."

She stepped away from him into the blackness of the cave and he immediately stopped her. "Nay, stay close, Daria. There still could be creatures there, and I do not want them to eat you or for you to lose yourself in the mountain. I am told some of the caves twist and curve back deep into the mountainside. To get lost would mean death."

She was back quickly, the jerkin hanging loosely around her. "Let us sit and eat some bread the farmer provided us."

Whilst they ate, he taught her the names of various foods and animals. She fell asleep even as she repeated *dafad,* or sheep.

He leaned back against the rocky wall of the cave and gathered her against him. His horse whinnied softly and the soft caw of the rooks filled the silence. He could even hear a woodpecker rapping on a tree somewhere near, and a waterfall loud and violent, slashing through a beech forest close by. She was right about the smells. Even in the dark cave, the smell of turf, bracken, water, and wind filled his nostrils. It was a wild smell, a savage smell, but one that fed and stimulated the senses.

He smiled as he fell asleep holding the girl who would be able to speak Welsh as well as a native if only she had enough time to learn.

It stopped raining near dawn and the sky was a soft rich pink in those brief magical minutes. He started to awaken Daria, when she said quite clearly in English, "I know you, know you deep inside me. It's passing strange and it makes me afraid, but for all that, it makes me feel wonderful."

He shook her awake. He didn't know what she was talking about, and something told him he didn't want to know.

They ate bread and cheese and drank the rest of the warm ale. Daria seemed not to remember her dream, that, or she didn't wish to speak of it. Dry and warm, they left their cave soon thereafter.

They rode through glades and thickets, through small twisted and lichened oaks, by boulders covered with moss. They passed naked rocks that looked wet even though the sun shone down strongly.

Roland continued to teach her Welsh. He felt a brief stab of jealousy at her talent, then grinned at his own vanity. It was good, this talent of hers; he didn't particularly relish having to shield a deaf-mute boy who was really a girl. Now at least she could say something when they met the Welsh, which they would surely do eventually.

And they met the Welsh sooner than Roland would have wished.

5

"*Afon,*" Roland said, pointing, "river." Then, "*Aber —* river mouth."

Daria dutifully repeated the words. She tapped Roland on the shoulder. "*Allt,*" she said, nodding to their left. "Wooded hill-side."

He swiveled about in the saddle and grinned at her. "You are very good," he said.

"Must I still be deaf and mute?"

"For the time being I think it the wisest course to follow. Be patient, Daria." He started to add that she would be home soon, but he knew her thoughts on that and so kept quiet. He wished he personally knew if Ralph of Colchester was a good man, a man of honor. Deep inside, though, Roland imagined that Ralph of Colchester could very likely be a troll and a monster and still Daria's uncle would wed her to him because he wanted to add to his own land holdings. It wouldn't matter to him if the man had wedded a dozen women and killed all of them.

He pulled up Cantor and let his destrier blow and drink from the cold river water. "Would you like to walk about a bit?"

She smiled gratefully and slid off Cantor's back. "Smell the air, Roland. And look at the sunlight on those maple leaves, 'tis magic, all those hues and shades."

She wrapped her arms around herself and twirled about in the small open meadow. *"Glyn,"* she called out, *"fflur!"* She pointed to some sweet-smelling honeysuckle. " 'Tis for fidelity, you know, and the ivy yon, 'tis for permanence."

He grinned at her like a besotted idiot, realized it, and turned away.

"Ah, I wish we could stay here forever!"

"Just wait for an hour or so — until it rains again. When you're wet and cold and thoroughly miserable, you'll change your mind quickly enough."

She waved away his words. "The gorse over there, it protects us against demons, or mayhap from the unending rain, if we wish it hard enough."

He didn't want to wish for anything right now except for the rest of his money. Then his wish for his own land, his own keep in the midst of the beautiful green hills in Cornwall, would come true. He watched her flit from a low yew bush to a lone birch, repeating the names in Welsh. So learning came easily to her. It meant nothing to him, not a thing. So she was bright and laughing. It meant nothing more than her ease of learning. His eyes were on her lips, then fell to her breasts and her hips. Nothing, he thought, turning quickly to pat Cantor's neck. It meant nothing. His destrier turned his head, his mouth wet, and nuzzled his master's hand. Roland said to his horse as he wiped his hand on his chausses, "You are the loyal one, the one who's always known what I wanted, what I needed. You I trust with my life, no one else, particularly not a female. Not even a female who is pretty and bright and sweet."

"You speak to your horse, sirrah?"

She was laughing, a dirty-faced urchin in boy's clothes, a limp woolen cap pulled low on her forehead. The dirt he'd rubbed on her face was long gone, replaced by new dirt, streaked and black, more authentic dirt, all of it Welsh. Even her smooth white hands were filthy. She didn't look at all like a boy to him.

"Aye, it's passing smart he is, and he tells

me 'tis nearly time for lunch."

Daria eyed the saddlebags hopefully.

"I'm sorry, but there's nothing left. I must do some hunting."

She looked back from whence they'd come, and slowly, regretfully, she shook her head. "Nay, I'm not all that hungry, Roland, truly. Can we not ride until late afternoon? Then can you hunt? I've wasted time here and I shouldn't have. I'm sorry."

"He's not after us, Daria. There was no one to betray us. Even if the farmer did tell the earl about us, he still didn't know where we were heading."

Still she shuddered even as she shook her head. "He'd know, somehow he'd find out. I just have this feeling." She added quickly, seeing him frown, "He's very smart."

Roland continued his frown, disliking himself even as the words came from his mouth. "So you admired him. Did you not wish to leave him, then? Did you wish to wed with him?"

Her head snapped up. "You are speaking like a fool, Roland!" And then, to her appalled surprise, she burst into tears. Roland stared at her.

The tension, he supposed, was finally too much for her. She'd finally succumbed, but still he was surprised. Until this moment, she'd shown unusual fortitude and grit. To fall into a woman's tears now — when the danger was past — seemed somehow very unlike her.

"Why am I a fool?"

She shook her head, swiped the back of her hand across her eyes, and turned away from him. "Nay, not a fool, just speaking like one." She dashed her hand across her eyes and sniffled loudly. "I'm sorry. Has Cantor drunk his fill?"

He gave her a long look, then said, "Aye." He gave her his hand and pulled her up behind him.

They were riding near to the River Usk and wood-clad hills rose up on either side of them, hills covered with thickets of beech and sessile oaks. Firs towered behind them, thin and high, and many narrow streams snaked through the land, most shallow and a pale stagnant brown under the bright sunlight. But even with the warm sun shining down, there was still the feel, the scent, the sound of water in the air — the streams burbling, distant waterfalls crashing and thudding over wet rocks, unseen water deep beneath the ground booming and gurgling. Daria shuddered. "It's overpowering," she said, and clasped her arms more tightly around Roland's back.

"Be thankful it isn't yet raining," he said. "Why am I a fool, Daria? Nay, *speak* like a fool."

He felt her tense up and knew to his toes that he shouldn't push her for an answer, but he was perverse, he knew it, had known it for most of his years. "Why?" he repeated.

"The earl is a frightening man. I don't believe him mad, not yet at least, but he is a strange sort of fanatic, and his moods shift dangerously. I would have rather wedded Ralph of Colchester's father or his grandfather than him."

"Ah."

He felt her arms tighten about his waist. "Roland, please don't take me back to my uncle. He doesn't worship God, even in a perverted fashion to suit himself. He worships only himself and sees himself as all-powerful, and he's more frightening than anyone because when he chooses to be cruel, his cruelty comes from deep within him, and it is pleasurable to him and so very cold."

"Then I should say you would be pleased to wed and leave Reymerstone and your uncle's malignant influence."

Again she stiffened, and he disliked himself for being hard, but he was being paid by the uncle to deliver the niece back to him, and with the money he would receive, he would buy his keep in Cornwall and he would live there and it would be his and never again would he bow to another's wishes unless it was his wish to do so. Daria said nothing more. That perverse part of him wished she would.

It was nearing midafternoon when she broke the silence. "I must stop for a moment. Please."

He nodded and pulled Cantor up. He dismounted, then held out his arms for her. She ignored him and slid down the destrier's left side.

"By God, get out of the way, quickly!"

Cantor jerked upward, whirling about to face the human who'd encroached, and he slashed out with his front hooves.

"Move, Daria!"

She fell backward over an outcropping stone and toppled into the grass onto her back.

Roland soothed his horse and looped his reins around a stubby yew branch.

He walked to her and stood over her, hands on hips for a moment, before he offered her his hand. "Don't ever do something so stupid again. You knew better, Daria."

She nodded, ignored his hand, and got slowly to her feet.

"You did it because you were angry with me. Kindly remember that you must be alive and well when you arrive at Reymerstone."

"Aye, that's true enough! If I die, then you will get no coin from my uncle, will you?"

He just looked at her for a long moment, then slowly nodded. "That's true. So take care of yourself."

"I am going into the trees," she said, so frustrated and angry with him and with their situation that she wanted to spit. He watched her walk slowly, limping a bit, into the rich humid-looking foliage. The smell of pine and damp moss was strong. He watched her until she disappeared, and he took stock of their position. Brownish hill-ridges protruded above the woods in the distance, and even in this small glade he could hear the rush of waterfalls gushing over slick naked rocks through the forest to the west. He saw a small herd of wild ponies on a far hillside, silhouetted against a thicket of pine trees, their long manes tangled and unkempt. They were aware of him and stood quietly watching. He walked slowly to a small twisted and lichened oak and leaned against it. Beside the oak stood several boulders fuzzed with moss, left in this unlikely spot long ago, as if tossed there by ancient storms or even more ancient gods. He whistled a song Dienwald de Fortenberry's fool, Crooky, had sung, smiling even as he added the silly words.

> Give up! Give in!
> Sweet Lord, 'tis no sin.
> Kiss her sweet mouth
> And make her sigh
> Give her pleasure, oh my, oh my.
>
> Give up! Give in!
> Sweet Lord, 'tis you who win.
> Kiss her throat and make her lie
> Upon your bed, oh my, oh my.

Surely it was an absurd song, but he sang it again, smiling more widely as he pictured Dienwald and his bride, Philippa, snug in his arms. Crooky had continued with various body parts, rolling his eyes and miming lewdly until Dienwald had kicked him soundly.

Roland heard a scream and stopped singing.

Tyberton Castle

The Earl of Clare leaned back against the cold stone wall, crossing his massive arms over his chest. The farmer was nearly dead, damn his perfidious soul to hell. He'd told his man to go easy, to hold up on the whip, but the blood lust had enthralled him and now the Welsh bastard was hanging limply from the iron manacles, his ribs heaving, his face gray, his eyes fading even as the earl looked at him dispassionately.

"Well, do you wish to continue with this torture or do you want to die quickly? Tell me the truth. Tell me where you got that horse and you'll not suffer more."

The farmer raised his eyes to the earl's implacable face, and he thought: *All I wanted was enough money to have four cows.* But it wasn't to be. He wanted to die. His body was so broken he couldn't have healed anyway, even if the torture stopped now. And the pain was too much, far too much. He said, his English broken and halting, "The man and the boy rode into Wales, 'tis all I know. His was a powerful black destrier, a warrior's mount, strong and enduring. I know not the man's name. He paid me to ride the horse in the opposite direction and leave it for you to find, but I didn't." He said sorrowfully to himself, "No, I was stupid and wanted to keep the horse, and thus I die for my stupidity."

That was true, the earl thought. "Come,

man, think! Surely he gave you a name. Come, and you'll die quickly, even the instant after you speak!"

"Roland," the farmer said after another strike of the thong. " 'Twas Roland!"

Edmond, Earl of Clare, stared at the man a moment longer, then nodded to his henchman. He pulled a dagger from his belt and slid it cleanly into the farmer's heart. The man slumped, his head falling on his chest, the manacles rattling as he went limp.

Who, Edmond wondered as he strode back into Tyberton's great hall, was Roland? A man hired by Damon, no doubt, to bring the girl back to him. Well, he wouldn't make it, that damned fake priest to whom he'd given his spiritual trust. But not all his trust. Deep inside he'd known the man was a fraud. He was too handsome, his body too well-honed for a man of exclusively divine concerns. He should have guessed it immediately when the castle women had wanted him so blatantly. And he'd gotten her away so very easily, the damned whoreson.

Edmond called MacLeod, his master-at-arms. He slapped his thick leather gauntlets against his thigh as he spoke. "Prepare a dozen men. We ride into Wales to fetch back the little mistress and the erstwhile priest. He stole her, took her against her will. We will rescue her. Bring enough provisions for several weeks. We ride hard."

MacLeod said nothing. It wasn't his business to disagree or question the lord or even think twice about his commands. The little mistress had left Tyberton willingly enough, everyone knew that, but they would find her, kill the sham priest, and bring her back to the earl's bed. They left Tyberton within the hour, the Earl of Clare at their head.

In Wales

Roland pulled both his sword and his dagger as he ran headlong toward the pine thicket. He heard a soft gurgling sound and felt his blood freeze. Had someone killed her?

He slowed, hearing low-pitched voices — two men, — and they had Daria. They spoke quietly, but he made out their words, the soft Welsh clear to him.

". . . to Llanrwst, quickly!"

"But the man, what to do with the man?"

"We'll be gone before he misses her. Leave him, leave him. Go quiet now. Quiet!"

Roland slipped between the pines until he reached a small clearing where a narrow stream sliced through the sodden grass. One man, tall and built like a mountain, had slung Daria over his shoulder. The other man, short and ragged as the Welsh ponies Roland had seen, was following close behind, glancing furtively over his shoulder every few moments.

Suddenly rain began to fall, slow drizzling rain that was gray and silent. One of the men cursed softly.

Roland followed as quietly as he could, but his boots squished in the wet grass. The rain thickened, coming down in dense sheets, blotting out the trees and the hills and adding to the sounds of a rushing waterfall not far distant. There were forlorn caws from rooks and kingfishers. This damned land — one minute the sun was shining brightly and now there was near-darkness and it was but midafternoon. Roland swiped rain from his eyes and crept after the men.

They made their way slowly but steadily to a small cave cut through boulders into the hillside. Roland drew back, watching them enter. He saw a lantern lit and a dull light issue forth. He drew closer, until he could hear the men speaking.

". . . damnable rain . . . *glaw, glaw* . . . always rain."

"Will ye take her, Myrddin? Now?"

"Nay, the girl's wet and nearly dead. Leave her there in a corner and cover her."

So they'd discovered she wasn't a boy. Not much of a discovery, since her disguise wouldn't have fooled Roland for an instant. These men either, evidently. Had they struck her hard? Roland didn't want to admit it, but his first thought was for her, not for the money he would lose if he didn't bring her back to her uncle alive and a virgin.

No, he said to himself. She was goods to be delivered, nothing more. She was a bundle to haul around and return safely to her uncle.

He pulled back and gave himself up to thought. It was still early; the men would have to split up for hunting. The huge man — his name was Myrddin, if Roland had heard the other man aright — didn't look like he would want to miss his supper. Roland was content to wait under an overhang of slick rock, sheltered from the endless gray rain.

It wasn't long before Myrddin emerged from the cave, cursed the rain in a way he'd good-naturedly curse a friend he saw nearly every day, then set off at a trot, his bow and arrow under his right arm. Slowly Roland made his way forward until he stood just outside the cave. He leaned forward until he could see the other man, the short one with the bowed legs. He was kneeling over Daria, staring at her. He slowly lifted the filthy blanket and continued to stare.

Roland suddenly saw the Earl of Clare in his mind's eye, saw his hand disappear beneath Daria's shift, knowing that he would penetrate her with his finger, and as Roland looked on now as another man was gaping at her, his hand moving closer to her breast, Roland couldn't stand it. He leaned nearly double and crossed the entrance into the cave as silently as a bat flying at midnight. The man didn't hear him. The fire the men had set was burning sluggishly, throwing off choking smoke, and Roland inhaled it and coughed.

The man whirled about, and Roland leapt on him. He was of greater size and strength, luckily, and his fingers closed in a death grip about the man's throat. He gurgled and his face darkened and his eyes bulged and still Roland squeezed, his rage overcoming his sense, until he heard Daria whisper, "Nay, Roland, do not kill him. Nay."

He was breathing harshly and released his hold from the man's throat. He rolled off him. "Are you all right?"

Daria took stock of herself and nodded. "Aye. They came upon me when I was preparing to return to you. The large one struck his fist against my head." She shook her head gently as she spoke. "Aye, I'll live, but we must leave here before he returns."

But Roland shook his head. He wanted to kill the man.

And Daria saw what he wanted and said quickly, "I'm frightened."

"You're safe with me. This lout planned to rape you and then hold you for his mountainous friend's pleasure. He's an outcast, a bandit, and I'll not let him live, not take the chance that he'll follow us and try to take you again."

She saw his logic, hated it, but kept still. "Go near to the entrance of the cave and keep watch for me. Don't turn around, do you understand me?" She obeyed him. He joined her quickly enough. Together they watched the fire in tense silence; then Roland rose and went outside. He said over his shoulder, "Stay still, and don't look back at that scum."

He waited outside under the overhang until his legs began to cramp. He shook himself, slapped his hands over his arms, cursed the endless cold rain, and continued to wait.

He heard a man's soft tread. Myrddin was mumbling to himself, and it was obvious he wasn't pleased. His Welsh was rough, yet still it was soft and lulling. "No game, nothing but rain, always rain, always rain." He repeated his words over and over and Roland wondered if he was a lackwit.

He waited, his dagger ready.

Myrddin paused, sniffed the air, then bellowed, a terrifying sound that made Roland start, thus giving away his presence.

"Bastard! Whoreson!" Myrddin was on him, swinging his heavy bow at his head. The man was enormous, stronger than Roland, but less skilled with weapons. But it didn't seem to matter in the slogging rain. Roland slipped and fell heavily, then rolled quickly, hearing the dull thud of the bow come down on a rock too near where his head had been. Myrddin slipped, but he didn't fall; he leaned sideways against an oak, pushed himself upright again, and this time he held a knife in his right hand.

He should have left with Daria, Roland thought wildly, after he'd slit the other man's throat. He'd been arrogant, much too sure of himself, and now, if he died, so would she, but not as cleanly or as quickly. Damn him for a fool.

The man was backing him against the glistening wet boulders, tossing the knife from his right hand to his left and back again. He was grinning.

126

Roland watched his eyes, and the instant he saw him ready to throw the knife, he hurled himself sideways. He heard the hiss of the blade through the rain and then the dull thud as it struck a rock and bounced off. Myrddin yelled in fury and jumped at Roland, leaping at the last instant to come down hard on his back.

His hands were around Roland's throat and he was squeezing. Roland felt an instant of stark panic, then forced himself to think. Slowly, even as he began to feel light-headed, he eased his knife upward. But he knew it was too late, knew it . . . knew it . . . Oh, God, he didn't want to die, not now . . .

Suddenly, through rain-blurred eyes, he saw Daria standing over Myrddin. He watched, disbelieving, as she brought a heavy rock down on his head. Myrddin lurched back, looked up at her, then seemed to sigh as he fell sideways into a patch of stagnant water.

Daria was on her knees beside him. "Roland, are you all right? Oh, your throat! Can you speak?"

"I'm all right," he said, his voice a harsh croak. "I'm all right." Slowly he rubbed his fingers to his throat and shook his head back and forth. That had been too close, far too close, and he owed his life to a woman. A woman he fully planned to dispose of as he would a horse or household furnishings. He looked up at her face, white and washed clean of dirt by the thick sheets of rain. "Thank you," he said. "Let's leave this place."

They were riding in the heart of the Black Mountains, into the valley of the Afon Honddu.

" 'Tis naught but solitude," Daria said, her voice hushed and awed at the stark desolation.

Roland merely nodded, so tired he could scarce think. "Wait until you see Llanthony Abbey. It was founded over one hundred and fifty years ago by the lord of Hereford, but the monks had no desire for such stark isolation or, as they said it, to 'sing to the wolves,' and thus migrated to Gloucester. In any case, there are still some stouthearted monks who brave this bleak wilderness. They'll take us in and we'll sleep dry and warm this night."

That sounded like a wonderful idea to Daria.

The prior met them outside the small church, and upon hearing that the gentleman and his young brother needed shelter, offered them a small room. The architecture was as austere and stark as the wilderness in which the building sat. Cold and unadorned, all of it, and Daria shivered in Roland's wake as the prior led them to the small meeting chamber where the remaining twenty-one monks took their meals. None were present, for it was late and the monks were at their prayers. Roland was relieved; even monks who hadn't been near other people for a very long time could, perchance, still see Daria as a female, and that would raise questions he didn't wish to deal with.

A small hooded monk brought them a thin soup and some black bread and left them alone. He was Brother Marcus, the prior said, but the man made no sign that he'd heard. The prior, having no more interest in them, also took his leave. The food tasted like ambrosia to Daria. She said nothing, merely ate everything offered to her. When she'd finished, she looked up to see Roland looking at her. His hand was poised in the air on the way up to his mouth.

"What's wrong? Have I done something to offend you?"

She spoke softly, in English, so no one could hear. Roland merely shook his head and continued eating his own meal.

"A bed," she said, "a real bed."

"Actually it will likely be a rough cot

made of straw. But it will be dry."

And it was. They had one candle, given to them by the same Brother Marcus. Roland closed the door to the small chamber with a sigh of relief. It held only a narrow cot with two blankets. Roland walked to it and poked it with his fist. "It is straw and looks damnably uncomfortable. But here are blankets, so we won't freeze."

"We?"

"Aye," he said absently as he tugged off his boots. "Ah," he said suddenly, looking up at her. "You're offended that you must sleep by my side? I don't understand you. You've slept by my side for the past two nights."

She said nothing. In truth, she thought it wonderful to sleep beside him in a bed. Quite different from their sleeping blankets in the forest and in a cave. "I don't mind, Roland, truly."

"Don't be a fool, Daria. I'm so tired it wouldn't matter if you were the most beautiful female in all of Wales and I the randiest of men. You don't mind, you say? Well, you should. You are a lady and a maid. 'Tis modest and right of you to protest. But it matters not. Come, get under the blankets. We leave early on the morrow."

She grinned at his perversity and slipped

under the blankets, wearing only her shift, thankfully dry. When he eased in beside her and sniffed out the candle, she lay stiffly beside him, not moving. The straw poked and prodded at her, and she shifted to find a more comfortable position. After several minutes of this, Roland said, "Come here, Daria, and lie against me. I'm cold, so you will warm me."

She eased over, coming against his side. She laid her head on his shoulder and gingerly placed her hand on his chest. This, she decided, was something she could become easily accustomed to, this having Roland beside her, holding her against him. She sighed and nestled closer. His arm tightened around her back.

Roland frowned into the darkness. He appreciated her trust, but she didn't have to flaunt it. Did she believe him impervious? "You aren't my little brother," he said, "so cease your wiggling about."

"No, 'tis certainly true," she said, and burrowed closer.

"Daria, I'm not made of stone. Damnation, cease your wiggling."

She grinned into the darkness. "But I'm cold, Roland."

He fell asleep before she did, but he awoke quickly enough when she began thrashing about. He shook his head, shaking away his own dreams. He gently rubbed her back, then lightly slapped her cheeks. "Wake up, come now, 'tis no time for a nightmare."

She awoke with a start and lurched up, gasping. "Oh!"

"You're quite all right. Hush, now."

"It was awful, those men and that huge one, Myrddin. He touched me and —" She ground to a painful halt.

"You're safe now," he said again, his words slow and deep. "No one will hurt you." His right hand was methodically rubbing her back. "I'll keep you safe."

It was dark, the middle of the night, and she gave voice to her bitterness. "You speak to me as though I were your child, Roland, but I am not. Of course you will keep me safe. You must have me alive, mustn't you? Otherwise my uncle will give you no coin."

"Quite true."

"I'm an heiress. I'll give you coin not to take me back."

"Don't be a fool, Daria. You have no access to your fortune. 'Tis well under your uncle's thumb. Accept what is, what must be, and do what a female must do — that is, accede to your guardian's dicta. You must be returned alive and a virgin." The moment he said that, he clamped down on his tongue. Damned imprudent mouth! Mayhap she would be too embarrassed to question him; mayhap she wouldn't have noticed what he'd said; mayhap . . .

She was fast as a snake. "What do you mean, a virgin? What does that have to do with anything?"

"Naught. I misspoke. Sleep now."

"What, Roland? Do you mean my uncle cares about my maidenhood? As much as did the Earl of Clare?"

"Go to sleep!"

She slammed her fist into his belly and he grunted. He grabbed her wrists and twisted onto his side, facing her. He couldn't see her face, but he could feel her warm breath against his cheek. "I said to go to sleep, Daria. You will not question me further."

"But you must tell me —"

"You don't obey well, do you?"

"Tell me," she said, her nose touching his. He remained silent. She continued slowly, "You mean my uncle stipulated I must be a virgin or he wouldn't want me back?"

"Don't be a fool. Be quiet!"

"If I'm not a maid, what did he say he would do?"

"All right, aye, 'tis the truth. He wants you returned a virgin. Are you satisfied now? Know, Daria, that you will be returned as much a maid as when you emerged from your mother's womb."

She digested his words, making no response. Because he didn't know her well, Roland felt relief at her quiescence. He rolled onto his back again, bringing her against his side. "Sleep now, Daria."

"All right, Roland," she said, and her mind was racing with ideas. What would her uncle Damon do if she weren't returned a virgin?

6

Roland pressed a gold coin in the prior's hand upon their leaving the following morning. The old man clutched the coin, stared at Roland in surprise, then speeded them on their way with a comprehensive holy blessing.

It wasn't raining and Daria breathed in deeply. "It smells so green and alive," she said.

"*Bore da,*" Roland said.

She butted her chin against his shoulder. "What?"

" 'Tis 'good morning.' Repeat it." And she did. Their lesson continued until Roland drew Cantor to a halt beside a burbling stream. They were high in the Wye Valley and the air was cool, the sky the lightest of blues.

"We'll be at Rhayader soon. They have a market, I'm told, and we'll buy some food."

"Am I still your brother?"

Roland merely nodded. "Keep your head down. You still don't look much like a little cockscomb to me." Just as she was beginning to smile at what she believed a scarce compliment, he added, "I don't feel like fighting any more men who decide you're female enough for them to enjoy."

Rhayader was a sleepy little town that looked more English than Welsh to Daria. There were many sheep about and few people. The market was sparse, most of the goods having been sold much earlier in the day. Roland purchased bread and cheese and some apples. They weren't approached or regarded warily. They were ignored for the most part. "We're outsiders," Roland told her. "It matters not that we're Welsh. We're not from here and that makes all the difference." She listened to him speak Welsh, marveling at how easily the words came to him, how he rolled the difficult sounds on his tongue, and looking, Daria thought, quite pleased with himself.

They ate their noonday meal on the banks of the Rhaidr Gyw, the Falls of the Wye, Roland translated for her, amidst waving wild grass and heather. It was beautiful and soft-smelling and the roar of the fierce rapids filled the silence. "This is a land more rare than the rarest jewel," Roland said as he chewed on his apple. "When it isn't raining, you want to stare, for the colors are more than just colors — look at the green of the Wye Valley, Daria, it looks soft and velvet it is so vivid."

"Where are we going, Roland?"

"We're traveling first to Wrexham, then to Lord Richard de Avenell's stronghold, Croyland. Lord Richard de Avenell is a Marcher Baron and Croyland lies just beyond the Welsh border, on the road to Chester."

She nodded. "How long will we remain there?"

"Not long," and that was all he would say. He saw that she would question him, and said quickly, *"Menyw,"* and touched his fingertip to her chin.

She repeated the word for "woman," then asked, "What is the word for 'wife'?"

Roland looked at her for a long moment, then shrugged. *"Gwrang."*

She repeated it several times. One never knew. Besides, it made him distinctly nervous and thus she repeated it again for good measure.

Roland fell silent then. He remained abstracted throughout the remainder of the day. They stayed the night under the overhang of a shallow cave. It wasn't raining and thus was pleasant.

"What ails you, Roland?" she asked him the following morning.

"Naught," he said shortly. "Tomorrow afternoon we will arrive in Wrexham."

They rode over a mountain that was topped with an ancient fort so old Daria thought it had probably been built before time began. They rode through wooded valleys and saw three waterfalls. It was magnificent, and Daria was enthusiastic until Roland's silence wore her down. They looked back on the Black Mountains, stark and forbidding even beneath a vibrant sun.

Daria was enjoying herself. This was a freedom she'd never known.

It was evident that Roland was not enjoying himself.

"Tell me of your family, Roland."

"I have a brother who is the Earl of Blackheath. He doesn't like me, has never approved of me. It matters not; you won't have to meet him. I have more uncles and aunts and cousins than I can even remember. Our stock is hardy and our men and women prolific." He fell silent again.

"Why don't you like me?"

He twisted about in his saddle and looked

at her. "Why should I not like you?"

"You won't speak to me."

He merely shrugged and click-clicked Cantor into a trot.

"And when you do deign to speak to me, your words are sharp."

"I'm weighing matters," he said, and she had to be content with that.

That night Roland stopped before dark, saying merely, "Cantor is blown. We must rest him."

But it was Roland who fell asleep even as the moon was beginning its rise into the clear Welsh heavens. Daria lay beside him, propped up on her elbow. His breathing was slow and deep. He didn't snore. She looked down at his face as he slept. He looked very young, she thought, all the worries smoothed from his face, and slowly, tentatively, she touched her fingers to his cheek, down along the line of his jaw to his square chin. There was black stubble and she smiled and wondered if the hair on his body was as dark as that on his head. She continued looking at him. It gave her a good deal of pleasure. His brows were naturally arched and black as sin. She wanted to smooth the black hair from his forehead, but hesitated. She didn't want him to awaken and spout angry words at her. She even enjoyed the shape of his ears.

She finally fell asleep snuggling against Roland's back. He wasn't awake to tell her nay.

She awoke with a start, jerking upright. The dream was vivid in her mind and it was alien. She remembered her feelings of knowledge, of deep and complete recognition, when she'd first seen Roland. Now she'd seen the dream he was dreaming. But how was that possible? She shook her head even as she silently questioned herself. She didn't understand how it could be so. She wasn't in his dream, nay, she was merely an observer, yet she seemed to know what he thought. The question was why Roland was presenting himself to her in these ways. She now thought she knew the answer, but she also knew she wouldn't say anything to him. He would believe her mad, or simply foolish, or both.

The following morning, the sky was overcast and both Daria and Roland knew that the rain would begin soon. There was nothing either of them could do about it save bear it.

She said suddenly, hoping to catch him off his guard, "I heard stories from my father, stories about the Holy Land. He said he'd been told it was all heat and white sand

and miserable fleas and poverty and children who were so hungry their bellies were bloated. He said the men were dark and bearded and wore white robes and turbans on their heads. He said the women were kept away from other men, held inside buildings with other women. Do you know anything of this, Roland?"

Roland's hands tightened on Cantor's reins. He'd dreamed of the Holy Land the previous night; he'd dreamed about a meeting he'd attended with Barbars himself and his chieftains, and they'd been in a royal tent set up within sight of Acre. But Daria couldn't know that. This was merely happenstance.

He said only, "What your father told you is true. Hush now, I must think."

Daria practiced her Welsh, forming sentences and repeating phrases he'd taught her the past days. *"Rydw i wedi blino,"* she said three times, until he turned to ask, "Is that just practice or are you really tired?"

"Nag ydw," she said, grinning, and firmly shook her head to match her words.

They entered a small church in Wrexham late that afternoon to get out of the rain. Even the building's warm-colored sandstone looked cold and dismal in the gray rain. They walked beneath the narrow Norman nave arcades, toward the cloisters.

There were few people in the church. It was damp and cheerless, no candles lit against the gloom. "It's dark as a well," Daria said aloud, trying to huddle farther into her cloak.

Roland said nothing. His head ached abominably; his throat felt scratchy; every muscle in his body throbbed and cramped. It pained him to breathe and to walk. Even his eyes hurt to focus. The illness had begun nearly two days before, but he'd ignored it, knowing he couldn't be ill, not now, not when he was responsible for Daria. But he was. It took all his resolution not to shudder and shiver beside her.

"Stop," he said finally, unable to take another step. He leaned against a stone arch. He closed his eyes, knowing that she was looking closely at him, knowing that at any moment she would guess the truth.

But he didn't have time for her to tell him so. He felt blackness tug at him. He fought it, but his fight was futile. He felt himself sliding down against the arch.

The Earl of Clare wondered if Roland had killed the two men, and decided he had. One lay rotting, his head in still green water; the other was curled up in death inside a close-by cave.

"Aye, he killed them, our pretty priest," he said. "But why? Did they attack him?" He paused and paled. Had the men raped Daria? And Roland had killed them because they had? No, he wouldn't accept that. No, he would assume that he'd killed them before they'd had a chance to do anything and left them here. He said aloud to MacLeod, "I wonder where our priest took Daria after he killed these louts? Why did they come into this filthy country? Has he friends here?"

MacLeod didn't know a single answer to the earl's spate of questions. What's more, he was beginning not to care. Like the other men, he was wet and miserable and cold and wanted nothing more than to return to Tyberton, to the stifling warm great hall with its fires filling the huge chamber with smoke, and drink warm spiced ale and fill his hands with soft woman's flesh.

"Do we bury them?" one of the men asked MacLeod.

He shook his head. "They're savages. Let them continue to rot in peace."

Daria knew he was ill, had known for the past day and a half, only she hadn't wanted to believe it and had made excuses to herself for his persistent silence. She'd asked him once that morning if he felt all right, and he had snapped at her, vicious and mean as a stray dog. And now he'd fallen unconscious from his illness. She dropped to her knees beside him. His forehead was hot; he was caught in the fever. His body shuddered even in his unconscious state. She looked about for help. She'd never felt more frightened in her life.

"Roland," she whispered, nearly frantic. "Roland, please, can you hear me?"

He was silent.

She was terrified, but not for herself. She was terrified for him, but of course he wouldn't care. It didn't matter now what he thought of her. He needed her.

When the black-robed Augustinian priest saw them, he hurried forward.

"Father," she whispered, "you must help me."

She realized she'd spoken partly in English, partly in Welsh.

He looked at her oddly and she quickly said, "He is Welsh and I am his wife and but half-Welsh. Do you understand English?"

He nodded. "Aye, for I lived many years in Hereford. What do you here?"

She looked him straight in his sharp, pale eyes. "My husband was taking me to his family in Chester when he fell ill. 'Tis all the rain and our hard pace. What am I to do?"

It was then she realized the priest had seen her as a boy, and she cursed herself silently. She'd forgotten and thought only to protect Roland, thinking a wife, in a priest's eyes, must have more favor than a woman not a man's wife. She said quickly, "I am dressed this way for protection. We were set on by outlaws and barely managed to get away. 'Twas my husband who got me these clothes."

"A reasonable thing to do. I am Father Murdough, and who are you and your husband?"

"His name is Alan; he is a freeholder, Father. Our farm is near to Leominster. Please help us."

He had no choice, for he was a man of God and he couldn't leave a man to die in his church. "Stay here. I will fetch my sexton to help us."

It seemed a decade had flowed by with Daria huddled over Roland, before her now-husband, still unconscious, was carried up three flights of stairs over the sexton's huge shoulder and laid upon a narrow bed in a small chamber beneath the eaves of Father Murdough's modest home beside the church.

"Have you coin, child?"

145

"Aye," Daria said. "In my husband's cloak. Will the sexton see to my husband's horse?"

The priest nodded absently. He'd seen that horse. It was a powerful destrier; unusual that a freeholder would own such an animal. Highly unusual. He wondered who this man really was. As for the woman, he doubted if she carried even a whiff of Welsh blood in her veins. He was glad she hadn't told him her name. He didn't want to know.

But that didn't matter now. Only the young man mattered. Father Murdough became brisk. "I will fetch a leech. The fever must be bled out of him if he is to survive. I will have my servant, Romila, bring blankets and water."

Daria, now frantic for Roland, managed to nod. Left alone with him, she saw that his clothes were damp and knew he must be made dry and warm. She would have to strip his clothes off, something she doubted he would approve of. She was unknotting his chausses when an old woman, tall and thin and proud-looking, her head topped with masses of white hair, entered, carrying blankets and a ewer of water. She had a lovely wide smile and full mouth of teeth. "Here, now," she said in low slurring Welsh, "wait a minute and I'll help ye!"

Together the women stripped oft Roland's damp clothes. When he was naked, sprawled on his back, the old woman took a thorough survey. "A fine man he is, aye, fine indeed, all lean and bone and muscle. No fat on this fine lad. Aye, and look at that rod of his! It must make ye as happy as a turtledove."

"You spoke English," Daria said blankly.

"Aye, the father told me to. Me, I come from Chester, and my husband is one of these savages. Aye, but he's a savage that keeps my old bones warm during the long winter nights. Aye, he's mine, he is."

As she spoke, Daria looked down at Roland, at his rod that must make her happy. It lay flaccid against the thick black hair of his groin. He was magnificent and she wished with all her heart that he could keep her warm during long winter nights for the rest of her life.

They quickly covered him, and the old woman said nothing about the reddened cheeks of the young man's wife. "He is so very hot," Daria said, her palm stroking Roland's face. "Please, he will be all right, will he not?"

Romila looked at the girl and nodded without hesitation. "Aye, he'll be well again, and like most men, he'll likely growl and complain until ye'll want to smash in his head, ye'll be so angry with him."

"I hope so," Daria said, and sat beside him. She smoothed the blankets at his throat. She couldn't seem to keep her hands still and they stroked his arms, his face, his hair.

When the leech arrived, a shrunken old man with wise eyes and clean hands, Daria felt hope.

She'd found a hoard of coins wrapped in a tunic in one of Roland's bags. When she paid the leech, he looked at her, clearly startled. "Who are ye, then?" he asked in deep slow Welsh.

"I am Gwen, sir, and I'm his wife."

The old man harrumphed loudly.

"Please, sir, will my husband live?"

"Ye ask me that? I have but one answer and I'll tell ye it on the morrow. Pray for yer husband, lass, and I'll be back in the morning."

It wasn't until the old man had left that Daria realized he'd begun by speaking Welsh to her and had then switched to English. She wasn't, she realized, much of a mummer, if even an old leech could see through her.

She returned to Roland's bedside. She looked at his still face. He was so familiar to her and she knew now that there was some sort of strange bond between them, a bond that he didn't feel, only she. She thought again of the men in their white robes that she'd seen in his dream. She'd been there observing, but she'd also been with him, felt what he'd felt, even understood the strange tongue they'd spoken. And she remembered that one of the dark-faced men had pulled him aside and said softly to him, "I know who you are and I will bring you down — when it pleases me — infidel dog!"

And Roland had thought in those moments: Well, damn, I will have to slit his miserable throat. Daria wondered if he had, and then she didn't wonder at all. He had; she knew it, knew it as well as she now knew him.

She laid her cheek against his heart and slept. He didn't stir until she woke him for some nourishing broth Romila brought early that evening. He ate because she forced him to. He turned his face away, but the spoon followed and he had no choice. When Daria was satisfied, she bathed his face and chest with a damp cool cloth.

The fever rose steadily and her fear kept apace. Near to midnight she offered her life in exchange for his, but she knew that such a request wouldn't find such merit in God's eyes. She was only a woman, her uncle Damon had once told her. What would God care what a silly woman wanted?

She wet more cloths and wiped him again and again. The heat from his body was intense; her fear grew and her prayers became more frequent and more impassioned. At exactly midnight, he opened his eyes and stared up at her.

"Roland? Oh, thank God, you're awake!"

He said nothing, merely looked at her. Then suddenly his expression was furious and he yelled, "Joan, you damned bitch! Get out of my sight before I wrap my fingers around your throat!"

He grabbed her wrist and twisted it hard. She cried out and pushed at him.

But he was strong, and now he was twisting and panting and muttering at her, "Aye, I loved you, I gave you my heart, I offered you everything that I was and would become. But you betrayed me and now you return to taunt me. Bitch, damned perfidious bitch!"

He released her wrist suddenly and slapped her, hard. She reeled back, falling to the floor. "Roland," she gasped, coming quickly onto her knees, "nay, don't move! Nay!"

He was lurching upward, flinging back the blankets. He rose, weaving until he gained his balance, and she stared up at him, terrified and amazed and joyous at the sight of him.

Then, just as suddenly as it had started, his spurt of energy was spent and he fell backward onto the bed. She managed to ease him onto his back again and covered him. An hour slowly passed. He sighed and opened his eyes again. Without warning, he reached up his hand and grabbed a thick tress of hair. "Joan, 'tis you. You won't have my soul again."

She leaned over him because his hold on her hair was painful, and clasped his shoulders. "Nay, Roland, nay, 'tis I!"

He was mumbling now, words she didn't understand, words in that strange guttural language he'd spoken in the dream. The language of the Muslims and the Arabs. Then he said to her, his voice deep and soft, "Forgive me, Lila, of course it's you. You could never be like Joan. Come to me now. I want your breasts in my hands and your hands on my belly. Yes, Lila, bring me your soft body."

Daria sucked in her breath, stunned and fascinated, but she didn't move. Roland raised his hand and now he gently stroked her breasts. "You are still clothed. What is this? Do you not desire me? Why are you still wearing clothes?"

He raised his other hand and caressed both breasts, weighing them in his palms, his thumbs moving slowly over her nipples. She stared down at him, at the intent expression on his face, at the gleam of pleasure in his dark eyes.

"Remove your silk jacket now. I want to feel you."

He believed her to be a woman he'd known in the Holy Land, a woman whose name was Lila. She didn't care, not now. She touched his hands, caressed them as his fingers caressed her breasts, and she could feel the urgency of his need, feel the desire that came from the depths of him.

And she knew then that nothing was more important in her life than this man. She knew that he would be the center of her life, knew that he would be with her until she died. Or, she thought with a pained moment of truth, it was what she wanted to believe. Still, with no hesitation Daria calmly unlaced the boy's tunic she wore. Roland wanted her breasts bare; she would give him whatever he wanted. She pulled the tunic over her head and tossed it to the floor. Thankfully, the chamber was very warm from the fire in the crude fireplace. She saw him smile, and he was looking at her breasts, at their motion as she moved back beside him.

"Come closer. Lean into my hands. Ah, yes, that is what I want. You feel like silk and . . . What is this? You want me, Lila? So quickly? Your nipples are tight, for me?"

She leaned over him, her breasts filling his hands, and whispered, "Aye, Roland, for you. I would be whatever you wished. Just tell me what to do."

His fingers stroked her and she moaned, then gasped, from her surprise. Never had a man touched her thus. She felt stranger still as he continued to explore her, and she knew that she was on the threshold of something wonderful, something she would like very much. She wasn't ignorant of what men did to women, for she had lived in her uncle's house for five long years. She knew very well what happened between men and women, her uncle had seen to that. He enjoyed flaunting his women in front of her. And she'd seen him naked, his rod standing out from his body, but she'd always felt only revulsion, deep, soul-searing revulsion. But not with Roland, never with Roland.

"Lila, bring your breasts to my face. I wish to suckle."

She stared down at him. This was something she knew nothing about. Suckle her? She couldn't imagine a man suckling a woman as if he were a babe. But it didn't matter. She lowered her body and felt his fingers again stroking her breasts, gently tugging at her nipples, and then his mouth was on her flesh and she drew in her breath with the wondrous feelings that were building deep inside her body. She closed her eyes, feeling his warm mouth, his wet tongue, and gloried in the sensations that were growing more intense low in her belly.

"Roland," she whispered, and her hands were on his bare shoulders, sliding beneath the blankets to his chest.

"So sweet," he said, his breath hot and urgent on her. His hands came around her and stroked down her back to her waist, then up again, his fingers tangling into her hair, pulling the braids free. "Lila, you still wear clothes." He sounded surprised and faintly displeased. "I want you naked and over me."

"I'm not Lila," she said even as she pulled off the boy's pants and hose and unfastened the chausses.

When she was naked, she slid down the blankets. She looked at his man's body, taut and hard and shadowed. She smiled and covered him with her body. At the feel of him beneath her, she felt something pass from him to her, something strong and gentle and demanding, something so powerful that for a moment it frightened her. Then she accepted it completely. But he must feel only his own building desire. He sighed at the feel of her body pressing against his. He slid his hands over her back until he was cupping her buttocks.

His breathing became quite suddenly fast and raw. "Bring me inside you, Lila."

He wanted her to bring his rod into her body? She lifted herself and gazed down the length of him. His member was swelled and hard and he moaned deeply, his hips jerking when she lightly touched her fingers to his hot flesh.

And again she felt this urgency in him, this overpowering need, and her fingers tightened around him. He was bucking now, moaning hoarsely. "Now, Lila. By Allah, my need is great. Wait no longer."

Still, Daria wasn't certain what to do. He was very large, surely too large to come inside her. She leaned down and kissed his hard belly. He flinched and moaned. She kissed him again, her mouth lower this time. When her lips touched his sex, his body heaved wildly, and then, suddenly, she saw a glorious naked woman with hair black as a night of sin who was straddling him and holding him between her hands and guiding him upward into her.

Daria cried out with the vividness of what she saw. She felt dizzy and frightened about the step she was taking, a step that was irrevocable. She was on her knees over him, staring down at him, and then she touched herself, felt the wetness of her flesh and knew it was to ease his way into her. She took him between her hands, ready, but he forestalled her. His fingers were on her belly, stroking her, kneading her, then lower until they sifted through the hair covering her woman's mound. She lurched straight up when his fingers delved through the slick flesh to find her, and she cried out.

"Ah," he said, and he sounded profoundly pleased with himself. "You are always ready for me, aren't you? Always ready to take me. I'm pleased. Shall I give you pleasure now? Before I come into you? Before you ride me wildly?"

"Nay, come into me now." She feared this pleasure he spoke so confidently about, feared what it would do to her. She held herself stiffly above him, feeling his fingers begin a rhythm on her flesh even as his other hand was pressing against her belly, and then he stopped.

"All right, I'll take you now, you're wet and ready for me." Daria no longer saw this

Lila, this other woman he believed her to be, this other woman who was no longer in his life. She was in the past, she didn't matter.

What mattered was now.

She closed her eyes a moment. He spoke again, and this time it was in that strange tongue, but more strangely still, she understood what he wanted and she felt no hesitation.

7

Daria knew if she did what he asked, she would no longer be a maid. She refused to consider the consequences more than she had already done. She raised herself above him again and took his man's rod in her hand. Slowly, so very slowly she pressed him against her, and felt him come easily inside her because she was slick and wet. He strained against her fingers. She eased down just a bit and took more of him. He was moaning, his hands were tightening on her hips, his fingers digging into her flesh. She felt herself stretch for him, felt the tension building in him, powerful and vigorous, and in herself as well, and knew the moment before he thrust upward that the pain was coming and she wouldn't like it. He grasped her hips hard and jerked her down on him even as he bucked his hips upward. The pain was a sharp burning stab that made her cry out, but nothing more, and then he was deep inside her, touching her womb, and it was something she couldn't have imagined. His urgency seemed to lessen and he began to move gently and slowly, nearly pulling out of her, then coming in deeply once more. His chest heaved with effort and sweat covered his brow, matting his hair, and he was murmuring over and over, "Nay, don't move, Lila, don't move! It's been so long, far too long . . . don't move!"

She held still, knowing everything was beyond her now, knowing whatever would come, she had done it to herself. She had set into motion her own future and she was the only one responsible. But she hadn't imagined his touching her like this, his body coming into hers, so deeply, so completely, possessing her so thoroughly. The pulsing, intense feelings of before had faded, lost in the pain of her ripped maidenhead, and they didn't return. But it didn't matter. Only he mattered. He was moaning now, harsh raw sounds from deep in his throat, and then he lifted her nearly off him. He held her above him, his rod barely inside her body, and stared up at her and smiled, and brought her down hard and fast, and she shuddered with the shock of it as she took him completely yet again. He clutched her to him then and jerked wildly.

"Roland," she said, and he looked at her, his eyes clear and bright and dark; then he closed his eyes, hiding the pain his control was costing him. "You aren't like yourself. I'm stretching you, I can feel it, and it's bringing me madness, this smallness. And I ripped you. How can that be? You aren't a maid. How can you still be so narrow? How can I hurt you? Have you found some cream that brings you a maid's tightness again? Or do you cry out with passion? Is that it, Lila, is it passion?"

" 'Tis passion, Roland. It could be naught else but passion with you."

He smiled again, a smile so sweet that she felt as if a fist were clutching around her heart. She hurt, deep inside, but it didn't matter. He wanted her and she would do anything for him. She rode him hard, for that was what his hands directed her to do, and as he jerked and moaned, his fingers wildly kneading her buttocks and belly, she said again, "I'm Daria. Please know me, at least for a moment, know 'tis me."

He suddenly froze and she felt him lurch upward, felt his seed spurt deep inside her. He was heaving, his breath fast and raw, and still she rode him until he whispered, "Enough, Lila. By Allah, you're good, so good. You've worn me down to my bones. I don't think I'll take Cena now. No, she must wait, even though she is hungry, I know, always hungry. You've reduced me to ashes and it was so good, so very, very good."

She stared down at him. He was deep inside her body and he was talking of two women in his bed. She slowly eased off him and saw his seed and her virgin's blood on her thighs and on his man's rod. She quickly pulled the blankets over him again and bathed herself with the cool water. She felt soreness deep inside her.

She returned to him and slipped beneath the covers to hold him to her.

It was during the night that she made up her mind not to say anything to him about what had passed between them. He hadn't known her. He'd believed her to be another woman, a mistress he'd known in a foreign land. It was then she rose and pulled down the blankets. She quickly bathed the blood and seed from his member. She held him gently, marveling at his differentness, at the beauty of him. She raised her eyes to his still face. "I love you, Roland. I will always love you and I will always belong to you and to no one else." She wished she knew the words in Welsh. She wished he could hear her, and she wished that he had smiled at her and known her as Daria.

She would be safe from his questions, if he chanced to remember what had happened, which she strongly doubted. If he did, he would believe it a dream, nothing more. She felt, oddly, content. He was the man destined for her and she'd given herself to him. That, she reminded herself, or she was as mad as her grandmother and seeing things because they were what she wanted to see. Or he was the man she'd been destined to have only for this night and then he would leave her, and all her precious knowledge of him, her deep *knowing*, had all been a lie, a sham. No, she wouldn't accept that.

Someday, perhaps, he would realize that he was tied to her. Perhaps someday he could care for her as she did for him.

She laid her palm on his forehead.

He was cool to the touch. The fever had broken.

So had her maidenhead.

Roland opened his eyes and stared around the small dismal chamber. He had no idea where he was. His head pounded but his stomach wasn't twisting and churning, nor was there the dreadful bone-aching pain that had dragged at his body and reduced him to the strength of an ant. He'd enjoyed excellent health his entire life, and the illness frightened him. It meant he wasn't in control; it meant he had to depend upon others. And he was vulnerable to anyone who took it into his head to do him in. He raised his hand and realized with something of a shock that he was still very weak. He turned his head ever so slightly at the sound of breathing. There was Daria, sitting on a lone chair, sewing a tunic — one of his tunics. She was still dressed as a boy, but her hair was loose and tumbling over her shoulders and down her back. Very beautiful hair, he thought inconsequentially. He'd forgotten how lovely her hair was, with all its dark rich colors. Her brows were as dark and finely arched above those green eyes of hers. Then he noticed that she was pale, very pale.

He felt his throat tighten, and said, "Daria, may I have some water?"

Her head jerked up and she smiled at him, a dazzling smile that would have brought an answering smile to his mouth if he'd had the strength. She bounded up from her chair and her abrupt movement made him wince.

He sipped at the cup of water as she held his head, so gently, as if he were naught but a babe. Again he felt fear, fear that he was helpless and out of control. She, a female, was succoring him, seeing to his needs, nurturing him. It wasn't to be borne, yet he didn't seem to have a choice for the moment. He sipped at the water. She seemed content to allow him all the time he wanted. He breathed in her scent, turned his face slightly so that his cheek was against her breast. She was soft, too soft, and that frightened him as well. He tried to pull away from her.

"Nay, Roland," she said, her breath sweet and warm on his face as she lightly stroked his cheek. "You're not ready to do battle in a tourney just yet."

"What do you know of my strength?"

To his chagrin, she smiled sweetly at him. "Romila told me you would be testy. She says that all strong men hate illness, hate being dependent on others."

That bit of philosophy drew him up. Damn her for being in the right of it. He realized he also hated being like everyone else, hated acting as he was expected to. "No, I don't mind it at all. Your breasts are soft against my face and —"

Water dripped down his chin. He tried for a cocky smile but couldn't manage it. For an instant he saw her expression change into one of wariness and something akin to fear. No, how could that be possible?

"Where are we? How long have I been ill?"

Her smile returned. She said nothing until she'd gently wiped his chin and given him more water to drink. Still, she held him, and he felt the soft thud of her heartbeat against his face. He wanted to stay there, warm in her arms, for a very long time.

"We're in Wrexham, in a small chamber in the priest's house. We've been here for nearly three days now. When you collapsed in the cathedral, Father Murdough helped us."

Roland chewed that over. "The priest then knows you are no boy."

"Aye. I told him you were my husband and that you were taking me to meet your family in Leominster. You're Welsh and a freeholder and I'm but half-Welsh, thus my lacks in the language."

Roland groaned.

"I told him that I was dressed as a boy because you believed it wise for my protection."

"I don't suppose the man of God agreed?"

She chuckled and he found himself smiling slightly in response. "He said aught about it, actually. He's a very accepting sort of priest. I am expecting the leech anytime now. He's not a fool and he has aided you. Do you really feel better, Roland?"

"Aye." He turned his head so he could see her face. "You're pale. Have you remained here, beside me, shut up in this dreary little chamber?"

"Had I not stayed with you, 'tis likely you would have tried to take over the cooking chores and bathe yourself and mend your own tunic."

He gave her an absent smile, then said, "We'll leave on the morrow, at dawn."

She was perfectly still for a moment. "No, we shan't. We won't leave until you have your strength back."

"You dare to tell me our plans?"

Her arms were around his shoulders and she hugged him slightly. "You sound churlish, Roland. Aye, you will do what is wise and not what is stupid. If I have to tie you down, you will remain here until the leech says you are well enough to travel without falling off Cantor's back."

"I don't suppose you've remembered the Earl of Clare and his desire for your fair person?"

"I've not forgotten," she said, and that was all.

His eyes hurt and he said irritably, "Dim the damned lights. I can scarce see."

"All right."

"You're being too agreeable. I distrust

that. A female who agrees with a man is having sport with him. Have you spent all my coins?"

She lightly passed her palm over his forehead and through his hair, tousling it, then smoothing it again, paying no heed to his sharp words.

"You aren't my mother, damn you, wench!"

"That," she said, gently pressing him onto his back and straightening over him, "is very true."

He gave a heartfelt sigh. "You are my penance. I wonder if the coin your uncle will pay me will suffice for my days in your tyrant's company."

"Be not sour-natured, Roland, it will do you no good. Now, if —"

He interrupted her. "I must relieve myself."

Daria nodded briskly. "I will fetch the chamber pot and assist you."

Roland looked at her with astonished loathing. "I don't need any help, only some privacy." When she didn't move, he gave her an evil look, threw back the blankets, and sat up. But he couldn't rise; he hadn't the strength. And he'd wanted to. He wanted to intimidate her with his size, mayhap frighten her with his bulging manhood. By all the saints, at present he couldn't intimidate a dwarf. He looked down at himself and knew that even his sex had betrayed him. His member wouldn't intimidate the shiest of maidens, and Daria had proved herself not at all shy. That in itself made him want to howl with humiliation.

Daria didn't draw back. She knew his body as well as she knew her own, for she'd cared for him completely for the past three days. She crossed her arms over her breasts and stared at him. "Will you rise now? Will I have the pleasure of seeing you collapse again? I doubt I have the strength to pick you up, so you will lie on the floor, naked as the day you came into the world, until I have fetched Romila. Two women would then haul you back into bed and see to your needs. Romila, I might add, much delights in examining your body, and she's frank in her assessments. Now, Roland, what say you to that?"

"I say you're a wasp and 'twas foul mischance that brought me to you."

She saw that he was trembling from weakness or perchance from a lingering chill, and forgot her show of mastery. "Roland, don't be foolishly proud. Let me help you. I would let you help me if I needed it."

He was damned if he did and damned

ever more if he didn't. He nodded. It was torture, every moment of it. Once he'd finished, he was tucked by her gentle hands back into the cot without a word being spoken. He closed his eyes. He considered slipping out whilst she slept and escaping her. He cursed her uncle's coin. He didn't want it, not if it meant that he had to relieve himself in front of her. She had turned her back, but it mattered not. 'Twas the same thing, and she'd known what he was doing. Indeed, before he'd regained his wits, he doubted not that she'd seen to it even then.

He was embarrassed beyond what he could tolerate, and there was naught, at the present, he could do about it. In the normal course of events, he didn't imagine that he would care in the least if she watched him doing anything at all; but he was helpless and weak, a pitiful specimen, and that made all the difference; that made it intolerable.

Daria watched him from beneath her lids. She was pretending to sew the rip in his tunic, but her eyes and her attention were focused on him. She wasn't certain she understood the depths of his feelings, but she accepted his anger, his sourness. She could only imagine what she would feel like if she were ill and had to relieve herself with his help.

When the leech arrived, she was profoundly thankful. He eyed Roland, spoke in soft Welsh to him, and seemed pleased. At one point, he gestured toward her, but Daria didn't understand his words or Roland's reply. She doubted her husband would be complimenting her.

And as Roland and the leech spoke, she felt free to look at him, and felt such a surge of relief that he was improved that she wanted to shout. When at last the leech turned to her, she was smiling despite her supposed husband's foul humor.

"Yer husband does well," the old man said. "He tells me he will leave on the morrow, and I told him if he does, he'll die and leave ye alone to the tender mercies of lawless bastards. He is now considering things." He paused, giving her a significant look, and Daria quickly paid him. "Nay, worry not, lass, he's not a stupid man." He gave her a small salute and took himself off.

"You give him *my* money, do you?"

"Since I have none of my own, there's no choice."

"So, you found where I'd hidden my coins and now you make free with them?"

"Perhaps I should have pleaded poverty and the priest could have dumped both of us in a ditch. As for the leech, of course I pay

170

him. To put up with your vile temper, he deserves all the coins I give him. Of course, since he's a man and not a simpleminded female, you accorded him more courtesy and attention!"

"You should have told me."

"You're right. I should have somehow roused you and asked humbly for your permission to use the coins. Such a pity I also am paying for the stabling and care of your destrier. Should I tell the priest to throw Cantor into a ditch, perhaps let him run loose until you are ready for him again?"

"You become a shrew, Daria."

"You are merely evil-tempered because you cannot bear the fact that you, my stalwart rescuer, are all too human. You aren't a god, Roland. You're only a man."

"So you have noticed that, have you?"

She gave him a smile that, had he but realized it, would have shown him just how much she did know. "Aye," she said. "Be patient, my l . . . have patience."

"How can I? The damned earl will come, and then what will you do? Tell him to be patient until I am well enough to protect you?"

She shook her head and spoke without thought. "I should protect you."

He snorted and lost some of his newly acquired healthy color. "No, say nothing more! Bring me food. I must get my strength back."

Daria considered starving him. He was ungrateful and a tyrant and seething all because he himself became ill. As if it were her fault. She sighed. Men were difficult creatures. "Very well. Please rest whilst I'm gone. I will return shortly with food for you." She marveled that she'd sounded so calm. She snapped the chamber door closed with a bit more force than was necessary and walked with a bit more pressure than was fitting for a priest's abode.

Romila took one look at her face and cackled. "Aye, yer pretty husband makes ye furious, eh?"

"Aye, I'd like to strangle him."

"He's a man, child, nothing more, nothing less. Feed him; he'll chirp in harmony again once his belly's full."

If Roland didn't chirp, he at least seemed to regain his calm after he'd eaten Romila's stewed beef and coarse brown bread covered with sweet butter.

"We leave on the morrow," he said, not bothering to look at her. He was calm and sure of himself and of her.

"No."

"In the afternoon."

"No."

"Daria, you will do as I tell you. I am not your husband but I am the man in charge of you, the man responsible for you and, thus you —"

"No. We won't leave until you are well, completely fit, and not before. I have hidden your clothes, Roland. If you behave as a half-wit, you will go naked as one. You cannot force me, nor can you threaten me. I won't let you go until your body is well again."

He cursed long and luridly, but Daria only smiled. He'd lost and he knew it. His foul language was just a man's adornment for his frustration. After he'd cursed himself out of words and into a near-stupor, he fell asleep and she moved to sit beside him. She lightly touched her fingers to his face, and leaning close, whispered, "You have no memory of two nights past, do you? I have wondered what I would do and say if you had. Would I have denied it and claimed it naught but a fevered dream? Or a fancy, mayhap? But it hurts nonetheless, Roland, very much. Now I find I'm disappointed that you don't have any memory of ridding me of my maidenhead.

"I do know, Roland, if you force me back to my uncle and he forces me to wed Ralph of Colchester, I would at least have had one night of love." She paused a moment, aware of tears pooling in her eyes. "Damn you, Roland. You are the most stubborn, the most obtuse of men. Mayhap I will simply inform my uncle that I am no longer a virgin and you are the man responsible. Then would I be safe from Ralph of Colchester?

"But at what cost? Would my uncle kill you? Kill me for my inheritance? Knowing Uncle Damon, I doubt he would have any scruples about doing away with both of us, but —"

"You carry on like a raucous kingfisher. What are you talking about? I try to sleep to regain my strength, but you babble on and on, numbing my ears."

She very slowly moved her fingers from his face. What had he heard? She tried to remember all of her soliloquy, but couldn't. A silly argument with herself, but it appeared he'd just heard meaningless sounds.

" 'Tis naught, Roland. Forgive me for disturbing you. Sleep."

He grumbled some more, but she didn't understand his complaints, which was probably just as well.

He slept soundly until late that night. After she'd fed him again and seen to his needs, which still caused him to curse and his expression to become taut with humiliation, she slipped into bed beside him, careful not to disturb him. But during the dark of the night, he found her and drew her against him. It was as if he knew her and accepted her and recognized also on a deep level that she was his and he would act as he pleased. His hands were on her hips; then she felt his fingers pushing between her thighs, skimming over her flesh to find her. She squirmed as his fingers probed, his middle finger easing high up inside her and his other fingers gently rubbing her swelled flesh. She turned her face into his shoulder, moaning through her clenched teeth, as her body shuddered with the intense feelings.

Then suddenly his breathing slowed and he fell back into a deep sleep, sprawled on his back, his fingers cupped over her hip. The frantic feelings slowly faded, and again she wondered where such feelings would lead.

She eased her hand down over him and discovered that his rod was full and heavy, but he hadn't moved to come into her. He hadn't had the strength, nor had he really awakened. What he'd done, he'd done simply because she was there beside him, a female whose flesh was eager for him. Had he realized it was her, Daria, he was holding and stroking, he would have probably fallen off the bed in his haste to get away from her. But he'd slept through his assault.

She didn't understand this sex business, particularly from the man's view. Touching her intimately, then stopping, never coming to consciousness. She awoke first the following morning and eased out of bed. She stared down at him and wanted to shout at the wondrous feelings that surged through her when she simply looked at him. "I love you, Roland," she whispered, then repeated in Welsh, *"Rwy'n dy garu di."* Romila had chuckled when Daria had asked her the words in Welsh the previous day, but had obligingly told her. Daria dressed hurriedly and left the chamber.

She wanted to visit his destrier and see that his care was proper. On the northern side of Wrexham cathedral, down a long narrow street, stood a public livery, a long low building built solidly of straw and dung and covered with a slate roof. Cantor was in the third stall and the toothless brawny individual who showed him to her babbled on about the amount of oats the horse was eating and how the beast had bitten him but good.

Daria finally paid him extra coins, and he beamed, scratching his armpit vigorously.

" 'Tis a fine bit of horseflesh," he said, speaking loudly and slowly to her in his own tongue. "Aye, 'tis true, and ye say yer husband be a freeholder?"

So much suspicion, she thought, nodding. She hadn't had time to think of a better lie, and this one wasn't serving her all that well. There was nothing for it but to stick to her story.

"Aye," the liveryman continued, " 'twere another couple of men in here earlier, and they asked me about this beauty. I told 'em yer husband were that, a freeholder."

Daria felt her guts twist painfully. She knew who the men were, she *knew.*

"They were *saeson,* the slimy louts."

Of course they were English; they were the Earl of Clare's men; she had no doubt of it. What she didn't know was what she should do about it. She scratched her own armpit, saying indifferently, "I wonder if they'll come back. Think you they want to buy the horse?"

The stableman sought his way through her clumsy Welsh, and nodded. "They're coming back," he said, and Daria knew everything had changed. Thank God the stableman didn't know their names or where they were staying. But the Earl of Clare would find out quickly enough. She ran her tongue over her dry mouth. Oh, God, what to do?

"Oh, aye," the stableman suddenly said. "There they be, yon!"

She turned to see two of the earl's men some thirty paces up the narrow street, speaking to a vegetable vendor. She recognized MacLeod, his master-at-arms. He was making descriptive movements with his hands as he spoke. Both men looked tired and impatient.

"I think I will take the horse for a gallop," Daria said.

"*Ond —*"

She waved away his objection and quickly saddled Cantor. The destrier, impatient and bored, neighed loudly, flinging his head up, and it required all her strength to get the bit between his teeth and the reins over his head. "I will return soon," she said to the stableman, and click-clicked Cantor from the stableyard. "I ride toward Leominster," she said, and prayed with all her might that he would repeat that to the earl's men.

As Cantor snorted and danced sideways through the crowded narrow streets of Wrexham, Daria stuffed her hair under her woolen cap. Did she look once again like a boy? She prayed so. She had no idea where she was going. She knew only that she had to lead them away from Roland.

She had coin and she had a strong horse.

She wasn't stupid and she could speak some Welsh. Aye, she thought, grimacing. Any robbers who caught her, she could tell them that she loved them. She would ride, she decided in that moment, to the castle called Croyland, to Lord Richard de Avenell. Surely he would assist her.

And what of Roland?

She closed her eyes over that thought. If the Earl of Clare found him, he would kill him. She had to lead him away; far away and quickly. Once they cleared the town, she gave Cantor his head. She knew from the position of the sun that they were riding northeast, toward Croyland, toward the English border.

What would Roland think when he realized she was gone?

8

It was raining, a cold fine spray that soaked Daria within minutes. She looked up at the angry gray sky and just shook her head at the endless misery of it.

She'd been riding for three hours now and hadn't seen a single man or woman in the past two. There were sheep, of course, sheep everywhere, and dark forests of sessile oak, thick twisted trees that looked wet to the touch even when it wasn't raining. The road she'd taken had become a rough path with yew bushes crowding on either side, many times their spiked leaves brushing against Cantor's flanks, making him prance sideways. She tried to keep him calm, his pace steady. His strength was great, his endurance greater.

She saw a flock of geese in a muddy field to her right and two badgers in a hedgerow beside her. No sign of the earl or his men. She prayed they were behind her, but far, far behind her.

The rain came down harder, in thick drenching sheets, and she huddled in wretched acceptance over Cantor's slick neck. She wondered if magically, once she gained England, the rain would cease. She couldn't be far from Chester, no, not very far now. And what of Roland? She shook her head. She couldn't worry about him now; worrying about herself had to be paramount.

Suddenly a hare sprang from a thicket in front of Cantor. The destrier reared back onto his hind legs, whinnying in surprise and anger, and Daria lost her hold and fell on her side into a puddle of water. She felt her bones jar with the impact, and for a moment she merely lay there, not wanting to move.

Cantor snorted over her, his mighty head lowered, mirroring her own misery. She tried to smile at being caught off-guard. But she couldn't find even a remnant of a smile. She scrambled slowly to her feet and leaned against Cantor's heaving side. He nudged at her and she pressed closer to him. She felt the vibrations against the soles of her leather shoes. Horses, and they were coming swiftly toward her. Soon they would come into view. It had to be the earl and his men.

She swung up onto Cantor's back and kicked his sides with the wet toes of her shoes. He bounded forward, only to stumble again. She was thrown sideways but kept on his back by wrapping his mane around her left wrist.

He was lame. She sat on his back, knowing it was over, yet unable to accept it. His head was lowered and he was blowing hard. There was no escape for her now.

She clearly heard the sounds of the horses' hooves now. Nearer and nearer, and there was naught she could do. Save wait. *What if they'd found Roland?*

She felt her mind bending and straining, and cursed herself with words she'd heard from Roland. What was she to do? And then she knew. After all, she hadn't the choice to play the fool; too much depended on her now.

She slid off Cantor's back and turned toward the oncoming horses. Even as she recognized the earl's big black Arab, she held herself ready, not moving, aware only that something deep inside her was flinching away from him, from who he was, and what he wanted from her.

I can't bear it if he touches me. I can't bear it. I'll shriek and kick and die if he touches me . . . if he touches me.

She raised her head and felt the cold

shards of rain strike her face. Sharp and stinging and cold, and she welcomed it.

The Earl of Clare raised his gauntleted hand. He stared at the rain-soaked boy who stood beside Roland's huge destrier. His hand clamped over his sword. Where was that damned bastard? In hiding amongst the yew bushes? Leaving Daria, dressed foolishly like a lad, to fend for herself?

He waved his men to a halt. He saw Daria give a start as she recognized him. He watched with growing bewilderment as her expression changed from fear to joy and relief. She was running toward him, not away.

He felt uncertainty as he dismounted from his destrier. He stood still and stiff, watching her race toward him. She was speaking, yelling to him, as she ran. Then she threw herself against him, her arms going around his back.

His hands fisted, yet he made no move against her. He was mired in confusion. She was babbling now, something about how he'd saved her! Saved her!

The earl clasped her upper arms in his hands and pushed her away from him. He shook her.

"What do you here?"

Those weren't the words he'd intended to

speak. He'd wanted to strike her, fling her to the muddy road, and strike her again for her perfidy. But he did nothing, merely stood there, saying again, "What do you here?"

She was stuttering, with cold, with fear, with relief . . . He didn't know; he didn't move, just listened as the words poured from her mouth.

"I escaped him, I stole his horse, but the wretched animal is lame and I thought you were he and you would catch me again and I was so frightened . . . so frightened."

The Earl of Clare felt the eyes of his tired men go from him to the shivering girl in front of him. Surely they were listening, but he could tell nothing of their opinions from their weary faces.

He realized suddenly that he didn't care what any of them thought.

"You say you escaped from Roland?"

"Roland? Is that the cur's name?" She shivered and flung herself against his chest again, pressing her cheek against the wet dank wool of his overtunic. "He is no priest, my lord. Please, don't let him catch me again! He told me his name was Charles, but I knew it wasn't."

"You struck me! You, Daria, not that whoreson."

She raised her face and gave him a look

184

that was unholy in its innocence. And, curse her, her voice was high and wavering, like a frightened girl's. "You were trying to ravish me and I wasn't your wife. What was I to do? I was taught to hold my virtue dear until I was wedded. I had no choice but to protect myself or I would have been cursed by God. Then that man — Roland — he came in and forced me to go with him. He's held me close to him, but finally he got drunk in Wrexham and I escaped him and took his horse."

"I only wanted you a bit before the priest married us!"

Her look was austere and severe. There was no more frightened girl in her aspect now. "A female has only her virtue to attest to her character," she said, speaking low, her voice sure and calm and guileless. "I had to fight you until I could fight no more. I would have been cursed by God had I simply given over to you. Surely you understand that, my lord, you must. A man of honor can't ravish an innocent maid, else he will lose all hope for forgiveness from the maid and from God. 'Tis what I was taught; 'tis what I believe. I couldn't allow you to shame me, and thus I did what I had to save myself."

The earl felt the impotent drag of uncertainty. He hated this not knowing, this no longer being confident and convinced of his actions. He'd raged and cursed and pushed his men until they were all so weary they could scarcely sit their horses. And here she was, blaming him! The bedraggled slip of a female was blaming him!

"Where is Roland?"

"I don't know. Somewhere in Wrexham, at least he was early this morning. He was in a sodden, drunken sleep when I escaped him, but he must know by now that I stole his horse. I found out what he intended to do with me. My uncle hired him, you know, offered him a great deal of coin to bring me back. Then my uncle would have me wedded to Ralph of Colchester." She shrugged. "I pray he won't try to find me, but I'm afraid, my lord, afraid that he will come after me again." She looked up at him, pathetic hope in her eyes. "Do you believe he will give up? Perhaps go back to England?"

"Mayhap," the earl said, but he was thinking: But not without his destrier. He looked up at the rain-bloated clouds, felt the endless trickles of rain snake down his back. He cursed. "Clyde," he shouted to one of his men. "We are close to the cave we came upon yesterday. We will spend the night there or at least shelter ourselves until this cursed rain stops."

The men moved quickly from the pitted muddy path. The earl turned back to the shivering girl still standing in front of him. "You're wet." He pulled a dry tunic from a saddlebag and wrapped it around her. "Keep this close about you. I don't wish you to die of a fever."

"His destrier is lame."

"One of my men will lead him." The earl wasn't about to abandon that horse.

The cave Clyde led them to was high-ceilinged and deep enough for the horses to be hobbled at the rear. Daria was settled near the fire, and slowly, teeth chattering every moment, she felt herself dry. She prayed that she'd fooled the earl. She prayed even more intensely that Roland was mending and that he would simply forget her and leave Wales and be safe. He still had enough coin to buy another horse, not one like Cantor, but still, he could buy his way to safety.

She realized that she would probably never see him again. So much for her knowledge of him. All her wondrous feelings, they'd been false, a lie, a dream woven of unreal cloth. She lowered her head to her hands and felt sobs ripping through her. She had no hold on him, none at all, even a hold of honor, for he didn't know that he'd taken hers.

What she'd said to the Earl of Clare wasn't true. Roland would leave Wales and he'd forget her and he'd forget about the money he would have had from her uncle. He wasn't stupid; he would know that the earl had taken her again. The Earl of Clare would bed her and discover she wasn't a virgin and kill her. For then he would know that Roland had bedded her. She couldn't begin to imagine his fury, for he would believe himself cheated and betrayed, though it had been he who had stolen her in the first place.

No, he'd decided that God had blessed him and approved what he'd planned for her. When the earl and God made a bargain, it was madness to try to break it.

She tried to choke back the sobs, but they broke through. She felt a man's large hand on her shoulder, but she couldn't stop her wailing.

"Hush," the man said, and she recognized MacLeod's voice, the earl's master-at-arms. "Ye'll make yerself ill. With this gut-soaking rain, 'tis not difficult."

"I'm so afraid."

"Aye, ye've reason to be, but the earl

seems bestruck wit' the sight of ye again. He'll not kill ye, at least not yet. Find ye cheer, lass — we're out of that filthy rain, and that's something to shout to the heavens about, eh?"

"Will he go back to Wrexham to find that man?"

"How do ye know we were in Wrexham?"

Oh God, I forgot, and my stupidity will finish me off. "I don't know, I just guessed you'd come from there. Where did you come from if not from Wrexham?"

MacLeod stared at her pale face, the red eyes, the damp masses of hair streaming down either side of her thin face. Such a pathetic little scrap. It seemed to him that the earl should view her as a daughter, not as a possible wife. He couldn't imagine taking the little wench to bed. She was too wretched, too woebegone, and in the baggy boy's clothes, she looked scarce a decent meal for a hardy man like the Earl of Clare.

"We came from Wrexham," he said, looking away from her into the fire. "We've ridden hard to find ye and that whoreson that took ye from Tyberton."

"Oh," she said, and wrapped her arms around her legs and eased closer to the fire.

"Where is the earl?"

MacLeod shrugged. "Speaking to the

men. Here, eat yer dinner. We bought the food at the market in Wrexham. 'Tis right that you eat afore ye lose yer boy's breeches."

MacLeod meant nothing by his words, but Daria saw the earl over her, pinning her down with his weight, hurting her, and she paled.

"Ye're thin, lass," he explained patiently. "Ye must eat something afore yer breeches fall to yer knees."

Daria smiled at him and chewed on the bread he handed her. "Thank you. *Diolch.*"

"So you learned some of this heathen tongue," the earl said as he eased down beside her. "I don't wish to hear it again." He picked up a thick slice of black bread and took a healthy bite. She watched him chew. "All right," she said. He didn't respond. He was staring at her and she knew that he was wondering about her, wondering if he should believe her. Finally, after he'd taken a goodly drink of ale, he said, "This man, Roland. I doubt he'll be witless enough to come after you again, Daria. However, he will come after his destrier. This time he won't find things so much to his liking. I will be ready for him."

"But how could he know that I found you? How could — ?"

"The man is one of Satan's tools. Also, he

isn't a fool. Who else would take you? He must guess that I would come after you. He'll know that I have you again. He'll know that I'm too strong for him, but still he will come. He'll want his destrier and thus he will come to Tyberton. And I will kill the whoreson there on my own lands, with God's blessing."

His horse but not me. The earl was certain she had not near the value of Cantor in Roland's eyes. Probably in his eyes as well. She wanted to laugh. If she was worth so much less than a horse, why couldn't she simply offer to give the earl Cantor, and be allowed to leave in peace?

She didn't know what to say, so she kept silent. The earl nodded, as if pleased. "You will take off your wet clothes. I don't wish you to become ill."

She turned to face him. Words stuck in her throat. She was frightened and just as angry that this man had such power over her, but she also knew that he wanted her docile and meek. She cleared her throat. She would gain her ends through subservient guile. "I beg you not to ravish me."

"It matters not. I will take you if I wish to."

"Please, my lord." She thought frantically, schemes tumbling wildly in her brain, for only a show of complete compliance seemed to touch him. "It will be as you wish, my lord. But it is . . . I have begun my monthly flow."

Her face was red with fear, not humiliation, but the Earl of Clare chose to believe that she was overcome with a maiden's embarrassment.

It pleased him, this sweet reticence, this guileless deference to him and his wishes. And her gentle confession, telling him of her woman's functions, the final proof of her purpose, gratified him. He felt all-powerful. He raised a hand and lightly patted her cheek. It required all her control not to flinch away from him. "You are still a virgin? That man didn't ravish you, did he?"

She shook her head and kept her gaze steady. He was searching out the lie, but she wouldn't let him see it in her eyes.

"Then I will wed you once we return to Tyberton. I won't distress you again, Daria, with my man's needs. Perhaps you were right to fight me so completely. Perhaps God willed your escape from me so that I would know his thoughts in this matter. Perhaps it is God's will that you not give yourself to me until you are my wife. I make my vow before God. You will remain a virgin until our wedding night. Then I will take you and you will be willing and sweet."

She thought she'd die with the relief of it. He saw it and frowned. "It isn't proper that you shouldn't want me in your bed. Accustom yourself, Daria, for I shall take you as surely as I will kill this Roland, and you will bear me a son before the coming winter wanes."

Pleased with the conclusion he'd wrought with his utterance, the earl turned and grunted something to MacLeod. Soon Daria was holding dry clothes and a blanket. The earl waved her to a darkened corner of the cave. As she changed into the dry clothing, she prayed that this time he would keep his word, that she would be safe from him. She prayed she had God on her side this time and that God would speak loudly to the earl.

It rained for a day and a half, sheets of wet cold rain. Daria wished she could simply succumb to Roland's complaint and die. The earl carried her in front of him, just as Roland had done. One of his men led Cantor. The horse no longer limped. The rain stopped for half a day, then began again, a cold muzzling drizzle. Upon their return to Tyberton, she almost felt relief. The rain stopped and the sun shone down, drying them. It was uncanny.

The day after their return, it was hot. Daria blessed the sweat that stood out on her brow. It felt wonderful.

And she kept her vigil for Roland.

He was well, he had to be. He was stubborn, obdurate, and he didn't give up. Aye, he would come to Tyberton — for his horse. But perhaps he could be convinced to take her with him again.

When she learned there was still no priest at Tyberton, she wanted to cry to the heavens in joy. She was safe from the earl until he had one fetched to marry them, safe, that is, if he would keep to his word.

Aye, safe. But for how long? Daria turned with a sigh from the narrow window as her maid, Ena, said, "Aye, he were in a fury, he were. Cursing and bellowing like the divil hisself, he was, and his men were sniggering behind their hands, laughing at how ye, naught but a bit of a female, had done him in." And Ena cackled as loudly as Romila. "Aye, they laughed at how he let his lust overcome his piety. But he left quick after ye. He tortured that farmer who'd held the pretty priest's horse for him. Then I heard the earl had a knife stuck atween the farmer's ribs, once he knew what was what. Aye, they left him in the dungeon to rot."

The man who'd wanted only a place of four cows — *lle pum buwch*.

Daria swallowed the bile that had risen in her throat. There was a knock on the door and then it opened, admitting one of the serving women.

It was her dinner on a covered tray. She was indeed to be kept a prisoner. The woman said nothing, merely stared hard at her for a moment, then dipped a curtsy.

Daria waved Ena toward the food. "I'm not hungry," she said, and turned away toward the window again.

The following morning the earl and a dozen of his men left to seek out a band of outlaws that had attacked the small English village of Newchurch, struck whilst the Earl of Clare had been traveling through Wales to find her. She was free, for a while at least. He'd also given orders that she was to be kept locked in her chamber. The earl had patted her cheek before he'd mounted his powerful destrier, but she'd seen the hunger in his eyes and flinched away from it. "Soon," he'd said, "soon now, and I'll have a priest here," and left.

It was midsummer, the ground baked dry from the sun, the sky clear of clouds, a startling bright blue.

And there was a priest now, the earl had told her the previous evening, a priest he'd found in Bristol after he'd searched long and hard, and he would arrive at Tyberton within a sennight. And he would marry her and then he would rape her and then kill her.

She wrapped her arms around her stomach. At least she hadn't been treated like a prisoner for the past week. The earl had returned flushed with victory over the outlaws. He'd hanged them, all those Welshmen who had still been breathing, that is.

It appeared the earl had given up his conviction that Roland would come for Cantor. She overheard him speaking of Roland to MacLeod and his voice was filled with contempt. "Aye, the pretty whoreson has judged even his destrier to be beyond his abilities to retrieve. He knows I'd kill him slowly and he knows I'd catch him. Back to England he's gone — Daria was right about that."

MacLeod had simply said, "But still . . ."

She knew the earl didn't completely trust her, but there was nothing more she could do to convince him. Indeed she wondered if she should even care. She'd begun to believe herself that Roland had returned to England. And if he hadn't, was he then dead? Was he near to Tyberton even now? No, probably not. Still, she remained meek and soft-spoken in the earl's presence, silent and cold when she was alone. She couldn't be certain that her once-trusted companion, Ena, wouldn't now betray her to the earl.

A single tear coursed swiftly down her cheek. She tasted the salt on her lips but didn't wipe her face. She didn't have the energy. She realized she was thirsty, but there was no water in the small carafe near her narrow bed. Slowly she made her way from her small chamber down the steep winding stone steps into the great hall. There were men lounging about playing draughts or trading jests. Women worked, scrubbing the trestle tables, scattering fresh rushes. No one paid her any heed. She didn't see the earl. She walked outside into the inner bailey.

It was the middle of the day, the time when, if possible, most of the people escaped to find some shade from the overpowering sun.

She walked to the cistern, standing there for a very long time, feeling the hot sun sink through her cold flesh, but there was no warmth deep inside her, only empty cold.

"What do you here?"

She heard the earl's distrust and forced a smile to her lips as she turned to face him. "I wanted a cup of fresh water from the well. It is hot and dry today."

He appeared to accept her words, and strode to the well. He fetched her a cup of water, watching her sip at it.

He said then, his voice filled with frustration and anger, "I have just gotten word that the king rides to Tyberton. He has been at Chepstow, thundering at the Earl of Hereford, I doubt not, and now he intends to come to me."

Daria didn't understand his mood. "But 'tis the king," she exclaimed. "That is an honor and a privilege to have him visit you, a sign of royal pleasure."

He snorted. "There is slight pleasure on either side. Longshanks holds little power here, and it irks him, for he wishes to grind all under his royal heel. He comes to pry and to spy and to threaten. Were I strong enough, would all the Marcher Barons but stand together, we'd send him back to that Sodom city he dwells in, that cesspit London. Let him breed with his whore, and keep away from here. We keep peace and hold the barbarians at bay.

"Aye, the king comes to seek out my strength. I know he would sell his miserable soul to the devil himself if he could wrest power from me, from all of us who keep England safe from the Welsh savages. He has no power here, ha! — no power west of the River Wye — and it isn't just for him to come!"

Whilst he was haranguing, it occurred to Daria that perhaps, just perhaps, the king could help her. Could she find him alone and plead with him for her release? Would he possibly believe her if she managed to see him? If he didn't aid her, would the earl then kill her? And what matter if he did? He would anyway, once he realized she wasn't a virgin.

She discovered that she was wringing her hands. What was she to do? "Drink your water," the earl said as he handed her another wooden cup.

The King of England sat back in his royal chair and looked at his dedicated secretary, Robert Burnell. The tent protected them from the hot noonday sun, and the king was basking in a good mood. He'd intimidated Hereford, the damned disloyal lout, and now he would arrive at Tyberton and make certain the Earl of Clare knew which way to step around his king. Burnell excused himself to seek some relief outside for a few minutes. His fingers were cramped from writing out the royal exhortations and he needed to stretch his muscles as well. When he returned, there was a strange look on his face, but his king didn't notice. He cleared his throat.

"Sire, there is a maimed old beggar outside who requests to speak with you. He claims to have information of vital importance." The king slewed about in his chair and pinned his secretary with a look that was so astonished that Burnell cleared his throat yet again. "Er, he appears harmless, sire."

Just as suddenly, Edward laughed. He'd just finished a fine meal and felt expansive from the two goblets of sweet wine he'd drunk. He watched Burnell fidget. Odd for a man of few nerves to fidget. "A maimed beggar, you say, Robbie? An old maimed beggar who begs to plead for a royal coin as opposed to a simple soldier's coin? A beggar who offers to share his begging with you if he gains coin from me? Speak you, Robbie, you seem deaf and mute and bereft of your wits as well."

The king was toying with him, Burnell thought, swept with relief for the absence of the royal temper. Edward was smiling, that wolfish charming smile of his that made everyone in his service grovel willingly. He stepped closer. " 'Tis not just a simple beggar, sire."

"I assumed this beggar you sponsor was fit for the king's time and presence. He is no common beggar, in short, but a beggar of royal persuasions, a beggar fit for . . ." Edward broke off, unable to find more glowing wit. "Bring me the fellow, Robbie! And I pray you have guessed aright, for if you haven't, I will cover you with the contents of your own ink pot."

Burnell had no intention of coming back into the king's presence. He left the royal tent. A miserable ancient relic shuffled in. By all the saints, the king thought, the old wretch stank more than a wet sheep and he looked ready to fall over and die, so appalling and pathetic was he. He gave a soft cackle and essayed a deep bow before the king. He sprang back up with no cracking of aged bones or joints.

"I understand it is a royal coin you wish," the king said, frowning mightily toward the beggar.

The old man cackled. "Nay, generous sire, 'tis a woman to warm my bed I wish, a woman wondrous fair with bounteous bosom and —"

The king stared at the old man, his cleverness momentarily extinguished.

"— aye, and a bounty of buttocks, mayhap. A woman as soft of flesh as a rabbit's belly and deep as a well for my mighty rod."

The king burst into laughter. "Shall I offer you first a woman to bathe you? You smell of slime and muck. Who are you, beggar? Not a common sort of vermin, I warrant, not from your polished impertinent speech. Come, I grow impatient with your antics."

"You are always impatient, sire. Your poor Robbie awaits just without, chewing his fingernails to their knuckles. 'Tis true, even a good tale is wasted on you, as is an excellent performance. I have heard it said that London's most wondrous mummers burst into tears at your inattention. Why —"

"Who are you, you miserable impertinent lout?" the royal personage roared as he rose to his full height. To his consternation, the beggar didn't quiver in fear, nor did he retreat even a frightened step. He gave him a filthy black grin and looked cockier than ever.

Then, just as suddenly, the beggar straightened and pulled off bits and pieces of his face. The king sucked in his breath, words failing him, at the hideous process.

Roland stood before him, tall, lean, proud of bearing, rubbing the back of his hand over his teeth. His teeth shone white and his hand shone black. The king shook his head. "I believe it not, and I know how well you can disguise yourself. My God, Roland, I have missed your impertinent insolent self!"

He embraced him. "By St. Andrew's knees, you must bathe," he said, and quickly stepped back.

"Aye, 'tis sheep dung and a few other disgusting things I found on my way here. I will keep my distance from your hallowed presence. I must ask you a favor, and then I will bathe. Have you time to attend to my plea, sire?"

"Robbie vowed you were a beggar worthy to plead before the royal presence. Still, Roland, if I said I didn't?"

"Why, then I should have to tell you of my adventures in Paris, where the ladies performed solemn rites and ceremonies upon my poor man's body with great enthusiasm and imagination. Ah, sire, these are bold and bawdy tales that will make you lick your royal lips."

"I wish to have both your plea and a full and complete accounting of your adventures."

Roland grinned at his king. "You are the answer to a poor needy beggar's prayers. I hadn't a notion of what to do, and you, like my chivalrous knight, come to my rescue, at least I hope that you will consider championing me."

"You make no sense, Roland. Sit, man!" he continued in a royal bellow. "Robbie, cease your fearful mutterings and come back in here. I need you to protect me from this rapacious beggar!"

"But my stench, sire —"

"It matters not. Just keep three feet between us and I shall survive your odor."

9

Daria stood at her post at the narrow window that gave onto the inner bailey. She knew such fear she could scarce bear it. The priest had arrived just an hour before, and the earl, impatient to have her sanctified in God's eyes, and in his bed, announced that their wedding ceremony would take place this very evening.

It was difficult to remain submissive, but she tried, asking in her softest voice, "But what of the king's visit, my lord? Don't you expect him to arrive shortly?"

"I pray the Almighty that his royal majesty takes his blessed time. He can arrive on the morrow. I will allow him to do that."

She kept her eyes lowered, and her brain squirreled with one idea after the other, each of them useless. The earl continued after a moment, "I have kept my vow, Daria. Forget not that I could have taken you at any time, but I held to my oath. I proved to you that I was to be trusted. I have shown you mine honor. You will have no more cause now to bend against me."

He had kept his oath; she'd give him that. She prayed for the king to arrive right now. She looked into the distance but saw no sign of anyone, just impenetrable forests and rolling hills.

The earl frowned down at her. "I wish you to gown yourself as befits the bride of the Earl of Clare. Do you understand me, Daria? I wish you to smile and show everyone that you come to me with a willing and submissive heart."

She nodded. He stared at her intently for a moment longer, then grabbed her, hauling her against him. He cupped her chin with his hand and pushed up her face. She closed her eyes, forcing herself not to struggle even when his mouth closed over hers. She felt his tongue, wet and probing, and wanted to gag. He released her and said, "I will wed you even though your dowry hasn't yet come from your loathsome uncle. But no matter his damned perfidy. I intend to petition the king for what should be mine and what will be mine, for once you are wedded to me, once I have taken you, even the king can't deny me your dowry, for I have right on my side." With those words, he actually rubbed his hands together, saying in triumph, "There's naught Damon Le Mark can do, for I will have the king with me. And he will yowl and whine and it will do him no good at all. Aye, at last I have won, and I like the feeling." He turned on his heel and left her. Daria stared after him, wondering at his mind.

She shook her head to clear it of the feel of him. Suddenly, from one instant to the next, she felt a sharpening of something inside her, an awareness, a renewed remembrance of something utterly vital to her, something . . . She looked down into the inner bailey, not really seeing anything or anyone specific, but still the feeling was there, that strange feeling, that knowledge that she'd known before. She wondered if her mind had finally snapped.

Then she saw him. A bent old man, with a head of scraggly thick white hair, shuffling in his rags toward the castle well. He was dragging his lame right leg. Stark joy welled up in her and she willed him to look up, whispering his name over and over as she stared hard at him. He did. She saw naught but a wrinkled old face until he smiled and she saw a mouth filled with rotted black teeth.

It couldn't be Roland, but she knew that it was. She waved frantically to him.

But he turned away from her with not a single sign to her, and continued his slow shuffling gait to the well.

His own mother wouldn't know him, she thought, and smiled. He'd come. He'd come for her . . . or for his destrier, perhaps both if she were lucky and Roland cared for her or cared equally for her uncle's money.

How could she speak to the ragged old beggar? Why had Arthur, the porter, allowed him to come into the castle? What ruse had he in mind this time? Her mind tumbled with questions, but mostly she just wanted to see him closely to ensure that he was completely well again. Ah, Roland, she thought, her step light and vigorous for the first time since the earl had brought her back to Tyberton nearly two months before.

When she reached the well, the old man was gone. Vanished. She stared about her, feeling despair weigh down upon her. Had she imagined him? Daria drew a deep breath and turned on her heel. She looked at her toes raise small clouds of dust. She didn't care if her new gown was as filthy as the ragged old man's clothing. She didn't care about anything except finding him.

Roland stood in the shade of one of the

barracks and watched her return slowly to the great hall, her step lagging. She'd recognized him instantly. It was impossible, yet she'd known him, and from a distance. It confused and confounded him, that recognition of hers — he couldn't comprehend or accept it. His heart pounded. She'd known him. For God's sake, how? His survival depended on his disguise, yet he hadn't fooled her for an instant.

He moved toward the cooking outbuilding, wanting to keep her in sight. One of the scullions came around the corner and Roland bent lower and scratched his armpit and mumbled to himself, turning a bit on his lame leg, and showing a wince of pain.

She'd known him. But how? The scullion gave him a look of scorn and pity combined, shrugged, then turned his back to relieve himself.

How was it possible? Would she give him away? Not likely, he thought. She was being forced to wed the Earl of Clare, this according to Otis, one of the stable lads. How Otis knew, Roland didn't question; everyone always knew everything in a keep's confines. He'd listened the entire day, and no one had paid any attention to an old beggar. De Clare had kept her locked in her tower chamber for many weeks whilst he'd gone off on one of his raids. Roland cursed at that. If only he could have returned here more quickly, if only he . . . It was too late now for recriminations. She was to be wedded to Clare this very evening. Roland closed his eyes a moment. The king wasn't due to arrive at Tyberton until the morrow. But tomorrow would be too late for all of them.

Clare would have wedded her, bedded her, and even the king himself wouldn't pull her away from a man whose wife she'd become, a wife whose maidenhead had been breached. And, Roland imagined, Clare had finally figured out that once wedded to Daria, he could get his hands on her huge dowry. He wondered if the earl had already taken her. Of course he had. There was no reason why he would not. There had been no priest here to gainsay him.

Roland cursed. They'd been so very close to escaping him before. If only he hadn't become ill . . . the genesis and the revelation of all their problems. Now she was no longer a maid and it was his fault. The situation called for a change of plan. He was adaptable and quick to revise. It had saved his life before. Now perhaps it would save Daria as well.

★ ★ ★

Ena's mind was murky, but she knew she was pleased about this, pleased that her little mistress would shortly be wedding the mighty Earl of Clare. She was too thin, but still she looked beautiful in the pale pink silk gown with its darker pink overtunic. Its long sleeves full at her wrists, its waist belted with a golden chain of fine links. Aye, she looked tasty and worthy of becoming the chatelaine of Tyberton. Aye, Ena was very pleased.

Daria's hair was long and loose, denoting a young girl coming to her marriage a virgin. There was a strange smile on Daria's face when Ena had insisted on this old custom, but she'd said nothing. She would have preferred to braid her hair tightly around her head. What would the earl have thought of that? she wondered.

"Ye're excited," Ena said, seeing the glitter in her young charge's eyes. "Aye, ye're ready to settle down now and forget yer pretty young priest. He left ye, and if it weren't fer the earl, ye'd be dead or worse by now. Nay, tell me no ties. I always guessed ye tried to escape, not the pap the earl spread about, curdling the cream even as he spoke the words. But things are the way they should be. Ye're a little lady and ye don't deserve a poor priest, no matter how pretty he was. Ralph of Colchester isn't here, so ye'll have the earl. Aye, all is well again."

Daria lowered her eyes. The old woman saw a lot even though she was becoming more and more vague. She didn't necessarily see the right things, at least in this instance, but still, she didn't want Ena announcing to the earl that the little mistress was all eager and impatient and ... The earl might well believe she'd released him from his oath and ravish her before the ceremony. Daria gave a restless gesture as Ena plaited in a final white daisy into her hair.

" 'Tis enough." Where was Roland? She felt the now-familiar fear that it was indeed only his destrier he'd come for. She was no longer important to him. He would no longer risk rescuing her. The coin wasn't enough. He'd realized the earl was right. He would have no chance in any case. But how would the old beggar steal his destrier?

"Yer veil, little mistress!"

Veil! Daria stared at the thick gold circlet with its flowing gauzy veil. It would be hot. On the other hand, it would blur her vision. She wouldn't be able to see the earl clearly; she could imagine and dream that ...

"Give it to me."

There was a knock on the chamber door. Before Daria could say anything, the door cracked open and two women entered, an older woman Daria didn't recognize and a very young one that she did. They entered furtively and quickly, the older woman closing the door behind her.

"What is this? What is it you wish?" The words were scarce out of Daria's mouth when she felt his presence, and she jerked up, staring at the two.

"Well," the older woman said, her eyes lowered, "I come to tell ye, little mistress, that the earl's a loud lout, telling all he's ready to tumble ye the instant the priest pronounces ye his bride."

"I'm ready," Daria said, excitement filling her. By all the saints, was she ready! "Shall we take Ena with us?"

The older woman shook her head. She looked toward Ena and said, "I need yer help, old witch."

"Who are ye calling an old witch!" Ena shrieked. "Here, now! What do ye want?"

Daria watched Roland put his arm about Ena, pull her close, and then lightly smack his fist into her jaw. Ena crumpled to the floor. "Tie her up quickly, Daria. As you probably know, she's defected to the earl's camp. We can't afford to take any chances."

The other woman was young Tilda, daughter of the castle blacksmith, all of fourteen years old and so beautiful that men stopped whatever they chanced to be doing to stare as she passed. She was a bit larger than Daria, her hair a bit lighter, but with the wedding finery, the veil . . .

"She wishes it," Roland said shortly before Daria could question him. "Quickly, out of those clothes whilst I tie up the old woman."

Within minutes Daria was arranging the veil over Tilda's lovely face. The young girl was shaking with excitement, but Daria was worried. Cora was of peasant stock. What would the earl do to her when he discovered the deception?

"Daria, quickly, put on your boy's clothes. And braid all that damnable hair of yours."

"Ah, Roland, you are such a fussy mother."

He grinned at her. "Didn't I fool you for the veriest instant?"

She shook her head. "Not even when you smiled up at me as a miserable old beggar with rotted black teeth."

And he remembered that first time he saw her, that astonishment in her eyes as she'd stared at him, a priest, that *knowledge*, and he frowned. And she'd fainted, as if seeing him had affected her in some way that he couldn't understand. But his disguises were foolproof. But then again, Daria wasn't a fool. He shook himself, tied up the old woman, and shoved her under the bed. Then he stood guard at the door until Daria emerged and touched his arm. "I'm ready."

He turned and saw that she was smiling up at him, complete trust in her eyes, that and complete . . . There was something different about her, something . . .

"Tilda, leave that veil on until you're commanded by the earl to remove it. Do you understand?"

The girl nodded. She was happy! "Thank you, Tilda." Daria gave her a quick hug, turned, and took Roland's hand.

"Keep your head down and don't say anything."

"This sounds very familiar, Roland."

"I'm your damned mother, silly twit."

All the castle servants and retainers were outside the keep, for the day was hot and dry and the Earl of Clare had provided kegs of ale and more food than most of the people saw for a year. There was much merriment and shouting and wild jests. She didn't see the earl.

"Aye," Roland said to a soldier who offered him a goblet of ale and asked him what he was about. "Just look ye at the little fiend.

Trying to peep at the earl's bride, he was. I'll strip off his hide, the little impertinence!"

And on and on his charade progressed, as Roland, confident as the pope himself, made his way through the throngs of people, initiating conversation with some, and thus making Daria's heart jump into her throat, and insulting the soldiers with friendly motherly taunts.

They made it to the gates. Arthur, the porter, was grinning widely, showing the wide space between his two front teeth. He was holding a mug of ale in his beefy hand and he waved them through without a look, without a question.

Daria pulled on his woman's sleeve. "Your horse! Cantor!"

Roland turned at that and gave her a ferocious frown. "Hush!"

Once they were without the castle walls, Roland took her hand and pulled her into a brisk walk.

"Thank you," she said.

"A mother is supposed to protect her son. Keep your tongue behind your teeth."

"But, Roland, you've left Cantor."

"Not for very long."

"Oh. The earl said you'd surely come for your destrier, but not —"

"But not for you?"

"That's what I thought as well until I saw you yesterday, and then I prayed that perhaps you would also take me."

"You forget, Daria, there is much coin awaiting me at Reymerstone. If I allowed the earl to wed you, I wouldn't gain a penny."

She felt a stab of pain so intense it nearly choked her. "I am still only a valuable bundle to you, to be delivered and then forgotten."

"You also left me to rot in the charge of that vicious leech and that officious woman Romila. At least you didn't steal all my coin or I would have had to pay Romila with my poor man's body. Old enough to be my mother, and she wanted me to bed her! I had to beg her for my clothes."

"I don't believe you! Romila told me how to deal with you and . . . I tried to save you! And I did!"

"You will weave your tales later, once we are far from Tyberton. Cease your chatter now and walk. I've a horse in that copse."

"Where are we going?"

"Why, to see the King and Queen of England, of course."

Edward and Eleanor stared at the older woman who was chewing on a stick, her sagging breasts thrust forward in her slovenly gown, her dirty hand firmly around the young boy's arm.

"Well, here he is, sire! All full of himself and crowing like a peacock once I told him the king wanted to see him."

Edward just shook his head and started to laugh. The queen looked at him oddly and said, "I don't understand, my lord, is this — ?"

"Aye, 'tis our Roland, an old shrew, with her son."

"Your highness," Roland said in his deep voice, and bowed to the queen. "And this is Daria, daughter of James of Fortescue, and niece of Damon Le Mark, Earl of Reymerstone. This is my second rescue of the lady and, I profoundly pray, the final one. The Earl of Clare desires her mightily."

Daria was overwhelmed. She started to speak but discovered that she had only a stutter. She gave an awkward curtsy in her boy's clothes.

"Your father was a fine man, Daria," the king said warmly. "We miss him sorely. As for you, I salute your disguise, Roland. Most resourceful. I shouldn't want you in my bed, however."

"I don't know," Eleanor said thoughtfully. " 'Tis a fine woman she appears to me, such experience of men she shows in her eyes, my lord husband. Save for that dark stubble on her jaws, I vow I'd confide in her on the instant."

Roland grinned at the queen, whose sweetness of expression rivaled her beauty and whose belly, he saw, was swelled yet again with another babe. "I thank you both for taking us in. I should like to resume my manhood and, your highness, if young Daria here could resume her gowns and ribbons?"

"Certainly," the queen said, and lightly clapped her hands together. "Come, child."

It was later in the afternoon when Daria saw Roland again. He was in men's clothes again and looked so beautiful she wanted to run to him and fling him to the ground. She wanted to kiss him and stroke him and tell him how much she loved him. He was speaking, however, to several of the king's soldiers, and she contented herself for the moment just looking at him. When one of the soldiers took himself off, she approached him and lightly touched her fingertip to his sleeve. He turned to look down at her and froze. Her look was intimate; there was no other way to describe it. And tender and . . . loving.

He took a backward step.

"Are you all right?"

"Aye," she said happily. "Do you think the earl has wedded Tilda yet? You don't think he'll harm her, do you?"

Roland shook his head. "I do think he'll bed her, though, and make her his mistress. She's a beautiful girl."

"You aren't objective; you are, after all, her mother. Are you well now, Roland? I was so worried about you and I didn't know what to do when the stableman told me of the men asking about Cantor."

"So that's what happened," he said. "I didn't know, couldn't understand, why you'd left so suddenly and with no word to anyone. I tried to search for you but managed only to get down the stairs and collapse again."

Her fingers tightened on his arm, caressing him now, and he frowned. "Daria, what is the matter with you?"

She realized what she was doing and in the same instant realized that he had no idea why she was doing it. She looked at him hungrily, then quickly released his arm and turned away from him. "Naught is wrong. What will happen now? How do you know the king and queen? They seem to be your friends. I heard someone say that we were traveling to Tyberton tomorrow. How can that be true? The earl will —"

He gently touched his fingertips to her mouth. "Trust me," he said. "All will be well and I will have my destrier back. And you will soon be on your way back to Reymerstone."

Her expression became stony, but he ignored it, turning away from her.

That evening, Queen Eleanor, having correctly judged Daria's feelings by simply asking her how she felt about Roland de Tournay, imputed similar feelings to Roland, for, after all, the girl was wealthy, quite lovely, and . . . The queen smiled, saying to Roland as she sipped at her sweet Aquitaine wine, "Do you wish to be wedded before you arrive at Tyberton, just to ensure that the earl won't scream down our royal ears?"

Roland dropped the braised rib to his trencher. He looked first to Daria, saw that she was staring openmouthed at the queen, and said quickly, "Your highness, I plan to return Daria to her uncle. It was a mission I accepted. I vowed I would return her to him a maid and otherwise unharmed. There is no question of marriage between us. I fear you have misunderstood the situation."

Eleanor cocked her head to one side in question as she turned to the king. Edward looked grave. " 'Tis you I don't understand, Roland. You are my friend and you are a man of honor. 'Tis true you accepted the mission to rescue Daria, but all of that has changed now. *You* changed it when you . . . well, never mind that now. You must realize that you can no longer return Daria to anyone, not now. You have a responsibility toward her. She is a lady, Roland, *your* lady."

Roland felt mired in confusion. He opened his mouth, but a servant appeared to fill the royal flagons with more sweet wine. Roland curbed his questions until the young man bowed his way out of the royal tent.

"I don't know what is happening here," Roland said, staring directly at Daria now. "She is my responsibility. I readily acknowledge it and accept that she will continue to be so until I return her to her uncle."

Daria was in her turn staring from the king to the queen and back again. They wanted Roland to wed her? All because she had confided in the queen that she loved him? Love had naught to do with anything. Even she knew that, not when it involved a dowry the size of hers.

But they fully expected Roland to wed her. Why?

She cleared her throat, saying before the king, whose complexion had reddened, could interrupt, "Nay, your highness, 'tis not for me to beg Roland to become my husband. 'Tis true I am passing fond of him, but that has naught to do with anything. Pray do not make him feel sorry because I told you of my feelings for him. He's not responsible for my feelings. He will do as he pleases; as for me, I will try to dissuade him from returning me to my uncle. Perchance I shall have to smash his head and escape him." As an attempt at wit, it failed utterly.

"But, my dear child," the queen began, only to stop when the king said coldly, "Roland, you cannot be lost to all honor, surely you must realize —" He paused as the queen lightly closed her fingers over his. She whispered something to him. His eyes narrowed, then sparkled.

Eleanor looked at Daria. She said in a very gentle voice, "Did you not tell him, my dear?"

Roland jumped to his feet. "This goes beyond all bounds! Tell me what, by all the saints?"

"Quiet, Roland," the king said.

Daria wanted to jump up and yell as loudly as Roland. What was happening here? "I don't understand, your highness. If you mean have I told him that I care for him, nay, I haven't. He wouldn't want to hear such words from me."

"Damnation, Daria! What are you mumbling about? What do you mean, I wouldn't care?"

The king leaned over and buffeted Roland's shoulder. "You're a virile warrior, as potent in bed as you are on the battlefield, Roland, and now you'll have yourself a wife. Don't struggle further against your fate. 'Tis about time, I think. The queen and I will act as godparents, and you —"

"Virile? What is this, what are you — ?" His voice fell off abruptly and he stared at Daria. Her face was washed of color now, her eyes wide, her pupils dilated, her hands tight fists in her lap. "Tell me," he said. "Tell me now or I will haul you outside and beat you senseless."

"Roland!"

"She will tell me what is happening here!" But he knew, indeed he knew what she would say, and it sickened him to his very soul.

"She is with child," the queen said.

Roland couldn't comprehend her words even though he knew they were the words she would speak. With child! "By all the saints, *whose* child?"

Daria only shook her head, but the queen knew no reticence. Her voice was sharp. "Yours, naturally, Roland!"

"Mine? But that isn't possible. I never —"
Again he stopped. All became clear to him.
The earl had had two months to ravish her,
and doubtless he had whenever he'd wished
to. God, the girl was pregnant with the Earl
of Clare's babe! He felt a wrenching pain in
his gut. He felt a spurt of hatred so strong
for the man he nearly choked on it. And
Daria hadn't told him, hadn't even hinted at
it, damn her! He wanted to strike her; he
wanted to yell and strike himself. Instead,
he drew a deep breath and said to the king,
"If you would forgive us for a moment, sire,
I would like to speak to Daria in private. As
you and the queen have guessed, I hadn't realized any of this. She hadn't told me a
thing. Daria, come outside."

She obeyed him instantly, her head down,
pale as death, the queen thought, watching
the couple leave the tent, as if she were
going to her execution.

The king stared after the man he'd known
for six years, the man who'd worked for him
tirelessly in the Holy Land, risking his life
with every breath he took, with every word
he spoke in Arabic, the man he trusted with
his life.

He turned to his wife. "There is some sort
of problem here, Eleanor?"

The queen looked as confused as her

spouse. "I didn't mention her pregnancy to her, Edward; the child isn't a wife, after all, and I had no wish to embarrass her. I assumed she knew she was with child, assumed that Roland was her lover. She conceived the child about two months ago, I'd say. It's very odd. She didn't know she was with child. Evidently she'd known no illness, no vomiting."

"Not so very odd," the king said. He leaned over and kissed his wife. He laid his hand on her swelled belly. "Do you not remember our first babe, Eleanor? 'Twas one of your women who suggested to you that you might be with child. You didn't know, hadn't guessed."

"You're right, dear lord. By the saints, whatever will we do? I had no idea both of them were ignorant of the fact."

"They will wed, as is fitting. They are both of the proper rank, they are both young and of good health, and you said the girl cares for him."

"She loves him."

The king waved that consideration away. "Roland will come about. He has no choice and he isn't a cruel man or an unjust one. She is a lady and he will wed her. She is also an heiress, and she will bring him sufficient dowry to buy the land and keep he wishes in

Cornwall. A good solution. I've worried about him and his future. In the near future I might even raise him to the rank of his sour-natured brother, the Earl of Blackheath."

The queen was chewing over the more romantic side of the situation. "The girl loves him more than . . . why, I cannot think of a good comparison, my lord, save to say that she loves Roland de Tournay as much as I do you, husband."

"Ah, well, that is sufficient, I should think," the king said, and sat back in his chair with satisfaction.

Outside the tent, Roland saw the several dozen soldiers posted around the royal tent and knew that he must contain his ire. He jerked her along with him, feeling her resistance. At the perimeter of the royal encampment, he paused and turned to her. Words and curses and confusion all whirled about in his mind, but he contented himself with, "Speak, Daria."

"I don't understand how the queen . . . Perhaps she is mistaken, because I haven't felt ill or . . . It must be very complicated —"

"Being with child is the simplest thing in the world! All that's required is that a man plow a woman, nothing more, not a single blessed thing!"

"I didn't know, I tell you! I suppose the queen recognized signs in me that I hadn't noticed. I haven't been very aware of things, Roland. A prisoner isn't, you know."

His hold tightened on her arm and she winced but made no sound. He shook her. "All right, you didn't know you carried a babe. Now you do know. It's true, isn't it? Have you had no monthly flow? Have your breasts swelled?"

She shook her head. He wouldn't stop; she knew him well enough to realize he would keep questioning her, keep pounding at her, until she told him the truth. Ah, the truth. That was the only thing he wouldn't believe. He had no memory of that night. What was she to do?

"Very well. Now, you will not lie to me. It will do neither of us any good. The earl had you, didn't he, took you before I got back to rescue you? Did he rape you when he first caught up with you? I thought that he would take you, for there was no priest to try to hold him back from going to your bed. It is his babe you carry. Why didn't you tell me he'd ravished you? Why? You know I still would have rescued you if you'd wished it."

"The earl didn't force me," she said, her voice low and dull.

He cursed and stomped away from her.

He yelled at her over his shoulder, "Damn you, Daria! A female is born with lies writhing in her mouth, just waiting for a gullible male to come within her orbit. More fool I! By all the saints, I will take you back to the Earl of Clare this very night! You said he didn't force you. Therefore you were willing. No wonder you left me in Wrexham. You couldn't before, but then I was too ill to know what you were about." He smote his forehead with his palm. "Will I never cease being a fool?"

"Evidently not."

He turned on her then, fury radiating from him. "There was no need for you to escape with me this second time, at least none that I can think of. He must have plowed your belly until you were well used to it. Unless you wanted me to punish him? I cannot fathom your mind, curse you! Tell me why you escaped with me. Why?"

10

"The earl didn't ravish me, nor did I give myself to him willingly. He made a vow that he wouldn't touch me until we were wedded, and he kept it. I believe he was quite proud of himself that he didn't break his oath. 'Tis not his child that grows in me."

Roland could but stare at her. He'd believed her guileless, candid, faultless as a child. But she wasn't a child. She was a woman and she was with child. Whose could it be? He'd been with her constantly, save when he'd been ill in Wrexham. If the earl had forced her, why didn't she admit it? Did she think he would blame her for that whoreson's violence? When he'd come to rescue her that second time, he'd fought the knowledge that the earl had raped her, for it had made no sense to him that he wouldn't have. But she was claiming that he hadn't taken her. He shook his head.

"Then who plowed your belly?"

She looked at him straightly. The time for deception was long over, as was the time for protecting him from the knowledge of what he'd done. He wanted the truth; very well, then, he would have it. "You did."

She winced as he laughed, even though she wasn't surprised at his reaction. He marveled aloud, "Such a lie as that can never work, Daria. A man knows when he takes a woman. It isn't something that passes unheeded like a belch. When is this babe of yours to arrive?"

"Since I know the precise day the babe was conceived, I can figure it out quickly enough."

"And just when was this precise day?"

"In Wrexham, over two months ago."

He'd been so very ill there; he hadn't protected her. "Were you ravished there? You went out alone and a man attacked you? You can admit it to me, Daria. I won't blame you, I swear it. Come, tell me. Were you ravished there?"

"No. You didn't ravish me."

"You tempt me to beat you, Daria. I order you to cease spinning your tales."

"When you were sick, you became delirious and you were dreaming of a woman —

no, women — whom you'd bedded in the Holy Land. I . . . well, I cared for you and I decided that I wanted you to be the man who would make me a woman."

He could only stare at her. "You're telling me that I took you — a virgin — and have no memory of it?"

"You believed I was Lila."

He drew back, stunned to his toes. "Lila," he repeated quietly. "She would have been naught more than a fevered dream. I couldn't have made it into something remotely real; I couldn't have taken you in her place, not unknowingly. It's absurd. I couldn't ever mistake you for her in any circumstance. You aren't a thing like her."

"No," she said sadly, turning from him, "you appeared to care for her mightily. And there was Cena too."

"Cena," he repeated, feeling like a parrot. Roland shook his head. This was lunacy, all of it, her lunacy, and she was trying to draw him into it. "Listen to me, Daria, and listen well. I don't remember any of this, and I'm not lying. I can't believe that a lady — a virgin — would allow me to breach her maidenhead without marriage . . . nay, you claim you even assisted me to take you?

"And just how many times did I — a man fevered and ill and tossing about out of his skull and evidently as randy as a goat — just how many times did I take you, Daria?"

"Just once."

"Ah, I see. And as a result of plowing your virgin's little belly, you are now with child."

"Yes." Daria was beginning to wonder if she could still believe herself. He'd demolished her quite thoroughly.

"And you expect me to believe this? Truly? Why are you doing this to me? What have I ever done to you to deserve such treatment? Why are you lying to me? Ah, I doubt not I was so fevered that I dreamed myself in other places with other people and that I may have spoken of people in my past, Lila and Cena included."

She looked at him. She was weary. She supposed it was the babe she carried that was pulling on her. She had nothing more to say, no proof to give him, no other arguments to present. He thought she was going to speak again, and slashed his hand through the air.

"No, Daria, no more. I'm tired of your lies. And now you've managed to seduce the king and queen with your charming innocence, though you and I both know it is all false. God, how could I be such a fool? Again and again it would appear, only this time you make me appear the villain, a liar without conscience."

"I'm only telling you the truth." He looked at her as if he hated her, and Daria felt such pain that she couldn't bear it. She'd known he wouldn't believe her, but still the reality of his feelings made her raw. She turned on her heel and broke into a run. She cared not where she ran, only that she get away from this man who hated her and despised her for a liar.

"Damn you, I'm not through!"

But Daria didn't slow even at his furious shout. She felt a stitch in her side but didn't stop. When his fingers closed about her arm, she cried out and turned on him, her fists pounding his chest. "Let me go! What care you where I go? Or what I do?"

"I don't," he said, his voice calm now. "Well, that's not precisely true. I do care. However, I told you once, I believe, that your uncle didn't want you back if you were no longer a virgin. And it's very easy to determine that, as you must remember."

She closed her eyes over the memory of the earl thrusting his finger inside her, pressing against her maidenhead. She shivered with the memory of it, the humiliation of it made more awful because Roland had been there, watching.

"I fancy your uncle would kill you were you to return to him now, for he would want your inheritance if he couldn't have the land from Ralph of Colchester. You're naught but an encumbrance to him now, Daria, nothing more. But you know that, don't you? Thus the reason for all your tales? You're simply trying to save yourself."

"And what am I to you?" She regretted the words the moment they were out of her mouth. Her face blanched.

He gave her a brutal look. "A mission to be accomplished, a possession to be returned to its rightful owner. Once valuable chattel, Daria, but now you are worthless."

"Stop it!" She slapped her hands against her ears to shut out his cruel words.

He clasped her wrists, pulling them away. "Tell me the truth, Daria." He shook her. "I'll help you, I swear it, but you must tell me the truth."

"I did tell you the truth! You were fevered. At first you thought I was a woman named Joan. You yelled at me and accused me of betraying you. I tried to reason with you, but it was no use. Then you spoke that strange language and you called me Lila and you wanted her to cover you, to allow you to come into her body. I didn't know what you meant, but you showed me. You wanted to suckle her breasts and you scolded me for still wearing clothes when you wanted me naked."

"And so," he said, his eyes hard and disbelieving, his voice filled with sarcasm, "you hurried to rip off your clothes, ready to do whatever I asked of you. There was a Joan — 'tis likely I would speak of the bitch if I was out of my head. But nothing else, Daria. An innocent young girl wouldn't allow a man to command her to sacrifice her maidenhead."

"And you spoke of Cena but said you were too fatigued for her. She would have to wait."

He tensed, resisting. But no, he could have spoken of both women. A fevered man could speak of any ghost or memory. A fevered man wasn't, however, strong enough to force a virgin to give over to him.

"I have told you the truth, Roland. That I did it was perhaps foolish, but I lo . . . I wanted you to be the first, I wanted to know you" — *to have your hands on me, feel you kissing me, holding me . . . I wanted the memory* — "if I was to be forced to wed with Ralph of Colchester, I wanted just the one time for myself, for there would be nothing more that I could have." There, now he had the truth, all of it. She watched the anger pale his eyes and tighten his expression.

He shook his head. It was foolishness and lies, all of it. "No. I cannot accept it. Why would you give yourself to me knowing that I believed you to be another woman? That I was speaking her name, seeing her, feeling her when I came into your body — knowing I believed it to be her when I kissed you and caressed you? It is absurd. No woman I have ever been with would do such a thing. And I have known many women, Daria. A woman would sooner stick a knife in the man's ribs and curse him to hell."

"Perhaps it is absurd. Perhaps I am absurd. I don't know. I haven't much experience with men and their ways, or ladies either, for that matter." She looked at him and her eyes were as sad as her voice as she said softly, "All I know is myself and what I feel." She drew a deep breath and blurted it out. "*Rydw i'n dy garu di*, Roland."

He stared down at her for a very long time. Finally he said, his voice emotionless, "Lying bitch." He turned from her and strode away, yelling over his shoulder, "Leave if you wish. I shan't stop you. By all the saints, I care not if I never gaze upon your face again. Return to your uncle, or, if you're afraid to, then return to the Earl of Clare. Perhaps he'll still want you if he hasn't plowed Tilda silly by now and finds he's forgotten all about you and your dowry and his hatred of your uncle."

He forced himself to keep walking. He forced himself not to turn back to her. She couldn't love him, damn her lying heart! She couldn't. It made no sense. *No more sense than her recognizing him instantly, no matter his disguise.* Who had told her the words in Welsh? He shook his head. He didn't care.

He knew he must return to the king and queen, explain somehow. Convince them of the truth without their believing Daria to be a conniving whore. . . . He cursed. What to do?

"The Earl of Reymerstone would kill me, and I wouldn't blame him. Worse, he would kill her as well, and he would do it without hesitation, without mercy."

Edward merely shrugged. "It isn't as if you were a peasant, Roland. Your family is as old as his, and —"

Roland interrupted his king. "You don't understand, sire. The man wanted Daria to wed Ralph of Colchester, and only him, because in return he would gain the lands he wants to add to his own."

"And then the Earl of Clare abducted her?"

Roland nodded.

"The story is complicated, is it not? Like one of your tales, Roland, with many twists and unexpected turns. Only this tale, well, it is up to you — regardless of all your protestations — to find a satisfactory ending."

"You refuse to believe that I am not the father of this child? Have you ever known me to lie to you?"

The king looked troubled. "No, I haven't. The queen is convinced that the girl is telling the truth. Listen, Roland. 'Tis possible that you took her believing her another, is it not?"

"Not that I can imagine. Can you imagine it yourself, sire?"

"No."

"She also claims that she is with child after but one plowing. One time and she becomes pregnant? I cannot credit that either."

At that the king smiled even as he shifted restlessly in his chair. "I can, Roland. It happens frequently. I can attest to that."

Roland fell silent. The king fell equally silent. He detested tangles like this. He wanted to face down the Earl of Clare and strip him of his power; he wanted to strip all the Marcher Barons of every drop of power they possessed; he, the King of England, wanted the power in Wales and he wanted to build castles to assert his power and bring the damned Welsh to their knees before him, their king . . . and here he was instead trying to solve a problem that had no apparent solution. None that was satisfying. Unless . . . "There is a way out of this perhaps. We can keep the girl with us until she is delivered of the babe. If the babe resembles you, then you can wed her. If it resembles the Earl of Clare — does he not have hair red as scarlet? — then it is proved."

"And what if the babe looks like no other? Or looks like its mother?"

The king cursed softly. "What do you think, Robbie?" Robert Burnell, silent to this point, looked decidedly uncomfortable. "Do you wish an opinion likely to conform to the Church?"

Roland snorted.

"Go ahead, Robbie."

"The Church would hold that the woman, regardless of her rank or supposed innocence, was the one culpable. It would be her fault and none other's. She would bear the censure and the condemnation and —"

"Hold! 'Tis enough, damn you."

"She would be viewed as a harlot, a deceiver, a stain on her family's honor —"

"Be quiet, I tell you!"

240

"But, Roland," the king said reasonably, "you claim it cannot be your babe. Thus, she lies. To protect whom? Robbie, what do you think Stephen Langton would have recommended?"

"He would have doubtless ruled that she be deprived of her dowry, and shunned and reviled by her family and all those who'd believed in her virtue."

Roland looked appalled. "If that were true, then she would die, the babe with her."

Robert Burnell shrugged. "Aye, very likely."

"I suppose the Church would also say that was proper — two dead — but the man responsible free and absolved!"

"The man is but weak of the flesh," Burnell said. "The woman is the evil one who plots to exploit the man's weakness."

"Such a testament to the mercy of God and his infinite fairness. It sickens me."

Roland rose swiftly to his feet and paced the vast interior of the royal tent. He cursed fluently in four languages.

"Very well," Edward said, watching Roland closely. His friend wasn't indifferent to the girl. He saw the likely result in that moment. Aloud he said, "I see two options. The first, she is returned to her uncle, and the second, she is returned to the Earl of

Clare. Are there others?"

Roland said on a sigh, "Her uncle will kill her if she's returned to him. If by chance the child she carries isn't the Earl of Clare's seed, why, then he would kill her too."

"As I inquired of you two," the king said patiently, "are there any other possibilities?"

There was dead silence. Roland could hear a soldier laughing from a goodly distance outside the royal tent. He could hear his own heart beating a slow steady rhythm. Then he laughed.

He turned, and the king knew in that moment that Roland had accepted the inevitable. But still, what if she carried another's child? He couldn't simply force his friend into a corner.

"Very well. I am the other option. I will wed her."

"But I have yet to see the Earl of Clare," Edward said, raising his hand. "Be reasonable, Roland. I can determine if he is the father and whether he will or will not abuse her. I am said to be a good judge of men. Well, let me judge this Earl of Clare. Perhaps he will want her, and if it is his babe she carries, then —"

"She claims to despise the earl. Even you wouldn't wish to hand her over to a man she hates. Nor is he a gentle man. He would abuse her endlessly, believe it, and once you were gone, who would there be to stop him?"

"But if she deserves his abuse, if she is lying for some reason unbeknownst to us, then his treatment of her will —"

"I will wed her," Roland repeated, and he looked defeated and very weary.

The king looked pleased, but he turned his head in time so that Roland did not remark upon it. Roland did care for the girl, regardless of the paternity of the babe she carried. She could bring him a goodly dowry; the King of England would see to it. The world was filled with bastards. Even his precious daughter, Philippa, was a bastard. It mattered not, not when there were money, land, and prestige involved. He would pray the child would be a female. Thus Roland wouldn't have to pass his worldly possessions down to another man's son.

"Aye," Roland said more to himself than to anyone else, "it is likely that the earl did rape her and she is too ashamed to admit to it." But why me? *Because she loves you, that's why. She believed she had no other choice.*

The king said nothing. He wasn't stupid. He nodded to Robert Burnell. "Send Eric to her majesty and inform her that we are to have a wedding right now, or as soon as Daria can be prepared."

Roland looked a moment as if he would protest; but he held his peace, resuming his pacing the tent. The king drank the remainder of the sweet Aquitaine wine. "The wine comes from Graelam de Moreton's father-in-law," he said to break the tense silence. "It is excellent. You will shortly be neighbors. And you will keep an eye on my dear daughter, Philippa, and that scoundrel husband of hers. Aye, de Fortenberry is a scoundrel, but the girl wanted him, wouldn't hear of anything else, as you well know. Wedded him, and that was that."

Roland was drawn from self-pity for a moment. "She didn't know of you when she wedded him, sire."

"More's the pity. Someone should have known. She looks like me, all that beautiful Plantagenet hair and those eyes of hers. Aye, someone should have known."

"De Fortenberry won't shame you."

"I will keep the royal eye on him nonetheless," the king said, and sat back in silence now to watch Roland continue his pacing.

His pacing stopped suddenly when the queen unexpectedly came into the tent. She looked worried.

The king rose quickly and went to her. They spoke softly together.

He frowned, then sighed, saying, as he turned to Roland, "Daria refuses to marry you."

"*What?*"

Eleanor said, "She refuses because you believe her a liar and naught more than chattel or a possession to be returned to her uncle for money. She claims she would rather go to a convent."

"I hadn't thought of that as a possibility," Edward said in a thoughtful voice. "Perhaps that is the best, perhaps —"

"It isn't the best! A convent would drain her of all spirit." He saw her suddenly in that small valley in Wales, breathing in the clear air, her arms wrapped around her, so happy in her freedom that he'd smiled as she'd danced. "No, she isn't fashioned for the religious existence. It is absurd. She is being willful. Damn her for an ungrateful wench!"

"But, Roland —"

"I shall thrash her, now! Have the priest readied. I will fetch her. Is she in your tent, your highness?"

"Aye, Roland, she is there," Eleanor said, and said not another word. When the king would have spoken, she clutched his arm.

"Damned female!" Roland muttered as

he strode from the royal presence without permission. "She besets me with her ingratitude, her pricks, and her thanklessness! Aye, I'll beat her!"

"All will be well now," the queen said, and smiled up at her husband.

Daria was alone in the queen's tent. She was sitting on a thick Flanders carpet, staring fixedly at the swirling red-and-purple patterns. Her arms were wrapped around her stomach. She knew she should rise, should prepare herself to leave. Would the king allow her to enter a convent? Would her uncle allow her to remain there? She'd heard that convents demanded huge amounts of money — indeed, dowries, because she would be the bride of God — to take a lady of her class. What if her uncle refused? She shook her head; she simply didn't know. Anything would be preferable to the Earl of Clare or Ralph of Colchester. Besides, she didn't want to die, and the earl would surely murder her once he discovered she no longer possessed a maidenhead. She thought of Roland and lowered her head. She felt tears well up and blinked them back. She swallowed. No, what had happened, she'd done, and it was she who would carry the responsibility.

When he strode into the tent, she raised

her head to face him, her expression not changing. She'd expected him to come; after all, hadn't he made a grand sacrifice? Wouldn't he now be angry to have it flung back in his face? But only for a little while. Then at least he would remember her fondly, for she'd released him from a gesture he'd hated to make in the first place. She couldn't make him pay for his generosity. She would have no honor if she did.

"Hello, Roland. What do you want?"

He didn't like her emotionless voice or the dullness in her eyes, nor did he like the fact that she was sitting cross-legged on the floor, her hair spilling down her back and over her shoulders.

He drew a deep steadying breath. He said quite calmly, "I want to know why you told the queen such nonsense."

She raised a brow at that but made no move to rise. She simply looked at him until he dropped to his haunches beside her. "Why, Daria?" He was three inches from her face. He didn't touch her.

"I am profoundly religious, Roland. No, you wouldn't believe that, would you? Very well, the truth. There is naught else but a convent. I wish to live. You said yourself that this would happen if you returned me to my uncle. He would kill me to have my inheritance. I know for a fact that the Earl of Clare, were he forced to wed me, would beat me and my unborn child to death, for he would know it wasn't his. It is not so hard to understand, is it? I don't particularly wish to die. I'm quite young, you know."

"I'm offering you another way. I won't kill you, nor will I beat you."

The pain threatened to choke her.

"You will marry me, Daria. Now, at once."

She shook her head. "Nay, I can't do that either."

"You believe I am lying? You believe I would beat you? Abuse you?"

"No."

"I shan't murder you, even if I do manage to gain your immense inheritance."

"I know."

"Then . . ." He growled in fury. "This is your grand gesture, isn't it? Free the poor man because he cares nothing for you? But first, bring him to his knees, make him grovel and plead, make him offer to do exactly what it is you wanted all the while. Then you scorn him? You are more perverse than that damned bitch Joan of Tenesby! I won't tolerate it, Daria, not for another instant!"

She had the damnable gall to simply sit there and shake her head.

For one of the few times in his life, Roland

knew such anger that he nearly choked on it. "By the saints, I will thrash you, Daria!"

He hauled her to her feet and flung himself onto the queen's chair. He dragged her over his thighs and brought his right palm down hard on her buttocks. She froze, then reared up frantically. She made no sound, but she struggled furiously. She was strong, he thought, as he brought his hand down again. He admired a silent fighter.

"Not even the smallest sound from you, eh? You're a stubborn wench. Should I pull up your gown and let you feel the heat of my palm on your bare flesh?" Before she could speak, if she would have spoken, Roland had bared her to the waist, ripping her gown and her shift. But he didn't strike her again. His hand remained raised in the air. He stared down at her buttocks, white and smooth and rounded, her long white legs, sleekly muscled. He swallowed. He moaned, then cursed. He shoved her off his legs and rose. He stood over her, panting, his hands on his hips. "Damn you, Daria. I would have remembered if I'd taken you, remembered your lovely buttocks at the very least. Now, prepare yourself, you stupid wench. You will wed me, and it will be tonight, before I change my mind, before I realize that you have shoved my honor down my throat. If you continue to refuse, I will beat you until you howl for mercy. No one will prevent me — don't think that anyone will!"

He said nothing more, merely strode to the tent opening. He turned and pointed his finger at her. "I mean it, Daria. You will wed me, and not another word out of your shrew's mouth."

11

The Benedictine priest Young Ansel, as he was affectionately called, exercised unflagging loyalty first to Robert Burnell and then to King Edward. He performed the marriage ceremony with as much dignity as his twenty-three years allotted him. His voice shook only a little when he spoke the soft Latin phrases. He thought the bride lovely and modest, and though she looked at him once, and that when he mispronounced a Latin word in his nervousness. A coincidence, he thought, swallowing. As for the groom, Young Ansel found him somewhat forbidding. For all his presence, he seemed absent from the proceedings.

Roland de Tournay was unwilling, Young Ansel finally realized, and wondered at it. He couldn't ask, of course; it would be considered an impertinence. Even though he was the king's second priest, Burnell had advised him never to take liberties. The royal temper had yet to consider him a friend.

Young Ansel looked at the bride more closely as he blessed the couple, and thought that perchance she was ill, so pale was she. He glanced over at Roland de Tournay, wondering if he saw how pale and still she was. But the knight was looking beyond Young Ansel's left shoulder, his face expressionless, his eyes cold. As he'd thought before, the groom seemed absent. He also looked miserable.

There were congratulations, exuberant and bawdy, because the king wished it so and his servants and soldiers willingly obeyed him. He wanted everything to appear as normal as possible. He wanted no talk about Roland, no talk about Daria. Even Robert Burnell managed to exclaim in modest enthusiasm several times. The queen hugged the bride and spoke softly to her. Young Ansel wondered what she said.

Eleanor was worried. As she gently held Daria, she said softly, "Do you feel ill, child?"

Daria shook her head against the queen's shoulder. She couldn't stand close to the queen because of her swollen belly. I will become like this, she thought blankly, and for a moment stared down at her own thin body. She'd known no illness from the babe as yet. How could there be a living being in her belly? So small? She wished her mother were here holding her. Perhaps her mother could make sense of it.

"You're afraid, then. Afraid of your new life, perhaps even of your new husband?"

"Aye."

"My sweet lord speaks so highly of Roland, has always done so. He's a man of honor and loyalty and he never treats his vows lightly. You're also an heiress and thus will bring much advantage to your husband. 'Tis important, you know. Have no fear, Daria."

"No."

The queen frowned over Daria's head at her husband. He was still loudly extolling Roland's good fortune, alternately buffeting Roland's shoulder as he gave him thorough advice and telling him he would soon be so rich he could well afford to assist his king. Edward raised his eyes at that moment and met his wife's gaze. He quieted, then said to Roland, "It is done. You are now a husband and soon you will be a father."

"It is amazing."

"It is done," Edward repeated. "All of us will go to Tyberton on the morrow. I wish the Earl of Clare to see you and know that

Daria is yours now and that he has no claim on her. I wish him to know that you have my favor."

Roland wished that as well. He nodded. He wondered how the earl would react. He wanted in odd moments for the man to become violent. He wanted to fight, to bash in his head, to relieve his frustration.

"I have had a tent prepared for you, my friend. You and your bride will spend the night there. I see the queen has released Daria. Come, we will dine now and drink to your health and your future."

There was nothing for it, Roland thought. He wanted to yell at the king that the last thing he wanted to do was spend the night with the girl who was with child and who was also his wife. He even managed to smile at Daria as he helped her into the chair beside his at the quickly erected banquet table. They were outside under the bright stars and the full moon. Torches lined the perimeter of the royal encampment. There were one hundred people milling about, eating their fill, turning at odd times to salute the bride and groom. All the food, Roland learned, came from the larders at Chepstow. He wondered if the Earl of Hereford would starve come winter. It appeared the king had stripped the castle granary bare. Perhaps in the misty future the king would visit him in Cornwall and delve with a free hand into his granary.

"Eat something, Daria."

She wanted to tell him that she would vomit if she did, but she said nothing, merely picked up a chunk of soft white bread and chewed it. When he turned away from her, she spit it onto the ground.

"You will be silent tomorrow."

"What do you mean?"

"I mean that we go to see the Earl of Clare. You will be silent and not flit and flutter about on me. I want neither your advice nor your protection, if that is what you're about now."

"I don't think I've ever fluttered about on you, Roland. As for my protection, 'tis true, I succeeded that one time."

He shrugged with masculine indifference. "Perhaps, perhaps not. Nor have you ever been silent. I wonder if the earl has guessed that you carry his child. I would imagine that his rage would know no bounds. Therefore, you must keep silent and let me deal with him."

"I don't carry the earl's child. Therefore he could have no rage, save the rage that he's been made to look the fool and he's lost all my dowry."

He just looked at her, thin-lipped, then tipped back his goblet and drank deeply of the red Aquitaine wine.

" 'Tis true, Roland. You must be careful, for I don't believe him entirely sane. Seeing you, the embodiment of his undoing, might make him act foolishly."

He made an elaborate pretense of turning to speak to Burnell. Inside, his stomach churned with anger at her. By all the saints, she'd gained what she wanted, so why did she continue to play the abused innocent? She infuriated him. He drank another goblet of wine. But he couldn't become drunk.

"You're very fertile if you indeed became with child with but one plowing."

"I am or you are."

He stiffened but his smile remained firmly in place. Did he really expect her to change her tune now?

"Then I'd best take my fill of you whilst you carry the babe. I'll be tired of you by the time the child is born and that will be just as well. I don't wish to have a dozen babes hanging on to me within as many years."

She wanted to yell at him; she wanted to howl at the glorious full moon. She did neither. She lowered her head and played with the bread on her trencher. He was trying on purpose to hurt her. She wouldn't let him see that he was succeeding.

"You have been so very kind to me, your majesty," Daria said later to the Queen of England. "I thank you, truly."

"Fret not, child. I will see you again. You and Roland will come to London, or perhaps my lord and I will visit Cornwall. Now, my dear, allow my ladies to prepare you for the night."

With those prosaic words, and not a bit of well-meant advice, the Queen of England left her to the ministrations of two ladies-in-waiting. The ladies weren't so reticent as their mistress. They'd drunk their share of wine and were thus giggling and giving Daria advice on making a man shudder madly with lust.

Roland paused outside the tent and listened to the women's laughter coming from within. And then he heard Daria's voice, puzzled and low, "Truly, Claudia, how do I do that? Just tell him to stick it into my mouth? Would I not choke? Would I not hurt him with my teeth?"

"Silly girl! Daria, you must stroke your hands over his body and follow your hands with your tongue and mouth. 'Tis a wonderful sound."

Roland's eyes widened. So the queen's ladies were as bawdy as any others. So they were educating Daria. Then his smile turned to a frown when she said, "Perhaps Roland won't like me to do that because I wouldn't do it well. Perhaps he would want another, more skilled and —"

"Daria, hush now. The only way for you to become skilled is to practice. Ask your husband if he minds that you practice on him. Then watch him lick his lips and watch his eyes grow large with anticipation."

Roland didn't hear what his wife said to that. His *wife*. It was almost more than a man of few years but vast experience could take in. He hadn't wanted a wife, not yet, not until his keep in Cornwall was in proper condition and he'd become . . . bored. He shook himself. Bored! He wouldn't ever become bored, and how could his mind assume that taking a wife was the cure for boredom anyway?

He pulled back the tent flap and chuckled at the drunken grins he received from the two women. Their thoughts were clearly writ on their faces, and his sex responded. He quickly turned to Daria. She simply stood where she was, staring at him. With new eyes, he thought. Was she seeing herself take his rod into her mouth?

Claudia poked her elbow into Daria's ribs. "Practice, my dear, practice!"

"Good night, Daria, and enjoy what God and the king have given you! The saints and women know there aren't many men as potent and well-formed as this one. Aye, he's a lovely lad, he is."

The two women eyed Roland through wistful drunk eyes, Claudia brushing her breasts against his arm as she went past him.

Daria stared, feeling no particular anger at the woman. They'd dipped freely into the wine, and Roland was a beautiful man. She supposed it made Claudia forget herself. Roland was standing there saying nothing, merely looking at her.

"Will you take their advice?"

Her face turned instantly red. "You . . . you heard what they told me to do?"

"Aye, I heard. 'Twas excellent advice."

She straightened her back and looked him squarely in the eye. "Then I will do it. But you must tell me what to do, Roland. I have no wish to offend you or perhaps hurt you."

"This is a very strange conversation," he said as he began stripping off his outer tunic. He tossed the wide leather belt onto the fur-covered floor. "The queen's ladies were most eager to teach you what to do to me."

"They seem to understand men," she said, frozen to the spot, watching as Roland matter-of-factly removed his tunic. There were three candles lit in the tent, in a brass holder sitting atop a small sandalwood table. There was a low cot covered with animal furs. There was nothing else in the tent. When Roland was bare to his waist, the candlelight casting darkening shadows over his body, Daria found herself staring openly at him. He was lean and firm, dark hair covering his chest. When she'd seen him in Wrexham he'd been ill and lying on his back. He'd been beautiful, she'd thought that very clearly, but she hadn't recognized the sheer strength of him, the tautness of his arms, the fluid motion of the muscles in his back and shoulders, the ridges of muscle over his belly. She swallowed, for now he was stripping off his chausses. He stopped then and looked at her. "Why do you stand there? Get off your clothes and into the bed."

She didn't move. As an order from a loving bridegroom, it lacked even a dollop of warmth.

He raised a dark eyebrow. "Since you carry a babe, I can assume that you have seen a naked man. I am no different from any of my fellows, Daria." He rose straight and tall and naked, and the look he gave her was mocking. She didn't want to look at him but she couldn't help it. Her eyes fell immediately to his groin. His man's rod lay flaccid in the bush of thick black hair.

But she knew he would grow large, very large, and he would want to thrust himself inside her body. She swallowed and turned her back to him.

She heard him chuckle. " 'Tis best to begin your caressing of me whilst I'm still in this state. Now, get off your clothes."

"All right." Quickly she doused the three candles, throwing the tent into gloom. The torches from without cast dim shadows into the interior, but at least he couldn't see her clearly. She was embarrassed. Before, he hadn't known *her*, hadn't really touched *her*, hadn't really taken *her*. But now he was well; now he was virile and eager; now he was her husband and would look at her.

"What are you doing?" She whirled about, consternation writ plain on her face.

"I'm merely lighting one candle. I don't wish to fumble in the darkness. Get off your clothes, Daria. I wish to see your breasts and your belly. I have paid dearly for the privilege. I will not tell you again."

With those emotionless words, he climbed into the narrow cot and pulled a fur to his waist. He crossed his arms behind his head and looked at her. Her hands stilled, then fell to her sides. She couldn't bring herself to remove her clothes in front of him; she didn't want to respond to his indifferent command. She was afraid; she knew he didn't want her, she knew that he would take her tonight simply because she was here, she belonged to him, and she could have been any woman to ease him.

Yet this man was her husband, and she must make the best of it. She tried again to untie the ribbons on her overtunic, but her fingers were clumsy and cold. Finally she loosened it enough to pull it over her head. Her gown was loose-fitting, but again she couldn't manage to unlace the strings that crisscrossed over her breasts.

Her husband simply lay there looking at her, his eyes hooded, just looking, as if he didn't really care, as if he simply wanted her to obey whatever order he gave her because he was the master and she wasn't, and because he was angry at her and wanted to punish her.

Suddenly it was simply too much. She looked at her shaking fingers, looked at him and saw that his expression was as cold as the waters of the North Sea, and whispered, "Nay, I cannot." She saw him jerk upright, and slowly, very slowly, she eased down to her knees. She felt tears sting her eyes; felt despair wash over her. She covered her face with her hands. And she cried silently.

Roland drew back as if he'd been struck. There was his bride, in a heap on the floor, crying! Damn her! Aloud he said furiously, "You have what you want, you cursed wench! And for whatever reason you wanted *me* as your husband, not the Earl of Clare, not God in a precious convent! Well, now you have me. Cease your damnable wailing. It but enrages me. A woman's tears mean naught; they're a sham. I won't stand it. Stop it now, Daria!"

She got a grip on herself. She was being foolish, and crying, indulging herself, her mother had told her, was something a girl shouldn't do with a man she loved because it wasn't honorable or honest. As if Roland would care. "Yes," she said, wiping her eyes with the back of her hand, "I'll stop crying. I'm sorry, Roland."

She rose slowly to her feet. He watched silently as she regained her control. She hiccuped even as she stripped off her gown. When she stood in the soft candlelight wearing only her thigh-length linen shift, he could see the faint outline of her nipples, the outline of dark hair at her groin. He wanted to see all of her. After all, he'd paid dearly for the right. "Remove the shift."

Her fingers went to the narrow straps on her shoulders, then stopped. "I cannot."

"Why can't you? You're certainly not a maid, so why this excessive modesty? Do you prefer that I strip the shift off you?"

"Nay. 'Tis the only one I have. I must be careful with it."

"Take it off, Daria. You are vexing me with your disobedience, and if you'll remember, you promised before God to obey me."

She felt humiliated. She searched for a shred of pride and managed to find enough so that she could stare straight ahead, not at him, and quickly pull off the shift. *Pretend you're alone; pretend he doesn't exist, that he doesn't lie there, watching you, seeing you.* And she didn't look at him, simply stared beyond him, feeling the soft linen shift pooling at her feet. She removed herself from the naked girl standing there for his examination, a man who was her husband, a man who disliked her heartily and believed her a liar and a female with no honor.

Roland stared at her, unable to help himself. He'd had no idea she was so very nicely shaped. Her breasts were high and full and as white as her belly, her nipples a pale pink. She was too thin. Her ribs were visible, and her breasts appeared almost too heavy for her slight torso, but he didn't mind that. He did wonder how she could be carrying a babe in that flat stomach of hers. He imagined she would begin to fill out soon enough. Her legs were long and sleekly muscled. He liked that. He remembered many of the women whose beds he'd shared whose bodies were white and soft, too soft. Daria was firm, and even in her thinness, she looked strong and able. He pictured her legs tightening around his flanks and felt his muscles tighten and his sex swell. He wanted her, but then again, he told himself silently, he would want any decent-looking female who was standing before him naked.

"Come here," he said. "Let me examine more closely what I have bought with my future."

"You forget that my money purchases a much nicer future than you expected."

"Aye, you do indeed improve my lot with your vast array of coin, but I pay with myself, Daria, and I keep paying until I die. I told you to come here. I am weary to my bones of your lies and protests, and I know I must take you at least once this night, even though I don't particularly wish to. It is my duty and I won't shirk it."

"You could pretend that I'm Lila again."

He sucked in his breath, rage and frustration pounding through him. "I told you once that you are nothing like her, more's the pity. If you don't come here, you will regret it."

Still she stood there in the center of the tent, naked and white and stiff as a lance. "Will you strike me as my uncle did? As the Earl of Clare did?"

His guts twisted at her words. It was rage at her now needless pretenses, nothing more. He rose from the bed and strode to her. He suddenly saw the fear in her eyes, and something else . . . She jerked back.

He clasped her upper arms tightly and pulled her against him. At the feel of her body against him, he felt a leaping of nearly painful need, felt his sex jutting against her belly. "Yes," he said as he grabbed a handful of her hair and pulled her face close to his, "yes, I will pretend you're Lila. Even if that fails, even if I recognize you, my wife, it still shouldn't be too difficult for me. I haven't had a woman for a long time, and even you will do." He kissed her closed lips, and he was hard and demanding. He was the master and he would prove it to her.

"I'm not Lila."

He released her, her quiet words flowing warmly into his mouth and into his soul, helpless words, despairing words.

He stepped back and looked at her face. She was not the girl he'd believed her to be. He pressed his open palm to her flat belly. "A babe is within, yet you are so small." His fingers kneaded her. "You say it is my babe, but I know that isn't true. You are a mystery to me, Daria. I remember the girl I rescued from the earl, the girl who traveled with me through Wales, the girl whose gift for languages rivals my own, the girl who was brave and fearless when those outlaws took her.

"And then there is the other Daria, the girl who has lies forming in her mind even as she thinks, and she, I fear, is the girl I married. Who are you, nay, what are you, and why have you done this to me?"

She closed her eyes against the pain. "I didn't wish it to be this way, I swear it to you, Roland. When you were ill, when you believed I was Lila, it was my decision to come to you, to give myself to you. I swore then to myself that you would never know, that I would never tell you, for I wanted no guilt from you, no pity. I even bathed my blood and your seed from you so that you wouldn't wonder. I was stupid, for it didn't occur to me that I could become pregnant. It never occurred to me that such a thing was possible."

He pushed her away from him. "Come to

sleep when it pleases you to do so."

He doused the candle, and as she stood there naked and shivering in the middle of the tent, she heard him burrow beneath the furs on the low bed, and she said, "You have so quickly forgotten your duty?"

He cursed her then, his voice low, his words crude. He rose and she felt his fingers close over her arm. He dragged her to the bed and threw her down upon her back.

"Well, wife, evidently you desire my body. Or will any man's body do? No matter, since I have no choice, it will have to be my man's body you endure. But it's all you will have of me. And know, Daria, that a man can plow any woman, it matters not to him. To see a woman's parted legs, that's all that is necessary for a man. That's all you will be to me — an encumbrance, a duty, a body to take until I tire and grow bored."

He came down over her then, his body pressing hers into the furs, and he kissed her hard, forcing her mouth to open, and when her lips parted, he thrust his tongue inside and she felt his anger, tasted it, and her body froze. He reared over her and laughed. "You regret your desire now, sweet wife? Well, 'tis a pity, for it's too late, for you are now mine legally and in the eyes of God. Open your legs and do it quickly, for I wish to be done with it. I look forward to losing myself in sleep and mayhap I will be lucky and dream about Lila and Cena, two women who were honest in their need for me, and hadn't a traitorous thought in their heads."

"Roland, please, don't do this. Please, don't hurt me, don't —" Her voice broke off on a gasp when he grasped her thighs and pulled them apart. "Let me see if you are ready for me. I have no wish to rend your woman's flesh, 'twill but make you hurt to walk and to ride, and thus prove an inconvenience to me." His fingers were probing at her, delving inside her, exploring, and she tried to pull away from him, to free herself from him, but his hand came down flat on her belly, holding her still and silent even as his finger slid inside her, stretching her, working her. She felt her flesh become damp and soft because her body recognized him and wanted him even though she wanted to weep with the pain of what he was doing to her.

"By all the saints," he said, his finger pressing more deeply into her. "You're small, but your body is hungry. I shan't force you. No, you shan't scream of ravishment to me, ever. I have never forced a woman in my life, and besides, with you, it would be impossible. You're eager as any wench, probably more so than the two ladies who advised you."

She tried to reach him just once more. "Please, Roland, don't do this to me, not in anger, not —"

But he was paying her no heed and she knew he was apart from her. He was between her thighs, spreading them wider still, bending her knees and lifting her hips with his hands, bringing her upward. "No pleasure for you, wife, save what you can gain for yourself. Actually, little enough for me. My duty . . . 'tis naught but my damned man's duty." And without warning, without another word, his fingers pried her open, and he thrust himself into her in one powerful stroke.

She yelled at the shock of him and the burning of her flesh as he plunged deep, spreading her for himself, and then she was crying, but she stuffed her fist into her mouth, waiting helplessly, waiting silently, for him to finish with her. He'd been right, there was no pleasure for her. She wondered dully in those moments if there was such pleasure to be had for a woman ever.

He was breathing hard, plunging repeatedly into her, pulling out, then thrusting deep again. Again and again, until she heard him suck in his breath as if he'd been struck.

Then he was hammering into her, deep, then shallow in short strokes, his hands frantically kneading her hips as he brought her higher for his penetration. Then he moaned, and she felt his seed come into her body. That was familiar to her, that deep joining that had eased her virgin's pain, for he'd belonged to her then, completely, and she'd possessed him.

She sobbed, unable to keep the sound to herself, not from any pain in her body, but from the pain in the very depths of her. For even in his man's possession of her, she was alone, deep within herself, as was he.

He was gasping for breath over her, his chest heaving from his exertion. He was still deep inside her and she could feel his member moving and shifting. There was still no pain, for his seed eased her and his member wasn't as swelled now. No, he hadn't ravished her body, but he had ravished her spirit.

"There," he said once he'd regained his breath, "I've done my man's duty by you, wife." He pulled out of her quickly, eagerly, and her body flinched in reply.

"What, Daria, no passionate little moans from you? No thanks for my taking you as you wished? Do you mean to tell me that you were unable to give yourself a woman's pleasure? You surprise me. Your body was more than willing to take me in and pull my seed from me. You're a stubborn girl, but no matter. I will sleep now. Do not disturb me further this night."

He climbed off her and fell upon his back. She felt him pull the furs up. Slowly, very slowly, she straightened her legs. Her muscles protested. She felt his seed seeping slowly from her body, but she was too uncaring of it, of him, of herself, to pay much heed.

She lay there quietly. She heard his breathing even into sleep. She realized that she should have never told him the truth. She'd placed the responsibility on his shoulders just as she'd sworn to herself that she wouldn't do. But it was his babe she carried. How could he believe her if he had no memory of it? Well, it was over now. She listened to his deep slow breathing and knew that she still loved him but that now it wasn't enough, this love of hers, not nearly enough. Mayhap it would never have been enough, in any circumstance. He hated her and there was no reason for him to cease doing so.

Unless the babe looked like him. Unless somehow he remembered that night in Wrexham. It was her only hope, a slim one she knew, for she herself looked nothing like her own mother or like her father. But there was nothing else for her.

12

There was complete silence in the great hall of Tyberton Castle. The Earl of Clare stood tight-mouthed, fury blotching his face, turning it as startling a red as his hair. He stared at the man who'd stolen Daria from him. The man who had made a fool of him twice. Hell and the devil, what was the damned knave doing with the king?

The earl said in a loud voice, "I see you have returned this man to me, sire. He's a thief and I will hang him this very day."

"Not as yet, my lord," Edward said pleasantly. "Not as yet. Come, have ale fetched. My queen is weary, as are her ladies." He added his famous Plantagenet smile, which had no discernible effect at all on the Earl of Clare. "I have a great thirst as well."

It was then that the earl saw Daria. He started toward her, then pulled himself upright. He held his peace. There were too many present to overhear him. He would wait.

After the queen, her ladies, and Daria were seated comfortably, the earl approached the king. To his chagrin, the whoreson Roland remained at the king's side, drinking from his flagon as if he had not a care in this world. He looked young and fit and strong — a warrior — not a pretty priest covered with a frayed cowl. How had the man gotten Daria away from him again? What kind of disguise had he used?

"I would beg to speak with you, sire. 'Tis important and regards this man here."

"Ah, yes," Edward said, his voice deep with amusement that the earl didn't hear, "I believe you wish to accuse this man of something?"

So the king wished the knave to remain. So be it. He drew himself up and contempt dripped from his voice. "Aye, he's a thief, sire, and he stole *her!*" He pointed a finger toward the queen's group of ladies. "Did he tell you that he pretended to be a Benedictine priest? That he, a savage and a heathen, even pretended to say a *Mass* for me? Not only did he rob me, sire, he blasphemed God's name and profaned the Church."

The king, diverted, turned to Roland.

"Did you really play the priest?"

"Aye."

"Did you do it well?"

"For the most part. Only Daria knew that I misspoke some of my Latin Mass. The earl here understands naught but what he speaks. I could have recited Latin declensions and it would have made him feel holy just the same. Nay, 'twas Daria who understood immediately I was a fraud."

"Daria! You call her Daria! 'Tis absurd! A female cannot understand God's word! You lie to me and to your king. I understood all your mistakes, but I am a good man, a tolerant man, and I merely believed you nervous in front of me, and I chose not to humiliate you. Aye, I willingly forgave your lapses. Sire, give him over to me and I will deal with him quickly and fairly." He panted himself to a halt, then, unable to help himself, yelled, "I demand that you turn the man over to me, sire!"

"Hold, my lord," Edward said. He shifted in his chair — the earl's own ornate carved chair — and continued mildly, "Listen well, for I grow bored with your plaints and your commands to your king. This man is Roland de Tournay. He is my man, sent by me and none other to rescue that girl, Daria, from your imprisonment. Her uncle, the Earl of

Reymerstone, pleaded for my help and I gave it. I told Roland to use whatever means necessary to accomplish his mission. Of course I didn't wish any blood to be shed, and he accomplished that as well."

Roland said not a word. He simply gazed at the king in admiration. He'd never believed the king so quick of wit before. He'd rather looked forward to this confrontation, but he'd assumed that the king would allow him to handle the earl, to do whatever he had to do, short of murdering the man.

He saw that the king was much enjoying his playacting. Roland, for the first time in their acquaintance of many years, remained silent. As for the Earl of Clare, he could not now make further demands, not after the king's explanation. Roland felt resentment at the king's interference, and some amusement, for the earl's hatred and immense frustration was very nearly a tangible thing, and there was naught the man could do, save silently choke on it.

Edward had no intention of allowing the two men to fight, for Roland would kill the earl, of that he had little doubt. He was younger, he was stronger, and he was smarter. And besides, he himself still needed the Earl of Clare, rot the man's miserable hide, needed him to fend off the

Welsh outlaws, until he could build his castles and assume control himself. Then the Earl of Clare could drown in a Welsh swamp with the king's blessing. He discounted his friendship with Roland de Tournay; it couldn't be a consideration in the royal decision. No, the king didn't want Clare dead now. Moreover, he'd gained advantage with Roland, for that talented fellow wouldn't be able to refuse his king anything, not after this. Why, he would even have Roland's fine destrier returned to him. He thought about the look on the earl's face were he to tell him that it was his, the king's, destrier, and he had merely loaned it to Roland. The earl would surely swallow his tongue in his rage.

The king smiled at the earl, a gracious smile. He didn't believe in pressing a man's face in offal unless it was necessary. A king could afford to be beneficent in victory; it was also in his noble character, unless, of course, he wished it otherwise. "So you see, my lord, Roland accomplished his mission. If he offended your religious feelings, I will reprimand him soundly. Further, it seems he became enamored with Daria and she with him. After he rescued her again — the second time, he played the bent old hag, did you know that? No, well, that time, he brought her to me. They were wedded last night, my lord, by mine own priest. He is, in fact, a Benedictine priest, I can attest to it."

For a long moment the earl simply stared, not at any person, but inward, and there he saw bleakness and rage. He couldn't accept it. He looked toward Daria, who stood next to the queen. This man, this Roland de Tournay, had wedded her and bedded her. "They left me with a peasant girl, garbed her as Daria for her wedding with me. If she hadn't giggled, I should have married the little slut!"

"She was most toothsome, my lord," Roland said. "I handpicked her myself."

The king grinned, then harrumphed and said, his voice serious, "This peasant girl, my lord, what have you done with her? Not harmed her, I trust."

The Earl of Clare turned a dull red, for certainly he'd bedded her, taken her with little delay; even as his servants and soldiers feasted, he'd taken her to his chamber and plowed her small belly. He'd hurt her, but not badly. What had she expected to happen to her once her lord had discovered the ruse? Any other man would have had her beaten to death. But it didn't matter. It wasn't at all the point. The earl shook himself much in the manner of a wet mongrel and bellowed, "Daria! Come here, immediately!"

Daria felt the queen's hand lightly squeeze her fingers to hold her quiet. The queen raised her head and smiled at the king. Both the queen and Daria wished they'd heard what had been said, but they hadn't.

"Aye," the king called, "let Daria come here. Let her tell the earl that she is wedded to Roland de Tournay, by her own will, with no royal coercion."

Daria rose slowly. She felt as if she were in a strange dream, filled with loud voices from people who weren't really there, weren't actually real. She walked across the cold stone floor of Tyberton's great hall, seeing the people who'd served her, who'd watched her, seeing some of them smirking now at their lord and his predicament, others gazing with hatred upon her. The queen had assured her earlier that the king wouldn't allow the two men to fight. She hadn't believed her before, but now she did. Further, no matter what Roland believed, no matter what he thought of her, she was his wife. She must not shame him. She stiffened her back and thrust up her chin. She didn't look at her husband.

She walked directly to the Earl of Clare.

"Yes, my lord?" she asked pleasantly. "You wished to speak to me?"

The earl stared down at her a moment. He wanted to strike her and pull her against him. She was pale, but even so, she didn't appear to have any fear of him. He'd strike her first, he thought, not hard, just with enough force to recall her to her duty to him; then he'd take her and hold her. He could feel the softness of her body, the narrowness of her when he'd penetrated her with his finger to find her maidenhead. She had no maidenhead now. She'd wedded Roland de Tournay. Blood pounded hard and fast in his head and in his groin. He said in a harsh voice, "You have truly wedded him? Willingly?"

"Aye. I am his wife."

"By all the saints! You lied to me when I caught up to you finally? You hadn't escaped him in Wrexham? You were not trying to find me?"

"That's correct, my lord. He'd fallen ill and would have been unable to fight you if you'd found us. I learned that you had arrived in Wrexham and had discovered Roland's destrier at the local stable. I had to save him from you, for I knew you would kill him with no hesitation. I took his destrier and led you away from him."

Roland didn't move. He didn't change expressions. He felt something move deep inside him, a feeling like the one he'd experienced the previous evening when his release had overtaken him. He'd wanted briefly to hold her tightly against him, caress her, and kiss her, and forget all else. But he'd managed to keep his mouth shut. He'd managed this time not to give a woman power over him. He'd managed to hold himself apart from the still and silent woman lying beneath him. He'd held steady; she'd already betrayed him once. She wouldn't betray him again.

Even if she wasn't lying about saving him, well, then, it still didn't matter. She'd lied about the other. There was no other explanation for it, the Earl of Clare had raped her the moment he'd recaptured her. And Roland felt the familiar rage with that knowledge. She had saved him; he accepted it as being plausible, though he'd never before known a woman with such initiative.

The Earl of Clare howled. "I offered you everything! Damn you, girl, you could have been a countess, not a simple knight's lady, doomed to poverty —"

"Oh, I shan't be poor, my lord," Daria said, interrupting him with great pleasure. "Don't you forget how you desired my dowry as much as my fair hand? My dowry and revenge against my uncle? Well, all is now Roland's."

Reason deserted him. The earl's fist struck her hard against her jaw. Daria staggered backward with the force of his blow, falling to the stone floor. Roland leapt upon the earl, his fist in his throat, his other fist striking low and hard in his belly. The earl yelled and stumbled backward, his balance lost. Roland didn't pause. He jumped at him, hurling him to his back with his fist hard in his chest. The earl's sword crashed loudly against the stone. Roland stood over him and hissed, "You strike someone with not a tenth of your strength. Well, I am her husband and I will protect her from such vermin as you." He kicked the earl hard in the ribs, then dropped to his knees, grabbed the earl by his tunic, jerked up his head, and pounded his face twice with his fist. He let his head drop back with a loud ugly thud.

"Enough, Roland," the king called. "Have some ale. That sort of work makes a man thirsty."

But Roland didn't heed the king. He saw the queen's ladies surrounding Daria, helping her to her feet, brushing off her gown. He strode to them and they fell away from her. He didn't touch her for a moment, just stood there before her, looking down at her.

"Look up at me, Daria."

She obeyed him. He clasped her upper arms in his hands.

The earl — the damnable sod — had struck her hard. Roland lightly touched her jaw. "You will look a witch come evening," he said. "But your eye won't blacken. Does it pain you much?"

She shook her head, but he knew it must hurt her. It pleased him, this unexpected stoicism of hers.

"Hold still." As gently as he could, he touched his fingertips to her jaw, probing, making certain it wasn't broken. She didn't move, didn't flinch once.

He saw that she was now looking beyond him to the still-fallen Earl of Clare. "Did you kill him?"

"Of course not. Do you believe me a madman?"

"I have never seen a man fight another as do you."

Roland grinned and rubbed the bruised knuckles of his left hand against his right palm.

"Aye, Roland," the king called out. "How come you to destroy another man with such strange motions?"

"A Muslim fellow in Acre taught me. He said that Christians and their notions of honorable fighting left him and his brothers roaring with laughter. They said English knights with their heavy, clumsy horses and their armor that baked them alive under the sun made them shake their heads with wonder. They could not understand how we could be so stupid. They weren't of course in Barbars' army. They were outlaws and street thieves."

The king, fortunately for all those present, chose to be amused. "Street thieves!" They heard a moan and the king nodded to several of the earl's retainers who had been standing frozen in place, not knowing what to do. They rushed to their master's side and assisted him.

"I cracked two of his ribs, made him impotent for a week, and severely bruised his throat, rendering speech difficult and painful for him, for three days, I'd say. Nothing that won't heal with time. Perhaps I should have made him permanently impotent. But the fellow doesn't have an heir. I found myself in sympathy with him at the last instant."

Daria looked from him to the king and back again. She saw her husband's dark eyes were sparkling with pleasure. He'd enjoyed hitting the Earl of Clare, pounding him to the stone floor. She touched her fingertips to her jaw. The pain flashed through her head and she closed her eyes a moment to gain control. To her surprise, she felt his arms go around her. He lifted her high in his arms. "My lady needs to rest," Roland announced to the assembled group. "Sire, if it pleases you, I will remove her to her former chamber, the small room where the earl held her prisoner for so many months. I doubt not that the earl will insist upon his king and queen having his own chamber. Pain tends to bring a greater measure of reason to a man."

Roland carried her up the winding narrow stairs to the upper level. The old woman Ena was crouched at the top of the stairs. When she saw Roland carrying her mistress, she stretched out a skinny arm and pointed a bony finger at him and howled, "Ye've hurt her!"

"Nay, old witch, your precious earl struck her. She will rest now, and your presence isn't necessary."

Daria said not a word. She wrapped her arms more tightly around Roland's neck. "He moved so quickly I didn't have time to avoid his fist."

"I know. I was so surprised at his stupidity that I, too, stared for a good second before I had sense enough to attack him." He eased her onto the narrow bed and straightened, looking down at her. He said awkwardly, "I'm sorry he struck you, Daria. I wasn't much of a protector."

She said nothing, merely nodded. Her head hurt and her jaw pulsed with pain.

"What you said to him — was it true? Did you truly lead him away from me?"

She heard the disbelief in his voice. She turned her head away from him. "Aye, it's true. I lied to him and pretended that I'd escaped you. I made him believe that I rejoiced at his finding me. He didn't see through it."

"Then he brought you back here and forced you, raped you. He got you with child then, didn't he?"

"No. He didn't touch me. I convinced him that we would both rot in hell if he forced me without marriage first. I told him he would ruin mine own honor if he took me without marriage first. I begged and pleaded. I prayed he would not be able to find a priest, and so he didn't, until that same day you came for me again. I was also fortunate that he left me for much of that time to search for Welsh outlaws."

"I see," Roland said, his voice emotionless. He strode across the small room to the window slit. He stood there gazing down into the inner bailey. This is where Daria had stood, helpless and a prisoner, for so many days. He turned suddenly and said, "Why don't you have sickness from the babe? I have heard it common in women to be ill." He shrugged. "To vomit, to feel weak. Are your breasts not sore?"

"I am tired more of the time, but nothing more."

"Your breasts are not sore? Did I hurt you last night?"

She couldn't bear it, this insistence of his, this distrust. "Leave me alone, Roland. You didn't hurt me last night, not physically. You merely made me feel defiled and helpless, worth less than nothing." There, she'd said what she felt. She watched him pale, but only for a moment. His eyes narrowed on her face and he said, his voice even, too even, "You are certain you are with child?"

So he wondered now if even that was a lie. A lie to trap him into marriage? She marveled at his mind, and said calmly enough, "I wasn't, but the queen was. When I doubted her, she laughed and told me she had considerable experience in matters of knowing when babes were in a woman's belly. Should you like to question her, Roland?"

"Sarcasm doesn't suit you, Daria."

"Your endless distrust doesn't suit me!"

His brows lowered and his dark eyes, so full of sparkling pleasure such a short time before, were now cold as a moonless night. "Remain here. I must return to the king." He strode to the door, then said over his shoulder, "It isn't true that you have no value at all. Do you so quickly forget all the wealth you bring me?" He left her then without another word, another look.

Daria had no idea of the time. Since it was the midsummer, it would remain light until very late in the evening. She was bored, but she didn't want to go to the great hall. Her jaw still throbbed, but not as much now. She stood by the open window slit, a spot where she'd spent so many hours, and stared down into the inner bailey. There weren't as many people about. It must be later than she'd thought. Her stomach growled and she crossed her arms over her belly. It was then, sudden as a streak of lightning, that her belly cramped, nausea flooded her, and she dashed to the chamber pot and vomited up what little food she'd eaten that day. She was heaving, her jaw aching ferociously after her exertion, kneeling on the floor over the pot, when the chamber door opened. She hadn't the energy to turn about, but she knew it was Roland. She heard him suck in his breath, heard him quicken his step to her. She felt his large hand on her shoulder.

She still didn't raise her head. Another wave of sickness hit her and she jerked and shuddered with dry heaves, since there was no more food in her belly. She felt weak and stupid and so listless that she didn't care at that moment if he was repelled at her illness. She remained still, bent over the chamber pot, breathing heavily, sweat trickling down her back and between her breasts.

"Come," he said, and slipped his hands beneath her armpits and raised her to her feet. She hadn't the strength to support herself and sagged. He half-dragged her to the bed and laid her down. She closed her eyes. She didn't want to see him, didn't want him to see her, not like this, not green and shaky and weak as a feeble old woman.

She felt a wet cloth on her face. Then he said, "Here, drink this. 'Tis naught but cool water."

She didn't want it, but she allowed him to raise her head and put the goblet to her lips. She sipped at the water, then felt her stomach twist. She gasped and jerked off the bed, back to the chamber pot.

Roland watched her, feeling more helpless than he had in his life. He watched her vomit up the water, then watched her body convulse and heave. He was out of his element in this; he turned and left her.

Daria didn't care, not about her husband's quick defection, not about anything, save the fierce knotting and unknotting in her belly. She finally slipped onto her side, her face against the cold stone floor. She didn't care about that either. It felt good, this coolness. She lay there, trapped in her weak body, content that she wasn't heaving into the pot. She wanted nothing more. Slowly, after some minutes, she lightly brought her hand to her belly. "My child," she said softly, feeling at once ridiculous and strangely content, "you have finally announced your presence to me. I but wish that you hadn't done it with such vigor."

The queen herself appeared, Roland behind her. "Ah, my poor child," Eleanor said, rueful sympathy in her voice.

"Place her on the bed, Roland. She will be better presently."

Daria didn't resist, nor did she acknowledge the queen's presence. She simply didn't care. She didn't look at her husband when he lifted her, cursing softly at the coldness of her body. "Move aside now and let her sip at this."

"Please, nothing," Daria said, her hand

swatting weakly at the flagon the queen held, but the queen would have none of it.

" 'Twill settle your belly, my dear. Trust me. Did I not tell you that my experience in these matters is vast? Drink, now. That's it. Slowly, just small sips. Very good. That's enough now. Just lie back and close your eyes."

The queen smiled at Roland. She was pleased with his reaction to his wife's illness. He'd come running into the great hall, interrupting the king, but not caring, so afraid was he for Daria. "Worry not, Roland. She will be fine. It is important that she eat lightly and very often. She has gone too long without eating, I suspect. This drink I gave her, I will give you the ingredients. When she is ill again, you will prepare this for her."

Roland sounded appalled. "She will be ill that violently again?"

"She is with child, Roland. 'Tis common, unfortunately, but it will pass soon. Another month or so and she will feel much better."

Daria nearly groaned aloud. Another month! She wanted to turn her face to the wall and sleep through that month.

"Now, my dear," the queen continued, "one of my ladies is bringing you some food. You must always eat slowly, and just a little. I will leave you now with your husband. He is as pale as you are, he was so frightened for you."

Roland looked as if he would protest that description, but he wisely kept his mouth shut. He had been afraid, it was true. He thanked the queen, accepted food from Damaris, and returned to his wife. She looked small and weak, lying there on her back, her arms limp at her sides, her eyes closed. Her thick braided hair looked damp with sweat, dull and heavy.

"Daria," he said. "Come, sit up and I will give you some food. Just a little, but you will do as the queen says."

"Please go away, Roland. Please. I don't want to eat, ever again, as long as I live."

"You must. If you don't, the babe will starve."

That was true, and she sighed. "All right, leave the food and you go away."

"Why? I've seen men vomit until they turned as white as a woman's belly. It is no reason for you to feel embarrassed, Daria. Come now and eat. I must return shortly to the king. He demands to be foremost in all his people's thoughts. He'll forgive me this lapse, but only this time."

She obeyed because she knew him well enough to realize that once Roland made up his mind to do something, he wouldn't bend or change it. She wanted to feed herself, but gave that up. She felt too weak.

He sat beside her, feeding her small chunks of white bread, dipping some of them into the meat gravy. And he spoke to distract her. "My destrier has grown fat and lazy, but I don't despair. Once we are in Cornwall I will work him until he is lean again." He wiped a trickle of gravy off her chin with his finger. He paused, then said, a touch of resentment in his voice, "The king has meddled again. He fears that your uncle will roast my body over live coals if I go to Reymerstone to announce my marriage to you and demand your dowry. Thus, the king will send Burnell and a dozen of his men to do the dirty work for me."

She felt such relief at this news she wanted to shout to the rafters with it. She knew Roland wouldn't like that, so said instead, "You wanted to see my uncle?" She looked both appalled and surprised. "You looked forward to confronting him?" She couldn't imagine anyone actually wishing to be in her uncle's presence. His sarcasm, his cruelty, his viciousness. She shuddered unconsciously.

"He won't hurt you again, so cease trembling when you speak of him. Aye, I wanted to see his face and dare him to gainsay me."

Roland gave a heartfelt sigh. "A pity, but what can I do? Edward must interfere, curse him. He enjoys playing the great mediator. In any case, you and I and several of the king's men will travel to Cornwall whilst poor Burnell travels east to Reymerstone. I have spoken to each of the men, and they wish to join my service. They have families in Cornwall, wish to return there, and the king, since he is wallowing in his peace-making, won't be offended."

Daria felt much better. The food settled in her stomach and she felt her strength returning. She finally looked at Roland. "Cornwall? You have family there? Your brother? We go to them?"

He shook his head. "Nay, my brother and all the family are near to York, in the northeast." He paused a moment and looked past her, seeing something she couldn't see, something that pleased him, something he wanted very much. "It's a beautiful old keep called Thispen-Ladock, owned by a man named Sir Thomas Ladock. It's not all that large and impressive, but Sir Thomas has no son or grandson. He has promised to sell it to me.

"The area around the keep is scarcely peopled. I want to build and charter a town and bring tradesmen there and farmers and blacksmiths." He broke off suddenly and closed his mouth. "I speak too freely." And too passionately, he added to himself.

"We will leave on the morrow."

"As you will," she said.

He rose. "I must return to the king to see what other pleasures he's planned for me. How sets your stomach?"

"I'm fine now."

He stood there frowning down at her. "Will you be able to travel?"

Was there another choice? she wondered. Would he leave her here? Drop her in a ditch somewhere? "Aye, I'll be fine."

He looked at her a moment longer, feeling uncertain, feeling guilt that she would have to travel, feeling resentment that he would have to go slowly so she wouldn't become too ill.

He said from the doorway, "Sleep now. I won't bother you tonight. I will go to argue with the king once again, but I don't think he will change his mind. He is the most stubborn man in all of England. He insists that someone will try to slit my throat unless I go directly to Cornwall, and he doesn't want that to happen until after I have sired my first —" His voice disappeared in a low curse. He was silent as death, and so was she. "We will leave early, if it pleases you."

She wondered, once he'd gone, what he would have done if she'd told him it didn't please her at all. So the king believed her a liar as well. It didn't particularly surprise her. He was a man, after all. Her stomach twisted suddenly and she tensed. Then her muscles eased again. She fell asleep still clothed and dreamed of her mother, abused by her uncle. What was she to do about her mother?

13

The morning air was thick with fog. Daria, bundled to her chin in one of her winter cloaks, waited silently for Roland to finish speaking to the king.

She'd already said good-bye to the queen, kissing Eleanor's hand as she curtsied deeply and thanking her with great sincerity for her care and advice. The queen had even prepared a large vial of the herb drink should she become ill again.

"You will be patient with Roland," the queen had said, hugging her, wishing she could spare her pain but knowing that she couldn't. She would pray that the babe closely resembled Roland; there was naught else she could do. "He is a proud man, loyal, and sound in judgment save, it appears, in the matters of the heart. I heard it said that once, many years before, he gave his heart to a girl who betrayed him. I know no more than that. My lord told me that, saying that Roland had been miserably unhappy at the time, and had confided only that much. It must have soured him, my lord said." She looked smug as she said that, pleased that her husband, King of England though he be, was faithful to her and only to her. Daria nearly burst out that the girl had been Joan of Tenesby, but she held her tongue. Roland wouldn't thank her to tell his secrets.

The queen added, "When you arrive in Cornwall I hope you will visit St. Erth Castle. It is where my husband's daughter lives with her husband, Dienwald de Fortenberry. Philippa is a sweet but spirited child and plants gray hairs in her husband's head. It will be your husband's decision, of course, to select where you will reside until he has managed to purchase this keep of his."

"He just told me of Thispen-Ladock last evening."

The queen said comfortably, "Worry not that he is closemouthed. He isn't in the habit of confiding in others. Roland will come to tell you many things before long. I am pleased the earl did not resist returning the clothing and household goods that you were carrying to Colchester when he abducted you. You and your Roland will be finely prepared once you move into your new keep."

Daria glanced back now, seeing that the pack mules disappeared into the fog, so thick it was. She did bring Roland many things for his new keep. She didn't bring him only herself. No, indeed, she brought him more coin than he needed, and rich furnishings, for at the time he was planning for her to wed with Colchester, her uncle's pride had been at stake. She remembered Roland's sour look at the sight of all the goods half an hour before. She'd wanted to slap him when he said, "I feel like a greedy merchant, traveling about with all my wares. Mayhap I can sell some of this to Graelam."

"The goods are mine," she'd said instead, so furious she was pale with it. "Don't you dare speak of selling what is mine. Some of the materials were stitched by my own mother."

He had looked up at her then, astride her mare, and he'd smiled and said, "Nay, sweet wife, you have nothing now. Did you not understand? All you have is a claim to my name and protection, and were I you, Daria, I would believe that both had a very hollow ring. All this rubbish, well, I shall do exactly as I please with it." He'd turned away from her then to speak to the men.

At least her belly was calm this morning, for she'd drunk some sweet goat's milk and eaten a piece of soft white bread. For that she was thankful. She allowed herself to know some excitement. After all, regardless of what Roland said or did, she was beginning a new life, one she hadn't known would exist such a short time before.

"Are you ready, Daria?"

She gave him a temperate smile. "Thank you for getting Henrietta for me," she said, patting her mare's neck as she spoke. She realized then that Roland wasn't looking at her, rather he was testing and pulling at the straps on her saddle. He looked up at her now as he also stroked her mare's neck, his fingers touching hers. "Your Henrietta is as fat as Cantor. No matter, both of them will be strong and lean within the week. You will tell me if you feel ill."

"Yes."

He lightly touched his hand to her thigh, nodded, and strode to the head of their small cavalcade. Daria turned and waved toward the keep. The queen, in her endless kindness, was very likely still gazing at her from one of the castle windows. She waved even as they rode from the inner bailey of

Tyberton. At the last moment, she turned again, and her eyes met the Earl of Clare's. There was no expression on his face; but his eyes — she flinched at the fury she saw in them. She shook off the bolt of panic she felt. After all, he had nothing more to do with her life. He couldn't harm her now. He couldn't strike her ever again. And, after all, if he hadn't abducted her, hadn't brought her to Tyberton, well then, she would never have met Roland. The vagaries of fate were something to think about.

The fog burned off within three hours and the day grew warm. Much to the men's surprise, Roland called a halt. He gave them no explanation, merely rode to where Daria sat her mare and pulled his destrier in beside her. He said nothing, just looked at her.

"Would you like to rest for a few minutes? Relieve yourself?"

She nodded.

"Which? Or both?"

She gave him a look and simply nodded again. He laughed, dismounted his horse, and clasped her about her waist, lifting her from her mare's back. "Are you certain you don't miss the old woman? I could send one of my men back to Tyberton for her if you wish it."

"Nay, she frightens me now. She is no

longer steady in her thinking. The earl won't harm her."

"Very well. There will likely be a willing wench to assist you once we reach Thispen-Ladock. Tell me when you are ready to leave again." He turned away to leave her in privacy.

Daria remembered the old woman's mumblings of the previous evening when she'd slipped into the bedchamber. She didn't cease shaking her head, back and forth, back and forth, as if she had no control over her own movement. "He's not an earl," Ena had said in her sour old voice, plucking up her skirts and shaking her head again. "He's a rogue, not to be trusted, at least not with you, little mistress."

"That's nonsense and I'll be pleased to hear no more from you!" The old woman merely scowled at her and took herself out of the bedchamber. Daria sighed. Just moments later, Ena had slipped back into the chamber and called out, her voice even more sour and shrill, "Not even an earl, and yet ye wedded him! Shame on ye, little mistress! Ye jest wanted a pretty face. Now, the Earl of Clare — he was a fine man . . . a bit rough, but it is as a man should be, not all kind and soft like yer pretty priest . . ."

Daria shut out the memory of Ena's

words. She turned and walked back to the horses. She wanted to sit beneath a tree and lean back and close her eyes, but she knew that Roland was likely pacing in his wish to be gone. She stretched, lightly touched her fingers to her flat belly. "I'm ready, Roland," she called out.

But it was Salin, a seasoned warrior of some thirty-odd years, who came to lift her back onto Henrietta's back. His face was intelligent and ugly, his hair thick and dark brown, curling around his large ears. He looked fierce and mean, but his voice was gentle.

"If you wish to stop again, mistress, you have but to call out to me."

"Thank you, Salin."

As she rode behind her husband, their pace slow and steady, Daria thought back to what Ena said once Daria had convinced the old woman to tell her what had happened to Tilda after she and Roland had left her in Daria's place.

" 'Twas a pity," the old woman said. "Aye, a rare pity, and the earl struck her hard, not on her face, for even he thought her beautiful, but he smashed his fist in her chest and cracked a rib, I think, by the screeches from the little slut. He knew it wasn't you, oh aye, right away he knew, and he struck her. The priest — a little worm with no guts — he said naught, merely stood there wringing his dirty hands. The earl then pulled the girl from the great hall and dragged her to his bedchamber. He plowed her good. Her cries were loud, and then there was nothing." Ena had spit then, a habit Daria hadn't noticed before. "She deserved it, of course, the little harlot. You should never have left, little mistress. The earl wouldn't have struck you."

Daria felt bile rise in her throat. She'd been so unthinking, so selfish, and all the while that poor girl was lying somewhere within the castle walls in pain.

"Aye, then the earl told her — leastwise that's what I heard one of his men saying — if she pleased him, he'd keep her, but only if she kept her cries behind her teeth. One of the women bandaged her ribs for her. I hid and he forgot about me," Ena added, her voice filled with her own cunning.

Daria felt the shift in the air. The hot summer breeze had cooled considerably, and black clouds were gathering overhead. It would rain, just as it had in Wales. She realized she viewed the coming rain with little dread, so used to the wet Wales days and nights she'd become during that short week with Roland. But the endless rain had made

Roland ill. Her brow furrowed with worry for him.

"What bothers you, Daria?"

She smiled at him, unable not to even though his voice was temperate at best. "It will rain, and I was remembering Wales." Her frown reappeared. "I was remembering that you sickened in all that rain."

"It wasn't the rain that sickened me."

She cocked her head to one side in question.

"I gave you my last tunic and thus wore a damp one for three days. The wet sank into my chest."

"You shouldn't have given me the tunic."

"Probably not, but I did. How do you feel?"

"I'm fine."

He rode beside her, silent now. But she felt the tension building up in him. She waited for his attack, knowing it was coming. Finally he said, "Why did you become ill so suddenly? You said you'd felt nothing before, no sickness of any kind, nothing at all. I don't understand how it could strike you with no warning, and then only after you learned you carried a babe."

"I wondered that as well. The queen said it was probably because I'd been so worried, so drawn into myself with other matters.

Once I knew about the babe, once I'd accepted it and recognized its presence, then my body acted as it should."

He only nodded. It would be foolish of him to begin an argument about what the queen herself had said. "There's a Cistercian abbey about three miles ahead. We will beg shelter there for the night."

The abbey was as old as the gnarled oaks that circled its perimeter. Jagged shards of stone were falling from the walls to lie on the fallow ground, unheeded and dangerous to the unwary. When a brother appeared at the front gate, Roland dismounted and spoke to him. Within minutes another came and motioned Daria to follow him. She looked at Roland, but he only nodded to her. The brother led her to a separate building well apart from the main abbey. It was gray and forbidding, low-roofed, its stone walls jagged and crumbling. They walked through a narrow damp corridor with a rough earthen floor to a small cold cell-chamber. It was more than dismal, it was miserably cold, and Daria found she couldn't stop shivering. The dinner brought to her by another cowled brother, who said nothing at all to her, consisted of a thin broth and hard black bread.

She looked at the broth with its layer of

grease congealed on the top, felt her stomach churn, and turned away to sit on the edge of the cot. The straw in the thin mattress was molded and damp and poked upward. She moved, but there was little relief.

Daria was hungry and cold and thoroughly miserable. Did God want women to be treated so poorly? Was that why they were shunted to dismal cells like these and hidden away? Were women to be punished for some reason she hadn't been taught?

She fell to shivering again, only to look up and see the congealed soup in front of her. Her stomach pitched, for she imagined herself sipping at that disgusting soup, and to her dismay, she heaved up the lunch she'd eaten earlier in the afternoon, barely reaching the cracked earthen pot in time. Her knees throbbed with pain, for she'd skidded on the hard dirt floor in her rush to get to the pot. She remained on her knees, her arms wrapped around her stomach, trying to breathe shallow breaths, to think of other things, to distract herself. In her mind's eye, she saw the farmer who'd helped her and Roland and she saw him horribly mutilated from the torture the Earl of Clare had inflicted on him. The cramps returned with a vengeance, and she retched and retched, her body shuddering with the effort, and she was trembling with weakness.

"Where is the vial the queen gave you?"

Daria didn't look up. She didn't know why he'd come. She wished he hadn't. She wanted to be alone and she wanted to die, by herself. She wanted no onlookers. She started to answer, but another spasm took her and she was beyond speech and thought for many moments.

Roland felt real fear in those moments, watching her shudder and heave with sickness, more fear than he'd felt the previous evening when she'd been ill. He said to Salin, who stood behind him, "Bring some water and clean cloths. Aye, and some decent food, some hot broth." He snorted at the soup on the tray. "If I had to eat that disgusting swill, I would vomit my guts up too. If the brothers say anything amiss, break their necks."

She felt his hands on her shoulders then and she tried to straighten, to show that she had some pride left, but all she could do was hang her head and tremble and shake, weak as an autumn leaf.

"Come," he said, and efficiently lifted her into his arms. Rather than laying her onto the narrow cot, he sat on the cot and held her on his lap. "This damned bed is harder than a moss-scraped rock in Wales."

Then he paused a moment, feeling the chill of the room.

Roland frowned. She couldn't remain here; she would sicken. The abbot had assured him that his wife would be fine, the lying whoreson. What to do? The abbey had such strict rules about females. Did they believe that the sight of a woman would make all the brothers swell with lust?

He felt Daria twist in his arms with another cramp. He held her more loosely, rocking her, telling her it would be all right, soon she would feel better. She quieted and he drew her more closely to his chest. She was shivering violently, and he cursed softly.

"I'll fetch you the queen's medicine now." He laid her on the cot and rose over her. She looked so pale it frightened him. And thin. He supposed he'd be thin too if he vomited all he ate. He shook his head and set himself to looking through her packets. He'd just given her some of the herb medicine when Salin returned.

Daria saw the look on the older man's face. His eyes were filled with pity. She hated it. She turned away, facing the wall.

"You will lie still for a few minutes, Daria, then eat. I don't want the broth to cool. Salin, I wish to speak to you outside."

"One of the brothers told me the chamber's a punishment cell," Salin said matter-of-factly when they were alone. "It's used only when one of the brothers commits a sin. He's whipped, then forced to remain in one of these chambers for several hours, never for an entire night. He would probably have to murder someone to be forced to do that. And as you now know, the chamber is also used for females who have the misfortune of needing to stop here for the night. Your lady will become truly ill if she remains in there."

"Punishment cell," Roland repeated blankly.

"Aye, I asked one of the brothers when you left. He said your wife would sicken but good if you left her here."

"It's raining," Roland said.

"Aye."

"It's their abbey and we can't break their rules, no matter how miserable they are. However, since I can't take her back to the main building, then I shall have to remain here. Fetch me all the extra blankets you can find. And, Salin, say nothing to our hosts."

The older man merely nodded and took his leave. Roland returned to his wife, who still lay on her side facing the grim rough stone wall, her legs drawn up. She hadn't vomited for a while, a good sign, he hoped.

"Now some broth, Daria."

Her only reply was a groan, but he didn't hear it. When she didn't move, he drew her up in his arms and fed her the broth very slowly, watching her expression.

She finally opened her eyes and looked at him, wonder in hers. "I feel just fine now. It is so very odd, this illness. I want to die and then I want to conquer a new land."

"No fights for you this night. I will remain here with you. If it weren't raining, I would stay outside these dismal ruins, but as it is, we must be glad for the shelter."

He continued to feed her and was relieved when the color began to return to her cheeks.

When Salin returned, his arms piled high with blankets, Daria began to smile. Then she giggled, for only his fierce dark eyes showed over the blankets, and Roland, so surprised at the unexpected sound, grinned at her.

He said to Salin, "See that all the men settle in, and don't let any of them do anything to annoy the brothers. If any of the brothers are bothersome, ignore them. The saints know we wouldn't want any of the monks punished and sent here to share the cell with us."

Roland doused the single candle not

many moments later. He lay on his side on the miserably uncomfortable cot and drew Daria against him, feeling her press her bottom against his belly. He bore most of the weight of the blankets. Without thinking, he lightly kissed Daria's ear. "Sleep well," he said, and pulled her even more tightly back against his chest and into the curve of his body.

Daria whispered, "Do you ever snore, Roland? Not just soft sounds, but snorting and blowing like a sickening horse?"

"I don't know. You will tell me."

"You should have to sleep in the same room with Ena. It is a torture in itself. She was once married, you know, many years ago. My mother told me that her husband left her because of the noises she made. He said it wasn't worth having the woman's body if he had to suffer along with it the sounds made by a pig and a horse."

Roland hugged her and she pushed her bottom more firmly against his belly. "Don't do that," he said, his voice sharp with sudden pain. "Don't."

She felt his swelled sex and held herself perfectly still. She didn't want him to humiliate her as he had on their wedding night. The memory of it brought back the pain of his anger, the pain of the shame he'd made her feel. She shook her head even as the thoughts twisted through her mind. She would forget that night. He'd been frustrated and angry and taken it out on her. He'd been kind to her since then. On the heels of those thoughts, Daria wondered if women always sought to excuse men when they behaved like ravening beasts.

Roland woke her immediately the following morning at dawn. The rain had stopped during the night but the sun was hidden behind thick gray clouds.

He was on the point of rolling off the cot, taking Daria with him, when he remembered her condition, and said quickly, "Don't move. Just lie there for a few minutes." He came up on his elbow and looked down at her face in the dim morning light. "What does your belly think this morning?"

"I don't know yet."

"I must go now, but you lie here until Salin brings you some warm milk to drink and some bread."

He eased off the cot, then rose to stand there. She grabbed his sleeve and he turned back to look down at her.

"Thank you, Roland. You are very kind."

His voice was stiff as his back after a night on the sorry cot. "You are my wife. I don't wish you to be excessively uncomfortable."

"Even though you believe it is another man's babe I carry?"

"Sound not bitter, Daria, you have no reason. Rest now, I will see you in a while."

Her stomach remained calm throughout the day. Roland drew their company to a halt every couple of hours, as if he knew almost to the minute when she needed to relieve herself or stretch her back and walk about.

That evening the sky was clear and Roland decided to bypass another abbey whose grim silhouette against the evening sky made even Salin grimace.

"We will camp in that copse of maple trees," he said, and it was done.

He didn't hold her that night, for it was warm and only a mild breeze sifted through the maple leaves overhead. Daria missed him, but she said nothing.

Two days later they mounted a rise, and in the distance Daria saw a beautiful Norman castle, its crenellated towers rising proud and strong above the thick stone walls.

"This is Graelam de Moreton's castle, Wolffeton. We will remain here until I have made our keep ready. His lady's name is Kassia."

"The queen thought you would bring me to St. Erth."

He merely shook his head. "You will

doubtless meet Dienwald and Philippa, but we will stay here for a time."

Daria looked around her. She loved Cornwall; it was savage and bleak and desolate, and it awakened all her senses, the stiff breeze from the sea ruffling her hair, its scent clean and salty. It wasn't a lonely place despite the barren desolation. It warmed her, this region, and she knew it as home.

"Is your keep far from here, Roland?"

"Nay, not far." He watched her breathe in deeply. "You don't mind the ruggedness of this place?"

"Oh, no, not at all, truly."

"Good, since it will be your home."

And she was pleased about that. He saw that she was pleased and wondered at the pleasure and anger it made him feel, both at the same time.

Unfortunately, she was doomed to meet the lord and lady of Wolffeton with her eyes closed and her belly heaving, for no sooner had Roland helped her down from Henrietta's back in the inner bailey of Wolffeton than she was vilely ill. She heard a man's deep voice and a woman's higher one, filled with concern and gentleness. She turned her face into Roland's shoulder and heard him whisper, "Don't be embarrassed. Kassia will see to your comfort."

Not ten minutes later, Daria was alone in a spacious chamber filled with bright light from three window slits, its stone floor covered with a supple wool rug from Flanders. The bed upon which she lay was so soft she sighed with delight, able to ignore her churning belly for a few moments.

She heard the woman say to her, "If you are ill again, the chamber pot is right here. Roland tells me you have some potion from the queen herself. Your husband is fetching it for you."

The woman said nothing more until Daria, her stomach eased, opened her eyes and managed to smile.

"My name is Kassia and I'm pleased that Roland has wedded and that you will remain with us for a while. And you are with child! How very fortunate you are. My own babe is but a month old. His name is Harry and he looks just like his dark-visaged warrior of a father. It's not fair, but of course Graelam merely grins in that superior way of his and says he is the stronger and thus his son must resemble him in all ways."

"It is good that he looks like his father," Daria said. "The child is lucky as well. His father will acknowledge him."

Kassia de Moreton, lady of Wolffeton, thought this a rather odd thing to say. She

317

cocked her head to one side in silent question. The young woman lying on her back, her face as pale as the white wimple that covered Kassia's hair, said nothing more. Her lips had become thin and Kassia worried that she would be ill again.

But Daria wasn't ill; her thoughts were bleak. She wanted to cry, but that solved naught. She could see her mother weeping silently, her hands covering her face, weeping that meant nothing to anyone, and certainly never changed anything.

"Would you like some warm ale, Daria?"

She forced a smile to her lips. "Aye, and I thank you."

"Please, call me Kassia."

Downstairs in Wolffeton's great hall, Kassia de Moreton said to her husband, "What do you make of all this, my lord?"

"Of Roland and his new wife? Why, I should like to see her when her face isn't green and when she isn't shuddering with illness."

"She is with child."

"Aye, Roland told me. Odd, the way he said it. Not the way a man should, I don't think."

"You mean, my lord, he didn't begin to strut about like a smug cock with his announcement?"

But Graelam didn't return her humor

with his own. He shook his head, looking thoughtful. "Something is amiss. Do you mind keeping the girl here whilst Roland travels to his keep — rather the keep he will soon own?"

"Not at all."

Later in the afternoon, Daria, embarrassed at her illness, emerged from the chamber feeling as wonderful as she had when Roland had become her husband. She was walking down the winding stone stairs when she met him coming up. She stood on the step above him.

He said nothing for a few moments, studying her face.

"I'm fine," she said quickly. "I'm sorry. This illness, it annoys me."

He still remained silent. Then he stepped up onto the step with her, pressing her against the stone wall. He felt the length of her legs, her soft belly, her breasts flattening against his chest. He raised his hand and absently began caressing the line of her jaw.

Daria began to tremble. She couldn't help it. She closed her eyes and leaned into him, wishing he would close his arms around her, wishing he would kiss her and tell her that he'd missed her and wanted her. "Roland," she said.

Roland said nothing.

He continued to stroke her jaw with his callused fingertip. When she unconsciously leaned her face against his hand, he withdrew, turned, and left her. He called over his shoulder, "If you are well enough, there is food for you in the great hall."

The main meal of the day at Wolffeton Castle was served in the late afternoon. The sun still shone outside, for it was deep summer. The hall was filled with laughter and jesting and howls of outraged humor.

Daria sat beside her husband, picking at her food. The herring was delicious, she knew it, but she was afraid to eat because she didn't want to become ill again, at least not today.

She heard Lord Graelam speaking to Roland about the king and his grandiose plans for castle-building in Wales. "So he is now visiting all the Marcher Barons. Eating them down to bare granaries and assessing their strength. Edward has always employed sound strategies."

Kassia turned to her new guest. "Try eating some of this soft bread soaked in the milk."

"I feel wonderful, truly, it's just that I wish to continue feeling this way. I don't like Roland to see me when . . . well, he is very kind about it, but . . ." Her voice dropped into nothing.

"But nothing," Kassia said briskly. "Now, tell me of your adventures. I overheard just a bit, and wish to know everything."

The evening passed pleasantly. Daria had begun to relax and to smile again. When Kassia excused herself to feed her babe, Harry, Roland turned to his wife and said, "Are you fatigued? Would you like to retire now?"

She nodded, feeling weariness tug at her.

Roland looked down at his empty trencher and said, "I will come to you tonight, since you are well. Prepare yourself for me. You belong to me, and if you aren't ill, then I wish to treat you as a man does his wife."

She hated the coldness of this, hated the man he became when he remembered himself her husband.

"What do you mean that I am *to prepare myself?* Do you wish me to stand naked in the middle of the chamber when you enter? Do you wish me to lie on my back with my legs parted? What is it you wish, Roland?"

He sucked in his breath, surprised at her attack. He wouldn't allow her sarcasm at his expense. "I wish you to cease your insolence, Daria. What I meant was simply that you know I intend to take you tonight, so be prepared for it."

"Will you treat me as you did on our wedding night or will you be gentle and tender and call me by another woman's name?"

"There was no other night save our wedding night, damn you! Lie no more, Daria, it annoys me!"

"Then you won't be gentle. You will take me without speaking a kind word to me. You will treat me like a slut who deserves naught else but your contempt."

He leaned close to her, for her voice had risen. "Speak softly, wife. I have no wish for our host to wonder why you become the shrew."

She rose, not waiting for him or one of the servants to assist her. She hissed down at him, "I won't *prepare* myself, Roland, as you so sweetly say it. I don't want you to come to me; I don't want you to treat me like a convenient body to be used by you. Sleep you with one of the castle wenches, I care not!"

She swept from the dais, leaving her husband to stare after her, half of him wanting to thrash her, the other half wanting to rip off her clothing and caress her and kiss her until she screamed for him to come into her.

Under his breath he said, "Damned unreasonable wench."

"I believe I have told you before, Roland, that women are the very devil."

Roland looked at the fierce warrior who sat on his right side and grinned reluctantly. "Your lady is sweet and guileless and tender as a ripe peach. You cannot mean her."

"No, but I did, at one time. 'Twas not too long ago. I misjudged her severely. I hurt her repeatedly. Now I would sever mine own arm before I would see her sprain her little finger."

Roland had nothing to say to that. He merely raised an incredulous brow.

"Your wife is upset — nay, she is but a bride. You are wedded less than a week. She isn't at all uncomely, Roland, and I assume that you found her much to your liking, since she is with child. So —"

"I don't wish to speak of the babe or of her."

"Ah, you simply wish to bend her to your will?"

" 'Tis a beginning. I begin to believe her well-broken, then she flings her sarcasm at my head. I like it not."

"The problem, Roland, is that a man's will seems to shift and change with the passing minutes and hours, particularly if the lady resides in his mind or in his spirit."

"I simply desire her, that is all. She resides nowhere, certainly not within any part of me. Any female would do just as well. Any female would probably do better, since Daria is so ignorant, she must be instructed to . . . well . . ."

To Roland's relief, Graelam de Moreton held his peace. Indeed, he turned to speak to his steward, a craggy-faced man named Blount.

Roland drank another flagon of ale in splendid silence, left to himself by his host. He chewed over his own feelings of ill use at the hands of a female who should be babbling her gratitude to him, who should be fully aware that she would be lying dead in a ditch if it weren't for his generosity. By all the saints, he'd tended her with compassion whenever she'd been ill. And here was Graelam quoting pithy words that were likely from some minstrel's lay. At last he bade his lord and lady a good night and strode from the great hall, his destination his wife's bed.

There would be no sarcasm from her mouth when he covered her.

14

Daria sat on a narrow chair close to one of the window slits. The night was clear, a half-moon glowing through an occasional cloud. A breeze cooled her brow. There was a lone dog in the inner bailey below. He occasionally raised his head and barked when a soldier strode by on his way to the Wolffeton barracks. Time passed.

Daria knew he would come to her eventually, so she wasn't startled when the chamber door opened and then quietly closed. Nor did she move.

She didn't wait for him to command her, but said only, not turning to face him, "I mean it, Roland. You will not shame me again." She was pleased her voice sounded firm in the silent chamber. She desperately wanted to look at him, to see if the expression on his face had gentled. His words told her of his expression as he said calmly, "I will do just as I please with you, Daria. You are my wife, my chattel, my possession. And what I please to do with you now is plow your belly."

She was glad that she wasn't facing him. She felt the night breeze flutter through the tendrils of hair on her forehead, felt the softness of the night on her face. "I remember the first time — I loved you so very much, you see, and there was nothing on this earth I wouldn't have done for you. I was terrified that you would die, terrified that you would be gone from me when I'd just found you. I wanted you, all of you, and that night I knew that you would teach me what it was like to be joined to the man I loved, and I was happy. When you were fevered and wanted me —"

"Nay, I have never wanted you," he said, and was thankful she hadn't turned, for she would see the lie in his eyes.

"Very well, you wanted that woman Lila. You didn't hurt me overly, even in your urgency, and I remember those feelings that were building deep inside me, low in my belly, I think, but then when you came into me, there was pain and the feelings left me." Now she turned to face him, her head cocked to one side in question.

"Were those feelings real, Roland? This woman's pleasure you speak about, is it real? I have wondered."

"When you take a lover, perhaps you will learn the answer."

She continued as if he hadn't spoken. "Then, just as you were about to spill your seed inside me, you stared up at me and your hands tightened about my waist, and in that instant I thought you recognized me, knew *me*, knew that you were joined to *me*, not that woman Lila."

Daria shrugged and turned back to the window slit. "Perhaps I was wrong; perhaps I wanted so much for you to whisper my name, to moan that you loved me. Perhaps you will never remember that instant in time when you were with me, when we were together, when you belonged to me —"

He laughed, a low, mocking laugh. "Remember a moment of time that is naught but an elaborate fancy of yours? A fabric you have woven of unreal cloth? If I remember aright, you say that you bathed my sex and groin afterward, that you — my embarrassed little virgin — wiped me free of your blood and my man's seed."

"That's right. There was no embarrassment. I'd cared for you because you were ill, and I loved you. Aye, I bathed you because I didn't want you to wonder and perhaps guess what had happened between us, and feel guilt and obligation for me. As I told you, it was my decision to give myself to you, and thus the responsibility was mine. But then it all went awry. For that, Roland, I am truly sorry. But the child, *our* child . . . I just wanted —"

He sliced his hand through the air. "Enough of your prattle, Daria. The saints know you've gotten exactly what you wanted, though I cannot see that I am such a prize to any woman. So you have me and my name; your child will have my name. And if it is a male child you birth, why, then, I will have my honor shoved down my throat to the day I die."

"Roland, would you have still not wanted to marry me if I had not been with child?"

He stared at her, for a moment non-plussed. He held himself silent over the words that wanted to pour out of his mouth. He said then, quietly, "If the king had still insisted that I marry you, then yes, I would have."

"And you would have been kinder to me when you took me?"

"Enough of this! I will hear no more of your ridiculous surmises, Daria. I will tell you that now — this instant — I want nothing more than to sink into your soft woman's flesh. Remove your clothing and lie on the bed. Be fast about it, I have not had a woman in a long time."

"You had me not very long ago."

"That duty hardly counted. It was a simple rutting, a coupling to be endured, little more. Perhaps I shall take my time this night and plow you until I am sated on your skinny body."

"No."

He walked to her then and very gently clasped her upper arms in his hands. He turned her around until she was facing him. His breath was warm on her face. His voice was as cold as his eyes as he said, "Never will you refuse me. Never."

"I'm refusing you now, Roland. I must. I cannot allow you to grind me beneath your heel, I cannot allow you to treat me like I'm worth naught but an afterthought."

"I'm the one ground down, Daria. There is a proverb my father used to throw into the breach at odd moments: and that is, a man must begin as he means to go on. You will not gainsay me; you will not willfully disobey me in anything. I won't tolerate that. I have paid too dear to allow it. I will force you, Daria, if you continue to refuse me."

She didn't move. Then, suddenly, she jerked free of him and dashed to the chamber door. She heard the chair crash to the floor, heard him trip over it. She was through the door in an instant, his flung-out arm missing her shoulder by inches.

"Where will you go?" he yelled after her. "You stupid girl, where will you go?"

He heard her dashing footsteps on the winding stone stairs. He heard a loud cry and a thud. His heart heaved to his throat, and he dashed to the top of the steps just outside the bedchamber door. He took them two at a time, nearly falling himself in his haste. Around the curve of the stairs, he saw Salin, consternation writ on his ugly face, bending down to where Daria lay slumped against the stair wall.

"What happened?"

"She flew into me," Salin said. "Then she bounced back and struck her head against the stone." He waited for Roland to rush to his wife, but he didn't come any nearer. He waited another few moments, then leaned down and picked her up. She was conscious now but her eyes were vague on his face.

"You're all right, little mistress," he said. "You just knocked the breath from yourself and lightly coshed your head." Salin didn't wait for a word from his master. He carried Daria into the chamber and laid her gently on the bed.

"Shall I fetch Lord Graelam's leech?"

"Nay. I shall see to her." Roland waited until Salin saw himself out, and then turned to close and lock the chamber door.

He returned to his dazed wife, methodically felt her arms and legs, then just as methodically began to remove her clothes. She gave him no fight now.

"I struck my head. It hurts dreadfully."

"I heard the crack, but there is naught but a small bruise forming. You're too stubborn to be sorely hurt by a knock on your head. If it hurts you, well, then, you deserve it, I should say."

"Will you force me now, Roland?"

He stilled, frowning down at her. "I don't want you; I should have to think of other women in splendid detail if I wished to regain my desire. As for stiffening my rod, I don't think it possible, at least not with you."

Still he continued to pull off her clothing. When she lay on her back, naked, he rose and simply stared down at her. He studied her, stroking his fingertips over his jaw, his expression one of indifference. "You're so very flat. 'Tis hard to believe a babe lies in that skinny belly of yours. Mayhap the father was a dwarf."

She lurched up, grabbed the half-filled

carafe from the table beside the bed, and flung it at him. It struck his chest, splashing a wide arc of water up onto his face.

But it cost her dearly, and she turned away, her eyes closed against the pain in her head. She cared not at the moment whether he would seek retribution or not. All had gone wrong. She heard him suck in his breath; then there was nothing. Finally she heard his footsteps going toward the chamber door. He said as he unlocked and opened the door, "I am leaving on the morrow. You will remain here with Lord Graelam and Lady Kassia. They will take care of you."

She sat up quickly, her heart pounding as fiercely as her head. He would leave her! "I would go with you, Roland. Please, take me with you, don't leave me here, it's not right. I'm your wife! You go to purchase your keep, do you not? I shan't be a problem for you. I won't be ill, I swear it. Surely you will need me, surely —"

"Need you? I need no sickly female to slow me down. You can't control when you vomit."

He didn't look at her again, merely walked from the chamber. She heard him say through the partially closed door, "Cover yourself. The sight of your breasts does nothing in particular for me, but one never knows. Some of Lord Graelam's men might be less fastidious than I."

Daria slowly pulled the covers over herself. Her head pounded from the blow she'd managed to give herself. At least it had kept him away from her, kept him from using her as a man would use a vessel from which to drink and slake his thirst.

He was leaving. Without her. She wondered if he would ever return for her.

She felt nausea, hot and urgent, well up in her. Her head forgotten, she leapt from the bed, making the chamber pot just in time.

Daria was awake when Roland left the following morning at dawn. She'd been awake for countless hours. She stood wrapped in her bedrobe, watching from one of the window slits as he mounted Cantor, spoke further to Lord Graelam, then finally motioned his men through the raised portcullis. As if she willed it to be, at the last moment he turned to look up. She waved to him frantically, wanting to call after him, wanting to beg him to take her with him . . . He turned back again, his expression never having changed at the sight of her.

Daria didn't leave her post at the window. He was going to his keep and purchase it with her dowry. Well, at least her father's vast wealth was bringing a measure of pleasure to someone other than her cursed uncle Damon.

She stood there a very long time. She was still standing there even as the inner bailey of Wolffeton began to fill with people at their work. There were so many people, so many animals everywhere, cows and dogs and pigs. But it wasn't at all like Tyberton or her uncle's castle, Reymerstone. She realized it was because the people were boisterous, loud. They were shouting at the top of their lungs and arguing and abusing each other. And they were laughing. Aye, that was it. The folk weren't doing their work with sullen faces and slumped shoulders and empty eyes. They were insulting each other in great good humor. Daria continued to watch. She wondered at the differences.

Then she saw Lady Kassia de Moreton, her likely unwilling hostess, emerge from the great hall. She was wearing an old gown and a white wool cloth over her head. She looked for all the world like another of the serving wenches. Behind her was an older man with a besotted grin on his face. He was carrying two trays piled high with sweet-smelling pastries, honey and almond, Daria thought, sniffing, her mouth suddenly watering. To her astonishment, Lady Kassia paused, gazed around the noisy den, then whistled as loud as any soldier. Within moments she and the older man were surrounded by the castle folk and their hands were swarming over the warm pastries on the trays.

Daria wished she could whistle like that. She could let it loose in Roland's ear when he next annoyed her. Daria smiled. It felt odd to smile, she realized, and forced herself to smile even more widely. She would very much like one of those warm pastries.

If her hostess was unwilling, Daria saw no sign of it. At the sight of her, Kassia smiled, waved her hand for her to come to her, then jerked off her white kerchief with the next movement of her hand. She looked like a small graceful dervish, her skirts twirling, her wide sleeves flying away from her wrists.

"Come, Daria, I've saved one of Cook's pastries for you. Yes, sit there and eat. Truly, you must break your fast, 'twill keep your stomach settled. Oh, my dear, you look tired. Did you not rest well? Your lord left very early this morning. You miss him, I suspect. Well, Roland is a handsome lout. When you've eaten, I will present my Harry to you and you must promise me to proclaim him the most beautiful babe in Christendom. He looks like his hulking father, which I insist isn't at all fair, but alas, no one heeds me. Ah, but I told you that already, didn't I? My lord is always telling me to slow down in my speech for I repeat myself."

Daria had no chance to reply to this outpouring, for Kassia had swept away from her, humming beneath her breath, speaking to the serving wenches, laughing, calling for more food for their guest.

By the afternoon Daria wanted to weep with sheer loneliness. How she could be lonely in a castle filled with people who were nothing but kind to her, she couldn't have said, but she was nevertheless. She spent time with Harry, duly complimenting him to his proud mother. He was a beautiful baby, and when she held him, she felt tears sting her eyes. Her babe — Roland's babe — would never know a father's pride. He would know only indifferent kindness at best and coldness at the worst. Roland would never be physically cruel. She knew that, though she didn't know how she knew it. He had certainly changed toward her.

She turned from her post on the eastern ramparts of Wolffeton Castle. There, in front of her, stood the lord of Wolffeton himself, Graelam de Moreton. She felt a shock of fear at his size, for he was a large man, a warrior of great skill she'd heard Roland say, and his expression wasn't naturally one of gentleness. He looked forbidding and ruthless. She thought of him with the slight gentle Kassia and wondered at it.

"You must be careful," were Graelam's first words to her. "Forgive me for startling you, Daria, but you must take care. You carry a babe, and the walkway here isn't all that wide."

He'd come to the ramparts to caution her to take care? She nodded solemnly. "Thank you, my lord."

Graelam turned to look out toward the sea. "Roland won't be gone long, not more than a sennight, I doubt. Then he will return and carry you back to his keep with him."

Only if he were forced to, she thought, but said only, "Where is this keep, my lord?"

His dark brow raised in surprise at her ignorance, but his voice was calm enough as he said, "Not more than fifteen miles to the northeast of Wolffeton. It's a tidy keep, not sprawling and dominating like Wolffeton with its sheer size, but still it is a home that will see the de Tournay line through many years. Roland is disappointed that it isn't closer to the sea, for he likes the smell of the salt and the feel of the sea winds on his face. The man whose family has held it for many years is old now and tired and has no male heirs. He was great friends with Roland's father and he wishes Roland to have the keep."

"I know it is called Thispen-Ladock and owned by Sir Thomas Ladock."

"Aye, combining the names of the two major families who have owned it since the time of William — and it is between the small villages of Killivose and Ennis. The largest village is Perranporth on the northern coast. Didn't Roland tell you of the keep and its location?"

She merely shook her head, and Graelam continued after a thoughtful moment. "There is little chance of invasion, thus there is little need for vast fortifications. There is little more than peace now, endless peace that drives a man distracted."

She laughed at his mournful tone and he stared at her, then grinned. "Mayhap I should move my family to the Welsh borders. The spirit of fighting always resides there."

"But only until King Edward manages to clip the wings of all the Marcher Barons, and he's determined to do it. Aye, he wants to begin his castle building as soon as possible. I fear we are to be cursed with naught but peace in the future."

"Despite Edward's plans, I don't agree. Englishmen and Frenchmen love nothing more than a violent dispute, and if there isn't a likely one in the offing, they will invent it and then they will rally about to bash heads. Don't forget the Scots or the Irish. They'd as soon cleave an Englishman's chest as speak to him. Now, allow me to assist you off this precarious perch. My Kassia sent me up here to be the knight to your damsel."

My Kassia.

That sounded very nice; it also sounded incongruous coming from a man who could with a single sword cleave a man and his horse in two. *My Kassia.*

To Daria's utter dismay, she burst into tears. She covered her face with her hands, so humiliated she couldn't bear it, yet the tears kept coming and she was gasping for breath as she tried to still them. She felt him then, standing before her for a moment, blocking out the warm sun; then his arms went around her and he drew her to him. His arms were gentle and his hand was even more gentle as he pressed her head to his shoulder.

" 'Tis the babe that upsets you so unexpectedly. You mustn't be ashamed, Daria, 'twill pass, you will see. My sweet Kassia suffered bouts of very strange feelings, some of them making me want to weep, others making me hold my sides with laughter."

" 'Tis not the babe!"

"Oh?"

" 'Tis Roland, my husband — the man who scorns me, the man who feels nothing but contempt for me, the man who wedded me because the king commanded it!"

Graelam had not a word to say to that. He wished devoutly that he was on the ground at this moment and his wife was magically in his place. He felt awash with protective feelings that he had no business feeling. He could still think of nothing to say to her. Her sobs had quieted but her shoulders still quivered.

"I'm sorry," he heard himself say. "Everything will be better soon." By all the saints, his thinking continued, 'twas a stupid, loutish thing to say, meaningless all in all. When he was nearing despair, she sniffed, trying to gain control of herself.

"No, 'tis I who am the sorry one," she said, wiping her eyes with her fisted hands as would a child. But she wasn't a child; she was a woman grown, who was married and carried a babe in her womb.

"Come," he said, inspiration returned. "Let us go to the great hall. Kassia will give you a goblet of milk. Aye, that will make you feel better."

When Kassia saw her husband's anguished look, she immediately set aside her task of the moment and shooed him willingly away. She escorted Daria to her chamber, scolding her all the way. "Now, you will tell me what is the matter with you. I will fix it if I can, even though my husband is always exhorting me to keep my tongue still and away from others' problems. Come, speak to me, Daria."

But Daria couldn't get the words out. Pride and misery stuck them in her throat. She remembered her unmeasured outburst to Lord Graelam and wished she could sink into the stone floor. She simply shook her head. " 'Tis but the babe," she said, "nothing more, just the babe," and Kassia knew with those few words that there would be no more forthcoming.

"Very well. You need to rest now. I will visit you later with some sweet white bread and some ale, or if you feel well enough, you can come to the great hall. We will see."

Daria, alone again, retreated to her bed and dutifully lay down. She lay there unmoving for a very long time. She was, after all, quite used to being by herself. Odd, though, how all the hours she'd spent alone hadn't taught her patience and serenity. When Daria finally rose, it was evening, and Kassia came for her with a smile. Daria managed one in return and followed her hostess to the great hall.

It was during the long night that followed that Daria came to a decision. Early the following morning, she approached Lord Graelam.

"My lord, I wish a favor from you. I ask that you lend me several of your men."

This was a surprise. Graelam looked closely at the girl standing in front of him, stiff and straight-backed. She was thin, pale, and looked resolute as a mule. "You wish to go somewhere?"

"Aye. I wish to go to my husband's keep. My place is with him, not here with you, a charge on your good nature. He will accept me; he must, for he is my husband. May I please borrow some men?"

What man could deny her such a request? But he shook his head; he'd promised Roland to keep his wife safe. Sending her off with some of his men, even though the area was secure to the best of his knowledge, wasn't what Roland would expect of him. "I'm sorry, but I cannot. You must remain here at Wolffeton until Roland returns for you."

If Roland returns, she thought, and turned away. His refusal was nothing more than she'd expected. He was a man of honor — and a man's honor only extended to another man, never to a woman.

She kept a smile on her face throughout the morning. Early in the afternoon she approached Kassia. "I wish to exercise my mare, Henrietta. Should I take a groom with me?"

It was the perfect approach and she caught Kassia off-guard. For a dreadful moment Daria feared that Kassia, rallying quickly, would insist upon accompanying her, but just as the request was about to issue forth from her mouth, a nurse came into the great hall with a squalling Harry in her arms.

Daria, two young grooms in attendance, rode from Wolffeton within the hour. She was careful that Lord Graelam was well-occupied on Wolffeton's vast training field and thus didn't see her leave.

The afternoon was hot, with the sun beating down overhead, but Daria didn't mind. She told her two grooms that she wished to ride northward along the rugged coast. Because they didn't know what was in her mind, they willingly agreed.

Daria stared at the stunted trees that grew close to the sea. The continuous sharp pounding gale winds bent them nearly double. They would veer eastward soon, she reckoned, near Perranporth. One of the grooms had obligingly told her of the location of her husband's keep, Thispen-Ladock. They had answered her guile and questions with prompt smiles and answers. She had fifteen miles to ride. She wasn't certain how long a time that would take, but she would do it. Her immediate problem was how to rid herself of Graelam de Moreton's two men now that she knew where to ride.

Two hours had passed when Daria, wanting to gnaw on her fingernails, finally called for a halt at the sight of the oak trees. A forest of them, thick and impenetrable. It was her best chance at losing her protectors, and she intended to take it now. She lowered her eyes, resurrecting a modest blush as she told them she had to take her ease for a few minutes in the copse of twisted oak trees.

They looked at each other but said nothing. They could not very well accompany her whilst she relieved herself. Daria thanked them sweetly, then dismounted Henrietta. She looked over her shoulder as she entered the forest, to see the men walking their horses, speaking intently to each other. She smiled. They'd believed her.

She walked Henrietta a good fifty feet into the thick forest, then quietly mounted again. She would be well gone before they realized she'd escaped them.

They, after all, had no idea that she even wanted to rid herself of them. She nudged Henrietta's fat sides and the mare quickened her pace, following the narrow trail through the forest.

Daria heard shouts, but they were far, far behind her. She saw the thinning of the oaks and knew that soon they would be through the forest, and Henrietta, if she hadn't grown too fat and lazy, would easily outdistance the grooms, even if they decided to try to follow her.

She rode another hour, finally slowing her mare's pace when she became winded. The salt air was harsh and wonderful against her face and the smells of the moss and the trees and the sea itself reminded her of Wales.

She saw a rough wooden sign to her left that was printed crudely: PERRANPORTH. She'd made good time. She decided to skirt the fishing village, just in case someone should try to stop her. She was a female alone, and she knew well enough what could happen to her.

She was hungry but ignored it.

She cut eastward away from the sea when the sun began to drift down in the distant west. She saw no one. It was as if she were the only one inhabiting this place. At first it comforted her, made her feel safe, but as time passed, she began to worry.

When she saw the smoke rising in the distance, she felt equal amounts of fear and hope. She slowed Henrietta to a walk, letting her pick her way over the rough, jagged-edged rocks. Finally she dismounted, tied her mare to a lone yew bush, and crept closer. It was a camp. She saw several women and about half a dozen men. The women were preparing the evening meal; the men were lounging about on the ground, some of them whittling, others sitting cross-legged, laughing with their comrades, others speaking to the women, their suggestions lewd in the extreme. Daria wondered if they were Gypsies. She'd never seen any, but it seemed possible. Then a large, well-garbed man came into her line of vision. He was fat and jolly-looking, his bald head shining even in the twilight.

He spoke to one of the men, slapped one of the women on her bottom, then reached his hand around and slid his fingers down her tunic. The woman squealed and laughed and rubbed her bottom against him.

Daria drew back.

She would continue on around their camp. She wanted to take no chance that they would try to hurt her or hold her for ransom. She'd spent many months a prisoner and had no intention of spending another moment as one.

She got quietly to her feet and turned to walk back to Henrietta, when the mare, seeing her mistress, raised her head and whinnied loudly.

"Shush! Do be quiet, Henrietta!" Daria ran to her mare and scrambled onto her back.

She wasn't fast enough. She heard shouts and calls and running boots. A man's hands grabbed her ankles and yanked her back down to the ground, catching her around the waist before she fell.

Daria fought. She fought without thinking, without hesitating. She fought as she remembered Roland fighting, with her elbow in the man's throat, her knee in his groin, twisting frantically to keep the man from getting a firm hold on her. The man bellowed with pain and rage as her fingers dug into his shoulder. Another man joined him and her arms were grabbed and pinned to her body.

15

Daria was panting, still wildly jerking and pulling, but the two men had a firm hold on her now. One of them whom she'd managed to gouge in the throat had raised his fist, blood in his eyes, when another man's voice shouted, "Hold, Alan! Don't strike her!"

"She nearly knocked my throat through my neck, the bitch! How could a little wench know how to do that?"

"Don't hit her," the man said again. It was the fat well-garbed man and he was walking as quickly as his bulk would allow toward them.

Daria quieted, trying to calm her heaving breath. She felt the roiling nausea in her belly, but managed to keep down her bile.

"Well, 'tis indeed a charming little pigeon," the fat man said, coming to a halt in front of Daria. "Pretty she is, and young, very young. Who are you, little pigeon?"

Should she tell him? Would she endanger Roland? What to do? He no longer looked quite so jolly as she'd initially thought when she first saw him.

"No words? I don't think you're a mute, are you?"

She shook her head, then said, "I'm afraid. Your men are hurting my arms."

"True, but you nearly brought my poor Alan low. A man doesn't like to have a woman do such things to him. It humiliates him to the point of violence. Release her, lads, but keep your eyes sharp."

Alan cursed and gave her arm a vicious twist before releasing her.

"Who are you?" the fat man asked again.

"My name is Daria."

"A lovely name, a very nice name withal, but by all the saints, it tells me little. Who is your family?"

"The Earl of Reymerstone is my uncle."

"She's naught but a vain little slut. She made up that name! She's a bitch and a liar!"

"Alan, please, my boy, calm yourself. If she's a liar, then I will return her to your fond embrace. As for her also being a slut and a bitch-well, I don't know if a woman's talents could grant her all that. Just because you haven't heard the name doesn't mean it can't exist. Where does your family live, my girl? Why are you here wandering about all alone? Ah, look at this very fine palfrey. Only fine oats and wheat in her fat belly, not sour swamp grass, I'll wager. You're not an impoverished little pigeon, are you?"

She knew the man could see the lies in her eyes but she couldn't hide her expressions or change them. Finally she blurted out, "I am the guest of Lord Graelam de Moreton! At least I was until early this afternoon."

"Another lie, Master Giles! The little bitch seeks to continue her deceit. I have heard that de Moreton is much pleased with his wife. He wouldn't have a little slut staying there under her nose."

The fat man, Master Giles, didn't chide Alan this time or tell him to be quiet. His eyes narrowed on her face and slowly, very slowly, he raised his arm. His hand was plump and white, too white for a man's hand, Daria thought, vaguely repelled. His fingertips with their longish nails lightly stroked over her throat. She flinched, wanting desperately to jerk away, but she held herself still, trying to remain outwardly calm at least. Suddenly, without any warning, the fat fingers dug with surprising strength back into her neck. The scream that gurgled at the back of her throat was choked down as the awful pain swept through her.

"The truth, little pigeon, or I will rip out your voice from your neck."

He was close to her, and she felt his breath, hot and sweet, on her face. She heard Alan laugh, heard a woman suck in her breath. She felt nausea in the pit of her belly, growing stronger, more insistent, rising, and she couldn't do anything about it this time. "Please . . ." His fingers eased off and she jerked back her head, grabbing her throat, gasping through the burning pain for air.

Then she twisted away, fell hard upon her knees, and vomited.

The fat man looked down at her and his voice was cold with disgust. "When she's finished throwing up her guts, bring her to the camp. I have many more questions for her. Mayhap we have a prize here, a quite valuable prize. And you, Alan, leave her alone; I want none of her pretty flesh bruised, none of her bones twisted. I have a feeling that we're all going to be pleased with her unexpected arrival."

Daria felt a tap on her shoulder. She could picture those fat white fingers and she shuddered, her stomach still roiling wildly.

"If you can hear me, girl, know that I will

have answers from you, true answers, else it won't be a pleasant future for you."

At the moment, Daria couldn't even imagine a future, much less a pleasant one. Her belly cramped and twisted. She remained on her knees, her head down, waiting for the nausea to leave her.

"Hurry up," Alan said, and he kicked her thigh.

"Don't bruise me, you wretched animal, you heard your fat master."

"Ha! More bile in your mouth, eh?" Suddenly he grabbed her elbow and jerked her to her feet. It was pride and nothing else that kept Daria upright.

She would have walked beside him, but he wanted to humiliate her and thus hurried his step, dragging her. She lurched like a drunken sot, trying desperately to keep her balance.

Alan released her when they reached the camp.

"Ah, little pigeon, do sit down." She looked up to see the fat Master Giles sitting on a finely carved chair, chewing on a tremendously large piece of fowl. He looked absurd, sitting there in the midst of a forest, in front of a fire, his ragged men and women around him.

"Who are you?"

"I? Why, I am Master Giles Fountenont, no reason to hide that. I am well-known in these parts — call me a princely fellow, a merchant, a man of a vast array of talents and resources, a man of ample parts as you see, and these are my people, loyal to their bones, all of them. Aren't you, sweetling?" He grasped a passing woman by her arm and pulled her onto his lap. She laughed and turned inward so that he would feed her a bit of the meat. Daria watched her rip off the meat with strong crooked teeth. "Off with you now, and bring this little wench something to eat. I don't want her to starve before I decide what's to be done with her. Aye, she's emptied her belly in fear. We must fill it again."

The woman slid off his fat legs and went to the cook pot that sat amid the fire embers. Master Giles said, "Aye, little pigeon. I am on my way to Truro to my own splendid lodgings there. This" — he waved about the forest — "all this is but a pleasant respite for me."

One of his men grunted and spit out a bone.

The woman brought Daria a thick piece of bread piled high with honey and a goblet of ale. Daria accepted it gratefully. After she'd drunk deeply, Master Giles said,

"Now, the truth, else Alan here will shred your nice gown and acquaint himself with your doubtless lovely body."

Daria didn't want Alan near her. The truth, then; there was no choice. She raised her chin unconsciously as she spoke. "I am wedded to Roland de Tournay. He left me at Wolffeton whilst he journeyed to his new keep. I missed him and wanted to join him. That's all. I would appreciate your help, Master Giles. My husband's keep is called Thispen-Ladock."

If Master Giles was at all surprised at this revelation, he didn't show it. "Ah, so he buys Sir Thomas Ladock's land. Well, well, a nice little keep with more stinking sheep than people to tend them. I have heard of your husband as well, a brave knight, I've heard it said, and popular with our king. Aye, this is an interesting tale you tell, little pigeon."

" 'Tis no tale, 'tis the truth."

Master Giles didn't doubt it for an instant. It was simply that he wasn't certain what to do about it. Truth be told, he was nearly bowled out of his chair at who she was. "Tell me, why did you leave de Moreton? And all alone? 'Tis not very clever of you."

Daria swallowed another piece of honeyed bread, giving herself time to think. But there was still no choice. Master Giles wasn't stupid. "My husband had ordered me to remain at Wolffeton, but I missed him sorely. I had to leave without Lord Graelam knowing it."

Master Giles heaved his bulk from his chair. He clapped his hands, and one of the women rushed forward. She handed him a wet cloth. He wiped his hands and face on it and tossed it back to her. Like a king he was, a king in a ragged kingdom. If Daria hadn't been so afraid, she would have laughed aloud at his pretensions.

"I will think about what to do with you, little pigeon." He walked away from her, saying over his shoulder, "Roland de Tournay. Aye, this is a problem that requires much thought."

One of the women handed Daria a blanket and told her to stay close to the fire.

But she wasn't to be left in peace. Alan came toward her sometime later, and in his hand he carried a long skinny rope. He dropped down beside her, and when she tried to draw back, he closed his fingers over her shoulder and squeezed.

"Onto your belly, you little bitch."

He didn't give her time to obey him, but roughly pulled her onto her stomach. He grabbed her hands and pulled them behind her. She felt the rope wrapping about her wrists, once then twice. Then he pulled the rope tight and she moaned aloud at the pain.

"There's no reason to torture her, Alan," a woman's voice said. "You're just angry because she hurt you. What would you have had her do — laugh and welcome you with a jest when you tried to capture her?"

Alan made a coarse remark and pulled the rope tighter.

He rose then, and she felt him looking down at her. Finally he left her alone.

Daria didn't move for a long time. Finally she rolled to her side, facing the dying fire. He hadn't covered her and it was becoming chilly. There was no sound now, no movement from the other men and women.

She fell asleep for mere minutes at a time, from exhaustion and from a numbing fear that was fast draining the spirit out of her. Her arms were numb, her position uncomfortable. Since there was nothing for her to do, she knew she had to make the best of it. She stared into the now-smoking embers. She listened to an owl and the answering whinny of a horse. She hoped Henrietta was all right, hoped they'd fed her mare. She hoped the babe was all right. She felt tears sting her eyes and swallowed. She'd meant only to join Roland; she hadn't meant to get herself into trouble. But she had, and now she was a prisoner again. All this tumult that had happened in the last six months of her life made her realize that the first seventeen years of her life had been rigidly uneventful, the days mundane and utterly predictable in their sameness despite the small cruelties of her uncle. She'd always been fed, provided with nice clothes to wear, learned her lessons in peace, and been bored withal. The boredom she'd known during her captivity with the Earl of Clare had always been underlain with fear. Now she'd brought fear down on her head again, all because she'd dashed heedlessly from safety and into the waiting arms of fat Master Giles, who was a villain, and strutted himself about like a royal prince.

She thought of Alan, ragged as the others, only more vicious, and shuddered. She thought of Master Giles and his white fat hands, and his oily voice, and the shudder turned into violent shaking.

The night was dark. Only a quarter-moon shone down from overhead. There was little wind, but still the leaves on the surrounding oak trees rippled and swayed, making her start with fear at the soft rustling noise.

She was awake in the deepest hour of the

night, just before dawn, for her bound arms were numb no longer. The pain was excruciating. She felt sorry for herself and wanted to weep. If she could have, she would have willingly kicked herself for being such a fool. She'd left the safety of Wolffeton, and for what? For a foolish girl's dream, a fantasy that had nothing to do with reality. Reality was being the prisoner of a spiteful man named Alan and a fat horrid man named Master Giles. She tried to breathe deeply and slowly, tried to turn her thoughts away from the pain in her arms. In the next instant a man's hand covered her mouth and his warm breath was near her ear. "Don't move. I'm here to save you. Don't make a sound or any sudden movements. Do you understand?"

Daria nodded. The hand raised from her mouth, and slowly, she turned over to look up into the shadowed face of a man bent over her who was a perfect stranger. He shook his head and she saw the sharp silver sheen of a knife. He looked as ruthless and hard as any man to her. Would he kill her? She felt the blade sink into the ropes around her wrists. She was free. She wanted to raise her arms but she found she couldn't. She stared up at him and he saw the pain and helplessness in her eyes.

The man merely shook his head at her again, grasped her around the waist, and lifted her. He walked silent as a shadow, carrying her over his shoulder. He stepped over one of Master Giles's sleeping men and the fellow never stirred.

He strode deep into the forest, then finally stopped and eased her to her feet, propping her up against an oak tree. "There," he said, and patted her cheek. "Work the feeling back into your hands and arms. Stay here and keep quiet. I have a meeting with Master Giles and it won't take very long." He started suddenly, then turned, his voice angry. "Philippa, no, damn you! Stay here with her, do you hear me? I demand that you obey me! By all the saints, I shouldn't have allowed you to come. I'm naught but a stupid whoreson and you're a meddlesome wench. I should have known that you —"

Daria heard a woman's low laugh interrupt the man's harangue; then suddenly she felt her legs simply fold beneath her. She heard the man say something, his voice sharp, but somehow distant from her; then she heard no more.

How much time had passed? Daria wondered. She didn't open her eyes; she was afraid to. She wasn't on the ground, she knew that. She was lying atop furs, and a warm blanket covered her. All that had happened trickled slowly into her mind. Still she didn't move. There was a lighted flambeau thrust into the ground near her, not really needed now, for the forest was filled with the soft gray lights of morning.

"You're awake."

It was the man who'd saved her. Slowly she opened her eyes. He was sitting beside her. He was younger than she'd first believed, but his face — it was hard and ruthless, his eyes cold. Like Roland's face when he'd come to believe her a liar. Had she fallen into the clutches of another scoundrel?

"Aye," she said, and was surprised that there was obvious fear in her voice. She was swamped with fear and cold. "Will you hurt me?"

His eyes warmed with surprise at her words. He tucked another blanket over her, saying in a soothing voice, "Just lie still. You've been through quite an ordeal. I've had dealings with Master Giles before, and he's a knave and an outlaw for all his pretty speeches and dainty manners. Did he deluge you with pretty speeches? Aye, I can see that he did — there's distaste in your eyes. Now, when you're ready, tell me who you are and how the fat old toad caught you."

He smiled then and it changed his face.

"You really won't hurt me?" He shook his head, saw that she was still frightened, and said easily, "Very well, let me begin. My name is Dienwald de Fortenberry and I suppose I am also something of a rogue, but no, I wouldn't hurt you. I saw you there, saw that villain Alan hurt you, but I couldn't get you free just then. I had to wait until they all slept. It took hours before the guards gave it up. No, I won't hurt you."

"I am Daria de Tournay, wife to Roland de Tournay."

Daria wasn't certain what she expected, but the man's eyes widened and he stared at her, silent for fully two minutes. Then he laughed deeply. "It is passing odd," he said at last. "Roland — your husband. That defies reason. Yea, passing odd, and it's delightful."

"You know my husband?"

"Aye, he saved my life not long ago. It was a magnificent bit of work — he threw a knife and it sliced cleanly through the fellow's heart. Needless to say I call him friend. So Roland has returned to Cornwall . . . aye, 'tis passing odd. Why aren't you with him?"

And so Daria told him her pitiful tale, not sparing herself, acknowledging her thoughtlessness. ". . . And so Graelam didn't know I'd left. I guess his two men will tell him. He won't be pleased; my husband won't be pleased either."

"Ah," Dienwald said. "Here is my wench of a wife. Philippa, come meet the girl who is wed to Roland."

There was laughter in his voice and Daria wondered at it.

Philippa de Fortenberry was a tall graceful girl of about Daria's age. She was wearing a wool cap and boy's clothing. Her face was intelligent, full of life, and her eyes the most beautiful blue Daria had ever seen. They were her father's eyes. She was meeting the king's daughter. "The queen told me all about you and the king called you his sweet Philippa. It's a pleasure to meet you. I only wish it could be somewhere else."

"Aye," Dienwald said after a moment, "that's true enough. My wench here is the king's daughter, blast her eyes, but since there's naught I can do about it, I shall just have to extol her endless virtues, at least when her father is within hearing. You're wondering how your husband sits in all this, I imagine. Well, Roland had been instructed by the king to come to Cornwall and marry Philippa. Unfortunately for the king and fortunately for Roland, she'd already wedded me. Which leaves two unfortunates, but I am too noble to repine openly. Of course I would have relinquished my claim to her large hand, but she convinced me that if I did so, she would lie down in a ditch and die."

Philippa de Fortenberry laughed, hissed something in her husband's ear, and punched his arm. "Ignore his braying, Daria. Like most men, he is naught but an ass, a wonderful rogue ass, but nonetheless . . . I am only relieved that we chanced upon you. All is well now."

"Why are you here? You're female, just like me, and yet you're dressed like a boy and you're with him. I don't understand."

" 'Tis all right. Dienwald doesn't understand either. You see, my dear, my husband needs me desperately. I tell him what stratagems to employ, how to proceed with his rescues, and how to execute a revenge. I am pleased that he performed according to my instructions. Aye, that foul cretin Master Giles has been served his comeuppance."

"What did you do to him? And all the others? There were two women and at least six men. And that horrible Alan."

Dienwald said, "Only one of them died, and the others, well, Daria, I vow they are at this moment more cold than embarrassed.

Can you imagine fat Master Giles seated on his princely chair, naked as a toad?"

"You took their clothes?"

Philippa and her husband were grinning like happy fools, nodding together. "Aye, and bound them tightly."

"That's wonderful! Oh, how I should love to walk up to Master Giles and laugh at him!"

"Perhaps we'd best not this time," Dienwald said. "Actually, if you're feeling all right now, we should catch up to your brave husband."

"You know," Philippa de Fortenberry said, her voice provocative as she swept her thick lashes over those brilliant eyes of hers, "I wonder now that I didn't accept Roland. Ah, such a noble creature, a man of such virile parts, such —"

Dienwald de Fortenberry rose in a swift movement, turned on his wife, and, wrapping his hands around her hips, lifted her high and tromped away with her.

Daria stared after him, disbelieving and sorely confused. These people were beyond strange. Well, she'd met the king's daughter and she was lovely, her blue eyes so bright and vivid and full of mischief and light.

She heard a yowl, part laughter, part fury. Several minutes passed before Dienwald re-

364

appeared. He was wiping his hands on his thighs. But he was now all business. "We must leave soon. As I said, we have nothing to fear from Master Giles and his oafs, at least for a while. But why tempt the capricious fates? I wish to deliver you safely to Roland. Where is he?"

" 'Tis not far, I don't think. He went to purchase lands and a keep called Thispen-Ladock."

"Ah, 'tis not far at all. Are you well enough to travel now?" Dienwald helped her to rise. "I do wonder what Graelam will say. I wish I could but see his face now, at this precise moment."

"Do you know everyone, sir?"

"Call me Dienwald. Actually, if you speak to my wife, she'll suggest other useful names to you. As for Graelam, it is his wife who knew me before her fierce husband did. So many tales lie in this head. And now you've added another. Also, we're a small society here in this part of Cornwall, so it isn't passing strange that we're all known to each other. What is passing strange is that we are all friends." He laughed at that.

"I am delighted that something lies in that head of yours," said Philippa, walking up to them. "Let me help you," she added, offering Daria her hand. She looked startled when Daria jerked away from her and rushed away, only to fall against a tree and vomit.

"Goodness, what did you say to her, wench?"

"Nothing, my lord husband. Oh dear, if she is ill —"

"We will travel slowly. There is no need to rush about now. Master Giles is taken care of." He rubbed his hands together and smiled a very evil smile.

Daria accepted the goblet of water from Philippa and washed out her mouth.

"I am with child," she said. "I'm not ill. The sickness comes and goes, and I hate it."

"I must say that Roland wasted no time in his duties," remarked Dienwald. "How long have you been wedded?"

"Not long," said Daria, and allowed Philippa to wipe a damp cloth over her face. "Thank you. That is wonderful. I'm all right now, truly. It's morning and the babe has but told me that he is ready to begin the day. Can we leave now to find my husband?"

She saw Philippa and her husband exchange glances; then Dienwald turned to her. "Aye, let us go now."

"My mare, Henrietta, Master Giles took her."

"I have all of Master Giles's horses. It is

sufficient repayment, I think, for his thievery."

"Don't forget all his clothes," added Philippa, sniggering behind her hand.

There were a dozen men in their troop, all of them in high spirits. Daria heard them saying:

". . . Did you see the expression on his fat face when the master told him to remove his tunic?"

". . . Did you see the woman's face when he did?"

". . . I thought she'd faint when he wore naught but his fat white skin."

". . . Aye, that little rod of his shriveled even more!"

". . . Master Giles won't cheat our master again, that's certain!"

On and on it went, and when Daria chanced to see Dienwald's face, she saw that he looked insufferably pleased with himself. The heavily clouded skies cleared and she saw her new host and hostess quite clearly now.

Philippa had pulled off her wool cap, and her hair, thick and lustrous and curly, of a dark honey color, tumbled down her back. She was laughing, riding close to her husband, and Daria saw that their hands were clasped between their horses. It hurt her to watch them. She remembered Wales, remembered those hours with Roland when he'd cared for her, laughed with her, complimented her when she repeated the Welsh words and phrases correctly . . .

Dienwald turned in his saddle and said, "We aren't far from Thispen-Ladock. Another hour. Do you feel all right, Daria?"

No, she wanted to shout at him. She couldn't begin to imagine what Roland would say when she arrived. She closed her eyes a moment, then squared her shoulders. "Aye, I'm fine," she called back, but Dienwald wasn't fooled for an instant.

"This is all passing strange," he said in a quiet voice to his wife. "Roland seduced her, got her with child, and married her? Why did he leave her at Wolffeton?"

"For that matter," Philippa said thoughtfully, "why did she leave to come to him? Is she simple? Surely she would realize the danger."

"Just as you did when you ran away from Beauchamp?"

One of her more colorful adventures that had turned out marvelously well. Philippa lowered her brow and giggled.

Dienwald squeezed her fingers and sighed deeply. "I feel for poor fat Master Giles. I dread to think what would have happened to the poor old bastard had you landed in his domain rather than mine."

Daria heard the two of them arguing, insulting each other, and laughing. She wished it didn't hurt. She turned her head and looked toward the vast expanse of rolling green hills and clumps of thick maple and oak forests. There were sheep everywhere, and wheat crops, the waving stalks turning the horizon gold. There were no more barren cliffs or naked rocks and bent trees. The land became more gentle with each passing mile. Daria was tired, she admitted it, but she wasn't about to ask her host to stop for her.

The girl, Philippa, wouldn't ask. She'd keep going until her husband dropped in his tracks first, even if it killed her.

Roland came to the fore of the keep's ramparts at the shout from one of his men.

"A cavalcade comes, master. I know not who it is."

Sir Thomas Ladock, old in heart if not in years, looked toward the oncoming riders, his dark eyes full of intelligence. "Why, I think it is Dienwald de Fortenberry. Do you not see his banner, Roland?"

"Dienwald!"

"Aye, I met the boy some years ago. His banner is distinctive — the eagle and the lion with the clashing swords between them. His father was a wild man — eager to fight, eager to love, and eager to laugh. Is Dienwald like his sire, Roland?"

Roland smiled. "Aye, he is."

"There is a woman — no, there are two women — riding with about a dozen men, I'd say," Salin called out.

Roland stared hard then, for he felt something strange stirring within him. It was an odd feeling; it had come from nowhere that he could fathom. It was simply there, and he waited for the feelings to become something tangible he could grasp. And as the cavalcade drew close, he saw his wife riding her mare on Dienwald's left. And there was Philippa on Dienwald's right, dressed in boy's clothes, her beautiful hair wild and free.

Roland said in the most measured voice he could manage, "It appears, Thomas, that you are shortly to meet my wife."

"Your wife," Sir Thomas repeated, staring toward the group of riders. "What is she doing with Dienwald?"

"I shudder to know the answer to that."

Salin smiled. "She missed you, my lord. And she came to you."

"Don't think she is so sweet and guileless, Salin. All women carry the scourge of Satan in them."

Sir Thomas, more astute in human nature than he cared to be, turned and looked long at the young man he wished had been his own son.

"Life is vastly unexpected," he said. "Let's descend, my boy, so that we may greet our guests."

16

Sir Thomas was fully aware that Roland was angry. His entire body had seemed to tighten, to become rigid, as Dienwald de Fortenberry's party had come closer. As the minutes passed, Thomas realized, oddly enough, that the young man's anger was directed at the slight girl astride the beautiful palfrey. His wife, he'd said. But why was he so displeased to see her? They'd not long been wedded. He remembered, so many years before, how he'd not let Constance out of his sight or bed for nearly three months. Something was decidedly wrong here. He looked at the young man, saw that he was closed as tightly as a clam, and said nothing.

Roland made no move toward his wife when the small cavalcade came to a halt in the inner bailey. It was Salin who lifted Daria from her palfrey's back. Roland introduced his guests to Sir Thomas, passing over his wife as if she weren't there. Roland continued to ignore his wife even after Thomas took her hand in his and bade her welcome to Thispen-Ladock. Dienwald's men were directed by Salin to the dilapidated barracks. Thomas led his guests into the great hall of Thispen-Ladock.

"You surprise me, Dienwald," Roland was saying to de Fortenberry, his voice sounding mildly defensive. "You are leagues from St. Erth. What do you here? Come you to spy on me?"

"Now, that's sport I hadn't considered. Nay, Roland, Philippa and I were out a-hunting fat two-legged prey and we found him in due course, along with your sweet wife."

"I see," Roland said, and turned to Thomas. He didn't see a thing and he was so furious that he couldn't bring himself to speak. His wife, his sweet, guileless wife, had convinced Dienwald and Philippa to bring her here to him. Ale was brought. Servants served it. No one said much of anything. Philippa looked from Daria to Roland, and she frowned. Daria sat silent, her head down, her hands clasped in her lap. This was her future home, she was thinking, and she was appalled. Her distress at Roland's obvious cold welcome was momentarily forgotten as she stared around her.

The great hall was damp and cold and its overhead wooden beams so blackened from years of smoke that it was impossible to see the roof. The trestle tables were battered and carved and laden with grease and bits of dried food. There were no lavers, no sweet-smelling rushes on the stone floor, no tapestries on the stone walls to contain the chill. It smelled old and rancid. She shivered.

"Are you cold?"

She looked up at her emotionless husband's voice and shook her head. She offered him a tentative smile, which he did not return. Roland, instead, turned to Dienwald. "Tell me about this fat prey of yours."

Philippa de Fortenberry laughed. " 'Tis a fine tale, Roland."

"Hush, wench, you'll ruin the humor of it if you rattle on. A tussle with Master Giles, Roland, a fat rogue I doubt you've met as yet. The fellow was near St. Erth one fine day when Philippa and I were away from the keep. We believe he probably waited until he saw us leave. He offered goods to Old Agnes and Crooky, and his oily tongue won them quickly to his way of thinking. In short, when Philippa and I returned some two days later, we owned supposedly fine bolts of cloth and the price paid had been wondrous low."

Philippa laughed again and said, "When we unfolded the cloth, we found that it was filled with moths and they'd already chewed it to bits. You should have heard Crooky, Roland, he broke into a song that burned even my ears! It seems that this cloth wasn't the same cloth Master Giles showed to Old Agnes, the cloth she had so very carefully examined. This was his special cloth, for replacement after his sale. Crooky then noticed that castle goods were missing, such as a gift from the queen — a beautiful wrought gold laver — and several necklaces from the king. Oddly enough, even Gorkel the Hideous believed oily Master Giles. He was overwrought to learn of his thievery. We ordered him to remain at St. Erth, else Master Giles might have found his flesh flayed from his fat body."

Who, Daria wondered, was Gorkel the Hideous? He sounded a monster, with such a name, but Philippa was laughing.

"So you and Dienwald rode after him," Sir Thomas said, much enjoying himself. He was sitting forward, his goblet of ale balanced on his knee.

"Aye," Dienwald said in a mournful voice, "but the wench here continued to call a halt every few hours, so it took us many days to catch up to Master Giles."

"I'm not a wench! I'm your wife!"

"Why?" Daria asked, "Why did you keep stopping?"

Dienwald gave her a wicked smile. "My wench here — my wench/wife — wished to ravish my poor man's body." He shrugged. "What could I do? To refuse her makes her cross and peevish — you may be certain that I've tried it. My men were most understanding of her needs and of my surrender. Indeed, once when I refused her for the third time, they begged me to give in to her. Ah, and so I did."

Philippa poked him in the ribs. "You will come to a very bad end, Dienwald."

"I already have, wench. I already have. Brought to my knees by a female giant who could have been used to make two quite proper-size wenches."

"I shall write my illustrious father and tell him that you show me no respect at all, that you wound me and mock me without respite —"

Roland interrupted. "The king, Philippa, is currently visiting the Marcher Barons. We left him at Tyberton, the stronghold of the Earl of Clare. You must hold your complaints against your rogue of a husband until the fall, when he and the queen will return to London again."

"Wound you, Philippa?" her husband inquired, his brows drawn together, his expression perplexed. "I thought it was many weeks now since it was a question of wounding, you being such a hearty wench, and —"

Philippa shrieked at him and clapped her hand over his mouth. "Forgive him, sir," she said to Sir Thomas, "his wagging tongue dances a fine dance at my expense and at your embarrassment."

Daria was smiling, she couldn't help herself, until she realized that Roland was looking at her. Her smile froze.

"So continue with your tale, Dienwald," Roland said pleasantly. "Finally you found Master Giles."

"Aye, in the Penrith oak forest not far from here. He had six men, one of them in particular a vicious lout, and two women. He'd just caught Daria and didn't know what to do with his prize. She was coming to see her husband, Roland, something that Philippa would do as well. Females! They have no sense, no means to weigh what they should or shouldn't do. They act because their feelings dictate they should, and we must come to the rescue."

Philippa wanted to continue with the jest, but she could feel the awful tension between Roland and Daria. She didn't know why there was such tension between them, but she wanted, oddly enough, to protect Daria.

Dienwald was also well aware of the strain between these two. "That vicious knave — Alan was his name — well, he was brutalizing your wife here —"

"You mean he raped her?"

Well, Dienwald thought, pleased with the gratifying violent reaction from Roland. He raised his hand. "Oh, no, I mean that he enjoyed causing her pain. Fat Master Giles chided him — part of their game, I suppose — and finally she was allowed to sleep, although Alan bound her wrists much too tightly. It was near to dawn that I slipped into their camp and brought her out."

"And then my dearest husband enjoyed himself, Roland. He stripped all Master Giles's people down to their skin and Master Giles as well. He left them there, bound, and we took their horses and their clothes and the cloth we had supposedly bought. Master Giles was bound naked to his throne!"

"A decent-enough punishment, I suppose," Thomas said. "Are you feeling all right now, my dear?" he asked, his eyes on

Daria. "A very frightening time for you."

"I'm fine, truly, sir."

"She wasn't earlier," Dienwald said. "She vomited until I believed she would fall over, so weak she was."

To his surprise, Roland's mobile features stiffened and he said, "Her vomiting is due to the babe she carries."

"So she said," Dienwald remarked. "You are to be congratulated for your swiftness, Roland."

"I call it wonderful potency," Philippa said with a mocking voice. "Virility, aye, that's it."

"Yea," Roland said, his eyes on his wife, "I am of a swiftness that defies my own logic."

Sir Thomas cleared his throat. He was vastly uncomfortable with all the eddies of tension that swirled around them. "You are all my guests. Had you come a sennight from now, you would be Roland's guests. Before you arrived, he and I were talking about the renaming of Thispen-Ladock."

"I'm not certain, sir —"

"Be quiet, Roland. You will begin your own dynasty, not continue mine. My family had their due of years. 'Tis now your turn. And that includes a name for your ancestral home." He turned to Daria. "Now that your wife is here, we can secure her opinion."

"I suppose Graelam and Kassia don't know that you ran away from Wolffeton?"

She shook her head. "Not when I did it. They must know now."

Roland felt full to bursting with bile. He said abruptly, "Excuse me, Thomas, Dienwald, but I would speak with my wife. Daria, come with me now. Philippa, I believe there is some bread and cheese. Tell a servant to fetch some."

Daria knew she had no choice, even though now she wanted nothing more than to remain in this dank gloomy great hall and sip at warm ale. She'd been through so much to get to him, and now that she was here, now that he was standing impatiently in front of her, she didn't want to move.

He took her arm and led her to the narrow winding stairs on the east side of the hall. The stairs were very steep and very narrow, more deeply and irregularly placed than any she'd ever before seen. Roland preceded her. There were three chambers along the bleak corridor, and he led her into the second. "This is where I sleep now; when the keep belongs to me — in seven days' time, as Thomas said — then I will remove myself to Thomas' chamber."

"And where will Sir Thomas go?"

"He will leave his keep and journey to

Dover. His daughter lives near Corfe Castle with her husband and many children. Thomas has no male heirs, thus the sale to me of Thispen-Ladock. But he needs coin for his daughter and her family, for his son-in-law is ill. When the king's men arrive from their meeting with your uncle, I will have enough coin to pay him."

"Will there be enough coin after you pay Sir Thomas for reparations on the keep here? It is in horrible condition."

It was true; he'd thought the same thing in much more explicit words, but her condemnation but added fuel to his smoldering fire.

"This is your home now, madam. I suggest you change your notions of what is horrible and what isn't. As to the remainder of the funds, why, you will have no say in how I wish to dispose of them. None at all. Now, you will tell me why you so foolishly left Wolffeton. You will make me understand why you scorned Kassia and Graelam and traveled by yourself. You will tell me why your stupidity passes all bounds known to man."

"I very nearly made it here safely." She shrugged, looking toward the narrow window slit that had a rough animal hide nailed over it. "I was merely unlucky to chance upon Master Giles's camp."

"Ha! I should say you were luckier than God's own angels to be rescued by Dienwald. The world is filled with the Master Giles sort. Do you have any idea, can you begin to guess, what could have happened to you?"

She looked down at her hands, for it hurt to look into his cold, furious face, a face she'd recognized from the first moment she'd seen him so long ago, it seemed. "I was a prisoner for many months, Roland. I had a very good idea of what could have happened."

"Still, it made no difference to you. Why did you do it, Daria? Why?"

She was twisting her hands together, she knew it, but couldn't still their frantic motion. Slowly she raised her head and said simply, "You're my husband. I wanted to be with you. I couldn't bear to be left in another's care, not really belonging, an unwanted guest."

The ring of truth was unmistakable and he flinched at it. "Damn you," he said, his voice low and deep, filled with frustration. "I can't very well take the time to return you to Wolffeton, not now." He strode away from her, pacing. He turned suddenly. "I suppose when you're not vomiting, you can be of some use here. The saints know the servants don't do a blessed thing, and what they do accomplish needs to be redone."

She said nothing to that, and it enraged him that she would sit there like a stone, taking his fury without returning any of it. "You're naught but a stupid sheep. You will remain here in this chamber until I send for you. Do you understand me?"

"Yea, I understand you."

He wanted her to rest for a while, but he realized that he'd made it sound an order. But he didn't correct himself. It would be wise of her to simply learn to obey him.

But why? she wondered as she watched him stride from the chamber. Why did he want her to stay here alone? Was he ashamed of her? Roland left the chamber without looking back at her. She tried to call up the Roland who'd been a Benedictine priest, the Roland who'd been her friend and her rescuer. But all there was now was the Roland who hated her and believed her a liar. She walked the confines of the chamber for the third time, then threw back her head. Was she to be a prisoner again? She left the room and made her way carefully down the stairs. As she neared the last curve, she heard Roland's voice. He was speaking quietly, but his words seared through her as if he'd shouted them at the top of his lungs.

"That one night — well, Gwyn, no more. My wife is here now."

"She's skinny and ye don't care for her," Daria heard a soft, very feminine voice say. "I saw how ye didn't want to look at her, how ye ignored her. I'll keep ye warm, master, and make ye happy. She'll not mind, that one —"

"That is perchance true, but the answer remains the same. Speak no more about it, Gwyn. See to dinner preparations now. We have guests, and I don't wish them to think this is a pigsty and the food they're served nothing more than swill."

The girl said something else, but Daria couldn't understand her words. The girl's name was Gwyn and Roland had taken her to his bed. He'd seen her naked and he'd kissed her and thrust himself into her body. She felt a pain so sharp, so deep, that she couldn't bear it. Slowly, holding her belly, Daria slipped down to sit on the cold stone step. A soft keening sound came from her throat.

It was that sound that Roland heard. He frowned, then strode up the stairs, coming to an abrupt halt. There sat his wife, leaning against the cold stone wall, her arms wrapped around her, her eyes closed tightly.

She'd overheard him speaking to Gwyn.

"So now, my faithless wife, you would add eavesdropping to your other talents."

She paid him no heed. He called her faithless? Another low keening sound came from her throat and her arms tightened around herself.

"It isn't well done of you, Daria. You disobey me yet again and leave the chamber when I commanded you to remain there. Well, now you know that I took the offered favors of another female. You also heard that I dismissed her because you are here now and I won't shame you. Just look at you! Sitting there like a rigid statue, bleating like a sheep —"

She flew at him, so quickly that he had no time to find another word, no time to move from her path, no time to see her fist flying toward him. Her fist struck him hard on the jaw and he lost his balance, crashing backward against the stone wall, stumbling on the lower stone step. She struck him again, yelling at him, "Bastard! Whoreson bastard! I'm not a bleating sheep! I'll not let you judge me so poorly again!" This time she struck him with her fist low in the belly, and he jerked forward even as he went crashing down the remaining few steps to sprawl on the stone floor of the great hall.

She was on him in an instant, coming

down onto her knees, striking his chest with her fists, yelling at him even louder. "I hate you! Unfaithful knave! Unspeakable cur! God, I hate you!"

Roland had knocked himself silly. It took him several moments to clear his head sufficiently to realize what was happening. Unlike Daria, he saw that the hall was filled with a score of people, Thomas and Dienwald included, and they were struck to silence by what they saw. They were watching his wife flail at him. They heard her screaming at him. Then he felt her hands go around his throat, and she was squeezing as hard as she could, her body trembling with the effort, silent now, so beyond rational thought that her eyes were blank and faraway.

Then she erupted again, even as she raised his head only to bang it down again to the stone floor, "You share what is mine and mine alone with another woman! You break faith with me, you break your vows! Then you call me a faithless wife! You call me a stupid sheep for saying naught about it! Well, no more, Roland. I'll kill you, I swear it, I'll kill you if ever you even touch another woman!"

No longer was she a stupid sheep, that was true. No longer was she a bleating sheep. He felt her fingers digging into his throat but she didn't have the strength to choke him, though her desire was great. He forgot about their audience. He slowly brought up his arms and grasped her wrists. He pulled them away from his throat.

She was trembling, shaking, but she was still screeching at him like a fishwife. "No more, Roland! I'll kill you, I'll kick you in the groin! I'll —"

He jerked her off him; then as gently as he could, he lowered her onto her back. He was over her in an instant, kneeing her legs apart, coming down to lie on top of her.

It was then Daria heard male laughter followed by more male laughter, and that was followed by lewd remarks, and then there was a woman laughing. It was then she saw all the people looking at them. It was then that she realized what had happened, and she looked up into her husband's face, her own as white as her belly.

"Will you hurt me now?"

"Hurt you? What do you think you've been doing to me? My head isn't a ripe melon, even though you seek to crack it open! Nay, even though you are a vicious killer, I shan't throttle you as you were trying to do to me. Now, wife, I think you've humiliated both of us quite enough. You've given a fine exhibition to everyone. I'm going to pull you up now, and if you dare attack me again, it will go badly for you. Do you understand me?"

"Aye, I understand."

He released her, and hauled her to her feet. In the next instant she drove her knee into his groin. Roland jerked upright, stared at her in stunned, horrified silence, then felt the waves of nausea flooding through him, felt the debilitating pain begin to grind him down. He grabbed his belly and sank to his knees, his body heaving.

The male laughter stopped. The lewd jests stopped. Daria, aware now of what she'd done, raised her head and saw that everyone was silent, staring at her, their expressions appalled and disbelieving. She was beyond thought now, beyond anything in her experience that could break through and guide her, and thus picked up her long skirts and ran from the great hall.

She heard Philippa shouting out her name, but she didn't slow. She ran and ran, stumbling once on uneven cobblestones, ran beneath the raised portcullis, through the narrow high tunnel that connected the inner bailey to the outer bailey, ran until she was at the open front gates of the outer bailey, and still she ran, holding her side and the ripping pain that was roiling through her. She was outside the keep now, and there were many people, but none tried to stop her. They paused in their duties and stared after her and called to her, but none made a move after her.

She ran until her legs collapsed beneath her, and then she fell on a soft grass-covered incline and rolled over and over until she reached the curved bottom of the ditch, and she lay there, not moving, not able to move in any case. She gasped for breath, afraid to move now because she was aware of the babe in her womb and she felt terrified that she'd harmed it with her mad dash from the keep, and her fall. She lay there until her breathing calmed. She lay there feeling the warm sun soak through her clothes, warming her flesh. She lay there knowing that when she did move there would be consequences that she didn't want to face. She quite simply wanted to die.

But she didn't die.

When Roland saw her lying there on her side, her cheek pressed against the soft green grass, her eyes closed, he thought she was dead. Fear raced through him and he skirted the steepest part of the incline until he could run to her without falling or skidding.

He dropped to his knees beside her, but he was afraid to touch her, afraid that she was hurt in some way he couldn't see.

"Daria."

She didn't want to open her eyes, but she did. Slowly she raised herself until she was on her knees in front of him.

"You're all right?"

She looked at him straightly, unaware of the grass stains covering one side of her face, unaware that her hair was filled with grass and twigs and was hanging loose down her back and over her shoulders, unaware that her gown was ripped and one sleeve hung down to her elbow.

And she said, "I hope you're no good to Gwyn anymore. I hope you're no good to any woman anymore."

Roland sucked in his breath, all his fear for her dissolved at her words.

She was gasping out the words, her eyes dilated, unheeding of him or what he could do to her. "I hope you return to the Holy Land and that you find Lila and Cena and tell them that you're no longer a man and that —"

He didn't strike her. He clapped his open hand over her mouth, shutting off her spate of words.

"Enough, damn you." He pulled her

against him and his face was close to hers, his breath hot on her flesh. "Now, madam wife, I am taking you back. You have caused quite a commotion. You have caused me no end of trouble, what with your violent attack on me and your irritating dash from the keep. You left Philippa telling me that your violence was caused by the babe, that you weren't thinking clearly because of it . . . by the saints, she was trying to protect you, even after you tried to bring me down."

"I did bring you down. You fell on your knees and I was the one who made you do it."

"Daria, I do recommend that you close your mouth and keep it closed. I would beat you, doubt it not, but I would do it carefully so that your child isn't harmed. Indeed, I would be more careful than you . . . tumbling down this incline like a half-wit. You defy logic, wench, you surely do. Now, will you come along with me willingly or do I beat you here?"

She wondered if he truly would strike her. If he did, would she cry and plead with him to stop? Would she grovel and whimper at his feet? She wouldn't. She would die before granting him such pleasure. "When you beat me, will you use your hand or a whip?"

Roland couldn't believe her words. Nor

could he believe the entire situation. Well, she'd finally shown spirit, more than he'd ever wished to see, more than his aching groin would ever have wanted. As to his emotionlessly spoken threats, it rocked him to his core that such things had come from his mouth. Never in his life had he struck a woman; he believed men who hurt women to be despicable, animals, of no account at all. But here he was telling her that he would beat her, and she'd accepted it, accepted it even though she should know he wasn't that kind of man, for she'd traveled through Wales with him, known him to prefer laughter to scowls, good dirty fighting to torture and cruelty. "I don't use whips, even on recalcitrant animals."

She dusted off her gown and straightened her back. She didn't speak again, nor did she look at him. She got to her feet and started walking back toward the keep. She felt her muscles begin to tighten and knew she would be painfully sore before too many more hours passed. Perhaps more than her muscles would be sore. Perhaps, if he beat her . . .

She noticed sheep now, so many of them that the air was filled with their scent. The trees that covered the gentle hillocks were green and thick and straight. The land was beautiful and soft, not harsh and savage and barren like the northern shore.

"How far inland are we here?"

Roland gaped at her. Was she simple, with this abrupt change of tone and subject? "About twelve miles."

"I miss the smell of the sea."

"So do I. Keep walking."

"Will you humiliate me in front of Dienwald and Philippa?"

"You attacked me in front of them. Why shouldn't I do the same to you?"

"Why did you take that girl to your bed?"

Roland shrugged. It was difficult to give an outward show of indifference, but he managed it. He shrugged again for good measure. "She is pretty, clean, and enthusiastic. I was in need of a woman, and she had many talents. She was available and willing."

"I see. So a wife is just another vessel for you to use. Every woman — every *comely* woman — is to be available, as is your wife. I don't like it, Roland, but I see now that there is naught I can do about it."

"You overheard me tell Gwyn that I wouldn't come to her again, that I wouldn't because my wife had come."

"I see. So it is in your man's code of honor not to disport with other females when your wife is present. I am gratified, sir, by this show of chastity and male honor. However, I care not now what you do. Take all the wenches that appeal to you, I care not. It keeps you from me, and I thank the saints for that. You've done naught but hurt me —"

'Twas just once, damn you! Our wedding night. 'Tis true, I wasn't as gentle as I could have been, but —"

"Nay, 'twas twice. Our wedding night and that first time, in Wrexham."

He cursed, long and fluently and loudly. Her words pushed him beyond sanity, beyond reason, and he was a man, astute and logical and not at all mean-spirited. Until he got near her, his wife, his damned lying wife.

"I should send you back to Wolffeton, but I doubt Graelam would want the keeping of you now. By God, he'd have to have you watched just as the Earl of Clare did. Nay, I shan't ask that of him. I wonder. Perhaps after several weeks, would you try to convince him that the babe you carry in your womb is his?"

He caught her wrist before she could strike him. He hauled her close and said very softly, not two inches from her nose, "Do not strike me again, Daria. I give you fair warning. Never again."

17

To the surmise of all the visitors present, the evening meal was delicious. The herring was baked to perfection, tender as snowflakes melting in the mouth, the slabs of beef spicy with herbs Daria couldn't identify. Whoever was the cook here deserved to be praised. The myriad rush torches that lined the stone walls cast vague shadows and softened the harshness of the great hall, and in this gentle light the lacks weren't all that noticeable. Indeed, Daria thought as she was savoring a particularly fine bite of stewed potatoes and turnips, it was warm and cozy. She swallowed blissfully, then grinned when she chanced to see Sir Thomas smiling at her.

"You are surprised at the quality of my food." He shook his head. "At my age, food is one of the few pleasures left. The cook is an individual I would send my men to protect. Aye, I wonder what your husband would say if I asked to take my cook with me when I leave."

"I think I should hunt the fellow down, Sir Thomas, and offer him the world to remain."

"Where did you find this god of a cook, Sir Thomas?" Dienwald called out over a mouthful of sweet almond bread dripping with dark amber honey. "Can I steal him away with me under the cover of darkness? Or perhaps steal him under cover of my large and beautiful wife?"

Daria laughed, as did everyone else. She hadn't believed earlier that she would ever want to eat again or even smile again, and here she was eating her head off and laughing until her ribs ached.

Tomorrow, she knew, Dienwald and Philippa would return to St. Erth, and she would be alone with her husband. She smiled at Sir Thomas. Perchance he'd choose to remain longer. At least he would be here until the king's men arrived with her dowry.

"Actually," Sir Thomas said, lifting a delicate herring fillet for all to see, "my wondrous cook is a bent old crone who tells me that her great-great-great-grandmother cooked for the Conqueror himself. Supposedly it was Mathilda herself who gave instructions to that long-ago Alice. You needn't worry that I'll steal her or that Dienwald will whisk her away. I believe all her magic lies here at Thispen-Ladock."

"I'm devoutly thankful for that," Daria said.

Roland was chewing thoughtfully on a piece of braised mutton. It was so tender that his mouth watered even as he chewed. "I don't know how you remain so thin, Sir Thomas. A man could become a stoat quickly enough."

"A young man newly wed, Roland? Fie on you! You will be far too busy, far too occupied with your new bride, to gain flesh on your belly."

"Aye, 'tis true," Dienwald called out. He stood suddenly and pulled up his tunic, baring his belly and his chest. "Look and feel pity for me, Roland. I was once possessed of a magnificent manly body, just weeks ago, in fact. But now my ribs stick out like barrel staves, my belly sinks into my back like a riverbed in a drought, and all because of the demands placed on me by my new wife. She works me harder than the meanest of our serfs work our oxen. This marvelous food keeps me alive, Sir Thomas, to toil at least another day in her demanding service. Then once again I shall have to avoid strong winds. And —"

Suddenly, without warning, Philippa de Fortenberry jumped to her feet, grabbed her husband's neck by his tunic, and stuffed a large handful of green peas into his open mouth. He sputtered and choked, spitting the peas in every direction. He turned on his wife, blood in his eye, and yelled, "My strength after this meal is awesome, Philippa. I can even reduce you, an oversize female with the strength of a female water buffalo, to begging within seconds."

Daria shook her head, she was laughing so hard. The two of them never seemed to tire of baiting each other.

"Begging for what, Dienwald?" Sir Thomas asked.

"Why, begging me to pleasure her, naturally."

Philippa squeaked, scooped up another handful of peas, but her husband was quicker. He reached down, grabbed her by the waist, and threw her over his arm. He kissed her then, hard and long, in front of the entire company. When he finally released her, she was laughing and pummeling at his chest. Only Daria saw the desire in her eyes, the flush on her cheeks, the softness of her open mouth as she looked into her husband's face.

Daria turned away, unable to bear their unity. She wondered if perhaps Philippa had known that Dienwald was meant for her and only for her, when she first saw him. The men were cheering and shouting out jests and trying to catch the serving wenches who were near to them, and they were successful most of the time because the women were laughing just as hard as the men and wanted to be caught and wooed so humorously.

Roland remarked to her, "There was a time when all wasn't a rainbow sky between them. But I remember that the anger that flared was all on Dienwald's side. As I recall, he was furious that she dared to have the king for a father."

Daria's head whipped up and she stared at him. "That makes no sense."

"When you come to know Dienwald, you will understand. Now, Daria, I have promised a game of chess to Sir Thomas. There is no reason for you to begin your duties as mistress of this keep until the morrow."

He was dismissing her, and she rose stiffly, both from hurt at his careless rejection, and from her sore muscles, and bade her good-nights.

Sir Thomas watched her walk slowly and gracefully from the great hall. Then he noticed she was limping slightly and he frowned.

"She fell," Roland said shortly, his eyes also following his wife's progress.

"Aye, so I heard from one of the women."

Roland cocked a black eyebrow.

"I heard she was running like a terrified little hen from the fox."

Roland said nothing.

"Did the fox catch the hen?"

"No, the hen brought herself low with no help from the fox. I see that Dienwald and Philippa are unaware of us, Sir Thomas, and likely to remain so. I venture to say they will shortly retire abovestairs. Shall we go to the chessboard?"

Daria was awake when Roland came into the chamber, quietly closing the door behind him, but she held herself very still. She didn't want to argue with him, didn't want to hear his cold emotionless orders, or, perhaps worse, his silent indifference, his contempt. She could see him clearly from the silver stream of the moonlight through the window slit; he was disrobing and she couldn't keep herself from watching him if she'd been ordered to. His movements were beautiful, supple and lithe, and as he turned or bent down, moonlight glittering off his back, his arms, the long shadowed line of his leg, she felt his grace touch her deeply.

She didn't move. She thought she heard him sigh, but wasn't certain. The bed gave under his weight. He settled on his side, his back to her. Within moments she heard him breathing deeply and evenly. Still she didn't move. She awoke during the night to the sound of rising winds. A storm would probably blow in from the sea before morning. But it was cold now, and would become colder soon. Slowly Daria curled up against her husband's back. His legs were drawn up and she fitted herself against him, snuggling closer, feeling the warmth of him, and settled her cheek against his back. She lightly laid her arm over his side onto his chest. His breathing didn't change.

She kissed his back and pressed closer. His flesh was smooth and firm and the muscle beneath solid. He was naked. She was wearing a shift, but it had ridden up and her legs were bare against his. In the dark, in the deep silence of the night, she could pretend that he loved her, pretend that he was once again the Roland who'd come to her as a priest, who'd saved her from those two bandits in Wales. Not that other Roland who was her husband.

She kissed his back again, savoring the

feel of his flesh, the scent of him, the taste of him. She wished she could tear off her shift and be naked against him, but she couldn't. She couldn't imagine what his reaction would be. He would leap from the bed, cursing her, or perhaps he would take her, as a man could a woman, and he would hurt her.

She closed her eyes against that pain. This moment of time was hers and she intended that it be what she wanted it to be. She would deal with tomorrow when it came. She fell asleep unaware that his hand clasped hers now.

Roland was fully aware of softness and warm breath against his back. He awoke alert, his eyes wide in the dull light of dawn. It wasn't yet raining, but the winds were high. Daria was pressed against his back. He felt the smoothness of her bare legs against his. He closed his eyes a moment, savoring the feel of her. He held her hand against his chest, his fingers lightly caressing hers. He supposed he'd held her hand all night, but he hadn't awakened before. He'd accepted her closeness, something that was odd, for he was a light sleeper, having learned through the years that a man drawn deep into sleep was very likely a dead man soon enough. But she'd lulled him.

He was hard as a stone. He wanted to

laugh at himself, at his randy body. Instead, he grimaced even as he very slowly turned to face her, drawing her close against him. Her shift rode higher; he felt her thighs against his. Felt her warm breath against his throat, her long hair tangled over his shoulder and chest. Her legs moved, twisting until his covered hers. He closed his arms around her back, drawing her closer to him.

His sex was near to bursting. He could simply ease her onto her back, come over her, and slide deep inside her, all within the space of a moment. The thought nearly sent him over the edge. But no, she wouldn't be ready to accept him. She'd be tight and cold and he would hurt her as he'd done the night of their wedding. No, he would control himself. He would make her ready; he would have her moaning for him before he sank his rod deep inside her. He would give her a woman's pleasure, he would make her tremble with the power of it, he would make her whimper as the spasms gained control of her, and he would control her and her body, and when she accepted him through her pleasure, then and only then would he take her. And she would accept him willingly because she would have no choice, for he would have conquered her body.

His touch light as a moth's wing, Roland's

fingers stroked over her back, smoothing the shift over her buttocks, his fingers curving inward, and he realized he hated the shift, hated anything between his fingers and her flesh. He shoved the stout linen upward, pausing only when she moaned against his throat, then burrowed more closely against him. His fingers splayed over her naked buttocks. In that moment, he was certain his seed would burst from his body. He couldn't believe he was so sorely tried at the mere touch of her flesh. He closed his eyes against the rampant wild sensations until he regained some semblance of control. He wanted to touch her, ease his fingers inside her and feel the tightness of her, the damp that his caressing would bring to her.

His fingers closed between her thighs, and to his surprise, her thighs opened and she was pressing back against his fingers, her back arching slightly, pressing her breasts more firmly against his chest. Was she awake? Did she know what she was doing? But then she sighed softly, and her buttocks were soft and relaxed again, and her breath was deep and even once more. He wondered at the dreams that were coming into her mind now, and he smiled, a nearly painful smile as he gently eased his middle finger inside her. He sucked in his breath, holding his finger still with a will he didn't know he possessed. The feel of her — it was something he couldn't have imagined, and yet he'd known many women, felt their bodies and caressed them with his fingers and his mouth, knowing them as well as it was possible to know a woman, but this was beyond his experience, beyond anything he'd ever felt, and it frightened him. Suddenly he shoved his finger upward, deep inside her, and he felt her muscles clenching around him, tightening and squeezing, and a harsh moan came from his mouth.

"Daria," he whispered, and he was kissing her temple, her cheek, nudging back her head with his other hand, kissing her lips, her throat. And his finger moved deep inside her, widening her for him, feeling the heat of her and wanting his member where his finger was, and his belly was cramping and hurting, his sex heavy and aching with his need. She was ready for him now, soft and moist, and all he had to do was ease her onto her back and draw her thighs apart . . .

But still he held back, even though he couldn't stop kissing her. He eased his finger very nearly out of her, then pushed and probed, sliding in deeply again, and she groaned, her body stiffening, then shuddering slightly. He wanted to shout with the pleasure of it. Then he touched her woman's flesh and found it hot and swelled. He couldn't wait further. He eased her onto her back and came over her, still kissing her face, and then he reared over her, coming up to his knees.

"Daria, wake up!"

Even as she focused on him over her, he pulled her shift up, baring her breasts.

Just as suddenly, he was covering her, and he was kissing her breasts, kneading them gently, sucking at last on her nipple, and she wanted to scream with the sensation of it. The dream had been making her wild, but the reality of Roland and his fingers and his mouth knew no comparison. She wanted him, no dream of him, no soft illusion of him.

But he couldn't wait, simply couldn't, and he slid down her body, parting her legs wide, and his mouth was on her as she wailed, a high, thin sound, and he smiled even as he felt himself near to bursting. She was tightening all over; he felt it, felt her thighs tensing around his shoulders, felt her fingers clutch his hair, heard the tearing moans from her throat. He raised his head just a bit, his breath hot on her swelled flesh, and he commanded her, "Daria, let go now. Let go and come to me."

She didn't understand his words, but her body did. Her flesh heaved with the knowledge, she opened the very depths of herself to him, fully and eagerly, and in the giving she found a pleasure that neared pain, so intense it was, so powerful and demanding, so urgent.

She screamed, but his hand was covering her mouth, and it freed her to cry out again and again, and her body bucked and heaved and she felt damp with sweat and loose and apart from herself, but it didn't matter, nothing outside them mattered, and it just went on and on. He raised his head and she wanted to weep with her body's disappointment, but only for an instant, for his hands were sliding beneath her hips, lifting her to him, and in the next instant his member was thrusting deep, filling her. She cried out again, her hips rising to pull him deeper, and the shocks of pleasure renewed and pulsed through her and her fingers dug into his arms, and she was lurching up to kiss him, and he met her then, even as he came into her, only to nearly withdraw again, and when he emptied himself into her, he covered her mouth with his and she took his moans and knew the dream could never rival the man.

He fell on top of her, his member still

deep inside her. Almost as soon as she felt the wonderful weight of him, he pulled back and she wanted to protest, but he was mumbling, "I don't wish to hurt your babe," and then he brought her with him onto her side and he was still inside her, only not so deep now, and she felt his words sear through her mind. *Your* babe. She wanted to weep with the pain of it, but her body was languid and soft and his body was against hers and he was gently rubbing his hands up and down her back, over her side, lightly touching her belly, then moving quickly away, to her breasts, weighing them and caressing them lightly, as if he'd guessed at their new tenderness.

"You liked that," he said, nibbling her earlobe. "You liked that very much."

"You're inside me, Roland. That is wondrous . . . you're a part of me."

"Aye, and I always will be. Every night I'll come deep inside you and you'll cry out to me to bring you more, and I won't disappoint you, Daria. Never again will you accuse me of misusing you. You now understand a woman's pleasure. I'll not let you forget it, not let you think another man can give you what I can. You screamed when I brought you to your release, and you screamed again when I came inside you. I liked that very much. Your breasts are as soft as the flesh between your white thighs. The way you feel . . ." His voice hitched and he fell silent.

She was exhausted from the force of this pleasure, and he seemed to know it. "Sleep now, dearling. Sleep."

And she did, knowing that he held her tight, knowing that in this she had pleased him, yet knowing too that in the end, nothing had changed between them. Except perhaps . . . aye, now perchance he would come to her with gentleness as he had to-night and there would be no more distrust and anger. He would come to her with pleasure for both of them.

When she awoke some hours later, she was alone. There was a basin of water and she quickly bathed and dressed and made her way down into the great hall. It was still fairly early and Dienwald and Philippa were seated at one of the trestle tables, eating and talking to Roland and Sir Thomas.

Dienwald looked up and saw Daria staring fixedly at her husband, her face flushed, her lips slightly parted. His grin was wicked as a devil's as he said loudly to his wife, "Would you observe that expression, wench . . . nay, not your own, Daria's. Now, I would say that she was well-pleasured last night. Is it true, Roland? Did you gladden your wife?"

"I cannot control him, Daria, forgive me. But I can offer him food so that he can keep up his strength and his mouth closed. Here, husband, chew on this wonderful honeyed pastry."

Just as suddenly, the odor of the sweet pastry sent her stomach roiling wildly and she gasped in distress and flew from the hall.

When she returned, Roland handed her a goblet of fresh milk. "Drink this slowly and then eat some of this bread. Alice told me it was just for you, made with special herbs that came from her great-great-great-grandmother, and it would make the babe happy as a little stoat."

Daria said nothing. She was embarrassed. The bread did settle her belly, and as she chewed slowly, she listened to her husband say, "I would certainly enjoy you extending your stay, Dienwald. I would put you to work. The eastern wall needs more men and labor than I have at present."

"You mistake the matter, Roland. I am a lazy lout, of no account at all. 'Tis my sweet wife here who is the worker. She pines to work. She languishes when she is not about some task. And she rides me constantly now to make repairs on St. Erth. She wears me down. Alas, Roland, I must return her to her home. I fear I cannot leave her to direct your reparations, for my son, Edmund, is more and more on her mind."

"Aye, the officious little tadpole," Philippa said fondly. She turned to Daria. "Once you've settled in and Roland grows bored with his domestication, then you must come to St. Erth and see this hornet husband of mine in his nest. It's a pleasing nest and he carps not overly."

"My uncle has no friends," Daria remarked later to Roland as they watched Dienwald, Philippa, and all their men ride from the keep. "No neighbor wants to see him even from a distance. He was always fighting, arguing, trying to steal their lands, debauch their daughters and wives, and I used to wonder when one of them would sneak into Reymerstone and slay all of us in our beds."

"The king's uncle, now dead, God bless his soul, bound men together here in Cornwall with his smooth wit and his unspoken power. Aye, if any of the lords hereabouts wanted to wage war on his neighbor, he would regret it, for the Duke of Cornwall acted swiftly. Dienwald was the only renegade, and he was only an occasional renegade. The duke chose to be amused by him.

And once Dienwald was wedded to the king's daughter, his fate was sealed. How do you feel, Daria?"

"Fine. Thank you for the milk and bread."

"Actually," he said, frowning into the distance, not looking at her, "I meant from last night. Was I too rough with you? I have heard it said that a woman's breasts grow very tender. I did not mean to give you pain, if indeed I did."

She shook her head quickly, and Roland, not hearing her speak, slewed his head around to look down at her. Her face was flushed.

His expression hardened. "You won't now pretend that you were forced or abused, will you?"

"If you won't pretend that, then I shan't either."

"Nay, I shan't pretend pain when there was naught but pleasure. You gave me great pleasure, I admit it."

He'd looked away from her again and she joined him in searching the horizon for nothing in particular.

"You are sweet," he said abruptly. "Your taste pleased me. If I think of tasting you, I grow hard and randy as one of our goats."

That was a surprise. "But it is only morning!"

"Look yon, Daria, to the southeast, at the base of that small hillock. There is a field of summer flowers there, thick as a woven mat, and warm and sweet. I would take you there and strip you naked. I would caress you and let you caress me and watch the sweat dew your soft flesh as the passion builds in you, and when you are twisting beneath me, I would taste you again and then press you down in the bed of fragrant flowers and sink into you."

He saw the pulse pounding in her throat, the heated color on her cheeks, the wild anticipation in her eyes. He smiled, pleased. There was no reason to argue with her, to constantly make her pale and draw back, no, there had been too much of that. He was wedded to her and that was an end to it. He would simply make the best of it; to discover that she was filled with passion would bring unexpected satisfaction to his future days and nights. *And what of the child? If it is a boy, he will be your heir and you will have to swallow your bile and your honor. . . .*

Roland shook his head. There was naught he could do to influence the sex of the child. Nothing. He wouldn't fret about it. He'd never really fretted in his life, yet he'd done more of it in the past weeks than he had imagined possible. It solved naught, this fretting, and it made him nervous and irritable. "Come," he said, his voice curt, "I'll introduce you to the keep servants. You are the mistress now and they must accustom themselves to the fact. It has been many years since a lady was in residence here. Sir Thomas tells me most of the keep servants are well-meaning, but they've grown lazy." He paused a moment. "I trust you have the training to oversee the work?"

"Aye, my mother did not neglect my household duties."

"But she found opportunity to teach you to read and to write. Very unusual, I should say. Did you know that Philippa is St. Erth's steward?"

"I have not been taught those duties. But if someone will but show me, then —"

"Nay, there is no need. You will meet my steward shortly. If he is a cheat, well, then, I will flail his buttocks and throw him into a ditch."

Daria grinned at that, then said, her voice diffident, "My mother, Roland. I worry about her. My uncle abused her, and since I was there she had no choice but to obey his wishes in all things."

"Think no more about it," he said, finality in his voice. Daria bit her lip, keeping her ire down.

★ ★ ★

Alice, the many-times-removed offspring of the Great Alice, had pain in her joints. Daria stood a moment in the cooking out-building, watching the old woman stir a stew with a long wooden spoon. It pained her, but Daria didn't know her well enough as yet to suggest a possible remedy. She praised her cooking, which was easy since her words were true, and settled back to hear advice on her pregnancy.

The advice journeyed through time back to the Great Alice herself, whence all knowledge began, Daria realized. She was close to nodding off when Alice, remembering her pastries, yelled, "By all the saints! Go ye, little mistress, and lie ye down. I'll send one of those lazy wenches with something fer ye to eat."

She slept away the afternoon. When she awoke, Roland was seated on the bed beside her. His look was intent and by far too serious for her peace of mind. Had he been there long? Just looking at her? What was he thinking?

"Hello," she said, and stretched. "Oh, dear, is it late? Have I slept long?"

"Long enough. How do you feel?"

She consulted her stomach and smiled. "Fine. Alice's bread boasts better results than the queen's herbs. Shall I rise now and see to your evening meal?"

"Nay, 'tis still early. You will remain here with me for a while. I've been watching you, Daria. I'm glad you're awake. I want to take you now."

The chamber was filled with sunlight, the high winds of the previous night had mellowed into a gentle breeze fit for a hot summer day. He wanted her now? When he'd spoken of the field of flowers, she'd felt the beauty of what he'd said, but not the embarrassment of it. "But it's very bright, Roland. There is a lot of light."

"I know. I want to part your white thighs and look at my wife. Now, let me assist you with your gown."

Her hair was loose and tumbled from her rest. He wrapped a thick tress around his wrist, slowly but inexorably drawing her face closer to his. "Look up at me, Daria."

She did, and he watched, fascinated, as her tongue lightly touched her lower lip. "You don't even realize that you make me want you, do you? Just looking at your pink tongue, and I'm harder than a stone." He laughed suddenly, released her hair, and began to undo the lace fastening down the front of her gown.

18

Even as he pulled and tugged at her clothes, his movements becoming more jerky, more clumsy as his need grew, Daria was thinking: And what of Gwyn? Am I simply to forget that he broke faith with me? And if I bedded with another man, what would he say? Would he even care? She shook her head at the unfairness of it, then felt the warm summer air on her bare flesh and looked up at him.

He was staring at her breasts.

"Am I as nice as Gwyn? Do I please you as much?"

Roland had forgotten Gwyn. He'd used her unthinkingly and he'd been left feeling he'd been very wrong, that he'd broken faith with his own honor. And, truth be told, he'd had no thought for Gwyn, for his wife had filled his mind even as he'd found his release. It was no excuse, he knew that, accepted it. Her unexpected words caught him off-guard and dug at his guilt, and made him angry at himself for feeling guilt. He was thinking her breasts more beautiful than any woman's he'd yet seen. His fingers itched to stroke the soft underflesh, to move gently over her nipples until they tautened, to make her shudder and moan with the feelings from it. He felt as though she'd doused him with freezing water.

"Not really," he said, and drew back, now looking at her face. "Gwyn's breasts are much fuller, her nipples a darker plum color and soft as velvet. Her breasts quivered, as if apart from her, when I caressed them, and they filled my open hands to overflowing."

She was unable to keep the pain his words brought her from showing on her face, but she had asked him. What had she expected? That he would tell her she was the most exquisite creature imaginable and that Gwyn was nothing? She tried to cover herself then, but he grabbed her wrists and pulled them down.

"Enough of this damned nonsense. Listen to me, Daria. You're my wife. I choose to look at you. Don't throw the other in my face again. It happened; it's over with. Now, wife, I don't want you ever to cover yourself in front of me unless I tell you it is all right."

"Will this other happen again, Roland? And again?"

He shook his head again, saying nothing.

Her breasts were heaving and she saw that he was staring at them again, still holding her wrists in front of her. Her gown was bunched at her waist. Suddenly he pushed her onto her back and came down beside her. He lowered his head and brushed his cheek against the underside of her breast, back and forth, slowly moving upward until his tongue touched her nipple and she felt a shock of such intense excitement plunge through her that she gasped aloud with the strength of it. And she felt humiliated because she'd gasped. His tongue played over her flesh and the feelings built, becoming more insistent, more urgent, making her thighs quiver.

"Please, Roland."

She didn't know if she was begging him to stop or begging him to continue caressing her with his mouth. She felt his fingers stroking her other breast, lifting it, and then his warm mouth closed over her other nipple and she lurched up. He laughed softly, his breath hot on her even hotter flesh, and she wanted to tell him to leave her, to go take his whore, that she didn't believe him, but what came from her mouth was a soft, pleading cry.

His splayed fingers slipped beneath her bunched gown and rested on her belly. He raised his head and looked into her face. "On your back, your belly is still flat. I can believe there isn't a babe in your womb."

She thought she saw a shaft of pain in his dark eyes, but he lowered his head again quickly to her breast and suckled her until she was shaking, her fingers digging into his upper arms, her head thrashing back and forth, her hips lifting and falling, wanting, wanting . . .

His fingers eased through the curls over her woman's mound and found her, and once again he raised his head to look down into her dazed eyes.

"Do you like that, Daria? My fingers on you? Do you know how you feel to me?"

His voice followed the cadence of his fingers: deep, caressing, rhythmic. She opened her mouth and a low moan emerged. He leaned down and kissed her, and his tongue eased into her mouth and she burst into her climax at that instant. She cried out and he took her cries deep within himself, reveling in the wild thrashing of her hips as his fingers kept to their rhythm. So much passion in her, he thought, dazed and triumphant with the evidence of it. He was hurting now, his body trembling with the force of his lust. He left her, unable to wait longer, and she was lying there, her legs sprawled, the gown in a tangle about her hips, her breasts heaving, and her eyes were bewildered and lost. Lost until he came over her, lifted her legs, and drove into her.

He thrust his tongue into her open mouth as his sex plunged more deeply inside her.

He felt the rippling pleasure as her fingers now dug into his back, and his pleasure built and built as she lurched and bucked frantically beneath him. He cried out into her mouth, his breath warm, his member so deep he touched her womb, and he found release so profound, so overwhelming, that it touched the deepest part of him.

He kept kissing her even though his body felt drugged with exhaustion. He needed to kiss her, craved to kiss her; he craved the taste and texture of her mouth. And she drew him to her, and he wasn't in any mood to fight it now. And he continued to kiss her, nibbling at her lower lip, touching his tongue to hers, feeling her delight when she initiated the touching.

Finally, sated, his body still sealed to hers, he knew he must regain control, control of himself, control of her. He raised his head and said, "There will be no more talk about

Gwyn. There will be no more talk about any women before Gwyn. Why should I seek out another woman when I have you? And you, Daria, are so passionate that I wonder how you remained a virgin for as long as you did. Of course, I really don't know about your virginity, do I?"

Shock made her reel, but she recovered herself quickly. "You were there when the Earl of Clare made me lie on my back, when he made me hold still, and he thrust his finger into me. You were there and you know I was a virgin, yet you wish to wound me. I hate you, Roland."

"I'm inside you, and you're wet and hot around me. Don't be a fool, Daria. There is no part of you, save your woman's perverse vanity, that could possibly hate me."

"Then I hate this need you seem to have to hurt me. I hate your cruelty, Roland. I don't understand why you do it."

He pulled out of her and rose, straightening his clothes with abrupt clumsy movements, for his body was sluggish and slow from the intensity of his release. He was, truth be told, angry at himself. The words had come unbidden from his mouth; her damned virginity — of course he'd stood there whilst the Earl of Clare had . . . He shook his head. He couldn't bear to think of that. *When she thinks about it, what does she feel?* More fretting, and now he'd shoved her away from him yet again. He didn't particularly understand why he'd baited her either. But it didn't matter. It put him back in control, firmly away from her. He smiled, but it wasn't a pleasant smile. At least he'd gained pleasure from her before he'd pushed her away, and pushed himself away as well. As to what it felt like to kiss her, he refused to be touched by it. "I thank you for the diversion. You wrung me out and it is a good feeling. Now, I think it wise for you to go to the hall and oversee the servants. I wouldn't want them to forget you are their mistress."

She lay there, her body still pulsing slightly with lazy shocks of pleasure. She watched him stride quickly to the door. He turned and said over his shoulder, "You are mistress here. See to your duties."

"Are you one of my duties?"

"Aye, and you've done well by me last night and today. Very well indeed. I shan't complain at your lack of skill. It will come. A wench with your enthusiasm will learn rapidly. And I am a good teacher. Aye, Daria, I am your first responsibility and you will see to me whenever I wish it." And he left her, and she thought she heard him whistling before the door closed behind him.

She was such a fool, she thought wearily as she rose from the bed, to think that he could possibly have changed with her arrival. She should have remained at Wolffeton. But to do what? To sit about doing nothing at all while Kassia went humming about her duties? Whilst Kassia laughed and teased her husband and nibbled his ear when she didn't believe anyone saw? No, staying there would have destroyed her.

Daria grinned then. By coming here she'd learned what passion was all about, and she quite liked it, even if Roland must needs ruin it after he was through with her. She more than quite liked it. Roland wasn't the only one to feel as though his body was shattering, flying out of control, yet demanding more and more until it was all chaos and sensation and nothing else mattered. He used her and she would use him. It was even. She wouldn't think of anything else. She would care for her babe when it was born, shower her love on her son or daughter. And she would use her husband and ignore his foul words.

It was true about passion, she thought again, her eyes closing as a vague tremor of feeling passed through her. It was beyond any experience that she could have imagined. If Roland thought of her as only a convenient receptacle for his lust, why, then, she would view him as a convenient . . . What? She wasn't certain how to divide up a man. She touched her fingertips to her lips. She could still feel him, feel his hunger, his urgency, and then his simple enjoyment of kissing her. He'd acted like a starving man. Ah, she loved to kiss him as well. Well, then, she was fortunate that she enjoyed his kisses. She didn't need anything else from him.

She felt his seed on her thighs, rose slowly from the bed and bathed herself, but the scent of him lingered and the scent of her as well, and she wanted to weep because there was no part of her, even her perverse vanity, that hated him.

What was she to do?

It was obvious to her now what she had to do. If any niggling feelings for her husband crept unasked into her mind, she would simply take him to her bed until the feelings disappeared and she was glutted with passion.

She went down into the great hall. Soon she would take things into hand. But not now, not whilst Sir Thomas was here. She quite liked him, she didn't wish to hurt him or make him feel an outsider. The servants

425

seemed to respond to her nicely, she realized with some relief by the time the evening meal had been justly consumed. She suspected that Old Alice, the resident autocrat, had dictated that she was the mistress and thus to be obeyed, bless her. Even Gwyn smiled at her, and did her bidding with satisfying speed.

There was no one to hold her in dislike save her husband.

Two weeks later, on the first Monday in August, the king's soldiers, led by Robert Burnell, arrived with Daria's dowry from the Earl of Reymerstone.

They also arrived with something else.

Burnell was weary to his bones, worried that the king was suffering from his absence, and relieved that the Earl of Reymerstone hadn't tried to murder him, though he'd seen the burning hate in the man's pale eyes, and known that it had been close for a time. Burnell didn't know if God had interceded on his behalf, but it made him feel blessed to believe it was so. The Earl of Reymerstone had allowed them to leave with a dozen mules, all laden with more goods that would have been Daria's had she married Ralph of Colchester. If Burnell hadn't insisted upon reading the marriage contract the earl had signed with Colchester, he never would have known about all the other goods. And that had made the earl all the more furious. Thank the good Lord he hadn't tried to murder them on their journey to Cornwall.

Daria looked from Robert Burnell's tired face toward the mules. There were coin, plate, jewels — she knew that there had been more that her uncle would have brought to her wedding. But so much more? Daria was stunned at the number of laden mules that came into the inner bailey, one after another.

So much, and now it belonged to Roland.

It was then that she saw her mother. Daria let out a yell and darted between people and animals and piles of refuse and deep gouges between cobblestones toward the woman who was bent over her palfrey.

"Mother! You're here! Oh, my!"

Roland turned quickly away from Burnell. "What the devil goes on . . . what is this, sir?"

The two men watched as Salin strode to the woman, and gently as he would handle a babe, lifted her from the mare's back. Roland saw his wife enfold the slighter woman, saw tears streaming down her face, saw her shoulders heaving as she kissed and hugged her mother.

"I had to bring Lady Fortescue, Roland,"

427

Burnell said, turning away from mother and daughter. "The earl — I saw him strike her viciously and repeatedly before I stopped him. It was after I'd made the demands, and he realized there was naught he could do — at least I prayed he wouldn't lose his head and murder me. He was yelling at her that he'd show her what he'd do to her bitch of a daughter when he got his hands on her. I knew he would kill her if I did not bring her away with me. She is still weak — several ribs are bruised, I think — and her wrist is hurt, but bound securely. She's a nice lady, Roland, soft-spoken and gentle."

Roland remembered the woman when he'd first gone to see the Earl of Reymerstone; he remembered the weariness in her eyes, the acceptance of things when there was no hope to change them. He felt a surge of guilt so powerful he shook with it. He should have instructed Burnell to bring Daria's mother away with him, but he hadn't thought of it. He'd been too locked into himself and his sense of abuse by the daughter's hand. He'd been nothing but a selfish lout.

"I'm glad you saved her." He nodded to Burnell and strode to Lady Fortescue.

"My lady," he said, and watched her try to straighten at his greeting, watched her try to offer him a curtsy.

"Nay, don't! Daria, your mother isn't feeling well. Take her to your solar. She must rest."

Daria saw her mother's bruised body a few minutes later in the solar when she helped her onto a narrow bed. She closed her eyes a moment, wishing more than anything that her uncle was present and that she had a knife. She would kill him. And she would enjoy it. She sent word to Alice, and a sweet-smelling warm potion of wine and herbs quickly arrived. Daria stayed with her mother until she slept. She smoothed back the vibrant red hair, still untouched by gray, saw the lines smooth from her mother's face. She lowered her head in her hands and wept. She should have demanded that Roland fetch her mother. But she hadn't. She'd been too consumed with herself, with the babe, with Roland's distrust of her. She'd been selfish, unforgivably selfish. After a long time Daria rose, straightened her gown, and called to Gwyn, who was cleaning in Sir Thomas's bedchamber. She asked her to remain with her mother.

"She's a beautiful lady," Gwyn whispered. "I'll see that she's all right."

Why should she have ever hated Gwyn? Daria wondered blankly as she walked down the winding stone steps.

★ ★ ★

Daria felt a bystander in the transaction between Burnell and her husband. She stood quietly in the great hall, watching the men bring in trunk after trunk. Sir Thomas, Robert Burnell, and her husband opened each trunk, commented on the goods, smiling sometimes, drinking ale. Then there came the leather coin pouches, and she watched as Roland solemnly passed the counted-out coins to Sir Thomas. The men embraced each other. Still she didn't move.

She heard Roland tell the men to take two of the trunks to his bedchamber. It was her bedchamber as well, but in important matters such as this, it was the man's. She'd learned that well enough during the past two weeks. The time had passed quickly, for there was so much newness at Thispen-Ladock, so many places to visit, so many new people to meet. Nor, Daria thought, as she saw to it that Burnell and the king's men were served quantities of ale and sweet buns from Alice's huge ovens, had she taken the reins in hand as yet. Actually, the reins had simply seemed to drift slowly yet surely there, and one day she was the mistress and all asked her for direction and orders. Roland had said nothing, nor had Sir Thomas. She seated herself finally, still saying naught. Her goods, her coin . . . but it was as if she wasn't even there.

" 'Tis incredible," Burnell said, sat back in his chair, and sighed deeply. His eyes remained closed as he bit into another sweet bun filled with raisins and almonds and nutmeg.

"Keep your thoughts away from my cook," Roland said, then laughed. "You will not seduce her from me even though you are a man of God."

"But the king, Roland, his belly would mellow from such wondrous food and —"

"He would become fat as a stoat, belch in foreign dignitaries' faces, sire no more children off the queen because he would be constantly eating, and she would be repelled, aye, Burnell, and he would die one day from gluttony, and England couldn't afford that loss, sir. And it would be your fault, all for lusting after my cook."

"Perhaps," Daria said, sitting forward, her eyes sparkling now, for the man who had spoken so humorously was the Roland she had met and known in Wales. "But what is a certainty, sir, is that Alice has no choice but to remain here. You see, she is tied to this place by bonds that go deeper than the spirit, all her skills derive from this earth and none other, and she told me that she

431

must remain here else she would lose all her knowledge and abilities."

"Ah," said Burnell, and frowned deeply.

Roland shot his wife a surprised look and she returned it limpidly.

"You are blessed with a golden tongue, wife," he said to her some moments later when Sir Thomas turned to speak to Burnell. "Poor Burnell!"

"Perhaps my lie was a bit more effective, but yours was by far more humorous, Roland. I'd forgotten how you could make me laugh."

"There isn't much to laugh about now, is there?"

"I suppose not, and I miss laughter. I miss it more than I minded the endless rain in Wales."

He gently clasped her face between his hands. He tilted up her chin and kissed her mouth. He continued kissing her, light, soft kisses that made her flesh warm. After a moment he released her, and to her surprise, he asked, "How is your mother?"

"Alice made a potion for her. She is sleeping soundly at present, and Gwyn is with her. She will fetch me when Mother awakens."

Roland picked up his goblet and began to examine the texture of the carvings on its surface. "I'm sorry about your mother, Daria."

She said even as she shook her head, "Nay, 'tis I who am at fault. I wasn't thinking clearly. I should have realized that my uncle was capable of —"

"Your mother is a beautiful woman. You look like her, you know, save that your hair isn't so strong and pure a red."

"True. I always thought I'd been diluted, though of course she would tell me that it was I who purified her." Daria pictured her mother's bruised body and suddenly, without warning, she burst into tears.

Roland saw the men turn to stare aghast at his wife. Conversation began to die. He waved a hand, then turned to her and said quietly, "I know you are hurt, hurt that you think you failed her, but you didn't. 'Twas I who failed her. Hush, now, Daria, else Burnell will tell the king that I abused you in front of everyone and with no provocation, and he will annul our marriage and take all your dowry from me. Sir Thomas will kick me out from my new home and I'll be cursed to wander the world again. Let me tell you that wandering grows tedious and I want no more of it."

His words were amusing and his voice was light and teasing, so she was able to ignore the truth of his words, and sniffed, wiping her eyes with the back of her hand.

"I'm sorry. I don't know why I did that."

"The babe," he said, not looking at her.

Daria hugged her arms around her belly. There was a slight roundness now and her waist was thickening. She wondered when he would look at her and be repelled.

"I haven't enjoyed you since this morning and my body is sorely deprived."

They were in their bedchamber. Daria closed her eyes, accepting more kisses, returning them with growing enthusiasm. When he caressed her and came into her body, he was kind and gentle and loving. If afterward he withdrew and became cold, well, it seemed it was her price to pay. She found she couldn't become cold as well as he did, so she said nothing, merely tried to pretend sleep as quickly as possible. Slowly, even as he continued kissing her, his hands still cupping her face, her hands lowered, stroking over his belly, lower, until her fingers closed about his swelling member. He moaned, his body jerking at her touch. Then he shoved against her fingers, and he was larger now, nearly too large for her hand, and she held him between her hands, lightly stroking him, gliding downward to touch the rest of him, and he was breathing hard and low and his kisses were deeper and more demanding and she continued to caress him until he jerked back from her, his chest heaving. She'd only touched him like this some three days before and she was more than pleased with her discovery. He'd said nothing about it, but his reaction when she touched him and caressed him with her hand was more than gratifying. She remembered the queen's ladies and their advice and knew that soon she would touch him with her mouth. She wondered how he would react to that.

He stared down at her now but his eyes closed suddenly as she squeezed both her hands around his member. He said her name softly, then, without warning, lifted her onto her back on a narrow table, knocking off the basin to the stone floor. It cracked, but he didn't notice. He jerked her hair free, threading his fingers through it until it hung down off the edge of the table, thick and tangled. He pulled her forward until her hips were at the edge of the table, her legs dangling. "Don't move, Daria."

She couldn't have moved in any case, for if she did, she would probably crash like the basin had to the stone floor. Her gown was tangled about her legs. She couldn't see him, but she could hear his breathing, and it was harsh and raw. Then he was over her, and he was lifting her legs and settling them over his shoulders, jerking away her gown, lifting her hips with his hands. He pulled her slightly forward, cradling her buttocks in his hands, and slid deeply into her. She cried out and he stopped.

"Do I hurt you?"

She shook her head.

He withdrew only when he knew if he didn't he would lose himself completely. He pulled out of her, his chest heaving, sweat filming his body. She felt his fingers on her, stroking over her inner thighs, moving closer, closer still, until he was touching her, caressing her, and then she felt his finger go deeply into her and she lifted her hips, nearly sobbing aloud with the wonder of it.

Then he lowered her legs and pushed her back on the table. He widened her thighs and brought his mouth down to her. He tried to hold her still, but he couldn't. She was wild and frantic, bucking against him, and he quickly lifted her and tossed her onto the narrow bed. When she wailed, her body going into frantic spasms, he came quickly into her again, and felt her legs close around his flanks, drawing him deeper and deeper still.

"Daria," he said, and let his release overtake him.

For many minutes neither of them moved.

"It is a good thing that Burnell brought the rest of my clothes. You are violent with my gowns, Roland."

He grunted, his mind still so blurred from the pleasure that he couldn't think.

As he came back to himself, Roland recognized that he was changing, and it frightened him. He was coming to need her, his wife, and seek her out. Not any deep part of him, not the spiritual part of him, but his body recognized her as its mate and his body's need seemed to grow stronger and more demanding. And it wasn't simply because she gave herself so sweetly to him — no, it was more, and more still, and it fretted him. It was as if this particular girl was meant to be his.

He withdrew his sex and his spirit from her. Then he withdrew his presence.

It was relatively simple to keep his distance from her, for Burnell wished to rest for several days and it was Roland's duty to show him the countryside and tell him his plans for Thispen-Ladock. As it was Daria's duty to provide for Burnell's pleasure, she was also occupied. And with her mother. He knew she spent many hours with Lady Fortescue. It wasn't until the last evening of Robert Burnell's stay that Lady Fortescue came into the great hall for the evening meal. She was lovely, he saw, her red hair warm and vibrant, her eyes bright and soft. Roland greeted her warmly. Sir Thomas insisted that she sit beside him.

At the close of the meal, which made everyone sigh with gluttonous pleasure, Roland rose from his chair, his goblet of ale raised high. He said to Sir Thomas, "You have provided me with my home and the home for my sons and my sons' sons. I thank you, Sir Thomas. You have given me land and a home that will remain in my spirit until the day I die. You have told me, Sir Thomas, that I must make Thispen-Ladock mine completely, that I must select a new name that will reflect what I am and my line. It was difficult to find such a name until I realized at last that I was a wanderer, and a lover of many lands. I saw the world, and I would bring the essence of what I saw here, to Cornwall, here to this keep, and all will come to know it as Chantry Hall. Chantry is the name of a man I knew in the Holy Land. He saved my life and he taught me that freedom of the spirit was the most precious of God's gifts to man. My thanks to you, Sir

Thomas, and to you, Robert Burnell."

"Hear! Hear!"

Daria stared at him, emptiness filling her even as her goblet overflowed with wine poured by an excited servant. The speech he'd just made was wonderful and fluent and moving. She hadn't known about it. She hadn't know about any of it.

She turned slightly and saw that her mother was looking at her, and she quickly lowered her eyes, raised her goblet, and sipped at the wine.

I am nothing more to him than one of the mules who brought his riches to him. She very slowly rose from her chair and walked from the great hall.

Only one remarked her leaving.

19

"It will rain soon. Do you miss Wales and the endless rain that soaked you to your soul?"

Daria didn't look back at him. She stood on the northern ramparts, wishing she could see the sea from its vantage point, but there was naught but the soft moonlight over the green rolling hills. It was warm this evening, the air heavy from the rain that would fall before midnight.

"Aye, I miss Wales," she said.

"Why did you leave the hall? I had thought it a good time to celebrate. I had thought Burnell would enjoy his final night if I filled it with laughter and jests and Alice's incredible array of food."

"Worry not, Roland. He is enjoying himself, as is everyone else."

"Why did you leave?"

She shrugged. "It didn't matter if I was

there or not, Roland. All this" — she turned then, spreading out her arms — "all this is yours. It has nothing to do with me. I hope you enjoy it, Roland, for to your mind, you've accepted dishonor and lies to gain it. I hope every sheep gives you delight, every shaft of wheat endless bliss."

"Your wishes for my joy warm me, Daria, but they seem a trifle incomplete. You don't wish me mindless pleasure from all the cows that graze the eastern acres?"

She thought her eyes would cross with fury, but she held on to herself, turning away from him, leaning on the stone ramparts. She swallowed, still saying nothing.

"Did you drink too much wine?"

She shook her head.

"Then you aren't ill?"

She was silent.

"You haven't vomited for nearly a week now. If you are feeling ill now, it isn't right. Speak to me."

She wondered how he knew that, but didn't say anything. She sighed deeply and turned once again to face her husband. "I'm not ill. I think I will go for a walk now. I bid you good night, Roland."

"What you will do, Daria, is return with me to the great hall and see to your guests."

"They are not my guests, Roland. They

are *yours;* they are here at *your* keep; they are here at *your* pleasure; they are enjoying *your* bounty, not mine. I have naught to do with anything. Don't lie to me about them being my guests. I am nothing here and they are nothing to me."

"It is a pity you removed yourself before I could finish my toast."

She looked at him warily, not willing to trust him an inch. "What do you mean?"

He flicked a piece of lint from the sleeve of his tunic. Her eyes followed the movement and she was looking at his long fingers when he said, "Without you — and your magnificent dowry, that is — I wouldn't be able to make needed repairs on the keep. Without you I wouldn't be able to increase my herds, hire more soldiers, bring in more peasants, and see to luxuries within the keep. Because of you, Daria, I am able to bring my home to its former glory now rather than in the misty future."

It *was* his home, just as all she had brought him through the marriage was his as well. She shoved him out of her way. Because she caught him off-guard, she was able to slip past him. She raced along the narrow rampart walkway to the wide ladder that rose from the inner bailey.

He watched her climb down the ladder.

442

She moved carefully, even in her anger, to protect the babe in her womb. He watched her dash across the inner bailey, gracefully avoiding refuse and puddles of water and two sleeping goats. He turned back and took her place at the rampart wall. He leaned his elbows on the rough stone. The night winds rose and the air thickened. He wondered, suddenly, without warning, what his father would think of him right at this moment. He saw his father's face after Roland had finally told him of Joan of Tenesby's treachery. He could still hear his deep soft voice as he said to his second son, "Listen, Roland, and listen well. You were played the fool, boy, but it didn't kill you. It hurt your heart and your pride, nothing more. It won't last, these sorrowing feelings. In the future, when you hear of the man who weds Joan of Tenesby, you will feel pity for the poor fellow, for he had not your luck. Nay, he will have gone blindly to his fate. You will tread more carefully now, and when it comes your time to wed, you will know what to seek and what to avoid in a wife. Honesty, Roland, honesty is a rare commodity in any human, man or woman. When you find honesty, then you will be the winner."

Honesty, Roland thought. *Honesty.* Rare

indeed, and he hadn't found it.

He turned away from the ramparts wall. No, he hadn't found honesty and he was himself becoming more dishonest with each passing day.

Just that morning, as the soft pearl lights of dawn had filled their small bedchamber, he had pulled Daria against him, then rolled on top of her. He'd felt the small roundness of her belly and it had driven him mad. He'd taken her quickly and left her. And he'd wondered if this child she carried would look like the Earl of Clare.

Katherine of Fortescue felt wonderful. She was sitting in the small apple and pear orchard at the rear of the keep. It was a warm day with a thick hot sun, but the dense branches of the apple tree shaded her well enough. She set another perfect stitch in the gown she was sewing for her daughter. She surprised herself by humming, something she hadn't done in so long she'd thought she had forgotten, but she hadn't. She hummed louder, charmed by the sound and by her nearly delirious sense of freedom, then burst into song. The gown dropped unheeded to her lap. Her voice was thin but true and she sang until she heard Sir Thomas chuckle behind her.

She turned to smile at him. "Do you come to silence the hideous noise, Sir Thomas?"

"Nay, I come to smile and feel my old bones warm."

"Old bones! You speak foolishness, sir! Why, you are still a young man."

"If it pleases you to say so, I shan't cavil." He seated himself beside her on the narrow stone bench. It had belonged to his grandmother. So many years had passed, so many events had shaped what he'd become now . . .

"I'm glad you haven't yet taken your leave," Katherine said, looking at Sir Thomas straightly.

"Roland has asked me to stay." He shrugged then, adding, "I cannot, in any case. Your sweet daughter . . ." His voice trailed off. "Nay, ask me not, Katherine, for I know not what trouble lies between them. I act as the block of wood between the two of them, a comfortable block, stolid and silent, and both of them look to that block for ease and safe conversation. Think you I should take my leave?"

She shook her head and set another perfect stitch.

"You are a woman of good judgment," he said, plucking a long piece of grass and wrapping it around his callused fingers.

"You don't meddle. You treat your son-in-law with respect and kindness. You don't frown your displeasure at him when you see your daughter's pale face. You don't try to tell your daughter what she does wrong and try to correct her."

Katherine grinned at him. "I am lazy, sir! Why should I work when Daria wishes to assume all the responsibility?"

"You lie, my lady. It is your wisdom that holds you silent, that and your love for your daughter."

"Like you, Sir Thomas, I shan't cavil if you wish to pay me compliments."

Sir Thomas said abruptly, "Are you healed?"

Her fingers stilled and she was silent for many moments.

"I'm sorry to distress you. It is just that I would kill the Earl of Reymerstone were he here. Indeed, I wonder if I shouldn't pay the bastard a visit when I leave here and show him the contempt I feel for his worthless soul."

Her hand shot out and closed over his clenched ones. "Damon Le Mark is a paltry creature, Sir Thomas. He knows no honor, no loyalty, and his treachery has rotted his soul. Ah, he knows pleasure because another's suffering gives it to him. Let him die in his own misery. And he will die as he deserves to, I know it."

"But he would have killed you had not Burnell brought you here!"

"I don't think so. He'd beaten me worse than that several times before."

Sir Thomas drew back, pain and shock contorting his features. "I must tell Roland. I must, for it is his right to avenge you."

"If you tell such a thing to Roland or to my daughter, I will call you a liar. Leave go, Sir Thomas. Another lady lived that meager life at Reymerstone. A new one, reborn if you will, sits here with you, humming and singing wildly as a berserk sparrow. This lady is happy and content and deems herself the luckiest of women. Sit here quietly for a moment and I will fetch you a flagon of ale. Should you like that, sir?"

Sir Thomas watched her walk gracefully toward the cooking outbuilding. He admired her. He thought her exquisite.

A week later Daria straightened from speaking to the dairymaid at the sound of horsemen arriving at the keep. She wiped her hands on her gown and walked quickly toward the inner bailey. It was Graelam de Moreton and three of his men. He looked like a pagan warrior, ruthless and overpowering in his black-and-silver mail, astride his huge destrier, and she felt an automatic frisson of fear. And then he smiled and shouted, "Roland! Bring your worthless hide over here so that I may tell you what Dienwald and Philippa have said about you!"

Roland was striding to him, yelling out insults in fine good humor, and clapped his shoulder after he'd dismounted his destrier. The two men embraced, then stepped apart, Lord Graelam saying to his man, "Rolfe, see to Demon. Where is your wife, Roland?"

"I am here, my lord."

She offered Graelam a deep curtsy.

Graelam stared at her silently for several moments. "My Kassia and I worried about you, Daria. What you did was foolish. My belly curdled with fear when the two grooms returned, red-faced, without you."

"I'm sorry, my lord. 'Twas thoughtless of me."

Graelam strode to her and very gently raised her chin in the palm of his gloved hand. He studied her face, not seeming to care that her husband stood not six feet from them, that the inner bailey was filled with chattering men and women and scampering children.

Roland said from behind them, his voice

sounding his irritation, "I sent you a message immediately, Graelam, that my wife was safe and with me."

Graelam turned then to Roland. He smiled even as he shrugged. "Kassia worries, Roland. She wanted me to come. She wanted me to ensure that Daria was comfortable in her new home and that the babe was settling in nicely as well. Thus you see me here awaiting your hospitality."

"Oh, dear! Please, my lord, come into the hall. My mother is here with us now and I wish you to meet her. Do you also know Sir Thomas?"

Roland found himself grinning reluctantly after his wife, who, after babbling like a cawing rook, picked up her skirts and dashed much too quickly, he thought, suddenly worried, across the crooked cobblestones and up the wide stone steps into the great hall.

"You've disconcerted my wife, Graelam. I believe it the unlikely combination of your fierce face and your gentle manner. How do your own lady and your squalling babe?"

"She is well, as is my son. I should apologize to you, Roland, but it never occurred to me that Daria was so unhappy at Wolffeton."

Roland was uncomfortable. He shrugged.

"Have Rolfe bring your men inside the hall. By now Daria has provided enough ale to quench the thirst of every man within our walls."

Roland turned and strode toward the hall. Graelam de Moreton followed more slowly behind him, thinking about what the devil he should do. His wife's words were still clear in his mind. "I'm worried, Graelam. There is strife between them, but there is caring as well, at least on Daria's side. Please discover what is wrong and fix it."

He shook his head. Kassia cherished this peculiar notion that he could fix anything, be it a war between two neighbors or squabbles between a man and his wife. There was trouble between Roland and Daria, no doubt about that. Graelam sighed. He preferred trying to fix the differences between two countries. He foresaw several days of watching Daria and Roland and trying to come up with some sort of solution that would please his wife, whatever the hell that could possibly be.

Daria sat alone in the solar, slowly and carefully grinding herbs just sprung up from her garden. It was a hot day and a line of sweat snaked down between her breasts. The sweet smell of rosemary filled her nostrils. She fanned herself with her hand and wished she could move closer to the window. But she couldn't. She'd spread the various herbs in small separate piles on the table in front of her, and any breeze or sudden disturbance would send the herbs wafting away in the hot air.

Her mother was likely with Sir Thomas. That was proving to be an interesting development, she thought as she transferred three pinches of rosemary to the fragrant dill. Days before, Sir Thomas had borrowed a dozen of Roland's men and they'd carried money to Sir Thomas's daughter and her family. At Roland's insistence, Sir Thomas had agreed to return to Chantry Hall. He was nothing loath, she thought, seeing her very lovely mother in her mind's eye, smiling up into Sir Thomas's weathered face. The man was besotted with her.

Daria added exactly three pinches of coarsely ground foxglove to a small batch of finely crushed poppy flowers. She had very little and must hoard her supply. She wondered how Roland was faring with the dour old farmer who held demesne lands at the northern boundaries of Chantry Hall. Roland had taken four men and ridden from the keep early that morning and should return soon now. She looked toward the window slit. The sun was settling down-ward. Yes, he should be returning soon now. . . . Just to see him, she thought, just to look at him whilst he spoke, to hear him laugh. I'm naught but a fool, she told her-self, knowing that it was true and knowing too that there was nothing she could do about it.

He hadn't touched her for a week now, not since he'd placed his hand on her belly and felt the slight bulge there. She paused in her work, remembering how he'd been frantic to leave her after he'd taken her. He was so distant from her now that he might as well be back in Wales. She shook her head, and wiped the film of perspiration from her forehead with the back of her hand. She wouldn't think of him now. There were other things to fill her mind and her time.

She began to sing softly as she added just a dollop of basil to a concoction to ease stomach cramps. The afternoon grew hotter and her fingers slowed in their tasks. Sud-denly, without warning, Daria froze where she sat, her fingers still, her eyes staring straight ahead. A huge door opened, right in front of her, and she saw herself passing through it into a field of dazzling white. The white was thick like fog, yet pure and dry, and it surrounded her yet didn't seem to really touch her. And there, as she stood silent and quiet, she saw Graelam. He was working on the eastern wall, dislodging old stone, lifting a mighty slab, turning to heave it away from him, then moving back to grasp another. Men were talking and looking at him as they in turn lifted the stones he'd heaved to them and in turn passed them to others. There was so much stone to be removed so that the wall could be rebuilt. She watched as he yelled something to one of the men, breaking his rhythm as he did so, his back turned to the wall. Suddenly there was a loud rumbling sound and the wall collapsed. Huge slabs toppled downward. She saw Graelam whip about, saw the stones strike his shoulders and chest, battering him to his knees. The stones rained down thick and hard, and covered him. The men surrounding him were yelling frantically, trying to escape danger from the avalanche of stone. Thick dust from the crumbling stone swirled about, filling the air with thick gray debris. And then there was awful silence. Just as suddenly, the white disappeared and she was back in her chair, her left hand still held out in front of her. Daria jumped to her feet, upending all the herbal portions, and dashed from the solar. She didn't doubt what she saw. It was the same sort of vision she'd had when she saw her father die so many years before.

She saw her mother speaking with one of the wenches in the inner bailey and screamed to her to follow. She raced to the eastern wall, and as she neared, she heard men shouting and yelling.

She ran until she reached the exact spot where Graelam had fallen. Men were hurling rocks aside, on their knees, digging frantically. She shoved several of the men aside and heaved the stones off him. Several smaller stones tumbled against her, striking her hard, but she ignored them, ignored the brief stabs of pain. She knew exactly where his face was and she knew she must clear it so he could breathe. She heard the men arguing, and someone tried to pull her away, but she turned and saw him draw back at the look on her face. She worked until she thought her arms would crumble as had the stone wall. She saw him. Finally his chest and head were clear. He lay on his side, his arms over his head to protect himself. He was perfectly still.

"No!" She screamed the word, and she heard herself as a child screaming the same word over and over after she'd seen her father fall and the horse crush his skull.

"Graelam!" She fell to her knees beside

him. The men, speechless and afraid, moved aside for her, making a circle around her. She grabbed Graelam's arm and heaved him over and onto his back.

"He's dead!" one of the men muttered. "Dead. There's naught ye can do, mistress."

"He's not dead," Daria said, and she slapped his face, hard, again and again. "You won't die! Graelam, damn you! No! You won't die, not like my father. I won't let you! No!" Still he didn't move, and she felt fury flood through her. She'd seen what had happened, yet she was to be impotent again. She wouldn't accept it. She pounded his chest with her fists, screaming at him, berating him not to die, not to leave his family, not like this. And she struck him again and again. She was trembling with fatigue and fear, yet her rage wouldn't let her stop. She pounded her fists again and again on his chest.

Then, suddenly, Graelam's chest heaved, and heaved again. Then he groaned, the most beautiful sound Daria had ever heard in her life.

She yelled with the relief of it. She'd won. He hadn't died. The vision hadn't shown her something beyond her control. It hadn't been a prediction, it had been a warning. She shook his massive shoulders, then grasped his face between her hands and stroked his brow, his jaw, his head. No damage as far as she could tell. Then he opened his eyes and looked up at her.

He frowned, his eyes narrowing in pain.

"Graelam," she said very quietly, her face close to his, "you're alive. My father died and there was naught I could do about it. But you lived. You lived, my lord!" She held him, her cheek pressed against his throat, speaking words, nonsense really, her voice becoming more slurred by the moment.

"What the devil is happening here!"

The men stumbled back to allow Roland through. He stopped cold at the sight of his wife on her knees holding Graelam and speaking to him in a singsong voice.

"Daria, what happened? Graelam, what —?"

She turned then and smiled up at him, tears glistening on her dust-streaked cheeks. "He'll live, Roland. It happened just like my father, but Graelam lived. It was a warning, not a prediction." She rose then, and said very calmly, "Please help Lord Graelam to the keep. His ribs are likely badly bruised. Be careful. Roland, I shall have Alice prepare a brew for him to ease his pain."

Without another word, she walked away from him, walked past her mother, her steps brisk and her head thrown back.

His questions would wait. Roland directed his men to lift Graelam. The men grunted and heaved in their burden. "Go easy," Roland said, and helped in the task. Once Graelam was lying on his bed, bared to the waist, Roland saw indeed that his ribs were bruised badly. He felt them, then nodded. "Daria is right. You will be fine, but sore as Satan for a good week. What happened, Graelam?"

"I was working on your damned wall, Roland. It collapsed suddenly, without warning, and the stone buried me. That's all." But it wasn't all, Graelam was thinking. Something very strange had occurred. It was as if he himself had quit being, but of course he hadn't. He'd been buried under the rubble . . . he remembered quite clearly the pain of the striking stones as they'd hit him; then he'd suddenly been separate from the pain, outside of it somehow, and he'd seemed to be surrounded by a very clear whiteness that was blinding yet somehow completely clear . . . nothing more, just . . . white, thick and impenetrable, yet clear. And then he'd heard Daria screaming at him, screaming that he wouldn't die, not like her father had died, that she wouldn't let him. And then he'd come back into the rawness of his body, even felt the pain of her fists hammering over and over again against his chest. And the white had receded, moving slowly away from him, then whooshing out of his sight in an instant of time, and he was awake and filled with life and pain and she was above him, babbling nonsense at him and stroking his face with her hands.

"What happened to Daria's father?"

Roland stared down at his friend.

"No, I'm not out of my head. What happened to him?"

"He died. In a tourney, some three years ago."

"I see." But he didn't, not really. He said very quietly, "Your wife saved my life, Roland."

"She pulled stones off you, that's true. But not all that many. The men hauled off the bulk of them."

"Nay, 'twas more . . . much more. The stones, they had already hurt me . . ." Graelam fell silent. He said nothing more until Daria entered, carrying a goblet in her hand. Her mother followed her, strips of cloth over her arms.

Daria paid no heed to her husband. She sat beside Graelam, smiled down at him, and said, "Drink this, my lord. It will take away the pain and make you sleep for a while. My mother will bind your ribs. Have you pain anywhere else?"

Graelam shook his head, his eyes never leaving her face. He drank the bittersweet brew. His head soon lolled on the pillow, but before he closed his eyes he said, "Thank you, Daria. Thank you for my life."

"What did he mean, Daria?"

She raised her head and looked at her husband. "I couldn't let him die. I couldn't let the vision end like it had with my father. I just couldn't. I have failed too many times in my life. I couldn't fail in this."

She stood then and straightened her gown. She left the chamber then, saying nothing more.

Roland said to Katherine, "Your daughter is behaving strangely. What is she talking about? I don't understand."

Katherine shook her head, motioning Roland to help her. Between them they managed to bind Graelam's ribs with strip after strip of stout white cloth.

Whilst Roland stripped off the remainder of Graelam's clothing and brought a light cover to his waist, Katherine walked to the small window slit and looked out.

"Stay a moment, Roland," Katherine said once he'd finished.

"I should go see to Daria."

"In a moment. Did she tell you about her father?"

"Only that he had died in a tourney in London just before Edward left for the Holy Land."

"There was something else. She saw her father die."

Roland stared at her. "I beg your pardon, my lady?"

"Daria saw him die, three days before word reached us that he'd been killed accidentally in that tourney in London."

"You mean she had some sort of vision?"

"Aye, I suppose that is as good a word as any. In any case, it happened."

Roland was thinking of her telling him that she'd known him the moment she'd first seen him. She'd recognized him deep within her. He shrugged, irritated, for it was the kind of thing a man couldn't touch, couldn't look at and say it was real or wasn't real. He didn't like this sort of talk. It was nonsense. Anything that smacked of visions belonged to prophets in mountain caves, not to young females.

"I realize it's difficult for you to accept, Roland. Just imagine what it is like for Daria. Evidently she saw Graelam being crushed by the stone wall. But somehow she brought him back."

"He was never dead! He was simply unconscious . . . and only for a few moments, nothing more."

"Perhaps," Katherine said. She gave him a sad smile. "Don't hurt her with this, Roland."

His head snapped up. He said, his voice quite cold and quite distant, "I'm not a monster."

He left her then, saying over his shoulder as he paused at the chamber door, "I will send Rolfe to attend his master. You must rest, Katherine."

Roland found Daria in the orchard. She was seated on what was now called Lady Katherine's bench. She was staring down at her hands, clasped in her lap.

He sat beside her, saying nothing.

"Lord Graelam is all right?"

"Aye, he will survive. He's sleeping now."

"Will you send a message to Kassia?"

"I probably should before Graelam regains his wits. He detests illness or weakness. But his wife should be told, just in case something goes wrong, just in case he is hurt internally and —"

"No, he isn't hurt internally."

Roland looked at her then, his eyes narrowed. "You have no way of being certain of that, Daria. No way at all. Why do you say it with such assurance?"

"I just know," she said, her voice now as distant as his.

"How do you know?"

"It matters not. I have much to do now, Roland. If you need me for naught else, then —"

He quickly grasped her wrist and pulled her back down. "I won't accuse you of being a witch, if you're afraid of that. My men just might be thinking that, though. You're not stupid, Daria. You know there might be talk. I want you to tell me exactly what you did so that I may combat it."

"I shoved the men aside and pulled off the stones myself. You see, I knew exactly what stones to shove aside to clear his head and his chest. Then I saw that he was motionless, that he wasn't breathing, and I was no longer just afraid. I was furious, so enraged that I couldn't control it. It is an odd reaction for me, but it happened. I was so angry that I struck his chest with my fists, again and again, and screamed at him like a shrew. That is likely what your men will gossip about. They will say that I lost all reason. But Graelam breathed again and he moaned and then he opened his eyes."

"He was merely unconscious."

"Yes, he was merely unconscious."

He looked at her profile, his mouth thinning. "You weren't there when the wall collapsed on him."

"No, I was in the solar mixing herbs."

"How did you know what had happened?"

"I saw it happen."

Roland was silent for many moments. He was aware of bees swarming about the apple tree behind him. He heard sparrows flapping their wings in the still hot air. The heavy smell of grass filled his nostrils. This should be a peaceful spot, but it wasn't. There were mysteries here, and things he didn't understand, and there was pain as well, and he knew he was the cause of it. He didn't know what to do. He didn't begin to know what to think about this. He rose and looked down at his wife.

"I must send a message to Kassia. Doubtless she will arrive shortly to see to her lord."

Daria merely nodded.

It was deep in the middle of the night. A storm was blowing in. Just as lightning streaked across the sky, Daria awoke, pain convulsing her belly, a cry erupting from her mouth.

20

Daria had never imagined such pain. It welled up in her, overpowering her, capturing all of her within it, and she couldn't stop it, couldn't control it. The pain shrieked in her belly, twisting and coiling, until the screams were pouring out of her mouth. She wrapped her arms around herself, drawing her knees up, but nothing helped. Then, suddenly, just as the pain had started, it stopped.

Roland lurched upright at her first cry. He'd just come into their bedchamber a short time before and was on the edge of sleep. "Daria!" He clasped her arms and tried to bring her about to face him, but her pain was keeping her apart from him, apart from understanding, apart from even the knowledge of him and his presence. So he held her until she quieted. She lay on her back, staring up at him, panting heavily.

"It's gone," she said, her voice low and harsh. "It was horrible but now it's gone."

"What pain? Where did you hurt?"

"My belly. Cramps, awful twisting cramps and —" Her eyes flew to his face. "Oh, no!"

Roland quickly lit several candles. He turned back to see her standing beside the bed, staring down at herself. He felt himself grow cold at the sight. Blood blotched red on her white shift, blood streaked down her legs, puddling at the floor between her feet.

She looked up at him, her eyes blank. "I don't understand." Another cramp seized her, and she fell to her knees with the force of it.

She was losing the child. She was bowed on her knees, crying out, jagged, tearing cries. He lifted her high in his arms and felt the vivid agony of her body as she twisted and heaved against his hold. He laid her onto her back, watching her immediately roll to her side, her legs drawn up, her arms around her belly.

"Hold on!" he shouted at her, then ran from the bedchamber, grabbing his bedrobe as he went.

He met Katherine in the narrow corridor. Her face was pale in the dim light.

"What's wrong, Roland?"

"It's the babe, she's losing the babe!"

Katherine ran past him. She stood over her daughter, wishing she could take the pain from her, magically take it into herself, but she couldn't, of course. She pushed sweat-soaked hair from her daughter's forehead, speaking to her softly. " 'Twill soon be over, Daria. Soon now. Don't frighten your husband so, daughter. But look at him, his face is as pale as the dawn light and your pain becomes his. Come, Daria, give him your hands and he will help you."

Roland moved automatically to do as Katherine bade. He was grateful for any instruction, for he felt so damnably helpless. He grasped his wife's fingers, then eased his hold so that she could grip his hands instead. She saw him, at last. "Roland, please make it stop!" She was gone from him for many moments, locked into the pain of her body.

Daria felt a mighty twisting that wound tighter and tighter, against all reason, crushing her within it, and she prayed in that instant for oblivion, for that thick whiteness she'd seen that afternoon. But she felt everything; nothing faded, nothing lost its sharpness. She felt the flood of liquid down her legs, and she knew then that she was losing the babe, losing her babe, Roland's babe. The wet was sticky and warm and she screamed at the ending of her child's life.

She screamed for herself and her own loss and she screamed for the loss of the unborn child. She was aware that someone's hands were on her body, warm water and cloths were touching her gently, and Roland was holding her face against his chest and she could feel the sharp loud rhythm of his heart and he was speaking to her, yet she didn't understand his words. Slowly, as the screams that clogged her mind and her throat finally pulled away from her, releasing her back into herself, she made out his words, soft but insistent, pulling at her, lulling her.

"Hush, Daria, hush now. You're all right. Everything is all right now. Hush." And he was rocking her, kissing her sweaty forehead, and for a moment in time she was comforted and allowed herself to heed his words and his gentleness, and gave herself over to him.

She heard her mother's voice. "I can see no damage done, Roland. Now I must get the bleeding slowed. Just remain as you are. Hold her and soothe her. Keep her as quiet as you can. Try to . . . comfort her."

He did, kissing his wife's temple, speaking to her endlessly of the farmer he'd visited and the man's four daughters who'd wanted to come back to Chantry Hall with him and serve his beautiful wife. Aye, they'd all heard of her, of her kindness, of her gentleness. He talked and talked, of nothing and everything, yet none of it was important and he knew it, but it didn't matter. Daria was quiet. He watched Katherine bathe the blood from her daughter, watched her make a thick pad of white cotton cloths and press it against her. He saw the crimson cloths on the floor beside the bed.

It was over.

Daria felt the smooth edge of a cup pressed against her closed lips. She opened her mouth at Roland's command and drank deep. She lolled back against her husband's arm, aware that the potion she'd drunk was drugged, aware now that Roland was stripping off her bloodied chemise and bathing the sweat from her body. She felt the soft cool material of her bedrobe as he wrapped it around her. When she was on her back, she opened her eyes to see her mother and Roland standing beside her. But they weren't looking at her, but at each other, and Katherine was saying quietly, "It isn't uncommon at all, Roland. She will heal and there will be other children for you. Also the vigorous activity this afternoon — she lost the child, but she did save Graelam. A choice God doubtless approved, Roland. It was no one's fault."

Roland was silent.

"It's for the best, Roland," Katherine said, unable to bear the empty pain of his silence. She really meant nothing by her words, just feeling so helpless that she said anything to ease him, for it hurt her to see him so shattered and withdrawn into himself. She wished he would say something, anything. But he remained silent. And she said again, " 'Tis for the best, Roland."

Daria felt darkness clouding her vision, closing over her mind, but she fought it. She laughed, a raw ugly sound. "Oh, Mother," she gasped, the words pouring out unbidden, "you're so very right. It is for the best. Roland's best. This child is dead and Roland is silent because he knows he must wait until he can yell his relief to the world — he is a man of some wisdom. He doesn't wish to shock you or any of our people, Mother, with his rejoicing." And she laughed and laughed until the tears streamed down her face and she was choking on them, and then suddenly she felt his hand strike her cheek and the laughter and tears died and she succumbed to the tug of the poppy juice. She saw her husband's face, drawn and white; then she saw nothing.

Roland stared down at his wife's pale face.

Bloodless, he thought blankly, his eyes going toward the soaked cloths. So much blood. "You're certain she will be all right, Katherine? She's so pale . . ."

"She's lost a goodly amount of blood, but withal, she's strong and fit. She'll come through this, Roland. She'll regain her strength and come back to you."

He continued to look at his wife's face, continued to listen to her breathing, continued to feel her damning words sear through him.

"What did she mean — that you would yell your relief?"

Roland looked up at Katherine of Fortescue. Slowly he shook his head. "She meant nothing," he said.

Katherine was tired, worried to her very soul, and thus she spoke harshly, without thought. "She meant something, all right. I'm not blind, Roland. There is strife between the two of you. My daughter is bitterly unhappy and you, well . . . you seem so distant with her, so removed from her. Damn you, what did she mean? What have you done to her?"

And Roland said simply, giving it up because he was so unutterably weary, "The king and queen know of it, but no one else. The child she carried wasn't mine."

Katherine drew back, so surprised that she dropped some of the bloodied cloths. "Not your child? That makes no sense at all! No, that couldn't be —"

"I don't know whose child it was. More than likely it was the Earl of Clare's, or perhaps another's, a man I never knew of. No, it wasn't her fault, I would swear to that. Daria is good and true. She would never betray me. She was raped." He paused, raising Daria's limp hand and pressing his mouth to her wrist.

Katherine continued to stare at him. He moved restlessly, saying more to himself than to her, "But you see, she insisted the child was mine. She refused to back down, even though all pointed to fabrication. I have assured her repeatedly of my protection, promised that I would think no less of her, and begged her to tell me who had taken her against her will, but she kept insisting that the child was mine, that she'd given me her virginity one night when I was ill, out of my head with fever. I don't understand her, but now it is over and there will be no more dissension between us."

Katherine wished desperately she hadn't pushed him. What he'd told her — it was something she would never have imagined. She guessed he would regret speaking the truth to her, feel anger at her for goading him, so she said nothing more. She felt exhaustion creeping into her very bones; she looked down at her daughter and knew she would sleep for many hours now, healing sleep. She nodded to Roland and left the bedchamber. When she opened the door, she saw Sir Thomas standing there. She wasn't surprised to see him. She smiled and said, "I would very much like to rest now, sir."

"I will assist you to your room, Katherine," Sir Thomas said, and gave her his arm.

Roland eased onto his back, and clasped his wife's wrist. He felt the pulse, strong and steady beneath his finger. She would live. He felt relief so profound that he shook with it.

No, he wouldn't be shouting his relief. He wouldn't be shouting at all. He wished he'd kept his mouth shut, but it was too late now.

Graelam de Moreton sat up in his bed, his wife standing over him, her hands on her hips. They looked to be in the midst of a colorful argument.

"If there are wagers to be made on the outcome of this conflict, my groats are on Kassia."

"Get out, you lout! And take me with you!"

"Nay, Roland," Kassia called out, laughter in her voice, "stay. Graelam becomes more and more unmanageable, but perchance you can convince him that he will be rendered impotent if he doesn't allow himself enough time to heal. I have told him that is what happens to men who don't obey their wives' common-sense instructions."

"That's her latest dire prediction," Graelam said. "I refuse to believe it. You don't, do you?"

Roland kept his expression steady. "I can see why she would be concerned," he said at last. "After all, you have always told me that your rod is a woman's bliss. Were something to happen to it, why, then, what would she do?"

Kassia gasped. "Roland, did he say that, truly?"

"Of course I didn't say any such thing!"

" 'Twas something like that, if I recall aright. Nay, you're right, Graelam. You told me that a man's rod was a measure of a warrior and that, therefore, you were as great as Charlemagne himself."

Graelam threw a carafe of water at Roland, then fell back against the pillows at the pain it brought him. He cursed fluently and with all the frustration in his soul.

He felt his wife's soft hands on his chest,

lightly stroking him, and the pain, incredibly, eased. He opened his eyes and looked up at her. "You think you are well in control, don't you, wife?"

She leaned down and kissed him. "Aye."

"He does better, Kassia?"

She gave her husband a long look, then raised her head. "He mends, Roland. I cannot, however, continue losing at draughts with him. He isn't altogether witless and must soon guess that I am allowing him to win."

Graelam smiled at that. "I improve, Roland. 'Tis just that I am so damnably bored! It's been two days now!"

"Lady Katherine tells me that you should be well enough to be out of your bed on the morrow."

"And Daria? When will she be up and about again?"

Roland shrugged, and bent to retrieve the wooden carafe from the floor.

"It's because of me that she lost the babe. I am sorry for it, Roland."

"Lady Katherine said it was God's will that you be saved. If that is the truth of it, then so be it. There is no blame here, Graelam. Rest now, and obey your wife. Daria does well enough. Kassia, when you wish to be relieved of this giant's company, you will send me word. Now, Rolfe awaits outside to see you, Graelam. Some matter of little importance, I imagine, but he doesn't wish you to feel impotent."

Roland left Graelam's chamber, his destination the stables. He wanted to clear his mind, to leave all the pain and hurt behind him for just a few hours.

Not that Daria had said anything to him. She'd said nothing. She'd slept throughout that day, awakening in the early evening to drink some beef broth prepared especially for her by Alice. Roland wanted to see her, hold her, perhaps, assure himself that she was all right, but when he had entered the room, it was as if she wasn't there. A pale copy of her lay in the bed, but Daria, *his* Daria, was gone. As was the babe. She'd looked at him, then turned away. He'd slept that night in the great hall, wrapped in a blanket, one of the castle dogs at his feet.

It was nearly dark in the bedchamber, yet she made no move to light a candle. The air was cooling finally after the intense heat of the day, and Daria pulled a light blanket over her. It brought her no pain to do so. She felt no pain at all, just a soreness and the damnable weakness.

Her mother came into the room quietly,

her stride light and graceful even though she carried a tray doubtless filled with an assortment of marvelous foods from Alice. Daria closed her eyes, but it was too late.

"Nay, love, pretend not with me. You must eat."

Daria felt the soft sting of candlelight against her eyelids. She didn't want to be awake, she didn't want to be *here*. She said aloud, her voice still raw and hoarse, "I wish I had died, Mother. It would have solved every problem."

"It would have solved your problem and only yours. You wouldn't be feeling a thing. But everyone else's?" At least she'd spoken, at last, Katherine thought, even though what she said made her mother's heart wither. She continued, speaking her mind. "You will bear your pain just as everyone around you bears his own. But that isn't the point, is it, Daria?"

"The point is that I have no more excuse to remain here, in *his* castle, eating *his* food, sleeping in *his* bed."

"It isn't a matter of excuses."

Roland's voice came from the doorway. Katherine whirled about, wondering how much he'd heard. As for Daria, she turned her face away, closing her eyes. Katherine watched him as he strode into the room. He looked tired, she thought. He said to her even as he looked only at his wife, "I will see that she eats, Katherine. Sir Thomas grows restive in your absence. I would appreciate your being our hostess until Daria is well again."

Katherine looked down at her daughter, then back at her son-in-law. She wanted to beg him to go gently, but his face was now closed, his eyes cold, as if he guessed she would press him again. She said nothing. Roland waited until the door closed after her; then he moved to stand beside the bed.

"You will eat your dinner."

Daria said nothing, nor did she move.

"You're not dead, Daria, so there are still problems abounding, and you must help to solve them, and that means that you must get out of that bed. I can't regain your strength for you. You must do it for yourself. Now, eat, or I will force the food down your throat. I won't tell you again."

When she didn't respond to him, he leaned down and clasped her under her arms and pulled her up. He smoothed the pillows behind her and straightened the covers. "Have I dislodged the cloths?"

"No."

"Do you have any pain?"

"No."

"Good. I will place the tray here and you will eat. I won't leave you alone until you have done so."

She turned to face him. For the past two days he'd kept his distance from her. Now it seemed that he was changing his tactics. His voice was cold, his face set. His dark eyes, so beautiful and deep, regarded her with no emotion at all. He looked tired, and she wondered what he'd done during the day.

Why was he bothering? Why was he playing the worried husband? It made no sense to her. He would likely gain an annulment, despite her pregnancy, since he would claim it had been another man's seed that had grown in her.

She said aloud now, "Why are you doing this? What do you want? I will give you an annulment, though I doubt anything I would say would have any bearing on it."

A black eyebrow shot up. "Eat some of these stewed carrots and beans."

Daria ate several bites of the stewed vegetables. They were delicious and she realized she was starving. Her mouth began to water. She took a bite of mutton, marinated in some sort of incredible dill sauce, and roasted until the meat was falling from the bone. She nearly moaned aloud at the wondrous taste of it.

She continued to eat. Roland merely watched her, saying nothing. He was so relieved, he could think of nothing to say in any case. She was still so very pale that it scared the devil out of him. He'd allowed her two days; nothing had changed. She'd fallen even more deeply into depression. She was retreating even further from him. He would allow her no more time, in the hopes she would regain her spirit. He would take over now.

"I vow eating Alice's cooking is preferable to dying," he said at last as she chewed on a hunk of soft white bread.

She continued to chew, looking straight ahead.

He wouldn't continue to let her ignore him. "Dying is the coward's way as well. It wouldn't solve any problems at all. You would just be buried with some of them, yet the feel of them would still exist and eat at others who still lived."

She looked at him then, her expression as closed as his own. "I care not about your problems, Roland. They are yours and thus you are responsible for them. I would that you leave me alone. I would that you would seek an annulment."

"It appears obvious to me that you will gain neither of your wishes. Don't tell me you wish to contemplate visiting a convent again?"

Daria closed her eyes and leaned her head back against the pillows. She wanted to shudder at the thought of a convent. Her belly was full, but she felt so tired, weary to the depths of her, and now he was baiting her.

"Please go."

"No. I've left you alone for two days. No longer. Now I will carry you to Graelam's bedchamber. He wishes to see you. His guilt is palpable and you must assuage it."

"*His guilt.* That is utterly absurd. It was my decision to try to save him, not his. If there is guilt to bear, it is mine and no one else's."

"That's what I told him, but he refuses to accept my word. Do you need to relieve yourself?"

She shook her head at that.

"Good. Let me take the tray, then." He paused, looking down at her. Katherine had braided her hair, but it was lank and lifeless. There were purple smudges under her eyes, but it was her eyes themselves that frightened him. They looked vague and lost. He shook himself. It made no sense. She would come around. He would make her come around. At least there was some color in her face now from the meal she'd eaten.

"I don't wish to see him."

"I don't care what you wish," he said. She didn't fight him, merely held herself stiffly until she didn't have any more strength, then laid her head on his shoulder as he carried her to Graelam's bedchamber.

Roland kicked the door open with his foot and called out, "I have brought you a treat, Graelam. What say you, Kassia? Shall I place my wife in bed with your husband? Perhaps we could begin a row of invalids. I would go find others. What do you think?"

"I think they're both too weak to shame us, Roland," Kassia said, and smoothed a place beside Graelam. "Place her here if you wish it." But Roland shook his head, saying, "Nay, I believe I shall continue to hold her. She's warm and soft. Bring that chair closer, Kassia."

Roland settled into the chair, his wife held close against his chest.

"Now, Graelam, as you see, my wife is mending. Unlike you, she is pliable and docile. I told her to eat, and she ate. She lies gentle and uncomplaining in my arms."

"Whilst you, husband," Kassia continued, sitting beside her husband, "carp and complain and make me want to throw that chair at your stubborn head."

Graelam stared at the pale-faced girl held in her husband's lap. With Kassia and Roland here, he would never come to know what was in her mind. Soon, he thought. On the morrow he would visit her. He said now, his voice gentle, "I'm glad you ate your dinner."

Daria nodded. She felt Roland's arms around her, holding her as if he cared about her. She felt his warmth, the hardness of his man's body, and wanted to weep. She felt pain so harsh it filled her and broke her completely, and she turned her face inward against his throat.

Roland felt her tears, felt the tremors in her body, yet she made no sound, just that awful racking of her body. He looked at Graelam and Kassia, their expressions appalled and concerned. "I will see you again," he said to Graelam, and carried his wife back to their bedchamber. He didn't release her, merely eased down on the bed, still holding her closely against him. "Are you cold?"

She didn't reply, just continued to cry without making a sound. It tore at him, this silent pain of hers. He spoke to her then, quietly, his voice pitched soft and deep. "If I could change what happened, I would, Daria. Doubt it not. I do not rejoice that you lost the babe, for I could have lost you as well. I want you to mend, to smile again, to come back to me. Please, don't weep."

"When you last took me, you felt the babe and hated me and you hated him."

Her voice was a whisper, and wet with hurt. He closed his eyes, remembering clearly that morning, remembering clearly how he'd felt when he'd touched the slight mound in her belly. He'd left her without a word. How had she felt?

"It isn't true that you don't rejoice."

"Daria, listen to me. I'm your husband. I have told you before and I will tell you again. I would protect you now with my life. Then I would have protected you with my life. It seems that ever since that first time I saw you, I was ready to protect you. I don't know why you won't name the father. Perhaps it is because you fear I would be killed by him, for I know you care for me. But it's no longer important. You are important, you and I and our life together."

She stopped crying then. These tears were for the child, his child, and for her, and for the emptiness in her heart. Slowly, for she was so very weak, she lifted herself to look at him. "I will say this just once more, Roland, then never again. The babe I carried was yours, conceived that night in

Wrexham. If you cannot bring yourself to believe in me, to believe that I would never lie to you, ever, then I wish you to seek an annulment. I don't wish to remain here."

"Daria —"

"No, make no more protestations. I had prayed the babe would come in its time and it would look like its father — like you, Roland — that it would be a son and he would be dark like you, his eyes so black they looked like a moonless night, that when he smiled, it would be your smile you would see smiling back at you. It was a hope that I held deep within me, praying that it would be so, praying that then you would realize that I hadn't lied to you. But God decided otherwise. Now there is nothing for you save my word to you." She broke off on a gasp.

"What's wrong?"

"The bleeding . . . oh, God!"

Roland quickly eased her onto her back. He jerked open her bedrobe and saw that the cloths had become dislodged and there was blood on her thighs. "Hold still," he said.

After he'd bathed her and replaced the cloths, he straightened over her. "Are you warm enough?"

She nodded, turning her face again from him.

"Salin told me today that he'd heard of a band of about ten men a day or so away from here, camping in the open. They weren't recognized."

She remained silent, locked away from him.

"From the description he got from a tinker, though, it sounds like your esteemed uncle. A tall blond-haired man with pale flesh and a destrier more powerful than any he'd seen before. I wonder if your uncle would be stupid enough to try to enter the keep and kill me. He's a fool if he believes he can accomplish it."

"My uncle would never attack you in the open. He is treacherous and he will find a way, doubt it not. He will seek to take something precious from you, and then he will use it as leverage against you. Perhaps jewels, perhaps coin."

"You are all that is precious to me and I vow he'll never come near you again."

He heard her draw in her breath.

He smiled down at her. "Would you like to play draughts with me now? Like Kassia, I could cheat so that you would win."

21

Graelam de Moreton waited patiently until Lady Katherine disappeared down the stairs, then walked down the narrow corridor, carefully and as slowly as an old man, his ribs pulling and aching. He slipped into the bedchamber, quietly closing the door after him.

Daria was lying on her back, her eyes closed, a thin cover drawn to her chest. He walked to the bed and stared down at her. Her dark hair was loose on the pillow. Beautiful hair, he thought, darker than Kassia's, yet mixed with the same vivid autumn colors. She was still too pale, her bones too prominent. As if sensing him, her eyes opened and her breath choked in her throat before she recognized him in the dim light.

"Lord Graelam! You startled me." She struggled up to her elbows. "Should you be out of your bed, my lord? Shall I call Kassia for you? Your ribs, surely they aren't healed sufficiently as yet. Shall —"

He smiled at her and gently pressed her back down. Her bones felt so very fragile under his hands. He sat beside her and lifted her hand, holding it between his two large ones. "I would speak to you," he said.

He saw her withdraw from him in that instant, her expression now carefully blank, her eyes wary, an invisible wall now firmly set between them.

"Nay, don't retreat, it's a coward's way and I know you aren't a coward, Daria. A coward wouldn't have thrown aside my men to get to me and heaved at those damned rocks until she was numb with the pain of it."

"Sometimes there's nothing left."

He snorted at that and said something so lurid she blinked, staring at him. He grinned at her and nodded. "Aye, my men told me what you did. Indeed they seem to talk of little else save your bravery. They were amazed, and yea, somewhat frightened, for you seemed possessed to them. Yet you saved me, and for that I think they will forgive you almost anything." He grinned. "My men are loyal."

"As is your wife."

"Very true. She would try to slit an enemy's throat were I threatened. She hasn't the physical strength, but her spirit is above boundless."

Daria said nothing more, and Graelam looked away from her, toward the window slit. "I know the truth."

"Nay!"

"There is humiliation in that one small word, Daria," he said, looking back at her. "No, your husband didn't confide in me, though I wish he had. Actually, I listened to your mother speaking to Roland. They didn't know I was there. She was upset and was pressing him, but he withdrew from her just as you have from me. This is a puzzle, this strange tale of yours, but not unsolvable. I'm surprised you would give up. I'm disappointed in you. It isn't the act of the woman who saved my wretched life."

"He won't believe me. Should I continue to protest my innocence until he retreats completely from me?"

"So, it's a matter of him not remembering that night. I wonder how to stimulate his memory."

"Nay, 'tis a matter of him refusing to believe me. I'm his wife and I love him, I always have, ever since the moment I first saw him disguised as a priest when he came to Tyberton to rescue me."

Graelam laughed, much to Daria's surprise. "Nay, don't look at me like I'm a monster with no feelings. It's just that early in my marriage to Kassia, there was a matter of discord between us. I didn't believe her innocence in a certain matter. And then, finally, it simply was no longer important, for I had come to love her. The truth came out later, but it didn't matter by then."

"There is a difference here. Roland doesn't love me and I doubt he ever will. The king forced him to wed me. Nay, more's the truth, his own honor forced him, for he did care about me; he felt sorry for me. He also wanted my dowry. And now there is no way I can prove the truth of my claim. You see, I swore to myself that Roland would never know. I didn't want him to feel guilty that he'd taken my virginity. I didn't want him to feel responsible for me, for all of it had been my idea. Then I was with child and everything changed. I was sorry for it, but there was naught I could do. And now there is no reason for him to trust me, to believe anything I say. There is no reason for him to ever care for me again."

"Why do you harp on that? Are you a shrew? Are you bitter-tongued and harsh? You haven't an answer, I see. Let me ask you this, Daria. Who does Roland believe to be the man who raped you?"

"Most likely the Earl of Clare. But if he didn't rape me, why then, Roland just accepts that another man must have, a man he doesn't know about, a man who must have attacked me in Wrexham whilst Roland was ill in his bed."

"So if I were to bring this Earl of Clare here and he denied having raped you, Roland still wouldn't be convinced?"

She shook her head.

Graelam stood slowly, for his every move brought pain from his bruised ribs. "You saw that wall collapse on me. You saw your father die. What is this with Roland?"

"It is just that when I saw him, I knew him. Deep inside, I knew him, recognized him as being part of me. I know it seems strange, mayhap even close to madness, but it is true."

"I doubt it not. I will leave you now, Daria. Please remember that a coward's way isn't your way. Do not disappoint me; do not disappoint yourself. I am in your debt. I always pay my debts, but I must consider all this very carefully. Aye, very carefully indeed."

He left her and she was again alone. And she pondered his words.

"Have you heard aught else?" Roland asked.

Salin shook his head. "He's gone to ground, the filthy whoreson. I don't like it, nor do I like the stories I've heard about the Earl of Reymerstone. I would take some men and search him out. I would like to split him."

It was Roland's turn to shake his head, and he did. "Nay, Salin, not yet. When it is time for the hunt, I will lead the pack. But I cannot leave yet, not until . . ."

His voice trailed off.

"Until your lady heals," Salin finished for him. "Gwyn told me she smiled this morning. 'Twas a matter of a new overtunic sewn for her by Lady Katherine."

Roland wished he'd seen that smile. Over a week had passed since she'd miscarried the babe. She seemed well again, though she was too thin and there were the dark smudges beneath her eyes. Yes, he wished he could have seen her smile. Either he or Graelam played chess with her in the evenings. Kassia refused to play against Daria, saying that women were too smart to go against each other. Roland wondered at Graelam's attitude toward Daria. He teased her and mocked her skills at chess and laughed at her until Daria began telling him he was a lout and a bore. Graelam only teased her more. And since two nights ago,

Roland had begun sleeping in his own bed again. But he'd made no move to touch his wife.

The previous evening he'd seen her looking at him and he'd returned her look before she had time to glance away. The pain in her eyes had smitten him deep. He'd wanted to say something to her, but she'd withdrawn immediately and he wasn't ready to scale that wall as yet, for, in truth, he didn't know what to say. His life had become a damnable tangled mess and he loathed it, yet he felt powerless to change it.

Both Salin and Roland looked up to see Lord Graelam de Moreton striding toward them across the inner bailey. He looked strong, fit, and fearsome in his black-and-silver mail. For a man who'd very nearly met his maker not too many days before, his appearance now bespoke something of a miracle. His men gazed upon him with looks approaching awe.

He was slapping his gloves against his thigh. He looked thoughtful and mildly worried.

"I believe you are healed, Graelam. Shall I buffet your ribs or shake your hand?"

Graelam grinned at Roland. "You will now have peace and perchance some success at chess, my friend, for I am leaving you. It is time I returned my wife to Wolffeton."

An odd way to say it, Roland thought. "And what do you then, Graelam?"

"Why, I'll rot in my own castle, what else?"

"I don't know," Roland said, frowning at him. "I don't know."

Graelam pulled on his gauntlets. "Mayhap I'll go a-raiding and steal some of Dienwald's sheep. He is a joy to behold when he's bulging with fury. Ah, and does Philippa ever make him bulge! Ah, my errant wife. Kassia! Come, dearling, and bid your good-byes to your kind host. Then you can bedevil me all the way back to Wolffeton."

Daria watched Graelam and Kassia and their soldiers ride from the keep. She wasn't particularly surprised when Lord Graelam suddenly turned in his saddle and looked for a long moment back at the castle. It seemed as if he was searching her out. She wondered at him. So fearsome a warrior, yet so kind to her. She would hate being his enemy, for she knew he would show no quarter. She felt suddenly unsteady and eased into a chair. The damnable weakness. It wouldn't leave her. Kassia had told her what to expect, at least what had happened to her after Harry's birth. Then she'd kissed her cheek, saying as she gripped her hands, "You saved my husband. For that I am in your debt for all time. I always pay my debts. Don't give up, Daria." Skirts swirling, Kassia had left her.

Chantry Hall was filled with people, shouting and laughing and buffeting each other, the children arguing and shrieking, and still Daria felt utterly alone even in the chaotic hall. She couldn't bear the furtive pitying looks, and thus remained alone in Roland's bedchamber much of the time. Daria rose now and pulled her new overtunic over her gown. It was a pale blue wool and very soft to the touch. She would show her husband her new finery. Perhaps he would smile.

He was speaking to Salin in the inner bailey, and both men looked ready to ride out. She paused on the bottom stone step of the great hall, the early-morning sunlight blazing down on her face, warming her. Roland looked up. He stared at her, unmoving. He said nothing. He raised his hand in a small salute, then turned on his heel and strode toward the stables, Salin at his side.

Ah, yes, he remained kind to her when he chanced to be with her. Nothing more.

But then again, she didn't expect much

more than that. She didn't see him at all during the days, for he worked beside his men to repair the eastern castle wall, the one that had collapsed on Graelam. It was nearly completed now. Time passed, and with the passing days, her strength returned. As for the interior of the keep, Daria worked diligently to see it cleaned, the trestle tables scrubbed, the lord and lady's chairs polished to a high sheen. And then, one morning she was able to see the thick oak beams crisscrossing high above the great hall. So many years of smoke had blackened them and it had taken hours of sweating and cursing to scrub them clean. She smiled, pleased with herself. Roland's keep was becoming almost pleasant. The reeds on the floor were sweet-smelling, the jakes had been thoroughly limed, and only a strong wind blowing in a westerly direction brought any noxious odors to the nose.

Now she needed to see the outbuildings whitewashed, needed to purchase goods and a few new furnishings for the great hall and its antechambers. The goods that had made up her dowry had added warmth, the two brass lavers gleaming, they were so highly polished, the chair cushions thick and soft, and the two tapestries sewn by her grandmother, on the far wall, giving color and protection from the damp. But she had to wait to purchase any further goods, for it required Roland's approval. She spent her afternoons sorting through herbs, mixing those potions she knew, sewing companionably with her mother, and giving instructions for the castle servants through Gwyn, the girl Roland had slept with, the girl who was friendly and quite nice, the girl Daria couldn't help but like.

She wore her new overtunic again, loosely sewn with wide sleeves, over one of her old gowns her mother had altered for her. She was too thin, but food still made her feel faintly ill. She girded the braided gold belt more firmly around her waist, pulling in the material. She brushed her hair and left it loose, thick and lustrous from washing, nearly to her waist.

Roland entered the bedchamber and came to an abrupt halt. She became still under his scrutiny.

"You're lovely."

"Thank you."

"I must see to some jewelry for you, Daria. Something delicate, perhaps emeralds to match your eyes."

She stared at him, wondering what was in his mind, wondering why he was speaking thus to her.

"I should prefer purchasing a few more goods for your castle, Roland."

"Oh?"

"Perhaps several more carpets, some cushions for your chair here in the bed-chamber, mayhap even a tapestry for the wall here, for the damp is very bad, Sir Thomas told me, during the winter months."

Roland appeared thoughtful for several minutes, then said, quite unexpectedly, "Did you know that Philippa is the steward for St. Erth?"

"Aye, you told me that once."

"Should you mind detailing our needs and balancing them against the coin we have remaining from your dowry and from my cache? Next year I suspect we will have excess wool to sell and that will make us more self-sufficient. Graelam and I spoke of which markets were best and which merchants in this area didn't try to steal your destrier from beneath you during the bargaining."

"You aren't jesting? I wouldn't have thought a man would approve such an activity for a woman."

Roland shrugged.

"I should very much like to do these things, Roland."

"When you have completed your entering, discuss it with me. Then we will decide what is to be done first."

She could but stare at him before the words blurted out. "Why are you being like this?"

"Like what?"

"Kind to me . . . as if you cared what —"

He cut her off, for he simply couldn't bear to hear the rest of her words. "There is work to be done and you are capable of doing it. Don't you believe yourself able to accomplish it?"

Her chin went up. "I am quite capable."

He smiled at her then, his dark eyes warm and approving, and Daria would willingly have cut even Lord Graelam's throat had he threatened her husband.

It was the second day of September. The air was crisp and cool. An early-autumn day it was, with a clear sky overhead and a bright sun that made the different colors of the countryside all the more vivid. Daria breathed in deeply. She came out of the great hall at the sound of shouting and stood on her tiptoes to see what was happening. There was her husband, stripped to the waist, breathing heavily, sweat glistening off him. He was circling another man, a huge lout who looked quite able to rip her husband into pieces. The men-at-arms had formed a large, loose circle around them and they were yelling and shouting. Daria froze when the other man suddenly lunged. Why were the men just standing there? Why weren't they helping Roland? She watched in mute horror as the man grabbed Roland around his waist and lifted him. She saw his massive arms bulge, the muscles flexing, and she knew he was strong enough to squeeze the life from her husband. Why, she wondered frantically, had she seen the wall collapse on Graelam and not seen her own husband about to meet his death? Why weren't his men doing anything?

She acted without thought, terror for Roland gripping her, making her frantic. She grabbed her skirts, pulling them above her knees, and dashed down the deep stone steps into the inner bailey. She was screaming as she ran. She reached the loose circle of men and began to curse them, pushing and shoving them aside until she was within the circle. She raised her fist at them, screaming, "Why aren't you doing something? You miserable cowards! You filthy whoresons! You will stand by and let him be crushed to death?" Several of the men who had heard her looked as if they'd turned into stone, staring at her, not moving a finger. Furious, she ignored them. She was so close to Roland and the huge man that she could hear their breathing, hear their lurid curses. Somehow Roland had gotten free, but just as she nearly yelled her relief, the huge tout lunged again, screaming a terrible curse, and Daria, all thought frozen within her, jumped on his back just as he grabbed for Roland.

She clutched him around his thick neck, yelling, pummeling the top of his head with her fist. "No! Don't you dare touch him! I'll kill you!" She managed to wrap her legs around him and she tried to choke the life from him, jerking his head back and crushing inward with her forearms. She squeezed her legs around him as he'd done to Roland with his arms, but it was nothing to him. She screamed and yelled and punched him, beyond thought, so furious and frightened that for many minutes she didn't realize that the man was standing perfectly still, not even trying to dislodge her from his back, and that there wasn't a whisper of a voice anywhere near them.

"Daria!"

Through the haze of fear, she heard her name. She shook her head, pounding the man's head as hard as she could.

"Daria! By all the saints, stop it!"

She looked up then and saw Roland standing beside her. She realized then that the man whose back she was clinging to like a demented fool was standing very quietly, not moving even a finger, just letting her strike him.

"Come, that's quite enough." Roland was holding out his arms to her.

"But I don't wish him to hurt you and . . . She sent her fist into the side of the man's head one more time.

"By all the saints, stop it! Rollo has few enough brains without you pounding the rest out of his head! Cease your attack! Come!"

She released her hold on the man's neck and dropped her legs from his waist. She flung out her arms and Roland caught her and lifted her down to stand on the cobblestones.

But she was still gripped in her unreasoning fear. But Roland seemed to be all right. She was crying now, not realizing it, her hands running over his face, down to his shoulders, touching him, probing at his flesh, assuring herself that he wasn't hurt. "I was so afraid . . . I thought he was killing you, he is so large and —"

It was the complete and utter silence that made her slow. Not a whisper of a sound.

Her voice dropped off and she became as still as everyone around her. Slowly she turned to look at the man. He was still standing quietly, just looking back at her, a curious blend of confusion and amazement writ on his ugly face. And all their people were now in a loose circle around her and Roland, staring at her and whispering behind their hands.

She raised her face. "Roland? He didn't hurt you? You're all right, truly? I don't understand."

Something was very wrong. She saw the myriad of emotions cross his expressive face. There was anger, oh, she could feel waves of anger flowing from him, but then it was gone, swept away by something else . . . something . . . He was laughing. He threw back his head and roared with laughter. Soon the entire inner bailey was filled with people who were howling with laughter, holding their sides, screaming with laughter. She stood there, not understanding. The huge man was now laughing as well, deep gritty laughter.

They were all laughing at her.

What had she done?

She realized at that moment that her gown was ripped under her left arm. Sweat was streaking down her face . . . nay, not just sweat, but tears of rage and fear at the man who'd been attacking Roland. One of her leather slippers lay on the ground near her. Her hair had come loose from its bound coil and was hanging over her shoulder. The laughter swelled, overwhelming her. She felt apart from all of them; she felt ridiculous; she felt a complete fool.

She cried out, a small broken cry, and grabbed her skirts yet again, and began running toward the narrow tunnel that connected the inner bailey to the outer bailey. The portcullis was raised and no one blocked her way.

"Daria! Wait!"

Roland's laughter died as quickly as it had sprung up. He looked at Rollo, the hulking fellow he'd been wrestling with.

"Thank you for not hurting her," he said. "All of you — back to your chores."

The laughter quieted a bit, but the men and women watched the master dash after his wife.

Salin said to Rollo, "Mayhap 'tis the best wrestling match I've ever seen. Mayhap it will bring an excellent result."

Rollo banged the side of his head with the heel of his hand, as if to clear it. He said with genuine surprise, "She jumped on my back and pounded my head. She tried to break my neck with those skinny little arms of hers."

"Aye, you'll have a bit of a black eye for your labors, but your neck's thicker than an oak tree. No danger she'd twist that part of you off."

Rollo shook his head, staring after Daria. "I could have killed her, yet she attacked me."

"Aye," Salin said. "He's her husband."

"A female attacking me," Rollo said, shaking his head. "I will leave now and return to my farm. Tell the master I will return whenever he wishes to continue our match. When I tell my wife of the little mistress attacking me, she will laugh until her eyes cross."

Roland gave up yelling after his wife. He would catch up with her soon enough. And he did, just outside the castle walls, just at the top of a slight hillock covered with thick green grass. He grabbed her arm, but she jerked free of him, and he stumbled at the same time and lost his balance and the two of them went tumbling over the side of the embankment down the grassy slope. They'd done this same tumble before, he thought blankly even as he fell. Roland tried to protect her, but it wasn't possible. They came to a halt at the bottom, Roland on his back and Daria on her side.

She lay there gasping for breath, quite un-hurt, at least in body. She was so humiliated that she regained her breath more quickly than she probably would have, and lurched to her feet. She saw Roland lying there, looking up at her, a huge grin on his face. She cried out and scrambled back up the slope, only to feel his hand around her ankle. He pulled, very gently, and she fell backward against his chest. He was still laughing. At her. She saw red and turned on him, crying out, smashing her fists into his chest.

"Stop it! You bastard, stop laughing at me!"

Roland stopped quickly enough. He pulled her against him, flattening her arms to her sides to protect himself, and held her still. "Hush," he said. "Hush."

"I'm not the one laughing! I hate you!"

"No you don't. Don't lie, it doesn't be-come you." And he chuckled, and in be-tween chuckles, he leaned down and lightly nipped at her bare throat. Her gown was now ripped nearly to her waist, and then he felt the hot smooth flesh of her shoulder against his mouth, he felt a surge of desire so strong he shook with it. No, he didn't want to laugh now. By all the saints, it had been so long, so very long.

He didn't think, just acted. He grasped the straps of her chemise and ripped them apart. He pulled the soft worn cotton to her waist, baring her breasts. She wasn't moving now.

"You're so damned beautiful."

He didn't touch her, just stared down at her heaving breasts. She gulped and tried to pull away from him, but he held her still, her arms still pinned to her sides.

"Are you well?" he said, and his voice was harsh and deep. "Inside, are you healed?"

But he didn't wait for her to answer. He couldn't. He leaned down and kissed her, hard, his hands cupping her face between his palms, holding her still for him. At the touch of his mouth against hers, Daria felt a great relief begin to fill her, but it changed and became something else, something urgent and frantic and wild.

"Part your lips. Yes, that's right. Touch my tongue, Daria. Ah . . . so sweet, so very sweet you are. Do you like my hands on your breasts?"

He was lightly stroking his fingertips over her breasts, lifting them in his palms, not yet touching her nipples, just stroking her lightly, as if to learn her. Then his hand dipped down to stroke over her ribs, then he was jerking away her gown, ripping it without hesitation, and finally it fell, pooling about her feet. He yanked at the chemise and then she was standing naked, supported by his arm, his hand stroking over her breasts, his mouth and tongue against hers.

She turned to him then, wanting more, wanting all of him now. When she pressed herself against him, his hands became frenzied on her back, sweeping downward to cup her buttocks. He lifted her, fitting her against himself, and she felt his urgency, felt the hardness of him, and he was so hot, so intensely alive, and he wanted her. A bolt of sheer lust went through her and she moaned against his mouth.

He set her away from him but her hands were on his clothes, pulling at the fastenings, and both of them were clumsily trying to strip him, but it took much more time than they'd thought it would.

But then, despite her help, Roland was naked and standing before her, and she hurled herself at him, pressing hard against him, flinging her arms around his neck, and she raised her face for a kiss and he gave her all his need and desire. Then he lifted her. "Wrap your legs around my waist, quickly. I'm going to come upward into you, Daria, deeply into you . . ." And she felt him fitting her legs around his flanks, felt his fingertips between her thighs, stroking upward until he found her. He parted her swelled woman's flesh with his fingers and she gasped and lurched, wanting to help him but not knowing how to. And he was breathing so harshly, and she was too, that neither of them heard the shouting. Then he was easing inside her, pushing upward, slowly, just a bit at a time, his body trembling at the control he tried to exert, and she was gasping at the feel of him, wanting more, yet it was tight and so sweet, the feel of him inside her . . .

"Roland! Daria!"

He shoved his full length into her, driving upward, kissing her breasts as she arched her back at the feel of him. "By all the saints," he gasped, and eased her down upon her back against the sweet-smelling grass. And he began to ride her hard and deep.

"Roland! Daria!"

He froze over her, a look of astonished chagrin coming over his features. "Oh, no," he said, and his voice was filled with pain. "By all the saints, I don't believe it." He began to curse.

She stared up at him, not understanding, until she heard their names shouted a third time.

He pulled out of her, his chest heaving, his member swelled and hard and wet from her. He looked for a moment utterly bewildered and uncertain of what he should do. Then he shook himself into action.

"Quickly, dearling, quickly. It's Sir Thomas and he draws very close." Roland saw that she was still held in thrall by her passion, and he ignored his own nakedness to help her dress again in her ripped clothes. "Hold them together. That's it. Are you all right now?"

She was holding the bodice of her gown together over her breasts and she was just looking up at him.

"Are you all right?"

She shook her head, no words in her mind, not a single one.

He smiled, a painful smile, and touched his fingertips to her mouth. "I know, dearling. This night there won't be any interruptions. By all the saints, you're lovely."

When Sir Thomas and Lady Katherine appeared at the top of the slope, it was to see Roland clumsily pulling on his clothes and Daria, standing there like a half-wit, watching him.

"I think," Sir Thomas said to Lady Katherine, "that our presence is more than a nuisance."

"You don't think he'll hurt her, do you?"

Sir Thomas smiled down at her. "Hurt her? I'll warrant he was making her wild with pleasure until we came along and ruined it all."

Katherine jerked just a bit at his words, and said slowly, "I don't think that's possible."

"So it was like that with you, was it? A pity. If you'll allow me, I will show you that a man can please you. Come, let's leave them. I daresay Roland won't particularly wish to converse with either of us at the moment. Actually, he is probably beyond putting two words together."

22

Roland couldn't clear his mind. He couldn't seem to focus on anything outside himself, outside her. His body was in control, or out of control, he thought blankly, his senses filled with her, her sweet wild scent, the tangled masses of hair tumbling down her back, her ripped gown showing patches of smooth white flesh. He grabbed her hand and pulled her around. He didn't care that they were in plain sight of the castle. He simply didn't think about it. He looked down at her mouth, soft and slightly parted, and moaned.

"Daria." He kissed her, pulling her up tightly against him, bringing her to her tiptoes. When she responded to him, arching upward, he trembled with the force of his need. He lifted her in his arms and strode toward a small copse of oak trees just to the east.

She wasn't pliant in his arms. She was as frantic and wild as he was. She kissed his chin, his mouth, his nose, wet, soft kisses that sent him into a near-frenzy. He felt her warm tongue on his ear, her sweet breath on his cheek. He started running. She wrapped her arms around his neck, choking him in her fervor to get closer to him.

Her ripped clothes became quickly shredded. He eased her down on her torn gown and found he couldn't wait. He came over her, parting her legs, bending her knees, and he nuzzled her white belly, kissing her, nipping light kisses, his hands stroking up and down the backs of her thighs, widening her legs, drawing nearer and nearer, and she was lifting her hips, wanting him there, closer . . .

When his mouth touched her, she cried out and lurched up, so astonished at what he was doing and how his actions made her feel that she was beyond words. "Hush, darling," he said, his breath hot on her flesh, or perhaps she was the one who was hot, for her need was beyond what she could have imagined, the roiling sensations were pushing her, making her twist and arch her back, making her legs tremble uncontrollably. It was beyond anything she could understand, and when he pressed his palm against her belly to hold her still, she lay there staring up at the sunlight that filtered through the oak leaves like silver spears. It was so beautiful, she thought, so very beautiful. But it wasn't the glistening sunlight that filled her senses, it was his mouth on her woman's flesh, and she wanted more and more. . . . Her breasts were heaving and her hands kneading his shoulders, pulling his head closer to her, and suddenly she spun out of herself, crying out again and again. Roland held her thighs, feeling the rippling spasms, the tightening of the sleek muscles. At each wrenching cry, he felt himself grow and swell, both his spirit and his member, for he reveled in her pleasure, the pleasure he was giving her. His groin was throbbing, painfully full with his need, but her release was more important, this wild pleasure of hers that went on and on and drew him into her, sending both of them beyond all thought. He gentled his mouth on her, drawing softly and slowly now, feeling her legs relax, feeling her entire body loosen, and he came up between her legs and said, "Daria, open your eyes. Look at me. I want you to see me coming into you."

He came into her powerfully, his entire body shuddering, not slowing in his pace, and he wrapped his arms around her thighs, lifting her and sending himself deeper inside her. His rhythm was hard and fast and deep, and he felt so frenzied, so out of control, he thought he would die of it. Suddenly he came out of her, the sensations too much, driving him too quickly. He lurched back and gently eased her legs off his shoulders. He pulled her upright to her knees, facing him. "I want to kiss you whilst I take you," he said, and pulled her legs around him and eased her down on his member. He closed his eyes at the feel of her. He kissed her, his tongue deep in her mouth just as his sex was deep in her belly. So deep inside her he was, she thought, and he was hers, in this precious moment he was hers and he was part of her, and there was nothing but him, and she was filled with him, and she was crying with the wonder of it.

He buried his face against her neck as he gained his release, trembling, then tensing incredibly, moaning against her throat, and she felt the wet of him deep within her and she held him as tightly as she could.

Roland lazily kissed her throat until his heart had slowed its furious pounding. Gently he eased her back onto the ground, covering her, his member still deep inside her. He lay over her, balancing himself on his elbows, looking down into her face. Her eyes were more green now than before, and he wondered how this could be so; green and vague and soft, and he saw himself reflected in her eyes and wondered if he filled her mind as he filled her belly. He prayed so, for she filled him. Her hair was tangled with stray twigs and bits of grass and small clods of dirt. Her cheeks were flushed and her lips warm and swelled. "You're beautiful," he said, and it was true. He kissed her mouth, remembering now when he'd first kissed her, he hadn't wanted to stop. Just to kiss her . . . and the instant she responded to him, he felt his member swelling again and he wanted her once more.

Very slowly he slid deep inside her, then withdrew almost completely, smiling when she lifted her hips to bring him back into her again.

"Can I give you pleasure again?"

"I don't know," she whispered, and pulled his head down. To kiss him. She loved his mouth, the texture of his flesh, the scent of him, as much as he craved her. Her body moved with his, unbidden, and when he quickened his thrusts, she dug her fingers into his back and moaned.

"I like the sound of that," he said, and eased his hand between them. To his besotted surprise, the moment his fingertips touched her, she grew frenzied, crying out, twisting beneath him, bucking upward, nearly throwing him off her in her passion. And she was crying out, quaking with the nearly painful feelings that held her, and he doubted there was a more beautiful sight in the world.

She shouted out his name in the moment of her release, and in that same instant he spewed his seed deep inside her, unable to wait, unable to do anything except to surrender to this joining, this incredible mating with her, with his wife.

It was many minutes before he could raise himself on his elbows. His muscles felt fluid. "I think you've killed me, wife."

To his pleasure, she flushed, and he laughed. He dipped his head down and kissed her mouth. How he loved to kiss her. It was many minutes before he raised his head again.

"I like to see you blush. It pleases me, but know, Daria, that a wife is expected to lose her head over her husband. 'Tis a requirement of marriage, I understand, this display of abandoned passion. Now, it appears you've twice lost your head, and that, wife . . . well, that makes me feel like a conquering warrior."

"What about your head?"

" 'Twasn't my head I lost, dearling. 'Twas all my seed."

She ducked her face into his chest and she breathed in deeply. He smelled of sweat and of the sweet earth and of her as well.

"What is this? Embarrassment from the most wanton of my women?"

"Women! I am your only woman, Roland."

"Aye, the females hereabout aren't all that comely, so perhaps I shall have to rely on you for my pleasure." He kissed her again, marveling as he did so how she drew him, charmed him with her mouth, her taste, and how he'd forgotten that during the past months, how he'd kept himself apart from her, not wanting to think of her, not wanting her to touch him in any way. He frowned as memories razed through his mind, memories he didn't want now.

She poked him in the ribs, bringing him back to her. "Nay, don't move, Roland!"

He sighed. "I'm sorry, sweetling, but you've depleted me, stripped me of my manliness, plundered my seed. I must rest for a while and garner my strength. Then you can have your way with me again."

"All right," she said, and snuggled against him. After a moment she raised her head and gave him a siren's smile, her green eyes so wicked he was again utterly charmed with her, this wife of his. "Will you need much time?"

He groaned loudly; then, because her mouth was there, just inches from his, he kissed her.

They were silent for some moments; then Roland said, his voice as neutral as a fool's smile, "Rollo is a huge fellow, a rock of a man, and stronger than an ox. Also, he is slow of foot and of reaction. That is what evens the contest."

"I don't wish to speak of that. I made a fool of myself."

She could feel him smiling. His entire body seemed to warm with his humor. "True, but had he been a knave, why, then, you would have saved me. Rather than being a fool, you would have been a heroine."

"I'm a fool and I can't go back. And look at me — my clothes are in tatters. Everyone will know what you have done to me!"

"Mayhap they'll think I beat you instead."

"But your clothes are in nearly as sorry a state. Nay, they'll know what we've done."

"That is a problem — the condition of our clothes. I will set my mind to finding a solution."

In the next moment, he was snoring loudly.

"Roland! Cease your noxious noises! You're pretending!"

He kissed her ear, nuzzling at her throat until she raised her head and gave him her mouth.

"It's odd, you know. I've always thought kissing a woman was pleasurable, but nothing more, really. But you, Daria, your mouth drives me mad with lust. Aye, I'll kiss you until God removes me from this miserable earth."

And as he kissed her, she lightly laid her hand on his hip. He jerked and kissed her harder. "And what will you do if I touch you here, Roland?" Her hand dipped to his flat hard belly. She could feel his muscles tensing, feel the crisp groin hair beneath her fingers and his smooth hot flesh. "And here?" she whispered into his mouth as her fingers lightly closed around his member.

Roland had not believed it possible, but at the touch of her warm fingers closing around him, he swelled until he was pressing against her palm, pushing, thrusting against her fingers.

"This is what I'll do," he said, and fell onto his back, bringing her over him. "Ride me, Daria. Take me."

She gave him that siren's smile again, her eyes crinkling with laughter and newly considered passion, and he shook with that smile and that look in her eyes, and he lifted his hips as she settled herself over him. When she took him and guided him upward into her, he closed his eyes and gave himself over to feelings he would never forget.

When she neared her release, he pushed her, and she went wild, bringing him with her.

"I shall surely die now," he said between gritted teeth, but he was still heaving upward, still clasping her hips in his hands, still touching her womb, and the stark intimacy of that touch held him captive for many moments. He was stunned at this mating. It should have been slow and tender, but it had been as frenzied as the first time.

"Killed by a greedy wife who wrings me out and tosses me away."

"I'm not tossing you anywhere," Daria said, stretching out over him. She nuzzled her face against his chest. "I can't even move, so how could I have the strength to heave you away?"

He was thoughtful for a moment. "This is very strange," he said at last. "Never in my life have I taken a woman so many times in so short a length of time."

She raised her head and frowned at him. "But I thought that perhaps we could —"

He slapped her buttocks. "You're lying and you just don't do it well."

"No, I'm teasing you, Roland. You enjoy me. I like that."

She looked so pleased with herself that he was obliged to chuckle. "Aye, I enjoy you. Now, however, we must see to ourselves, somehow, before Salin sends out a party to search for us."

"Must I try to stand up?"

"Aye, and so must I."

"My legs are wobbly and I can't feel any bones."

His felt just as unsteady, but he only smiled as he helped her up. They stood facing each other, dirty as urchins, smiling, smelling of sweat and sex and grass. He cupped her breasts in his hands, and she, smiling a slightly crazed smile, cupped his member between her hands and felt the heat of him warm her to her heart.

He sighed and stepped back. "There's no hope for it," he said, glancing about at their strewn torn clothes.

No one said anything when the master and mistress came into the inner bailey looking like they'd been attacked and rolled in the dirt.

Roland had stroked his fingers through her tangled hair, but it had done little good.

Daria was very aware that a multitude of eyes were staring at them and knowing what had happened. And if they didn't know immediately, her downcast eyes and the bright flush on her cheeks gave them away. Roland, curse him, was smiling like a fool.

She quickened her step and looked at her toes. Her other slipper had somehow disappeared. Roland chuckled beside her, then leaned down to whisper in her ear, "Such energy, wife. I thought I'd drained you of every ounce, but no, here you are ready to race me to our bedchamber."

"I'm a woman, Roland. I have great endurance."

"And I'm a man and filled with vigor."

He leaned down, cupping the back of her neck in his hand, and kissed her, in front of all their people, in front of the children, in front of all the dogs and cats and goats, and because kissing him was more wonderful than nearly anything else she could imagine, Daria kissed him back, pressing upward against him.

She dimly heard a raucous cheer and flushed from her hairline to her dirty toes.

He continued to kiss her until he was satisfied with his result. Then he raised his head and gave her the most insolent grin imaginable. And he said softly, smiling down at her flushed face, "You're mine, all mine. Never forget that, ever. Have water fetched for us. I shall join you in our bedchamber very shortly."

"I would say that things have improved between your daughter and Roland."

Katherine turned smiling eyes to Sir Thomas. "Aye, it would appear so. She looks so . . . at ease with herself."

"She has the look of a woman well and truly pleasured, Katherine. Her eyes appear even greener. Were her father's eyes that startling color?"

"Nay, her grandmother had eyes as green as spring grass. She shares nothing at all with her father."

"You should be proud of her. She's a lovely girl. If she continues to be so well-pleased with her husband, I doubt not that another babe will soon grow in her belly."

Oddly enough, Roland shared that thought nearly at the same time. He was watching Daria chew on a braised meat bone with great thoroughness. Her teeth were white, her tongue pink, her concentration profound. He wanted her again; he wanted her to kiss and fondle his member with such absorption as she was giving that damned meat bone.

It was perplexing, this effect she had on him, and as mystifying as it was belated. He'd kept his distance from her, both mentally and physically, since their marriage. Until today. Until she'd run out of the great hall screeching at the top of her lungs and jumped on Rollo's back, uncaring about herself, wanting only to save her husband. A woman who didn't love a man wouldn't do that. Even as he'd felt anger, then amusement, in the depths of him, he'd felt valued, he'd felt incredibly cherished. And now everything had shifted, changing even before he'd had time to question it, and, he suspected, this damned change was irrevocable. He'd never before considered himself a man to be a slave to his phallus, as were some men he'd known. Even when he'd been in the Holy Land and played the indulgent owner of six women, each of whom was eager to do nothing but please him, he hadn't been controlled by lust. And yet here was his wife, too thin, but with flesh softer than a summer rain, her cheeks rosy from the sweet wine she'd been drinking, and he wanted to jerk the meat bone out of her hand and pull up her gown and take her here, right now, this very instant. He was hard and swelled, and he was vastly relieved that the full-cut tunic covered him. He shifted painfully in his chair.

If he continued to want her, she would soon be again with child. His child this time. He sat back, listening to all the voices that filled the great hall, blending together in a low rumble, the individual words indecipherable. It was pleasant, all this noise, and it gave him peace, strangely enough. He looked over at Lady Katherine and Sir Thomas. Thomas was smitten, no doubt about that, besotted to the roots of his grizzled hair. He wondered about Katherine. Perhaps they would wed. If that happened, he hoped they would remain at Chantry Hall. The idea of having a large family surrounding him was satisfying. It made him feel needed; it made him feel like he belonged. Finally there was a place for him and he would fill it with those he cared about and those who cared about him.

Roland took a slow drink of his wine. He replied to a question from one of his men. As he spoke, he heard Daria's clear laughter. It warmed him more than the sweet wine. Then, quite suddenly and unbidden, he remembered walking beside her into the cathedral in Wrexham to get out of the endless Welsh rain. He was sicker than the devil's dog, aye, he remembered that. He'd felt weak, and his throat was raw and his head pounded and he'd wanted to puke. He remembered desperately trying to keep control of himself, but he couldn't. He remembered clearly when his mind blanked away and he was sliding to the floor. He remembered nothing else. But he should remember more, and he didn't understand why he couldn't. He frowned as he emptied his flagon.

Why couldn't he remember anything else? Two days were missing from his life. Two days until he'd come to himself to see Daria standing over him, and he remembered the feelings of humiliation when he'd had to relieve himself but was too weak to see to it without her help. But even much of that time was blurred and indistinct in his mind. He saw an older woman standing over him, smiling and giving him an evil potion to drink. Her name was Romila and she hadn't told him Daria was gone, disappeared, until he'd threatened to go search for her. What had he done in those two days? Had he possibly taken his wife's virginity during one of those two nights?

Graelam de Moreton felt good, for at least ten more seconds. He felt very good during those seconds, for under guard on the eastern side of his camp was the Earl of

Reymerstone. Then he heard a woman's voice and he started to his feet, dropping the wooden goblet of ale, when he recognized that the voice belonged to Kassia. And then she was striding up to him as if she were conqueror of the damned world, dressed like a boy in tunic and hose, a feathered cap over her hair, and she was laughing. When she got five feet away from him, she let out a whooping yell and hurled herself at him.

He caught her, holding her tightly to him. She was laughing and babbling, her words tumbling to and fro, saying things about paying her debt to Daria, and here he was doing the same thing, and they'd more than paid back their obligation, and wasn't it wonderful.

Graelam shook his head, set his wife away from him, and tried to look fearsome. It wasn't difficult, for he was stripped down to a loincloth, preparing to bathe his sweating, dirty face and body. He was large and hard, and when he wished to, his expression could be as frightening as the devil's.

"Oh," Kassia said, looking at him from his toes to his mouth. "Oh," she said again, and she smiled up at him brilliantly. "You're nearly naked, Graelam."

He clasped her waist between his hands and lifted her. When her nose was right in front of his nose, he said, "You are here in my camp, a wild and lonely place that lies twenty miles from Wolffeton, a place you shouldn't be, and you are garbed like a silly boy in clothes you shouldn't be wearing, and you are grinning like a half-witted wench. I heard your wild babbling but understood it not. Now, madam, you will tell me what the hell you're doing here and why —"

She laughed, leaning forward to kiss him. "I will tell you everything, my dear lord, if you will but let my feet touch the ground again. I should love some ale. This tracking makes one vastly thirsty."

"Kassia!"

She danced away from him, and he watched her, shaking his head, knowing she would tell him everything in her own good time. He commenced with his bathing. When he felt her take the wet cloth from his hand, he smiled, and gave a contented moan as she scrubbed his back.

He was naked now and they were alone in his tent and she was standing between his legs, her fingers massaging his scalp.

"I was worried about you, Graelam."

" 'Twas naught to worry even little Harry. The Earl of Reymerstone wasn't expecting me, needless to say. I took him and his men with no bloodshed. He lies yon in a tent with

Rolfe and three of my soldiers guarding him. He's a very unhappy man at this moment, and likely confused as to why I, a stranger to him, would take him prisoner."

She leaned down and kissed him. "Let the lout suffer awhile longer."

"And will you tell me what you've done, Kassia?" he asked, all calm inquiry. "Clearly this time."

"Aye, I will tell you, my lord. I have the Earl of Clare with me, and four of his men."

"You what?"

His incredulous reaction warmed her to her fingertips. She grinned hugely. "I owed Daria a debt for saving your life. You were going after the Earl of Reymerstone, but what was I to do? Oh, yes, I overheard Rolfe speaking of it, that's how I found out. There was a shortage of enemies. Then the most wonderful news came to Wolffeton whilst you were gone. The Earl of Clare — that Marcher Baron who'd held her captive for all those months — had come into Cornwall to try to recapture her. Nay, Graelam, don't bellow at me! Please, heed me, my lord, for I have right and reason on my side."

Graelam's face was white and grim. He couldn't believe his ears, couldn't believe what his wife — this cocky little twit — was telling him. "Continue," he said, but he wasn't at all certain he wanted to hear the rest of it.

Kassia, happily, was unaware of her husband's mental upheaval, and continued, "I saw it as a sign from God, Graelam, surely you must understand that. You were gone and thus I saw it as a divine signal for me to act. It was my opportunity to repay my debt to Daria. None of my men — your men — were hurt. The Earl of Clare lies bound and in some discomfort in the small copse just beyond your camp. The man has the reddest hair, did you know that? The fool had thought to sneak into Chantry Hall, steal Daria away, and disappear like a thief of some brilliance. I told him that I wouldn't allow that. He's equally as unhappy as the Earl of Reymerstone, I daresay."

Graelam stared at his wife, at his delicate, white-skinned, very small wife. "I should beat you," he said, his eyes darkening.

"I pray that you don't, my lord, for I am very weary from my hunting."

He rose, towering above her, his naked body gleaming in the lone candlelight, and pulled on a bedrobe. As he belted it, he heard her say from behind him, "I would prefer you naked, husband. Just to look at you makes me hungry for you, not for a boring meal."

He turned on her, roaring, "You won't make me forget your reckless stupidity, Kassia! Don't try your woman's wile on me!" He paused, eyeing her, then said, "There is some bread and meat left from our supper. I will have one of the men bring it to you. Remain in this tent or it will go badly for you." With those threatening words that didn't make Kassia tremble in the least bit, Graelam strode out of his tent. He quickly found Rolfe, his master-at-arms.

Rolfe grinned at him. "Nay, my lord, don't bite off my tongue. Your lady took him fairly, and your men protected her well. I've bedded him down on the western side of the camp. Both our knaves are well-guarded, my lord."

Graelam could manage nothing more than a grunt. Rolfe chuckled. "I don't lie to you. Your men did guard her well, my lord. Indeed, they much enjoyed themselves, taking the Earl of Clare and hearing your lady crow in triumph. Would you like to sit down and drink a bit of this wine? It's from Lady Kassia's father. It will warm your innards, my lord, and make you smile."

Graelam, knowing there was nothing for it, did as Rolfe suggested. Rolfe asked, "What will ye do with the foul churls, my lord?"

"Ah," Graelam said, and sat back against the trunk of an oak tree. "We have a surfeit of earls, both so black of soul I doubt the sun will rise fully on the morrow. It's amusing. I suppose we could ransom them for a goodly sum, ransom them, that is, if there is anyone who cares whether they live or rot."

"They were both after revenge," Rolfe said, shaking his head at the wickedness.

"I'll take both of them to Roland. Then my debt to Daria is paid."

Rolfe grinned over the rim of his goblet. "Don't forget your lady, my lord. She'll ride beside you, proud as a little peahen, for after all, she did catch the Earl of Clare. She now considers her debt paid as well. Did you know that Clare has the reddest hair I've ever seen on a man?" Rolfe shook his head, continuing when his master remained silent, "And neither knows the other is here. Do they know of each other, I wonder?"

"Indeed they do. They're mortal enemies, from what Roland told me."

"Now, that's interesting. What will Roland de Tournay do with two earls?"

"If he's wise, he'll kill them both. But knowing Roland, I venture to think he'll devise a punishment that will make both of them howl into eternity. He's got a devious mind, Rolfe."

"Like your wife's, my lord?"

Graelam gave him a sour look. "Aye, just like my damned wife's." He rose to his feet and stretched. The smell of the sea was sharp tonight and the wind was rising. Dark clouds scuttled across the sky, covering the three-quarter moon, then leaving it to shine brilliantly. Graelam breathed in deeply, bade Rolfe and his other men good night, and strode back to his tent.

His wife was waiting for him, just as he'd ordered her to, only she was quite naked and lying in his narrow cot.

He heard her giggle even as he stripped off his bedrobe.

23

Kassia de Moreton gave her husband a wounded look. "You didn't tell me they knew each other, Graelam."

"Villains usually do," Graelam said.

"I wonder what would happen if we simply left them alone together."

"They'd probably kill each other. Roland told me that there is bone-deep hatred between them. Evidently Damon Le Mark killed Edmond of Clare's brother some years ago. I know not more. Mayhap Roland will tell us what is between them."

The two earls stood separated by the width of Chantry Hall's inner bailey, each surrounded by both Graelam and Roland's men. As for Roland, he and Daria were staring from Graelam to his small wife, who stood by his side, straight and proud and tousled in her boy's clothes. What was left of her braids was still tucked up under her cap.

Roland shook his head, still looking dazed. "I know no more than that, Graelam."

Beside him, Daria said, her voice bewildered, "You mean each of you captured one of them . . . to pay back your debt to *me?*" At Kassia's pleased nod, Daria said, "But there is no debt! If I made you think you were ever indebted to me, I should be hung up by my toes and flayed —"

"Hush, Daria," Graelam said. " 'Tis done. The two men were here in Cornwall, and each was up to no good. They are evil, and they deserve whatever punishment Roland decides to mete out to them. My wife and I, well, we simply eased matters for your husband here. Nothing more."

Lady Katherine stood behind her daughter, her eyes on Damon Le Mark. Just seeing him again made her tighten inside with fear, made her throat dry and her hands clammy. Daria could feel her mother's rigidity. She turned and said quickly, her voice low and soothing, "Mother, nay, don't be frightened of him. Damon can't hurt either of us, ever again. He's bound, Mother! Look at him!"

Katherine heard her daughter's voice as if from afar. "He was coming here to kill you and your husband. Doubt it not, Daria."

"Of course he was," Roland said cheerfully. "He failed, Katherine. Do as Daria says — look at him. Isn't he now a pathetic specimen? A man like him who's been stripped of all his fine power has nothing much left. Power gave him the illusion of substance. Now he's of no importance at all. Believe me, Katherine, and don't fear him ever again."

Daria was staring at her husband with wonder. She saw her mother draw a very deep breath, and the dreadful gray pallor began to leave her cheeks. She saw Sir Thomas gently take her hand into his gnarled one and lightly squeeze it. To her delight, her mother turned and smiled up at Sir Thomas.

Roland nodded. "Now, come inside, all of you. Aye, Graelam, bring even that ragged boy there with all the hair. I should like to hear why you appear so bewitched with a skinny lad who hasn't even the years to grow a beard yet."

"The little lad only appears skinny in these absurd garments," Graelam said. "Without them, it's a very different lad. And with the proper encouragement, why, 'tis a lad with much promise."

"That's quite enough," Kassia said. "Ho, Daria! Come rescue me from this loutish humor."

But Roland held tightly to Daria's hand. "Come into the hall and tell us how all this comes about."

"Will I hear counsel to tell me to thrash the little one here?" Graelam asked of no one in particular.

"There are better things to do to a wife," Roland said. He clasped Daria's fingers more firmly and pulled her closer. "Of course, that path leads to exhaustion and near-collapse and besottedness."

Graelam looked at them thoughtfully. It took only his departure to bring the two of them together? He'd been the one standing in their path? It was a lowering thought. He saw that Kassia was also remarking this new closeness with the same surprise.

Once they were seated at a trestle table, goblets of wine in their hands brought by a beaming Gwyn, Kassia said simply, "As I said, we are repaying our debt to you, Daria, nothing more. My husband hunted the Earl of Reymerstone, and I, well, I was fortunate enough to learn that the Earl of Clare was in Cornwall as well. Both wanted to take you. As for Roland, I doubt not they had bloody revenge in mind for him."

Roland felt the slight tremor go through her body as she said, "I don't want you to think that way! I don't want a reward, because I did naught more than anyone else would have done!"

Graelam smiled. "Does this mean that you wish us to let the earls go free?"

Daria stared at him, suddenly mute.

"He's got you there, dearling. No, Graelam, and we both thank you, even though we wish you hadn't endangered yourselves."

"The only danger that will come to my wife now is from my hand on her buttocks. Listen, Daria, you saved my life. As for Kassia here, well, she fancied that my life was also worth something to her."

Roland laughed. "Whilst I sit on my arse safely within the walls of my castle, the two of you are out capturing treacherous rogues and bringing them to me. For judgment? This will take some thought."

Graelam nodded. Kassia said, shaking her head, "Nay, Roland, they are here for Daria's judgment. It is her debt we repay." She turned to smile at her husband. "We do hope, however, that neither of you have any more enemies lurking just beyond the hills. I try to keep my husband safe."

"I do not. Do you, husband?"

Roland looked thoughtful for a very long time before he finally shook his head. "Any more knaves would be a scruffy lot, unworthy of your exalted attention, Graelam."

"Good," Graelam said. "I've a fancy to rot a bit within my castles walls for a while."

Kassia leaned forward, pulling off her boy's cap as she did so. "Can you tell us more about these two men, Roland?"

"As I told Graelam, Damon Le Mark murdered the Earl of Clare's brother some years ago. Clare never forgot and his hatred grew. That was why he kidnapped Daria. It was his revenge. But then he wanted to take her to wive and he wanted her dowry as well. As the Earl of Clare himself told me, it would have to satisfy him."

Daria continued. "Damon knew the real reasons for my kidnapping, but he didn't tell Roland. He made up some tale that Roland never believed."

Katherine said very quietly, "No, he wouldn't tell the truth, even if he had a choice. He didn't even tell me, and that I don't understand at all, for it would have tormented me to hell, and thus afforded him great pleasure."

Everyone turned to Lady Katherine in surprise. "What do you mean, Mother?"

"I mean that Damon should have told me what had happened. He would have enjoyed my misery. I simply wonder why he chose not to."

"You knew the Earl of Clare had kidnapped me. You knew he wanted to wed me."

"No, I didn't know that he wanted to wed you. Damon didn't tell me about that." She shook her head. She looked pale and very, very sad. Then she smiled, a bittersweet smile that held a good deal of acceptance. "The truth is sometimes difficult, Daria. But now it is your right to know. It is true that Damon Le Mark did indeed murder Edmond of Clare's brother. His name was David and he was young and innocent, as was I, and we fell in love. It was so many years ago. My parents had promised me to Reymerstone's half-brother, Daria, but I didn't want him. I wanted only David. Of course, what a girl wants makes no difference to anything. I was forced to wed James of Fortescue anyway. But before I became his wife, I went to David. It's probable that David is your real father, my love. The Earl of Clare is thus your uncle. Damon found out about this some time ago, possibly from his half-brother, for my husband never believed you were the product of his seed. Damon caught David some five years ago and murdered him. He sent word to his half-brother of what he had done, and my husband rejoiced. He laughed when he told me. Even though they were but half-

540

brothers, you see, they were very close. They were very much alike in many ways save that James was skilled in arms and fighting. He was seen as honorable and brave. But it was his conceit that he held up for all to see as his honor, and most were fooled by it, including you, my daughter."

There was utter silence in the hall. Sir Thomas coughed.

"If the Earl of Clare had but looked at Daria, he would have seen that her eyes are very nearly identical to his brother David's. But evidently he didn't see any resemblance. His brother never told him about me or about his daughter. David protected both of us, Daria. But of course Damon knew."

"So that's why my father ignored me, why he never kissed me or petted me or told me he loved me."

Katherine nodded. "I'm sorry, Daria. Every time he looked at you, he would then turn to me and his hatred made me shrivel. He never struck you. He never hurt you. I told him if he did I would kill him. Not with a knife, but with poisons. He believed me, for he knew I had the recipe for many of your grandmother's potions. But then he was killed and we were at Damon Le Mark's mercy."

Roland remembered the sad-eyed Katherine when he'd first visited Reymerstone.

So Damon had avenged his half-brother by taking his wife to his bed and by murdering her lover. He probably believed it a fitting punishment for her infidelity. It was more punishment than anyone should have to bear. He too found himself wondering why Damon Le Mark hadn't taunted Katherine with the possible marriage between her daughter and her daughter's uncle, the Earl of Clare. Then it occurred to Roland that he hadn't because such knowledge might have gotten back to Colchester, and Damon Le Mark had wanted that marriage more than anything.

Roland turned to his wife. He couldn't bear the anguish here, the years of secret, unspoken pain. He said, his voice light, "What say you, wife? Do you want their ears chopped off? Shall we make them into eunuchs? Do you want me to run them through?"

"Nay," she said, shaking her head. She looked at him then, and she was very pale, her eyes bewildered. "I very nearly married my uncle."

"Yes, but you didn't." *But your uncle raped you, didn't he, and you could have delivered a child born of incest.*

Katherine said, "I didn't realize that the Earl of Clare could possibly think of wedding Daria, it never came into my mind, else I would have gone mad. I'm sorry, child, truly, but I didn't want you to know the truth and perhaps despise me for it and —"

Suddenly Daria laughed, deep, raw laughter that was ugly in its pain. It rang out in the great hall and the anguish of it was more than Roland could bear. He shouted, as he grasped her upper arms and shook her, "Daria, stop it!"

But she couldn't. She covered her mouth with her hand but the laughter still came out, muffled and deep and wrenching. She gasped for breath as she choked out the words. "It is too much, Roland, far too much. Don't any of you understand?" Her laughter was dying now but her voice was sharper, more shrill. "Don't you see? My God, if I hadn't lost that babe, if I had birthed the babe, it still could have looked like the Earl of Clare, for he would have been the babe's uncle!" Laughter spewed out of her mouth. Roland stared at her.

"Aye, 'tis true," she said, her voice now oddly singsong, "and then you would never have believed me, Roland, never. You would have looked at that babe and remarked, 'Aye, look at all that red hair. The Earl of Clare is the babe's father and I am vindicated in my belief that my wife is a liar!' "

Daria broke free, whirled about, and looked one last time at her husband. He was still staring at her, his face very pale, his hands now fisted at his sides.

"There's no winning, Roland, at least not for me. It is over and I have lost." She turned to Katherine. "You won't berate yourself again, Mother. Now, if it is truly my judgment, then what I wish is this: I want the two of them put together. I want the two of them to fight it out. Each deserves to fight the other. If the Earl of Clare hadn't been a coward, he wouldn't have kidnapped me, he would have met Damon and challenged him as a man of honor should face another man who is his enemy. As for Damon Le Mark, he is despicable. He should have told Roland the truth about my birth, but he kept silent. He cared not what became of me; he cared not if my uncle bedded me. Perhaps he even thought it would be a fine jest on my mother and on the Earl of Clare, but he wouldn't have said anything, not until it had been done."

Daria looked straight at Roland and laughed. "One more time for my lie, Roland, then never will you hear me protest again. The Earl of Clare didn't bed me, no one save you did. He humiliated me but he didn't bed me. Now, are my wishes to be considered?"

Roland felt mired in the swirling tensions surrounding him. They were also within him and he didn't like it. So the Earl of Clare hadn't raped her. He believed that now. Daria was incapable of fostering such a deception in the face of learning that the Earl of Clare had been of her blood, her damned uncle, by all the saints. It still left him puzzled and beset by confusion. Her laughter and her pain made him raw.

He nodded slowly. "It will be as you wish."

Graelam said then, "And if one kills the other? What would you have done with the one who wins?"

Daria said quite without emotion, "He will go free."

Roland nodded his agreement, but in the next instant he shared a look with Graelam and a silent pact was made.

The afternoon was hot, the early-fall wind harshly dry and chafing.

Daria knew she would never forget the looks on the two men's faces, the fury, the raw hatred. They'd been stripped down to loincloths and given swords, maces, and axes.

She didn't want to watch, but she did, as did her mother. The scores of people surrounding the two men were silent. Daria knew that by now all of Chantry Hall knew what she'd screamed in the great hall.

All of them knew that her two uncles would fight to the death.

Both men were her uncles. It was insane. She looked at her mother, hoping she was all right, but she couldn't tell, for there was no sign, no expression, on Katherine's face.

She heard the sudden ringing of the heavy battle swords. She heard the curses of the two men as they lunged and withdrew from each other. She could feel the poison of their hatred for each other.

It didn't last long, though it seemed an eternity. Damon Le Mark fought bravely, with all the enmity in his soul, but he was no opponent for the Earl of Clare, whose fighting skills were honed daily on the Welsh outlaws. She saw the Earl of Clare lift the sword with both hands, saw the sword descend, and knew that Damon Le Mark was dead. At the last instant, just as Damon Le Mark jerked sideways, then back, the Earl of Clare used the sword as a spear instead, sending it straight ahead. It sliced through Damon Le Mark's chest and came out the back, flinging him onto his side on the ground. He was dead before he rolled to his back.

There was a shock of silence. The Earl of Clare stood over his dead enemy, and he was smiling. She couldn't believe what happened then. She watched her husband, now stripped to his loincloth, step into the circle, a battle sword in his hand. As he lifted it, he grinned and yelled at the Earl of Clare, "Did you know, you filthy whoreson, that Daria is your niece? She is of your flesh, you damned fool! Your brother, David, was her father! Had I not taken her from you, you would have committed the gravest sin in God's eyes! What say you to that, you stupid sod?"

The Earl of Clare calmed his breathing. He looked at the young man before him, knew him for a dangerous warrior, and wanted to kill him. The humiliation Roland had meted out to him at Tyberton was a raw wound. Roland had thrashed him like a mewling pup, in front of the king, in front of all his men and servants. Well, now he had a sword. He'd killed Reymerstone and now he would kill this impudent bastard. "You lie," he shouted. "I would have surely recognized her if she had been of mine own blood. She is not!"

Graelam started forward, fury writ on his face. "Roland, this is not for you to do!" he yelled. "Damn you, come out of there! It was to be my turn!"

But it was too late. The two men faced each other. The earl, his red hair blazing in the hot afternoon sun, was the larger of the two, a massive man whose power was evident in each movement he made with the heavy sword. He'd but slightly exerted himself to kill the Earl of Reymerstone. He looked at the young man who was dark as a Muslim, and smiled. He knew that after he killed Roland he would himself be killed, but for now he didn't care. He would have his revenge. He roared and lunged, only to have Roland feint to the left. He was left panting, feeling like a fool, his sword slicing through air.

Daria looked at her husband. He was more slightly built, leaner, his body hard and taut, but he was strong and agile and very fast. He'd dropped the battle sword and was now swinging an ax in his right hand. Then he tossed the ax to his left hand and back and forth, taunting the Earl of Clare, until he bellowed like an enraged bull, and charged Roland again. Roland danced lightly to the side and struck suddenly, fiercely, with the ax. It thudded loudly against the earl's sword. Roland looked surprised; then he gave the earl a look of approval before quickly spinning to the left out of the range of the earl's pounding sword.

Daria touched her hand to Graelam's sleeve. "Nay," she said quietly, "he will be all right. He will kill the earl."

"You cannot possibly know —" Graelam's impatient voice dropped off. He stared at Daria.

"He will kill him," she said again, her eyes never leaving her husband. "Nay, I'm not seeing a vision. I saw him fight the Earl of Clare in the presence of the king at Tyberton. He is very skilled, and what he does is unexpected."

"He's an evil fighter," Graelam said after a moment watching Roland. "That's true. Look at that! Aye, Roland fights with his brains."

"He also learned tricks from outlaws in the Holy Land."

The Earl of Clare was bearing down on Roland, trying to corner him, striking again and again, not letting up, forcing him back with the raw power of his strength.

Suddenly Roland tossed the ax aside. Salin slipped a long slender-bladed knife into his hand and Daria heard Graelam heave a heartfelt sigh. " 'Tis over now," he said.

"How do you know that?"

"Just watch."

Roland slipped away from the earl, dodging right; then he turned on the balls of his bare feet, and fast as lightning, reached out and sliced a clean diagonal line through the thick red hair on the earl's chest. The earl looked down blankly at the oozing bloody line that marked his chest and howled with fury. "I'll kill you, you whoreson!"

Roland laughed. "Again, you bastard!" He spun about, his arm extended, and he struck so quickly it was a blur. Now a bloody red X stood out on the earl's chest.

The earl was so beside himself with rage he began to hammer with the mighty sword, wildly slicing it from side to side in a wide swath.

Graelam said quietly, "He's no longer thinking. He is reacting, nothing more. He doesn't realize that his incredible strength isn't an asset. He doesn't realize he won't touch Roland. Roland has learned that his brain is his best weapon."

Daria watched Roland lightly back away from the earl, not coming to a stop until he was a good fifteen feet from him. The earl was yelling, howling his fury, and he was readying to charge, his sword raised above his head.

Slowly, very slowly, Roland aimed the knife and released it with a smooth flip of his wrist. It sang through the still air and thudded softly into the earl's chest, just at the point where the X crossed.

Edmond of Clare stared down at the quivering pale ivory handle that still vibrated from the strength and speed of Roland's throw.

He looked up then, first at Roland, then toward Daria. "I wanted your dowry, not you," he said. "You're not of my blood, I would have known if you were, for David kept nothing from me. He would have told me. Nay, you're naught but —" He crumpled where he stood.

Roland was covered with sweat and dirt and he had a huge satisfied smile on his face.

"Nay, berate me not, Graelam," he called out with great relish. " 'Tis over now, and he was mine, not yours, not anyone else's." He turned to his wife. "Be ready to leave Chantry Hall at first light tomorrow morning. Pack enough clothing for a month. Speak to Alice and have her prepare ample food supplies for us and seven men." He was still grinning when he turned to Sir Thomas. "Thomas, you will see to Chantry Hall's safety whilst we're gone. And, Katherine, worry not about your daughter."

"No," Katherine said slowly. "I don't think I shall now."

"Where are we going, Roland?"

Roland walked to where his wife stood, and he looked down at her, saying nothing for a very long time. Finally he raised his fingers and cupped her chin. "We go to Wales."

"Why?"

He leaned down, saying very quietly, so only she could hear his words, "I took your virginity, yet I have no memory of it. I want that memory back, Daria. I want the knowledge of your eyes upon me when I came into you that first time. I want my awareness of you when I first touched your womb."

They reached Wrexham twelve days later. Incredibly, it had rained only twice. Incredibly, they'd met no outlaws. Incredibly, Roland was whistling when they entered the Wrexham cathedral.

Daria was praying hard. She didn't know what to expect, but praying seemed the best approach.

Romila opened the door at Roland's pounding. She was grumbling about louts bothering until she recognized him. Then she smiled widely, rubbing her hands together as she looked him over from head to toe. "Aye, oh, aye, 'tis the pretty lad whose body and face have provided romantic fodder for all the girls in Wrexham. I've told them of your endowments, my lad, described to them how your flesh feels beneath a woman's hand. Ah, when I told them about the size of your rod . . . Is it you, Daria? Well, well. What do you here? What —"

And on and on she went, and Roland just smiled at her and listened to her babbling. Daria said nothing.

After a time, Roland asked if Romila would take him upstairs to the chamber where he'd been in bed for nearly two weeks.

"Nay, Daria, I wish to go alone," he said to his wife when she would have followed. She nodded, and watched the two of them climb the narrow filthy stairs. She wondered, half-smiling, if Romila would try to seduce him once in the bedchamber.

Salin said from behind her, "Roland is a fair man."

She only nodded and began her prayers again.

Upstairs, Roland stood in the middle of the small airless chamber. He looked at the bed where he'd spent hours he didn't remember at all, and more hours he did remember that he couldn't begin to count. He looked at the chamber pot in the corner and shook his head at those memories. He turned to Romila, cutting off her outpourings of vulgar suggestions. "When I was brought here, I was out of my senses?"

"Aye, ye were, me lad."

He looked toward the window and saw Daria standing there, quiet and still, looking out onto the courtyard below. He looked at the chair. He remembered clearly Daria sitting in that chair, sewing on one of his tunics.

"Yer little wife took good care of ye. Even when ye were a testy lad, she only smiled and shook her head and loved ye. O' course, she did ask my advice now and again, and I told her ye'd be in fine form again soon."

He remembered the spoon touching his mouth, remembered Daria's soft voice telling him to eat, telling him he must regain his strength.

"Aye, oh, aye," Romila said, her voice wistful and teasing at the same time. Then she laughed aloud, raucous and loud. "And I remember more than I should, ye randy goat!"

Roland turned slowly to face her. "What do you mean?"

Romila cackled and looked again down his body. "Aye, a randy goat ye were even when ye were out of yer head with the fever and yelling strange things in savage tongues. I knew ye'd not been married to yer little wife long, but still I couldn't believe that ye had such a dreadful need in yer manhood! Men and their seed — always wanting to spill it, no matter if they're dying."

And Roland said again, his heart pounding slow dull beats, "What do you mean?"

"I mean that yer randy body didn't know ye was frightful sick, oh, no, ye horny pretty lad!" She laughed again and looked at him as if she'd like to throw him on the bed and rip off his clothes.

"You do?" he said.

"Oh, aye, me pretty boy. I come up that night, for yer little wife was so tired and so frantic with worry for ye that I was worried about her, and then I stopped outside the door and heard this moaning and groaning and I heard her cry out, and I opened the door, all afeared that ye was dying, and there ye were, holding her on top of ye, lurching yer rod into her, and she was crying, and then ye moaned deep and took her but good. Aye, ye made her ride ye hard." Romila stopped, smiling fondly at Roland. "I like a man whose rod isn't struck down along with his body. Aye, yer a bonnie lad."

"Thank you," Roland said blankly. He flung his arms around Romila, lifted her high, even though she weighed about the same as he did; then, as he lowered her, he gave her a loud smacking kiss on her mouth.

"Thank you," he said again. As he made his way back down the stairs, he thought: By all the saints, I wish I could remember. Just a moment of it, just an instant. He wondered if perhaps someday he would.

Not that it mattered. Not that what Romila had told him mattered all that much. It struck him then that he wanted to spend the night here, with Daria, in that bed. He wanted her on top of him and he wanted to take her again, here, just as he'd taken her so long ago.

He whistled.

At nearly midnight, a howling storm blew up and the animal hide that covered the window thudded and flapped loudly. On the narrow bed, Roland was sprawled on his back, looking up at his beautiful wife, naked, her hair loose down her back, watching her come down on him, then move as she wished to, then arch her back, bringing him so deep into her that he thought he'd die from the pleasure of it.

He saw nothing but his wife, Daria. As he watched her reach her pleasure, he told her, "I love you, Daria, and you will never doubt me."

She yelled her release, and he grinned, wondering if Romila stood outside the door listening to them, cackling like a witch. Then he moaned, and he forgot all save his enjoyment of his wife.

Epilogue

London, England

That hot September afternoon when two peers of the realm had met in the outer bailey of a little-known castle in Cornwall to fight each other to the death didn't reach the ears of the king until well into October. The tale was, much to the king's displeasure, little embellished by the king's son-in-law, Dienwald de Fortenberry, whose mournful expression showed his disappointment at not having been present at the fight. Not that it mattered to anyone.

Both men were long dead and no one really cared now who had killed whom and how. But the king, in a flash of unpredictability, decided he wanted the details, all of them, and he quickly realized that Dienwald wasn't being completely frank with him. He knew that Roland was involved, as was Graelam de Moreton. He was angered, yet at the same time the king was pleased that the three men felt loyalty to each other. But shouldn't they also trust their king, the lame

558

louts? They should; it was their duty to do so.

He considered threatening Dienwald with torture for lying to him, his dear papa-in-law, for he knew that Dienwald was withholding all the doubtlessly interesting parts of the truth from him. Then he looked at his daughter, Philippa, saw that she was grinning at him and knowing that there wasn't anything he could do. He held to his kingly control, then yelled for wine.

The king wasn't angry beyond his second goblet of wine, for after all, he now had two very rich holdings in his royal, always needy hands. Neither earl had left an heir, much to the king's joy — Burnell had quickly found that out — save for a cousin to Reymerstone who was a puling boy and not worthy of either the title or the lands. The king gave guardianship of Tyberton to one of his own trusted knights with the admonition that the moment he ever thought of himself as an arrogant Marcher baron, his king would ensure that his ale was poisoned. He'd thought to reward his son-in-law with Reymerstone, then decided he hadn't yet proved himself sufficiently loyal to his king.

After the first of the year, the king recalled the tale again, and decided he would discover what had happened from the horse's mouth. He sent a messenger to Chantry Hall, insisting that Roland de Tournay and his wife visit London and give the royal ears a full accounting.

Roland sent a return message by the king's soldier:

Sire:

I beg your indulgence and forgiveness, but Daria and I cannot travel to London to bask in your royal presence for some months yet. She is with child. We would ask that you receive us in the late summer.

"Humph," the king said when Robert Burnell had finished reading the brief letter. Then he looked up, puzzled. "But I thought she was already with child, Robbie. Shouldn't she be birthing it by now? I remember Roland wedded her because she was pregnant. Don't you recall, the queen told us of it?"

"She miscarried the babe, sire, late last summer I believe I was told."

The king wondered for a bitter moment how Burnell seemed to know everything, even insignificant detail such as the miscarrying of a babe by one of his Cornish baron's wives, but he was too proud to ask.

"That is what I thought," the king said. "I must tell the queen there's to be another child. She will be gratified. She is most fond of Daria and Roland, you know."

"Aye, sire, she is."

The king looked suddenly very pleased with himself. "The child Daria miscarried, it was the Earl of Clare's, was it not, Robbie? Do you not remember? He'd forced himself upon her and Roland, despite the fact, insisted upon wedding her?"

"Aye, sire, your memory is flawless and surpasses all that is imaginable."

The king smiled his beautiful Plantagenet smile. "Do you jerk at my royal leg, Robbie?"

"I, sire? Nay, I would never be guilty of something so ignoble."

The king rubbed his hands together and rose. "Well, that's that. I have lands I sorely needed and a cartload of coin for my coffers. My subjects appear to have sorted things out amongst themselves. You look tired, Robbie. Why don't you rest a bit this afternoon?"

It sounded a fine suggestion to Robert Burnell, and he nodded.

The king turned to leave the chamber, then smacked the palm of his hand against his forehead. "I almost forgot! Bring your writing materials, Robbie, there's a delegation from some Scottish fool wishing to beg our royal favor."

Burnell sighed, then smiled. "Aye, sire. Immediately."

Chantry Hall, Cornwall

Roland and Daria stood on the northern ramparts of Chantry Hall, looking over the rolling hills dotted with at least one hundred sheep chewing at the sparse winter grasses. It was early January, but the air was crisp rather than cold and the sky blue and clear. It was a Cornwall day that delighted every man and woman living within its boundaries.

"It warms the heart," Roland said, waving an expansive arm toward his sheep.

"It also gives a very peculiar order to the air," said his wife as she drew her thick cloak more closely around her.

Roland hugged her to his side, kissed her temple, then pointed eastward toward the king's departing messenger, Florin, who'd spent the night and imbibed too much ale. "I wonder what Edward will say when he receives my missive."

Daria laughed. "If Florin arrives intact with it! Husband, your reply to your king bordered on the cocky. It was rather in

Dienwald's insolent style, I think."

"Ha! Dienwald slinked about when the king taxed him in October about our two dead earls, fumbled all over himself and in general laid claim to being a better fool than Crooky."

"That's what Philippa said, not Dienwald."

"As I recall, he smacked her bottom for that. Do you think the king also wrote to Graelam and Kassia?"

"We will be certain to ask when they are next here." Daria turned and smiled up at her husband.

"Do you feel well, sweeting? Our babe sits content in your womb?" He drew her against him as he spoke, and gently rubbed his palm over her swelling belly.

"Aye, both of us are filled with well-being and both of us are getting quite hungry."

Roland gave her a mournful look. "If you had told me that but a few months ago I would have considered your hunger to be of a more felicitous nature. I would have lifted you over my shoulder and carried you into our western pasture and loved you amongst the eglantine and bluebells. But now I must play the forbearing husband, all patience and long-enduring, whilst my babe gleans all your attention. It is difficult, Daria, for I am young and lusty and filled with lavish excesses and —"

She grabbed his ears and pulled his face down, nipping the tip of his nose, kissing his mouth again and again. "There is no eglantine now, Roland, but there are pine cones in the forest. What say you, husband? Are you all words and plaints or will you give me deeds?"

"And I thought I was the only one suffering from excesses," he said, and lifted her high against him, her feet off the rampart wooden walkway. "No forest bed for you, Daria, but a soft bed where you will be winsome and soft and so dear to me I want to weep with it."

"You become a poet, Roland. I think first I shall have Alice prepare her wonderful mulled wine. 'Tis to dull your randy senses so I may have you energetic yet controlled in your excesses."

He looked at her with such love that Daria forgot her attempts at wit and every other scrap of humor that had come into her brain. He eased her back down and she leaned against him, hugging her arms tightly around his back.

"Life is sweet with you, Roland. Life is all I could wish it to be."

"Even with the smelly sheep and us

standing downwind from them?"

"Aye, even that. Come now, my lord husband."

"If our king but knew who the cocky one really was at Chantry Hall I vow he would knit me with fine words until I died."

"I will tell Philippa. Then we will see."

"I shall tell Dienwald." Roland paused, adding on a wide grin, "I haven't the faintest idea what Dienwald would do."

"Show me what you would do."

"Let us get to it then," Roland said and led her down from the ramparts and into the great hall.

The employees of Thorndike Press hope you have enjoyed this Large Print book. All our Large Print titles are designed for easy reading, and all our books are made to last. Other Thorndike Press Large Print books are available at your library, through selected bookstores, or directly from us.

For information about titles, please call:

(800) 223-1244
(800) 223-6121

To share your comments, please write:

Publisher
Thorndike Press
P.O. Box 159
Thorndike, Maine 04986